CHASE
the
BUTTER
FLIES

CHASE *the* BUTTER FLIES

International Bestselling Author
MONICA JAMES

Cover Design: Perfect Pear Creative Covers
Editing: Editing 4 Indies

Interior Design and Formatting by:

www.emtippettsbookdesigns.com

Follow me on:
www.authormonicajames.com

Dedication

This is for you, Papa. I'll see you when I see you.

Author's Note

This book was written a while ago, and although I had luck finding publishers overseas who loved it, I didn't have the same luck finding an English publisher. So, I sat on it, not really knowing what to do with it.

It didn't really "fit" into one specific genre, which for me, as a writer, is frustrating, but by the same token, it was also liberating. I knew that if I waited, one day the time would be right to release this book.

And now is that time.

On July 8th 2019, I lost my dad. No words can ever describe the loss and sadness I feel, and will feel for the rest of my life.

Chase the Butterflies is dedicated to him. This is my way to share a part of my dad with the world. By reading this, you keep his memory alive, so, I thank you from the bottom of my heart.

Never give up on your dreams…anything is possible.

Happy reading.

Love,

Monica xoxo

Does the flap of a butterfly's wings in Brazil set off a tornado in Texas?

The Butterfly Effect~ Edward Lorenz

Prologue

"Hold up, I have to tie my laces."

"*Again*? Do you need reminding? *Over, under, around, and through. Meet Mr. Bunny Rabbit, pull and through.*"

Bryan arches a sculptured, dark brow while I mute my chuckles behind my hand.

"Turn around, would you? I can't do this with you looking at me."

Folding my arms across my chest, I tap my foot against the pavement. "Can't do what? Tie your laces? What are you, five?" I can't keep the humor from my tone as I peer down at him crouched on the floor.

"Tori, please, just this one time, can you do what you're told?"

I've never been able to say no to Bryan. "Fine, have it your way, but you really should learn how to do double knots."

"Ha-ha, very funny. You're lucky it's your birthday."

I can't keep the smile from my cheeks. "Exactly, and right now, you're wasting precious birthday time. Twenty-seven will soon be twenty-eight at the rate you're going."

Twenty-seven.

It's hard to believe that this time yesterday, I was twenty-six. I don't feel any different, and I know I look the same. The only thing that's changed is that my love for Bryan has grown. It's been ten years since he asked me to prom, and it's been ten years since I met my happily ever after.

"What are…?" But the words catch in my throat when I see Bryan on one knee, extending a red velvet box my way.

To cement the gravity of what I'm seeing, the box hinges whine open as he reveals an enormous diamond ring snuggled amongst white silk.

"Th-That's a ring," I stupidly state, my eyes as big as saucers.

"I know."

I point at the box, my finger trembling. "Why are you holding it?"

"Because I want you to marry me." There isn't a pause or slight hesitation to his affirmation.

"Now?" I really need to stop talking, but I'm afraid once I do, I'll start crying.

"Maybe not right this second, but hopefully soon." He

smirks. The sight has my stomach somersaulting.

I want to say so many things, but there are simply no words to express how happy I am. The ring is the most beautiful thing I've ever seen—its sparkle rivaling the bright moonlight above us.

"So…want to marry me?" His laid-back attitude is so typical of Bryan while I'm on the verge of hyperventilating.

"I-I…" A simple yes seems so ordinary.

"Victoria?" Small furrows crinkle across Bryan's brow when I stand, speechless, my mouth gaped open. "Will you marry me?" Every girl wishes to hear those words—they're the words that slap me into gear.

This explains him having to tie his laces seven times throughout the night. He chickened out all those times prior, but now, this is real. This is really happening. "Yes, I will marry you. A million yeses!" I cry, tears rolling down my cheeks.

"You'll marry me?" he asks, and I'm surprised he'd think my answer would be anything but yes.

I nod, a loud sob escaping me.

"Oh, Tori!" He springs up and throws his arms around me, twirling me high in the air. I can't contain my laughter and tears.

When my feet finally touch the ground, he reaches for my finger and slips the ring onto it. It's a perfect fit.

"I love you so much. You've just made me the happiest man alive." We kiss and hug and laugh for how long, I'm not sure. But everything is perfect; it's how things are supposed to be.

As we walk to our car, I can't stop admiring the ring on my finger. I wiggle my left hand out in front of me. It's so surreal. The brutal wind hastily picks up speed, howling behind us as I lean into Bryan's side, stealing his warmth. When our black Jeep comes into view, I breathe out a sigh of relief. It's eerie being out here alone as the usually busy street is now completely deserted.

"Are you going to call your mom?" Bryan asks, wrapping his arm tightly around me, cocooning me in his signature fragrance.

"First thing tomorrow morning." I yawn, wondering how late it is. "But I'm going to call Matilda as soon as we get to the car." My sister would have my neck if she found out after Mom.

Bryan kisses the top of my head, a gesture which wraps me in a protective sound bubble. That safety is shattered however when I hear a bottle skate along the pavement. I turn to look over my shoulder, my eyes straining in the dark, but I can't see anyone behind us. I inhale deeply, relieved. But that relief is short-lived when I bump straight into a pungent-smelling mass. I yelp, my hands automatically raised in surrender as I apologize profusely for not looking where I'm going.

"Nice ring," sneers a stranger, his yellowed, long teeth akin to that of a sewer rat.

Bryan instantly pulls me to the left, dragging me away. I don't know why, but I suddenly tremble, sensing something bad, something life-changing on the horizon.

"Keep walking," Bryan whispers into my ear, our rushed footsteps highlighting our need to get away. Our Jeep is mere feet away when an excruciating pain tears through my skull and down my neck as my head jars backward with a sharp tug. I immediately pull my head forward, but my long hair is snagged on something. Or *someone*.

The next few seconds blur by, not knowing what's happening until Bryan is screaming, frantically trying to unsnag me. I yank and pull, my fingers tugging at my roots, hysterically attempting to pry myself free. I don't have time to scream because before a sound leaves my trembling lips, I feel something sharp press against the small of my back. My body instantly relaxes, and a strangled cry leaves my lungs as an arm presses over my windpipe.

This can't be happening.

"Give me the keys." The stench of rot surrounds me. I sniff back my tears. My gaze lands on Bryan, who has his hands raised, his eyes pleading with my assailant to let me go.

"Here…now let her go." He lowers his arm and extends it forward, unfurling his fist to reveal the set of keys.

But that won't do. "Not so fast." His breath is warm…too warm, like rancid milk. "Toss them over."

Bryan does as he demands, no questions asked. I can see the terror in his eyes as he nods that it'll be okay. But it won't. Nothing ever will.

"Now pick them up," he hisses in my ear, his lips too close to the shell. I whimper, my heart hammering so fast within my chest I'm afraid it'll spill out onto the asphalt.

Just as I bend forward, he cackles a cruel, maniacal laugh. He tightens his hold around my neck, pressing so firmly into my throat I struggle to breathe. My hands fly up, clawing at him to release me.

"Let her go!" Bryan roars, charging forward, fists clenched by his side. He stops dead in his tracks when the cool metal shifts from my back and is placed at my temple.

"Bryan…" I plead, I want to shout out, beg him to help me, but my cries would be in vain. There's no one out here but us. No one can hear me scream. "Run," I sob, hot tears scoring my flesh as they betray my fears. I fight helplessly, as his hold is so strong.

"No, I won't leave you!" He doesn't hide his horror that I'm sacrificing myself for him. But why should we both suffer? The hard probing into my lower back is an indication the keys are suddenly not what this vile creature is after.

"Yes, why don't you run home." He laps the side of my face in one long, slow lick. Bryan gnashes his teeth, advancing forward with a growl.

I thrash about madly, attempting to break free, but struggling only makes him force his forearm deep against my windpipe. I gag, slowly being robbed of breath. The metal against my skin feels slick and hot, the warmth from my skin heating the barrel.

My body goes lax, as I know I can't fight him off.

"That's it, princess. This will hurt a lot less if you don't fight me." I surrender, but I intend on fighting like a pit bull when he lets down his guard.

Bryan's eyes are filled with tears, matching the ones pooling in mine. "I love you," I whisper, gasping for breath when my attacker wraps his large hand around my throat and begins dragging me backward. I have no choice but to go with him.

I scratch at his fingers, afraid I'll pass out if he doesn't loosen his hold, but it only encourages him to press harder.

"Tori, no!" Bryan's cries are my final undoing, and I relax my body, on the cusp of surrendering for good. I can't stomach his pain. His pain hurts more than my own. My eyes are locked on his as I'm hauled away, and the best night of my life quickly becomes the worst, and quite possibly, my last.

"You follow us, and I swear to god, I will kill you both." All I can do is submit for Bryan's safety. The gun waves out in front of me, making no secret it will kill both of us if we revolt.

As we round the corner and I'm dragged down a dirty, dark alleyway and brutally shoved up against a wall, face first, I think about Bryan and me, and all the hours, minutes, seconds spent together. There are countless moments in time, but now, they aren't enough. It'll never be enough.

The hem of my dress is yanked up, my underwear gets ripped from my body, exposing my bare behind. As my hand gets crushed against the brick wall, my ring catches the moonlight, drawing attention to the fact that one day I could have been Mrs. Bryan Moore. But I know now that may never be.

"Scream all you want. I like it when they scream." Someone is about to take my decency, and I don't even know his name. He shoves a hand between us, groping, fondling.

"Just don't hurt Bryan." It's my final plea.

"You're in no position to make demands." He tugs at the ring on my finger, making it clear he wants to take everything from me.

His deplorable action sparks the pit bull in me, and a surge of anger courses through my veins. I refuse to be a victim. I act on pure instinct and strike my head backward, connecting with something that makes a noise akin to an orange being run over by a truck.

Bedlam suddenly breaks loose as I screech, turning around and charging for the bastard, who is clutching his bleeding nose in his cupped palms. "You fucking bitch!"

My screams resonate off the walls as I rush forward, ready to inflict whatever pain and retribution I can. However, heavy footsteps pounding against the concrete make me lift my eyes, relieved, but also scared to see two figures running toward me. Bryan trails behind a shadowed form. He must have called for help.

I dodge my offender, running like the wind toward my cloaked protector, who seems more intent on saving me than my own fiancé, who is lagging behind. Bryan looks scared, hesitant even. The fact he isn't running full speed hurts. But I can focus on that later.

"Run!" I shriek, not wanting my champion to get hurt. Why do I feel an unexpected connection to him?

I'm yards away, but his pace never falters. He's so intent on saving me, I could cry in relief. This is it. It's really over. I'm going to be okay. I'm feet away but am vacantly filled with terror when my masked protector bellows, "Watch out!" before I hear a click and two deafening gunshots, and then…everything fades to black.

*The butterfly develops through a process called metamorphosis. This means **transformation.***

The First Stage: Egg

One

Nine Months Later

"I'm so sorry, Tori. I couldn't protect you like I promised I would."

I remember staring blankly out the window of our once cherished home, feeling nothing but numbness.

"I wish I could have been the man you deserved, needed. I just...I fucked up. I'll never forgive myself for what I did."

These are all excuses, lies.

"I can't stay here. There are just too many...memories. I can't live in this home any longer. Forgive me. I tried to stay strong, but I just can't. You're so...distant. Cold. You don't want to come back to me."

"You're a fucking coward!" I scream. It's the only thing I've said to him in months.

Tears stung his eyes, and without a single word, he closed

the door to our home, to our future, without even saying goodbye.

A chair is still a chair even when there's no one sitting there.

But what happens when the chair in question is the same chair which broke apart your life because you found your fiancé screwing your sister on it—or, more accurately, over it. Looking down at the malevolent object, I realize I should have left it back in Bridgeport as I did with my ex-fiancé.

The silk feels smooth and regal as I run my finger along the top, bringing back happy memories of when this chair sat in front of our bay window, overlooking the immaculate landscaped gardens and vibrant vine maple trees. I lost count of how many hours I spent snuggled in this chair, reading my favorite books, or more commonly, correcting my third-grade students' papers.

I felt like a queen sitting on her throne when Bryan would sneak in with a chai tea in hand, placing it down in front of me, before kissing me lovingly on the brow. He then left just as quietly as he entered.

When the tea and kisses stopped, I should have known something was askew. But I was so preoccupied with trying to pull through the hardest time of my life that I missed all the warning signs. But even if I did, would I have wanted to know? I'm ashamed that the answer is no.

I'm a coward, I know that, but sometimes, ignorance is truly bliss. I would give anything to wipe away the memory of coming home to find my fiancé screwing someone who supposedly was family.

The constant nightmares of the night that changed my life forever seemed like a walk in the park compared to having my heart broken by two people I loved most in this world. Whether it was the sheer terror or the betrayal, I'll never know, but I was sick right then and there, disrupting an orgasm that was rightfully mine when I caught them.

I wanted to believe that by some miracle my soul mate wasn't having an affair with my sister, but brutal acts of violence, they turn you into a survivor. They force you to face hardships that most times you're not ready to face.

So I refused to allow my fight for survival to be in vain. My empty chest wouldn't allow it either. I moved out that same night. I expected some kind of explanation, an apology from either Matilda or Bryan, but all I got was a slap in the face, and by slap, I mean three weeks later, our four-bedroom, foursquare-style home was on the market and sold within the month. It was prime real estate, the realtor had said, but to me, it was a wasteland where my dreams had gone to die. I didn't object when I saw the FOR SALE sign because I couldn't live in a home which entombed too many bitter memories.

I hadn't spoken to Bryan for months. I knew it wasn't his fault, but I lost interest in day-to-day activities. I was a shell of the person I once was. I felt cut off and detached from my family and friends. I should have felt something, anything—I mean, I had been assaulted and then caught my fiancé cheating with my own flesh and blood, but funnily enough, I just felt numb.

Today is the first day in my new house—a run-down, isolated waterfront home in northeastern Connecticut, the place I moved to when I was fourteen. It may not be much to look at, but with two acres of untouched land, it's perfect to escape the commotion I've just lived through.

I promised myself that with a new home comes new memories. Slumping into the revolting chair, the chair which caused this trip down misery lane, I grasp that I'm a fool for ever believing that I could do this. It's been endless days since this all started, but it still feels like day one.

My miserable reflection stares back at me from the grimy window, a reflection of someone who doesn't resemble me. My chestnut brown hair is short and styled into a bob, just past my ears. The style seems to emphasize my enormous hazel eyes which were never this big, but violence and heartache turned me into someone I no longer recognize.

I miss my long hair. I suppose I miss a lot of things. Clutching at the shorter strands, I appreciate that my hair can grow back. It can grow healthy and long, and I can almost forget why I wear it short. The same can't be said for the reoccurring nightmares which knock at my mind every time I close my eyes.

But I was going to get better. I was determined to live. But the thing about PTSD is that it doesn't discriminate—it hates us all. My determination may have saved my life, but it didn't save my relationship. It tore it apart. I could see it every time Bryan looked at me. I was a victim. In his eyes, he failed me. He couldn't protect me. I made him feel less of a man. If he ever confessed to the affair, it would have been one of the spineless reasons he used for why he cheated with Matilda in the first place. She made him feel wanted.

I tried to talk to him, to tell him how I felt, but every time I opened my mouth, the words would get caught in my throat. I closed myself off to him, and I didn't understand why. I think a part of me blamed him for not fighting harder. We drifted apart, regardless of how hard I tried to stay anchored. The doctors said it was normal after everything I'd been through, but I felt anything but normal.

So I suppose one can't blame me for looking at this chair with nothing but contempt and…violence. I will never associate anything good with this piece of furniture because this, just like the past ten years of my life, has been one big fucking joke. But unlike my memories, which I cannot set on fire, I can however, burn this chair.

The tranquility I once experienced, even the numbness I felt when this entire shitstorm started, begins to slowly ebb away, and unexpectedly, my composure, my indifference, floats away, and all I'm left with is murderous, spiteful rage.

I jump up like the chair is on fire. Images of this immaculate white settee being *literally* set on fire stokes my inner anger, and

I move before my brain can chastise me for being so reckless. I'm sick of being cool, calm, and collected. I'm sick of not screaming from the rooftops about what a lying, cowardly scumbag my ex-fiancé is, and how my sister betrayed me beyond belief. But most of all, I'm sick of the hand I've been dealt. Why me? What did I do to deserve this? I have no direction. I have no freaking clue what comes next.

But what I do know is that my future starts with burning this bloody chair.

I won't rule out that I'm currently possessed because I can't believe my small, feeble frame of one hundred and twenty-five pounds is dragging this antique wooden chair across the slippery floorboards. But running on pure adrenaline and fury allows you to become the strongest person in the world.

Reaching for a perfectly positioned bottle of whiskey off the kitchen counter, I toe open the glass doors which lead out into my large backyard. Hauling with all my might, I pull the chair. It drags noisily down the weathered stairs, but I keep on persevering; only stopping when my body shudders in near defeat. I'm breathless, my entire body screams from exhaustion, and my brow is covered in sweat, but I don't allow that to stop me as I hunt through the pockets of my butterfly print sundress to find my pack of matches and joint.

Once my fingers pass over my lifelines, I lunge for the bottle of Jameson that is sitting on the couch cushions and unscrew the lid. Taking a quick swig, I then commence to pour the brown liquid all over the pristine chair, its dirty color staining the white shade perfectly. I only stop when there is a shot left in the bottle.

Unable to wait, I drag the match along the striker and watch it sizzle to life a second later. The flickering flame burns in sync with my frantic heart, but suddenly, my insanity comes to a screeching halt, and I gasp, appalled at what I was going to do.

What will my neighbors across the lake think of me? Not even in my home for twenty-four hours and already I'm disturbing the peace with my need for vengeance. The flame fizzles out, and I sigh, hating how weak I am.

Gulping down the last of my alcohol, I stand mute, my eyes fixated on the chair and everything it represents. The joint is my only reprieve, the only thing which got me through the nightmares and the breakup of my relationship.

"Victoria, I really wish you wouldn't smoke that." I can hear Bryan scolding me loud and clear.

I was too afraid to push the boundaries, wanting to please the only man I had ever loved. And in return, he crapped all over my loyalty and made me feel a fool.

The cool breeze licks at my heated skin, and the sensation sends a sudden zing through me. I know what I have to do.

Looking over my shoulder, I ignore the feeling I'm being watched, and proclaim, "No more reservations, Victoria. From this day forward, I demand you to change. You survived the hardest few months of your life, and it's your turn to be free. It's your turn to live."

Placing the smoke between my lips, I pull out another match and strike it, shielding it with my trembling hand as I light the joint. Sucking in a deep, heavy drag, I feel my insides automatically chill and bask in the afterglow that helps me forget what a mess I am.

The flame soon burns my fingers, but instead of blowing it out, I squeeze my eyes shut and flick the match into the unknown. A moment later, the unknown makes itself known, and just like I predicted, when my past goes up in flames, nothing has ever felt sweeter.

"Welcome home, Victoria Armstrong. Here's to the new you."

Two

Fire.

As I complacently stand, watching one of my most prized pieces of furniture go up in flames, I can appreciate why so many tribes around the world look at fire as a miracle. I only just refrain from doing a traditional Aboriginal fire dance around the flaming fireball, as I don't want to move, just in case I miss anything.

Fire takes and gives, and at the moment, it's giving me great pleasure by taking away my pain.

I'm too transfixed on the flames and what they represent to notice a hooded figure jogging toward me and blending into the shadows until I see movement from the corner of my eye. Squinting, I focus on where I'm almost certain someone is shrouded behind an enormous pine tree. Before I have a chance to question my sanity, the shape emerges, confirming that some stranger *is* currently in my yard.

From their tall, towering frame and bulky, muscular build, it's safe to assume my assailant is a man, which makes me shriek and thrust the Jameson bottle out, wielding it like a weapon.

I should run inside, lock my doors, and call the police, but the fact I have a blazing chair in my backyard, which is crackling loudly and burning brighter by the minute, has me standing my ground and endeavoring to sound confident as I yell, "Who's there? You've got three seconds to get off my property before I call the police!"…*on my cell, which is uselessly sitting upstairs*, I silently add.

My empty threats fall on deaf ears, however, as my intruder suddenly stalks toward me. His dark gray hood is pulled over his head, concealing his downturned face. I don't know why—because Lord knows I should be—but I'm not scared. I have an inexplicable sense of excitement and anticipation coursing through my veins, and all I can think is I want—no *need*—to see his face. He's across my yard in five huge strides and standing before me in seconds.

I tilt my head to the side and hold my breath when a large hand reaches out and cautiously lowers the bottle, which I'm still waving around. For some unexplained reason, my arm falls willingly by my side. The firestorm has taken a back seat because all I can concentrate on is the way the fair skin of his long-fingered hands contrasts the shadows of the night as he raises them and slowly removes the hood from his head. A silver chain with a small pendant hanging off the end comes free with the movement, catching the shine of the moon.

With a measured, calculated speed, he lifts his chiseled chin, and I'm suddenly pinned with the deepest blue stare of a handsome man, who exudes nothing but confidence and allure. His angular jawline is coated in a dark five o'clock shadow, setting off his sexy, rebellious look. The moon is full, and the flames provide the light I need to see he is just as transfixed by me as I am by him.

His dark brown hair is longer on top, messily styled as though he's passed those long fingers through it. He looks rugged and dangerous, someone who looks like trouble, so I pull myself together because I've just been openly ogling the handsome stranger who quite possibly could be a serial killer.

But serial killer or not, I've never seen someone this… mesmerizing before. I know that word is a little vague, but it's the only one fit to describe the stranger standing in my backyard. The stranger who has stoked a tiny fire in me, a fire I didn't even know existed.

"Hi."

His deep, gruff voice makes me instantly remember where I am, so I stop admiring his broad chest to focus on his attractive grin.

His cockiness titillates me. "Hi," I reply a moment later after licking my suddenly dry lips. However, realizing I should probably address the issue at hand, I ask, "Who are you, and why are you standing in my yard?"

The corner of his mouth tips up into a hint of a smile, and the simple gesture makes me wonder how he'd look with both corners lifted—handsome, no doubt.

"I'm Jude." I nod, waiting for him to continue. "I live across the pond," he goes on to explain, gesturing with his head to a humble but arresting looking white house across the lake.

His comment has my cheeks bursting into flames. Have the neighbors sent him over to investigate who the new weirdo is? What a way to announce my arrival to the neighborhood.

I look over his shoulder at the smoldering mess I've made. "I'm really sorry about the pyromania. Please let everyone know their houses are safe. I'm not usually this crazy. Well, only on Fridays. And maybe every second full moon," I add, cringing at how ridiculous I sound.

But Jude surprises me when he smiles. I was right—complete heartbreaker.

"No one sent me over," he clarifies, shaking his head.

"Oh?" Looking down at his black Nikes, black sweats, and gray sweater, I realize he's dressed to blend into the shadows, not stand out, leading the neighborhood watch patrol. "Well, that's a relief." Not thinking, I draw the joint up to my lips and take a much-needed hit.

"But that might change once Henry gets a whiff of you breaking all the rules."

I cock an eyebrow, not following. "Who's Henry?"

Jude looks toward an enormous, double story house, blowing out an exaggerated breath. "Henry is one of those do-gooders. You know the type—goes to church every Sunday, drives a hybrid, separates his colors from his whites."

"Henry needs to lighten up," I quip, blowing out a plume of smoke.

A dimple presses into his right, whiskered cheek. "He certainly does. But I guess he has to be an uptight asshole… seeing as he's the sheriff."

I almost inhale my joint the moment I hear the word sheriff. Thumping on my chest, I wheeze, "Is he home right now?"

He nods coolly while taunting, "Yeah. That's kind of why I'm standing in your backyard."

I toss the joint to the ground, stomping on it and hissing when it burns the pad of my foot. But my pain can wait as I currently have an inferno to deal with. "Bloody hell," I curse under my breath, my Australian accent breaking through when I panic.

Looking around my barren yard, I wonder if the garden shed has a hose, or some kind of watering device to douse these flames fast enough so that my neighbor, who just happens to be the sheriff, won't awake to the flames of hell licking at his bedroom window.

I take off in a dead sprint, almost winding myself because I can't remember the last time I actually ran after I got sick.

When I get to the garden shed, I cuss because the double doors are locked with a rusted padlock. "Shit. You son of a bitch!" I groan, pulling on the sealed doors in vain.

A husky laugh behind me reminds me I have company, and I turn, not at all impressed to see Jude smiling. "What are you doing?" he questions, folding his arms over his impressive chest.

"Just in case you hadn't noticed, a huge fireball is currently lighting up my backyard."

"I noticed," he smugly replies and continues to stand there, grinning.

I take a deep breath. "Well, how about you stop standing around like a stunned mullet, and help me figure out how I'm going to put it out without having to call the fire department?"

His voice is smooth, honeyed as he laughs. "A stunned mullet? What the hell is that?"

"It's an Australian thing," I grumble. "And right now, you're the epitome of one."

"How long have you been in the States?" he asks calmly, ignoring my panic.

This is the worst time to make conversation, but I suppose he's trying to be neighborly. "I moved from Darwin, Australia when I was fourteen," I reply absentmindedly.

"I've always wanted to visit Australia. Surf those awesome waves." I can't believe he's talking about my home country in my time of crisis. I grunt in response.

There is no way I can push this thing into the lake. I expelled all my energy dragging this abomination out here in the first place. I really should have thought this through before I lit up my backyard like a damned Christmas tree on steroids. I'm actually surprised Henry hasn't woken up to the fact a huge bonfire is burning in the vicinity of his home.

As I'm strategizing ways I can get rid of this problem without having to call the fire department, I fail to notice the fireball traveling farther and farther down the dock. It's not until I hear a splash and a sizzling hiss do I see my problem sinking like a dead weight to a watery grave.

"I'm pretty sure a stunned mullet couldn't do that," Jude proudly states, standing by the dock's edge, calmly watching the water boil and sputter. I, on the other hand, feel like I'm losing my mind.

Unanticipated hysterical laughter bubbles from my throat, and I end up cackling manically like a crazy person. Tears slide down my cheeks, but I don't bother wiping them away. My actions tonight have no doubt cemented my insanity, and I'm pretty sure Jude is seconds away from paddling across that pond and getting the hell outta Dodge.

When will this roller coaster of emotions end? One minute, I think I've got a handle on everything, then the next…well, the next, I'm almost setting my house on fire. I'm losing my mind.

"Thank you, Jude," I say when I can finally catch my breath. I walk over to where he stands. "I owe you."

He doesn't turn to face me, though, as his eyes are still riveted to the spot where my sad, burned-out chair has sunk to the bottom of the lake. "Why did you burn it?" he asks, his voice unexpectedly poignant.

I rub my bare arms. I've suddenly caught a chill. "Some things are better off as ashes."

We stand side by side, our gazes fixed to the spot that seems to captivate us both. I've only just met this man, but I feel an inexplicable comfort around him. It's a feeling I haven't felt in a very long time, which frightens me.

But I don't need any more hitches as my life is complicated enough. So with that thought in mind, I clear my throat. The sound seems to jar Jude from whatever pensive thoughts he's lost in. "Thanks again. I really appreciate it."

"My pleasure…" He pauses. "I don't know your name."

Telling him my name is harmless, I reprimand myself. *What's in a name?* I squash down the significance of that quote. "I'm Victoria."

He nods in approval. "Victoria. I like it."

"Thanks." I have no idea why I'm thanking him for liking my name. I guess I'm just filling the tangible static because that's a far better option than questioning why I'm suddenly nervous around a complete stranger.

Thankfully, he's the one to fill the silence. "Sorry for messing up your serenity."

Looking at what's left of the smoldering chair, I wave him

off. "Don't even worry about it. It'll take some time before I reach the complete serenity stage." As if on cue, the back porch light fizzles out, leaving us at the mercy of the full moon.

"Well, if you ever need me, you know where I live." The invitation isn't sleazy, it's genuine.

That weighty feeling that the night is drawing to a close lingers in the air, but still, neither of us appear to want to say good night. Remembering my promise to start afresh, I ignore the mysterious pull, and say, "It was nice meeting you."

I shuffle my feet nervously and bite the inside of my cheek as he watches me closely. I desperately want to find out what he's thinking, but why does it matter? I'm not interested in getting to know anyone. I moved away from civilization for a reason—I'm here to focus on me and me alone.

With that attitude, that's exactly what my future holds—me alone.

"Good night." It appears he wants to say something else. Just when I'm about to ask if everything is okay, his face turns nostalgic. His heavy footsteps sound on the dock before he disappears down my driveway just as quietly as he appeared.

I stand rooted to the spot, unable to tear my eyes away from the place he once stood. Call me crazy, but from the brief minutes spent with Jude, I have a hunch that he's someone with a past just as blackened as mine. The old me would have asked him if he needed a friendly ear, but that old me is dead and gone. The new me has no interest in making friends or even making conversation. I just want to be left alone.

Walking up the creaky backstairs, I slam the back door shut behind me and lean against it, closing my eyes. I hate this constant feeling of apathy weighing me down, but better this than leaving myself open for new heartache.

Pushing off the door, I hunt through my small fridge and snatch a bottle of white wine. Switching off the lights, I climb the stairs to my room, too tired to even process that across the lake, just past a tree, lies the bedroom window of someone who I'm almost certain is going to be trouble.

Three

I wake with a start, convinced an earthquake is rocking my neighborhood, and my home is the epicenter.

Looking down at the non-moving floor, I realize my "earthquake" is actually my iPhone vibrating loudly against the floorboards. The movement rattles the empty bottle of wine, and I groan. This is not how I wanted to wake up Saturday morning in my new home—hung over and questioning if I was wearing any clothes. Peering down, I see I'm still in yesterday's dress—the dress I passed out in after polishing off a bottle of Sauvignon Blanc in twenty minutes.

To stop the racket, I have no other choice but to pick up my cell. I bark, "Hello?" without bothering to look at the screen.

"Well, good morning to you, too."

Jerking the phone away from my ear, I have no idea who

the caller is. "Who is this?"

A small giggle passes through the speaker. "It's Charley McMann. We went to high school together."

Charley McMann? How on earth did she get my number? We were best friends during high school but drifted apart when she moved away to attend Juilliard in New York. It appears she's back in town.

"How are you?" Sitting up slowly, I attempt to join the land of the living as I gulp down a bottle of water.

"Cold."

"Cold? Where are you?"

"Standing outside your front door."

"How do you know where I live?"

"You know this place; everyone loves to gossip."

She's right. I'm sure the word has spread amongst the desperate and dateless that Bryan is now a single man. Or maybe not. He could be living the perfect life with my sister. I wouldn't know, as I refuse to acknowledge either of them.

"Can you let me in?"

Charley was a great friend. Maybe this is exactly what I need to start afresh. New friends and new experiences. It's worth a shot.

"Sure, give me a second."

Swinging my legs to the side, I place my feet onto the floorboards, the cool texture sending a shiver down my spine. Since that night, I've always been cold. There is a constant chill to my bones, no matter how hard I try to get warm.

My wobbly legs make it down the stairs as I open the door. Before me stands my once best friend, Charley McMann. "I can't believe you're here," I stupidly exclaim into the phone.

Charley chuckles, snapping her phone shut. "Where else would I be?"

She's aged extraordinarily well and looks just like she did the day we said goodbye. I self-consciously run a hand through my bird's nest, but I know nothing can tame that beast.

"How're you holding up?" she asks sympathetically. That's the one thing I liked about Charley; she was never one for small talk.

"Honestly, I should just buy shares in Kleenex."

Her full lips tip into a small smile. "Cry that asshole out of your system." Without warning, she steps forward and hugs me tightly. I don't know why, but her kindness has my tears resurfacing. It feels nice to cry, as I don't allow myself this reprieve often.

I half laugh, half sob into her shoulder, and once I feel composed enough, I pull away, wiping my eyes. I'm not embarrassed she caught me crying. I've known Charley since I first moved to Connecticut. We met at Paradise Valley High School and became best friends immediately.

She was there through thick and thin, always a shoulder to cry on, no matter what.

"Come inside." Looking at the collar of her couture-looking

sundress, I blanch. "Sorry I used you as a tissue. I promise your garments are safe from now on."

She laughs, wiping away the tears which have gathered in the corner of her eyes. Some things never change as Charley was always a sympathetic crier.

When she steps into my bleak home, she looks from left to right, but doesn't pass judgment on my barren surroundings. It's old, ratty, and barely functioning, but it'll do.

"Shit," I curse as we walk into my kitchen. "I don't have any coffee."

"I thought as much." Charley reaches into her blue bag, pulling out two disposable cups, a jar of ground coffee, and some creamer.

"You're a lifesaver. I'll just take a quick shower. The kitchen stuff is in there, I think." I tentatively point at a lone box in the corner, unsure if there's pots in there or pants. I dumped my stuff anywhere, as it's not like I had a method to my madness when I packed up my life into a handful of boxes and threw them into the small moving trailer.

She waves me off and goes to work on sorting out my mess by ripping open the mystery box. "Go, I'll find what I need." I nod before lumbering up the stairs and heading straight for the bathroom.

I strip off, avoiding the mirror above the sink, and dive into the small, outdated shower, turning the faucet to hot. The pipes whine and grumble, but eventually, lukewarm water splutters from the showerhead. The pressure is lousy, but the water feels divine against my aching flesh, reminding me of last night's weird yet exciting proceedings.

I can't deny that some unexplained static was bouncing between Jude and me. He *is* incredibly attractive, so I'm sure it's just a normal reaction to seeing a handsome guy. But is it? I wouldn't know. Bryan was my first everything, and I've never experienced a weird static with anyone other than him.

It's hard to think back on our relationship with anything other than hatred, but the butterflies *were* there. They were there the moment I saw him chasing the ball as star quarterback in high school. Too bad those butterflies turned out to be moths in disguise.

Regardless of this static, I'm not in the right frame of mind to be thinking about this. But I can't help but wonder what secrets lay behind those sorrowful blue eyes. I know there's something…more.

So much for not thinking about this.

Switching off the water, I quickly dry off and step into my bedroom in nothing but a towel. My eyes land on the open window where the flimsy lace curtain flaps gently in the light breeze—the window that sits in line with Jude's.

I tighten the towel around my body and ensure I'm not flashing any inner leg as I dash over to the two boxes sitting near my closet. Tearing open the box, I pull out my denim cutoffs and a tank. The smaller box to the right contains my underwear, so I hunt through it.

Meeting someone as perfect as Jude has made me feel incomplete, which I know is ridiculous. But I don't feel how I once did when looking into the mirror. When I look at the angry, red scar sliced across my chest, it reminds me of all the things I've lost.

That night, it wasn't enough that my attacker took my soul. He also took a part of me physically when a bullet lodged deeply into my chest. The doctors said I was lucky because if the bullet was two millimeters to the right, I would be dead. But I don't feel lucky. I'm not only scarred emotionally, but physically as well.

I aptly strip off, ensuring to steer clear of the window as I dress. When I'm good to go, I run my fingers through my damp hair and bounce down the stairs the moment I smell coffee waft through the air.

"You're a godsend." She chuckles and passes me a cup, which I gratefully accept.

I lean my elbows on the counter and cradle my cup, lost in thought.

"I read what happened to you in the papers. I'm so sorry, Tori. You didn't deserve that. And then Bryan…" She frowns, shaking her head.

I reach for her hand. "Thanks, I'll be okay. I *need* to live a normal life, and to do that, I have to start living."

She squeezes my fingers. "I've always admired your

strength." Tears sting my eyes, and I discreetly wipe them away with the back of my hand. "Okay." She lets out a loud breath. "Enough with the sads. I've decided you're having a housewarming party."

"Um, no," I reply without delay. "I'm not here to make friends." She flutters her eyelashes playfully. "Charley," I warn. "I don't need or want a housewarming."

My plea falls on deaf ears. "You don't have to do a thing. I'll organize everything. It'll be small. I promise."

"Uh-huh," I reply, unconvinced. I have a feeling Charley's "small" is one hundred plus guests.

When she sees my apprehension, she raises three fingers. "Scout's honor."

I can't help but laugh. "You were never a Girl Scout."

She shrugs, unperturbed. "I know, but I would have totally rocked the outfit if I was."

How can I argue with that? "Okay, fine. But twenty people max." I point my finger at her to emphasize how serious I am.

She ignores me and jumps up and down, clapping. "You won't regret it. It'll be so fun."

"And no gifts."

"Nonsense. Your bleak home will thank you."

I don't bother arguing.

She reaches for her cell. "Now, is there anyone you *don't* want me to invite?"

"Everyone," I grumble, sipping my coffee. "I don't do social events—especially now. I just want to blend into the background and be incognito. Not the center of attention."

Charley stops typing and frowns. "After everything you've been through, you deserve some attention. Let loose. This is a part of being the new you."

Scraping my fingernail over the paper cup, I confess, "I don't know who I want to be. That night, I don't…remember much. Flashes come back to me through nightmares, but I can't recount what happened. The doctors, they tell me I got shot. The scars I bear also confirm this. But I don't remember anything."

"What can you remember?" The room suddenly turns stale, still.

Closing my eyes, I inhale deeply. It's the same scenario I dream about every night. A dark alleyway, my heart about to explode from my chest, a hooded savior, whose face I never see, screaming at me to watch out. Then I wake in a sweat. I've been told what happens next, but I can't remember. Is there something wrong with me? Who was the man who saved me? Who was willing to risk his life for me, while my fiancé lagged behind?

"Tori, are you all right?"

My eyes snap open, focusing on Charley's fingers gently squeezing my forearm. "I just wish I could remember. I feel like something is missing, and I don't know what."

She bites her glossy lip, allowing my purge.

I chew the inside of my cheek to stop the tears. "I'm just so scared…all the time. I feel helpless. I should have done more. I pushed Bryan away because a part of me hates him, and I don't know why." I sip my coffee, but my palate suddenly demands something stronger.

"And…your sister?" she apprehensively asks. Now I definitely need the booze.

"I don't have a sister. She gave that right up the moment she thought my husband was suitable shagging material." My tone is sharp, and I regret snapping. Rubbing my brow, I exhale loudly. "I don't know who I'm madder at; her or Bryan."

Charley shakes her head, disgusted. "Both." She reaches into her bag and pulls out a mini bar-sized bottle of vodka. She unscrews the lid and takes a swig, offering me the rest.

As I tap my finger against the label, I realize she's right. One betrayal is just as bad as the other.

"It'll get better. Each day will get easier."

I nod half-heartedly, not so sure.

"If you ever wanted to talk, you know I'm here. I know we drifted apart, but I never stopped thinking about you. You were a great friend to me. Sometimes, I wish I never moved away."

I can't help but frown because she sounds so glum. I try to lighten the mood. "You were a great friend too. We did get up to loads of mischief, didn't we?"

She smiles broadly, almost nostalgic. "We sure did."

"So did you become the world-famous dancer you were

determined to be?"

She lowers her eyes and chews on her bottom lip. "Things change. What was once important doesn't seem so important anymore."

Her vague response is clue enough that she doesn't want to talk about her past, which I will respect, as I know the feeling all too well.

"Thanks for being here, Charley. I really appreciate it." Deciding to let down my guard, I confess, "I just need to move on. My heart still aches…" Will I ever stop hurting? "I'm a mess, I know that, but that's why I moved here. To work on myself and to start over." *Away from memories I wish I could forget*, I silently add. "You being here helps."

I'm in the midst of tossing back the vodka when I see her eyes widen as she stares over my shoulder. "What?" I screech, sweeping my shoulder frantically, afraid a spider is crawling all over me. A shiver spreads like wildfire. Why can't I brush the feeling that someone is always standing behind me?

"*Who* is that?"

"Who is who?" I ask, confused.

"That," she replies, pointing behind me and pulling at her glossy bottom lip.

I have no idea what has captured her undivided attention, but when I turn around and see the object of her affection, I understand why her jaw has just dropped onto my kitchen counter.

"That's Jude," I say, watching curiously as he stands by the lake, hands on hips.

"*Who* is Jude, and how do you know him? Dear Lord, he kind of looks like Scott Eastwood. All dreamy and so brawny."

I can't help the small chuckle that escapes me. Good to see I'm not the only one affected by his looks. "He lives across the lake," I explain. "I met him last night when he kindly gave me the heads-up not to burn my possessions or smoke weed in the vicinity of Henry, the county sheriff."

Charley gasps. "I don't even know how to process that sentence."

My gaze never wavers from Jude, who looks even better in the daylight. He's wearing blue jeans and a white tee, showcasing his impressive muscular arms and summer tan. The sunshine catches the light chestnut in his hair, contrasting the woven strands of darkened brown.

"Introduce me," Charley says, snapping me from rubbernecking.

"Why?" I ask a little too heatedly, turning back to face her.

When her mouth parts and she smirks, I kick myself for not being a little more tactful. "I just meant, why do you want to meet him?"

"Because he's hot," she replies, fanning herself. "And so… big," she settles for after fishing for the right word.

The reason I moved out here in the wilderness was to stay away from big, hot, handsome men. What are the odds I now live near one? "If you want to meet him, then be my guest," I foolishly suggest, as I believe that'll discourage Charley and she'll let the matter drop.

But I should have known she never backs down from a challenge.

"Charley, no!" I scold, but she brushes past me and yanks open the door before I have a chance to stop her from charging down the stairs. The noise alerts Jude.

With no other choice, I throw back the vodka and follow my determined best friend.

This is so embarrassing, and I have no idea why. But I stand tall, hoping I look semi-composed instead of displaying how nervous I feel. I'm a few feet away when I hear Charley gush, "Tori didn't tell me you came with the house."

Jude smiles broadly while I feel a pinch of jealousy. I dismiss it instantly.

"I'm Charley, Tori's best friend." She extends her manicured hand.

"Nice to meet you, Charley. I'm Jude." He politely shakes her hand.

"Oh my…" She gasps. "Firm grip you have there."

And that's my cue to intervene. "Good morning, Jude." I raise my eyes upward at my ridiculous friend who is still shaking his hand.

The moment he hears my voice, he drops Charley's hand and focuses that stormy gaze my way. "Good morning, Victoria."

My name has never sounded so smooth.

I need to stop this now. Mentally slapping myself, I smile. "So, not to sound like a broken record, but what are you doing in my yard?"

He grins, a dimple hugging his cheek. "I figured I owed you."

"Owed me what?"

"Well, considering I ruined your side of the lake, I figure it's my job to clean it."

"It might be hard to clean a lake," I tease, hating the way I respond to him.

He catches me completely unaware when he steps forward and wraps his fingers around my wrist. The charge sizzles all the way to my toes. "Maybe I could cut your grass then?"

I gulp.

I know I'm slender, but my wrist looks dwarfed by his humongous hand. "Thank you for the offer, but you've already done enough." And I'm not just talking about him saving me from Henry, the neighborhood vigilante.

Only when Charley clears her throat do I realize Jude is still holding my wrist, gently stroking his finger over my sudden racing pulse. His touch feels surprisingly good, but regardless, I should probably break contact. He must be able to sense my retreat because before I can move away, he pulls me toward him so we're standing inches apart. He's tall, I'm guessing six foot three. My modest frame of five foot four is eclipsed by his enormous frame.

He watches me closely, and when I'm graced with a sexy, slow smirk, I feel my cheeks heat and my legs get heavy. My original thought of him being trouble has just been confirmed. But funnily enough, I'm reveling in the disorder.

"Unless you know how to unclog my pipes, you're wasting my time." Charley snorts while I feel my cheeks burst into flames. That probably wasn't the best thing to say as it sounded awfully flirty. I didn't even know I could do flirty. But I just did, and even though I'm mortified beyond belief, it actually felt kind of liberating.

Jude smirks; his longer canines making him appear sweet, but dangerous all at the same time. "It's been a while since I've unclogged anyone's pipes, but I'll try my best." This situation really can't get any more embarrassing, as I think we're talking in innuendoes. I remove my wrist, thankful when he lets me go.

It's impossible to look over his broad shoulder, even if I stand on tippy toes, so I playfully shove past him while he chuckles. The moment I walk down the dock, I remember him pushing the chair into the water like it weighed nothing at all.

"Thanks again for helping me last night," I say over my shoulder.

I see that he's followed me. He remains pensive before he replies, "No problem. Try not to set anything else on fire, though." He winks, and I redden once again.

"Hold up," Charley says, reminding me that we've got

company as she also joins us. "What do you mean, anything else? What have you set on fire?" She stands near me, grinning curiously.

"Well…" I rub the back of my neck. "I sort of set a chair on fire," I shamefully confess.

"Sort of?" Jude exclaims. "Those flames would have been seen by the good Lord himself."

"Oh, shut up." Without thinking, I playfully slap his arm. A stunned wheeze escapes me when my hand is met with solid, contoured, defined muscle.

I remove my hand with lightning-quick speed, feeling my heart thump to a wound-up drumbeat.

"What are you doing next weekend?" Charley asks a second later.

Jude appears to be mentally calculating through his plans. "Nothing really."

"Fantastic, because we're having a housewarming at Tori's place. You should come." I'm still standing wordless, watching the conversational ping pong bounce between Jude and Charley.

I don't know whether I should thank her or cuss her out, but when Jude grins, I know I owe her a thank you for seeing that smile once again. "Sure, I'd love to come."

Before I have a chance to even get my head around anything, Charley is entering my cell number into Jude's phone. I need to speak up. I need to thank him for getting rid of the evidence, but there will be no housewarming because I'm busy—busy attempting to piece my life back together.

"There is no house…"

But I'm rudely cut off when Charley interrupts me. "There is no housewarming without lots of food and beer. Make sure you come with a big appetite for fun."

I don't even bother correcting her because she's thought this all through.

"Okay, I'll be there," Jude says, watching me closely. "Just let me know the details." He holds up his phone, cementing the fact he has my number and can call or text anytime he wants.

My breath gets caught in my throat, and I'm suddenly finding it hard to breathe. "I need to run to the store." My voice is high pitched and flighty, revealing I'm seconds away from crumbling into a mess.

Jude nods, his watchful eyes most likely detecting my apprehension. His insight into my discomfort makes me spin abruptly and march briskly to the stairs. I charge up them, needing to hide away from those inquisitive eyes. Sadly, my dilapidated home decides to surrender, and the moment I climb the second to last step, it caves out beneath me. I trip forward as one leg is dangling through the hole where the rickety step once sat.

"Holy shit!" I curse, desperately clutching at the unsteady railing, attempting to pull myself up before I fall straight through. Just as I boost myself up, a set of strong arms wraps around my middle, lifts me up, and walks me to safe ground. It happens quite quickly, and I'm too indebted to Jude for saving my life to realize he has his arms folded across my chest.

It takes my brain all of three seconds to realize this is the first time I've allowed anyone to touch me in months. As I think about why that is, hot, angry tears sting my eyes. I latch onto his wrist and force his arm off me. I find my footing on solid ground while Jude wobbles and latches onto the railing.

"Whoa! Is that any way to thank me for saving your life?" He regains his balance, standing inches away.

I know he's joking and trying to make light of the sudden stale mood, but I never asked him to be my knight in shining armor. I moved out here to get away from uncomfortable situations such as this one.

I don't want complications. I just want simple. And the way I feel when I'm around Jude is anything but simple. I don't know why, but I just know he's trouble.

"Thank you," I bark. Even to my ears, it sounds abrupt. "But no one asked you to. I don't need you coming to my rescue. I can look after myself."

A frown quickly replaces Jude's smile. His walls are firmly erected as he replies, "Don't worry, it won't happen again."

"Good." I'm rocking the shit out of my resting bitch face right now.

We stand staring at one another, the tension crackling between us. He doesn't hide his annoyance at my discourtesy, and a small part of me is annoyed at myself for being so closed off to a friendship with this man. He's been nothing but nice to me, going out of his way to be neighborly, and all I've done is behave like a crazy person.

"I'll see you around, Victoria," he says, breaking the silence. I nod, afraid of what my voice would sound like if I replied. He gives me one final look before darting down the stairs, two at a time, to avoid the missing step.

When he's no longer in sight, I gingerly meet Charley's stare. I know what she's about to say, but I don't want to hear it. "Save it, Charley."

Of course, she doesn't listen and charges up the steps to stop me from going inside and locking her out. "Tori, there's nothing wrong with you making friends. I understand it's too early for you to be thinking about a relationship, but Jude, or any other guy for that matter, is not Bryan."

His name is akin to nails running down a blackboard and my mood is further sullied. "It doesn't matter either way. I'm not interested in getting to know anybody. I moved out here for a fresh start, and that start doesn't include my snooping neighbor."

"He was hardly snooping," she corrects. "He was just being nice."

"Well, he can be nice on his side of the lake." My tone has more bite than I intended, but I know Charley. If I don't stress how strongly I feel about this, she'll play cupid and end up inviting him over for dinner. "I'm going into town. Do you need anything?"

She reads my dismissal but smirks. "*I* don't need anything, but you may want to pop into the animal shelter." When I cock a puzzled brow, she clarifies, "Because at this rate, you're going to need an army of cats to fill your crazy cat lady quota."

Playfully rolling my eyes, I enter my home, but not before replying over my shoulder, "Lucky for me, cats don't talk back."

Four

My beat-up Honda coughs out a black cloud of smoke as I kill the engine. I'm actually surprised it made the leg over here and that I didn't need to call AAA. As I exit my car, I understand why they call this part of the state The Quiet Corner. The semi-rural town is more rustic than suburbia, and I love it. It's the exact reason I chose to move here. With the population coming in at just over twelve thousand, it's large enough not to be noticed, but small and boring enough that folks just keep driving by.

The quiet stretch of dated stores provides the essentials for a one-stop shop. There are a few people going about their daily duties, hands filled with groceries, busy to get from point A to B. I lower my head, not interested in getting to know my fellow townsfolk, because after this morning, I really just want to be left alone. I know it can't stay this way forever because if I want to get back into teaching, then I'll have no other choice but to socialize. But for now, I'm content being in my own company.

The bell above the glass door chimes as I enter the musty smelling store. It's bigger than I thought it would be, and I'm thrilled to see they have a small furniture section to the far left. The trailer I rented was big enough to fit the spare double bed, a bar fridge, a few boxes, and the infamous chair, which is now no longer. I can't help but think about where it sits, sunken to the bottom of the lake. I also can't help but think about the reason it's no longer in my yard.

Shaking my head, hoping to dispel all thoughts of Jude, I smile politely at the uninterested blonde teenager behind the register engrossed in her gossip magazine. My eyes are instantly drawn to a blood red chesterfield throne. The gold border with its carved, intricate pattern is completely lavish and totally unnecessary, but I want it. White stuffing is poking through a small tear in the arm, but the imperfection contrasts the flawlessness of my previous chair, and for some unexplained reason, it's perfect. There isn't a price tag, so I do a quick sweep of the store, grabbing a chipped dinner set, some glasses, and a few other kitchen supplies.

With both hands filled, I place everything onto the counter, disturbing the jaded girl. "How much for all of this and that dining table and chairs…and that red seat?"

In response, she pops her pink gum and continues reading

her magazine.

"Is twenty-five dollars all right?"

When she chooses to ignore me, I reach into my back pocket and place the cash onto the counter. Just as I'm about to ask if this amount suffices, the phone rings. She answers it and turns her back to me, giggling at whatever the caller just said.

Well, that was rude, but I shouldn't expect much less, as there isn't an app for manners.

Once I'm done boxing up my kitchenware, I tackle the table and chairs, which are much lighter than I thought. Carrying them to the trailer is easy enough; it's the damn seat that provides the challenge, as it's heavier than I thought it would be. It's also awkward to carry.

I take a deep breath and haul the chair with everything I have. The fact I need another to replace the one I burned spurs me on, and before I know it, I'm stumbling out the door. Stopping for just a second, I use my adrenaline punch to lift it up and place it alongside the table and chairs in the trailer. Locking the doors, I place my hands on my hips and bend low, gulping in fresh air and filling my depleted lungs.

I hate that I'm still so weak. The doctors said this was natural, that it'll take a while for my body to be what it once was. I used to be a runner, fastest in track, but now I can barely climb a set of stairs without gasping for breath. Well, that stops today. I have a lake right outside my home. As of tomorrow, I'm going to see how many miles it is to the other side of the lake.

I'm no longer a victim. I survived for a reason, and that reason was to live.

When I hear the unkind, appalling words, "Hey, retard," my living starts right now.

Up ahead, I see a small group of teenage boys, who look like wannabe James Deans, surrounding a younger boy. He is clearly terrified, thumping his little fists against them, desperate to escape. But the circle around him grows tighter and smaller, imprisoning him in a cage of five callous bullies.

"Retard, give me your money!"

"He doesn't have any money. His dad is a deadbeat."

"I'm sure his grandpa gave him some cash." They continue to taunt, pushing and shoving him until he's screaming, attempting to break free. When the biggest of the group pushes him so hard he falls to the ground with a sickening thud, I see red.

"Hey!" I shout, charging over. My warning falls on deaf ears, however, and only seems to encourage them to be crueler.

They bend low and begin a malicious chant. "Retard! Retard! Retard!" This has the petrified boy curling into a ball as he begins crying.

"Stop it, you little buggers! Leave him alone." I yank at the arm of the ringleader, who spins around, stunned that someone is reprimanding him.

My threat thankfully has some impact, and I shove past them and tend to the crying boy on the pavement. I crouch down in front of him. "Hello. My name is Victoria. I won't hurt you. Are you okay?"

But he doesn't flinch. He doesn't even appear to hear me.

Deciding that touch may be the best form of therapy, I gently place my palm on his back. Sadly, it doesn't have the effect I'd hoped for. He springs up, his blue eyes wide as he screams. The screech is deafening, almost off-key. When he begins mumbling guttural sounds, I know why he didn't respond to my words.

"See, told you he's a retard."

Turning to glare at all of them, I spit, "What is the matter with you? He's deaf! Now go away before I walk over to that corner store and ask where you all live. I'm sure your parents will be interested to know that you've all skipped school." That shuts them up real quick, and they eventually turn and leave.

I don't know sign language, but his minimal language skills make me believe he's been deaf for a long while. "Hi." I place up my hand. "I'm Victoria. What's your name?" I'm hoping he can read my lips, but he cocks his head to the side, frightened.

My soul weeps for this brown-haired, blue-eyed boy. "Where's your mommy?" The word which hurts my heart seems to do the same to the boy, whose lower lip trembles. "You've lost your mommy?" I ask, trying to piece this puzzle together. When he continues staring at me, watching my lips closely, I repeat, "Mommy? You've lost her?"

As I extend my hand out to comfort him, he suddenly jumps up and slaps my arm away. I pull back, stunned. What did I say? Just as I open my mouth, ready to ask about his mom, he shakes his head violently and screams. The force of the sound has me jarring backward, confused about what I said that has set him off.

I don't have time to find out, though, because before I say another word, he pushes past me and runs down the sidewalk and around behind the corner store. I shoot up and follow in hot pursuit, afraid he's going to get himself hurt. But when I turn the corner, he's vanished into dense woodlands.

"Shit!" I curse, debating whether I should follow. Bearing in mind the last time I tried to comfort him backfired, I think the wise thing to do would be to call the police. Sprinting back to the thrift shop, the bell whines as I shove open the door.

"Can you please call the police?" My desperate plea doesn't rattle her in the slightest. Annoyed with her apathy, I explain, "A little boy, around eight years old, just ran off into the woods. I'm concerned about him, as he was clearly upset." She blows a pink bubble, it pops, just like my last nerve. "And he's deaf! Call the police now. Please. He could be in trouble. Or he might get lost."

She yawns, my melodramatics apparently boring her. Just as I'm about to reach over the counter and call 911 myself, an older lady strolls in. "Good afternoon, Mrs. Silverdale."

"Hello, Brittney. Can you call the station? Young Angus has run off into the woods again."

Brittney nods, frowning. "Sure." She reaches under the

counter, producing an old-fashioned phone. The rustic charm is now grating on my nerves.

When I hear her ask for the sheriff, I know that's my cue to leave. I have no desire to meet my neighbor, especially when I quite possibly might have scared a hearing-impaired little boy into the woods. And if by chance the sheriff smelled the weed wafting over the waters or caught a glimpse of the flaming inferno outside his window, then I'll definitely be in his bad books. I don't need to add this to the mix. I'm out the door before she hangs up.

On the short drive home, I can't help but think that for a town labeled The Quiet Corner, I sure as hell have created a thunderous noise.

Birds fly from their perches as I curse like a sailor.

Buying this chair may have seemed like a good idea at the time, but now I'm wishing I'd bought the fondue set instead. I have managed to get it out of the trailer, but dragging it across my overgrown lawn and to the front door is the problem.

"You better feel like clouds under my bum." I'm huffing and puffing, determined to get this thing inside, but it's not budging an inch.

Needing a break, I head inside for a glass of water. My cell sounds, indicating I have a voice message. Reaching for it off the counter, I dial voicemail, hoping it's someone with some muscle to help me on my quest.

But it's not.

The pause should have hinted at who the caller is.

"…Tori, please listen. I…this is hard for me, too. We never meant to hurt you. We both missed you so much. I talk to you every day even though I know you won't talk back. I'm sorry, please forgive me. I need you. I miss my sister. Please…"

My fingers tremble as I end the call. I've heard enough. I just can't deal with this…ever.

Matilda's voice brings back so many memories and her excuses cement the fact that she and Bryan are dead to me. I won't cry. A treacherous tear spills free, but I wipe it away quickly.

Needing a distraction, I finish my water and head back outside. With a new surge of adrenaline, I pick up the chair. However, when I hear, "Do you need a hand?" my determination turns to gratitude because I'm only going to make it a few more steps.

Peering around the chair, my appreciation turns to dread when I see a tall, fairly attractive, older gentleman in uniform. In my utter shock, my grip loosens, and I drop the chair leg onto my foot. "You little bastard!" I shout, shooting up and hopping around as I grab my injured foot. It's a knee-jerk reaction, but probably not the best to have, seeing as I have a police officer staring at me like I've lost my mind.

Today can blow me.

"Miss, are you all right?" he asks apprehensively, resting his hands on his hips. I have no doubt that this move was intentional, as he's now in reach of his mace and gun.

"Yes, I'm fine," I reply, placing both feet on the ground. Putting on my semi-sane face, I smile, but it feels like a scowl instead. My answer appears to appease him however, and he nods.

His nametag reads *Sands*. Looks like I've finally met my infamous neighbor. I don't know why, but he makes me nervous. He certainly has an air of authority and discipline surrounding him. No wonder he was made sheriff.

"Can I help you?" I ask, unsure if this is a friendly visit, or if he's here to arrest me for disturbing the peace.

"I'm Sheriff Henry Sands. I live across the lake."

I play dumb. "It's nice to meet you, Sheriff Sands. It's good to know the sheriff is my neighbor. But I'm sure it's a safe neighborhood. I'm Victoria Armstrong." I'm rambling because he doesn't say anything. He just continues staring at me, sizing me up.

I extend my hand, but drop it quickly when Henry says, "I know who you are, Ms. Armstrong."

"Oh?" I gulp.

"Yes," he replies before he strolls over to the patrol car and opens the passenger door. He's so refined, so formal, I suddenly believe he's here to haul my ass off to jail.

I watch eyes wide. Does he want me to get in? "I…"

I don't get a chance to beg him to go easy on me because when he produces a cardboard box and I see the items I purchased from the thrift store inside, I exhale loudly. The sound has him raising an eyebrow. Thankfully, he doesn't address my jumpiness. "I believe this is yours." His polished shoes swish through the long blades of grass, soiling their shine as he walks over to me and hands me the box.

"Yes, it is. Thanks. How'd you know it was mine?"

"Good detective work," he replies, making me even edgier. I smile, but it's strained. "A report came in about a boy named Angus wandering off into the woods."

"Oh, that was me who called. He got rather spooked and ran off. I wanted to chase after him, but thought it best I call the police. I hope that was okay?" I question when he gives nothing away.

He runs a hand through his thick brown hair. It's graying at the temples, giving him a distinguished look. "Yes, that's what we're here for, but in the future, it's best you don't run off."

"I hardly ran," I reply, not appreciating his tone. I don't care who he is. I won't be made to feel like a criminal when I've done nothing wrong, and on my property no less.

He nods with a stiff upper lip. "I saw you. I was on patrol just around the corner."

There is no point in arguing with him, so I simply nod with a sour smile. "Thanks again for bringing this over." I lift the box, the items rattling inside. It's a silent dismissal, one I hope he gets loud and clear.

"Where would you like the chair?"

The chair is the least on my concerns. "It's fine. I'll just leave it out here for the moment until I decide what I want to do with it."

He frowns, but thankfully doesn't argue. "Okay. It was nice meeting you, Ms. Armstrong."

"You too…" *Not.* I want this uncomfortable situation to be over with, so I turn, ready to run into the safety of my home. I only make it three steps because if I continue walking, I'm afraid I'll fall over my feet.

"Will you come over for dinner tonight?"

"D-Dinner?" The word gets caught in my throat. His statement was just that. It was phrased as a question, but in reality, I know I don't have a choice. However, that doesn't sway me in saying yes. "I would love to come but—"

"Great. Dinner is at seven."

"Sheriff Sands, I couldn't impose," I reply, turning around to face him. Looking down at his hand, I see he's wearing a simple, gold wedding band. I'm hoping this approach will work. "I'm sure your wife would want a little more notice for a dinner guest."

However, Henry Sands doesn't take no for an answer. He is also someone accustomed to getting his own way. "Nonsense. My Jillian makes enough food to feed an army. And besides…"

His pause has the hair on the back of my neck standing on end. "It's the least we can do."

"I'm not following." Is this some welcome to the neighborhood soirée?

Pulling up his belt, he states, "You helped out our grandson. To show our gratitude, we'd like to have you over."

Breaking bread is the last thing on my mind. "Grandson?" I shake my head, completely lost in translation.

This is the first time I've seen Henry's hardnosed demeanor shift. When he mentions just *who* his grandson is, all the pieces come together. "Yes, the young boy, Angus…he's my grandson."

Five

S o much for this place being a small, sleepy, quiet town where I could start over with no drama or complications. So far, I've had nothing but drama and complications.

Locking the back door, I amble down the creaky stairs, not at all interested in having dinner with the Sands. I have no idea what I'm going to say to them.

A small, weathered motorboat, which has seen better days, is tied to the long wooden dock. I can picture whoever lived here before me running along the lush grass and cannon balling into the clear water. Laughter would have filled the long summer nights. I imagine many happy memories made here.

In its prime, this home would have been thriving, the envy of all the neighbors, but now, it's just a run-down shell of what it once was. In a weird way, that's why I fell in love with it. I can see its potential, even if others can't.

The faded red boat is the most practical form of transportation, and probably more fun than driving to Henry's place, but I don't trust that old-fashioned motor, so it looks like I'll be taking the Honda. My car starts with a splutter, and I know it won't be long until it kicks the bucket for good.

I pull onto the graveled private road, thankful it's only used by the locals. The sun is at half mast, illuminating the tranquility of my neighborhood. White oak trees border the road, lined up like regimented soldiers, adding bursts of color of yellowish green to a deep jade. I take in the surrounding houses. Some are small, while others are lavish in size—it's a mixed community, but overall, every home looks loved.

I can't help but slow down to a crawl when Jude's home comes into view. It's a modest, two-story house, with a well-maintained front yard. I wonder if Jude is happy here—if he likes being a part of a small community such as this one. Something tells me he's not really the type to host a Sunday roast, however.

When a light flicks on in the front window, I yelp and floor the accelerator in panic. My tires kick up the dirt as I fishtail down the road. I don't know why I feel so anxious around him, but whatever the reason, I'm not interested in dissecting.

Looking at the numbers on the letterboxes, I come to a stop when I'm in front of Henry's house, or should I say palace. His home is by far the biggest and most extravagant in the neighborhood.

Locking the car, I walk up the wide steps and wipe my sweaty palms onto my jeans. I take a deep breath before ringing the doorbell. It sounds loudly inside, cementing the fact I'm now committed to stay.

When the door opens, I try my best to appear delighted to be here. "Hi, Henry. I hope I'm not too early?"

He looks casual, which I wasn't expecting, in blue jeans, a navy polo, and boots. He also smells of fresh scented cologne. "Not at all. You're right on time. Please come in."

Once he steps aside, revealing the fortress behind him, it's time to enter the lion's den. The high walls are a pristine white, offset by modern works of art. He leads me through the living room, which is adorned with the entire contents of an IKEA catalog.

"I hope you drink chardonnay," he says, his voice echoing off the hallway walls.

"Yes, that's great. Thanks," I reply, still in awe of my surroundings.

He leads me into the open-plan kitchen with adjoining dining room where I stand, feeling so unbefitting. I watch as he hunts through the silver refrigerator and produces a bottle of wine. There is an elegant invitation stuck to the fridge with a mock police badge magnet. It appears there is an upcoming police ball, and Henry is the guest of honor.

"Thirty-five years on the force. That's some accomplishment.

Congratulations."

Henry looks at the invite, his chest puffing out in pride. "Thank you. It should be a great night. I hear over three hundred fellow officers will be in attendance."

"Wow, it'll be Christmas for all the felons in town." It's a joke, but Henry doesn't find it funny.

"Jillian is just upstairs changing," he explains, reaching for three wine goblets from a cupboard above the monster stove, which is littered with bubbling pots and pans. It smells absolutely delicious and my stomach rumbles in delight.

As he opens the wine, the far wall covered with a few photo frames catches my eye, so I wander over, needing to do something other than stand around uncomfortably. I'm instantly drawn to the gold-crusted frame holding a portrait of Henry, a pregnant young woman, and an attractive lady whom I assume is Jillian.

The woman in the photo must be his daughter, as her brown eyes and dark mahogany hair are akin to Henry's. Even though they're all smiling, I can see that her smile is staged. There is no happiness or warmth behind her eyes, and I can't help but wonder why.

"That's my daughter, Rosemary," Henry says from behind me.

"It's a really beautiful photograph." I turn to face him, seeing him stare longingly at the picture.

"Thank you. It's one of my favorites. Reminds me of the

good times. It was taken one week before Angus was born." His heavy sigh hints that Angus's condition weighs deeply on him.

"He's a remarkable boy," I say, scanning over the numerous pictures of him. There is no doubt the Sands love their grandson, but I detect something troublesome lingering beneath the surface.

"He is." When there is an uncomfortable silence, he changes the subject. "Where are you from? I sense a hint of an accent."

He passes me the wine which I gratefully accept. "From Darwin, Australia, originally, but I've been in the U.S. for roughly thirteen years."

"Where did you live before you moved here?" I know he's only trying to make conversation, but his questions feel like the inquisition.

"In Bridgeport." He sips his wine, nodding, hinting I'm to go on. "I taught elementary." It's all I'm willing to share.

Looking down at my ringless finger, Henry puts two and two together. "So you moved here for a fresh start?"

"Something like that," I reply, before gulping down my wine. We stand in silence as Henry appears to digest what I just told him.

I breathe out a sigh of relief when Henry's gaze turns soft. "There she is, my love."

Looking over Henry's broad shoulder, I see the lady in the photo is indeed Jillian. Her warm nature instantly puts me at ease, but there is something buried behind her bottle green eyes.

"Thank you so much for having me over for dinner. And at short notice, nonetheless." I want to make it clear I didn't invite myself over. Henry doesn't seem to appreciate the jab.

Jillian simply smiles. "I hope you like lamb. It's Henry's favorite."

Henry leaves Jillian to dish up dinner as he leads the way through the archway and into the impressive dining room. The double glass doors are open, revealing a magnificent view of the lake.

The gigantic table is set with sparkling crystal and gold-rimmed tableware. The silver forks and knives appear methodically placed with an equal space between each set. A beautiful bunch of mixed wildflowers are placed in the center of the table. Everything is positioned with military precision and decorated in a stark white. There are no colors or different shapes or sizes. Everything is meticulous, but that perfection contradicts how imperfect this home really is.

We sit silently, obviously both meeting the quota of things to say.

He clears his throat. "You said you taught elementary?" I nod. "Pinewood is actually looking for a teacher because Ms. Hillier is due to go on maternity leave soon. If you're interested, I could pass your details onto the principal."

"That would be great, thank you so much." I haven't worked since the attack, but now that I'm better, stepping into a role I feel so comfortable in is a good way to claim back my life and independence.

Maybe Henry isn't so bad after all.

Jillian enters the room, hands filled with food. "I hope you're hungry." With a newfound appetite for food and life, my mood picks up, and I finally loosen up.

"Do you mind if we say grace?" he asks.

"Oh, no, of course not." I'm not a religious person, seeing as in my time of need, my prayers seem to have gone unheard. But that doesn't mean I'll stand in the way of others embracing whatever faith they believe in.

Jillian smiles and bows her head, placing her interlaced hands on the tabletop. I mimic her, hoping I don't look as amateur as I feel. She clears her throat. "Thank you, Lord, for the food we are about to receive. Bless our family and friends, especially those who are unable to be here today." When Henry shifts in his seat, I wonder what's wrong. "I ask that you watch over our daughter, Rose. Wherever she may be…please let her be safe and know that we love and miss her so much."

I now understand Henry's reaction to the photograph. It appears that moment in time was a happy one because he actually knew where his daughter was, unlike now.

His jaw hardens. "Shall we eat?" His clipped tone displays the fact he's not appreciative of Jillian airing their dirty laundry at the dinner table. I, on the other hand, admire her strength and honesty.

As we eat in silence, I can't help but wonder what happened to Rosemary, because I now understand why Angus freaked out when I mentioned his mom. From his reaction, it's safe to assume he doesn't associate fond memories with her, which makes me all the more curious. Did she abandon him? My stomach drops at the thought.

"Victoria is a teacher," Henry says to Jillian, shaking me from my thoughts. "I was going to talk to Principal Washman, see if he's found a replacement for Ms. Hillier yet."

I wish I could show more appreciation, but I can't stop thinking about Angus. Once upon a time, I was so desperate to have a baby. I tried everything from having sex while in sync with the lunar cycle to drinking "miracle" herbal tonics, but nothing worked. So the thought of abandoning an innocent child such as Angus has me wondering what kind of a person Rose is.

Curiosity gets the better of me.

Swallowing my lamb, I ask, "Does Angus attend Pinewood?" The room suddenly turns stale.

I peer over at Henry, whose jaw appears clenched. "No, he does not," he replies with delay. "He attends some school for the *disabled*. His father insists on ostracizing him more than he already is. That school is only interested in robbing people blind." His tone and expression highlight the fact he doesn't approve of his grandson's schooling. But it's understandable Angus would attend a school catered to someone of his uniqueness.

"Oh, Henry, why…" Jillian is unable to finish her sentence, though, as Henry's glass slams loudly onto the table.

"You will not mention him in this house, Jill. You know how I feel about him." He makes a tight fist around his napkin, glaring at her. "He's the reason my Rose isn't sitting there." My eyes widen when he points at the seat I'm currently occupying. "I know he knows where she is, but he refuses to tell me."

Jillian sniffs, masking her sorrow as she shakily drinks her wine, while I'm wishing I could swap seats. "I miss you so much." No doubt she's talking about Rose. "None of this makes any sense."

The already uncomfortable evening has just taken a turn for the worse, and I'm counting down the minutes until I can leave.

Henry hacks into his meat, while I peer across the table, silently apologizing to Jillian for unintentionally opening a can of worms.

When I unlock my car and jump inside, I let out the breath I've been holding all night. I quickly wave at Henry, who is standing on his front porch. As I drive away, I watch his frame grow smaller and smaller in my mirror. I suddenly have images of T-1000 in *Terminator 2*, latching onto the back of my car, attempting to stop me from fleeing.

Thanks to my curiosity, the conversation at the dinner table consisted of mere grunts and uncomfortable silences. Henry's outburst seemed to ruin all our appetites, and after I passed on apple pie and coffee, my hosts understood I was desperate to leave.

My heart broke for Jillian, as her anguish over her missing daughter was clearly evident. She barely spoke a word all night. But Henry appeared angry, ready to play the blame game and not look at the fact his daughter up and left her young, hearing impaired child behind.

Lost in my head, I don't see a pair of glowing eyes until it's too late. Screaming, I swerve to avoid hitting whatever critter is on the road, but the move costs me as I end up caught in a ditch. As I attempt to accelerate, my car rattles and splutters, and with a final gurgle, it dies.

"No, no, no!" I yell, thumping the steering wheel with my palms. I try the ignition, but it clicks over—she's officially scrap metal.

Unbuckling my belt, I snatch my bag off the passenger seat, mumbling every expletive word I can think of. It's pitch black out, and with no street lights, all I have for guidance is the moon. I don't even bother locking my car as I commence my journey home.

Looking into the heavens, the clear night sky is littered

with twinkling lights. Each star flashing before me is a potential wishing beacon, promising the believer that it indeed holds the power to make all of one's wishes come true. Right now, I wish for a sign that I'm doing the right thing because I suddenly feel so lost. In no way do I want to go back to the life I lived with Bryan, but he was familiar, safe. I'm starting over, and I'm afraid I'll be eaten alive by the Henry Sands of this world for breakfast.

Please, universe, give me a sign.

Muted voices catch on the light breeze, alerting me to the fact I'm no longer alone. Fearfully looking ahead, I see a car without any headlights on stopped about half a mile away. It all looks extremely suspicious when a hooded figure emerges from the driver's side.

If this is my sign, then I don't know what that's saying for my future.

Deciding to take my chances, I confidently keep walking, ensuring to keep my head down and not make eye contact. My footsteps seem amplified out here in the open, especially because it's so quiet. I quicken my step. As I get within a few hundred feet of the car, the voices cease, and I can feel the strangers watching me. My eyes are still peeled to the ground as I try to blend into the shadows.

My breathing is fast and choppy, giving away my fear. But my house is only a few yards away. If this is my sign from the universe, no matter how obscure, then I'm going to embrace it and discover what it all means. I hustle past the car and its occupants, minding my business and only focusing on getting home.

Once I reach my house, I sprint around the back, inhaling deeply as I stop in the middle of my yard to catch my breath. The blood whooshes through my ears, resulting in an exhilarating head rush. Bending at the waist, I gulp in mouthfuls of air, somehow titillated by the entire situation. The feeling reminds me of last night—of when I met Jude.

"What happened to your car?"

"Sweet baby Jesus!" I yelp when I hear a voice sneak up behind me. Spinning around quickly, my excitement turns to dread when I see the hooded figure I saw out on the road is now standing in my yard.

"It's me," the figure says, unshrouding his face when he reads my panic.

"Jude?" I question, my heart racing at a billion miles a minute.

"Yes, it's me," he clarifies, walking closer, hands raised in surrender. This time, I don't have a bottle of whiskey to protect me.

"What are you doing here?" The moonlight reveals his smirk. It appears this question is a common one between us. I've known this man for all of twenty-four hours, and all I'm left with are more questions than answers.

But if he is my sign from the universe, I want a recount.

He must be able to read the conflict in my eyes because

he pulls his shoulders back. I can read his withdrawal, and for some unexplained reason, I don't want him to go. "My car died!" I state, replying to his earlier question. "I swerved to avoid hitting an animal, and well, my sympathy has left me without a car." The words rush out of me, as I'm afraid he's going to leave.

He thankfully stays rooted to the spot. "You could have called me. I'd have come get you."

"I don't have your number," I stupidly reply. Wow, that sounded like a come on. I'm about to backtrack, but my excuse dies in my throat.

As he steps toward me, his commanding presence fills my yard. His demeanor seeps confidence and control. Jude is a man who demands attention, and he's certainly got mine.

He simply extends out his hand, indicating he wants my phone. Looking briefly into the sky, a star twinkles brighter than any others. A shooting star then flashes across the sphere.

Damn this to hell.

Searching through my bag, I pull out my iPhone and hand it to him. As he enters his number, I turn to look at the lake. Henry's glowing house is now an eyesore, as I know what goes on behind closed doors.

"Why did you burn that chair?"

The mention of the chair spikes my temper. "Because, like I said, some things are better off as ashes."

"Most people would have left the chair behind, or maybe given it to Goodwill. Not set it on fire in their backyard. But you're not most people. You're…" His pause makes me wonder what he was going to say.

"I'm what?" I ask, turning to face him. "Crazy?" I offer, filling in the blanks when he looks at the ground.

His hair flicks forward, shrouding his face, so I can't read what's going on behind those eyes. "Different," he corrects a second later.

"Different?"

He nods. "So why?" he presses when I'm trying to decode what he means by his response.

"Why what?"

Finally looking up and meeting my gaze, he elucidates, "Why did you burn it? Or should I ask, why did you keep it?"

Memories of Bryan and Matilda, memories of my fiancé screwing my sister while she screamed out that she loved him punch me in the guts and I feel a whirlwind circling within my soul.

Jude senses my impending explosion and continues to push. "Tell me, and be honest with yourself."

The walls start closing in on me, and I suddenly feel hot. I frantically need to claw my way out of this uncomfortable situation. "I have to go." I try to push Jude away, but he stands his ground as he grips onto my bicep. The pressure isn't punishing, and I could break free at any time. But I don't.

"It's a simple question." His breath fans across my cheeks.

"No, it's really not."

His eyes turn curious, but they also fall poignant. "Why are you holding onto the past? Burn it. Burn it just like you did that chair."

I can't breathe.

I'm no longer in my yard; I'm back in Bridgeport, weakly climbing my front steps. The door is unlocked, and I don't hear the cries until I slip off my shoes.

"Bryan?" I gently call out, my head close to exploding after a simple walk around the neighborhood.

The cries get louder and louder.

"Matilda?"

I know what's happening, but my brain goes into survival mode. It doesn't want to believe the truth.

The slapping of flesh, the impassioned moans, the amorous words all point to one thing. But that thing—no, it's not happening. But it is. Pushing open the heavy door, I see my fiancé driving into someone who looks like my sister but surely, it can't be her.

But as she screams, "I love you, Bryan!" I know it is.

They haven't seen me; I've crept in quieter than a mouse. Bryan's eyes are closed, his head thrown back, his length slamming in and out of my sister as she's sprawled over my chair, my most favorite chair in the world. I'm numb. There simply are no words. But funnily enough, all I can think of while I watch my fiancé fuck my sister is why did they have to use this chair? Why not the couch, or the bed? Why did they choose this chair?

That chair—it represents all I've lost, and all I'll never achieve.

That motherfucking chair.

Months of anger bursts out of me; anger I didn't even know was there. I thought I had a handle on this, but I was wrong. So, so wrong.

I shove at Jude, who stumbles backward, his face painted with shock. But he pushed these buttons. He wanted the truth? Well, here it is. "I kept it as a reminder of who I'll never be again! Of what I'll never allow myself to become!"

"And what's that?"

"A victim! I'm done being fate's bitch. I'm a survivor, and burning that chair proves it." I need to shut up, but I can't. I've kept this bottled up for so long it's now seeping down the sides. "You're right, I am different. Most women would have screamed, shouted, and cried about the injustices of the world, but I didn't. I was too busy trying to survive. I've lived through an assault, a near fatal gunshot wound, continuous nightmares of the most horrific event I've ever experienced, and a cheating fiancé and sister. I thought by moving here I could start fresh, but why is the pain, the betrayal"—I thump my fist over my heart—"still here? Why do I constantly think, why me? What did I do to deserve this?"

By this stage, I'm sobbing, the hot tears scoring my flesh. But I don't care. It feels good to cry. I've tried to be strong, tried to move on, but my heart is grieving—grieving for the person I wanted to be.

"Victoria," Jude consoles, but I'm suddenly embarrassed—

he knows it all. He now knows my secrets. He knows I'm incomplete.

I need to get out of here.

"I'm sorry. I wish I could have—" He suddenly pauses, his eyes searching mine, the remorse clear in the blue depths.

I wipe my nose with the back of my hand. "Are you still so eager to help me when I'm in distress?"

Even though he looks sorry for pushing, he nods firmly. "Yes. Always. That won't change."

"Why?" I ask, my voice merely a whisper.

Smiling sadly, he steps forward apprehensively, approaching me as he would a crazed tiger. I feel warm and safe wrapped in his presence. I haven't felt this way for so long. With a calculated, unhurried speed, he wipes away a stray tear with his thumb. "Because you're different. I knew it the first moment I saw you. You're strong." Taking a deep breath, he goes on to confess, "And what makes you different…makes you beautiful."

I can't even comprehend his declaration—it's simply too much. In a warped way, *this* is the beginning of the new me. Once I face my demons, only then can I let go.

I remain motionless as he slips my cell into my hand without another word. Before he goes, he graces me with words of hope. "I think we're going to be great friends."

He then leaves me standing alone, his words on a loop because funnily enough, we appear to be two birds of a feather.

Six

I don't feel as ridiculous as I thought I would.

Peering into the mirror behind the bathroom door, I adjust my blue polka dot tankini, thankful the neckline isn't too low because it hides my scar perfectly. This two-piece bathing suit was a gift from Matilda. She said I should flaunt my assets. Just because I lost my will to live didn't mean I had to dress like a nun—an insensitive comment from someone who was perfect and clueless.

There was never any doubt Matilda and I were sisters. Some even confused us for twins. But she was always the curvier, prettier one, and I was fine with that. I had Bryan. He was all I ever needed. Too bad he was all Matilda needed too.

I have no idea what they are doing or if they're still together. I don't even know if they ever were. Matilda confessed when I weakly answered her numerous calls, saying she never meant to fall in love with Bryan. What happened to me took a toll on everyone, and it appears the way she decided to grieve was by having sex with my fiancé.

My parents now live in Reno after deciding to live out their twilight years in the Biggest Little City in the World. That was the plan for Bryan and me, too. Maybe not live in Reno, but we'd talk about retiring someplace quiet where we could look back on our amazing life with nothing but fond memories. But that'll never happen.

My mom is desperate for me to reconcile with Matilda, saying blood is thicker than water. However, I'm not the one she should be giving her sermon to. My dad is more understanding, giving me the time I need to heal. And after last night, I think I might be at the starting line.

Reaching for a towel off the rack, I'm looking forward to taking a swim and building up my strength and stamina to what it once was. My strength is shining through—wearing this bathing suit is proof of it.

The brilliant sunrays kiss my pale skin, warming my body from head to toe as I step outside. The blades of grass under my bare feet connect me to Mother Nature. I feel alive.

Jude's comment from last night replays in my mind. He thinks I'm beautiful. It appears he sees something in me that I've missed. He now knows my secrets, yet he still thinks I'm someone worth knowing. Why?

It's way too early for such philosophical thoughts, so I walk down the dock and toss my towel onto the edge. The water looks crisp and still, welcoming me into its depth and promising an opportunity of rebirth.

I was once a strong swimmer, but looking at my lanky arms, I wonder if I'll sink to the bottom of the lake like my chair. Peering into the watery depths, I wonder if that would be so bad. There were many times I wanted to die. Death would be the easy option. I wouldn't hurt. I wouldn't have to live with the constant ache of remembering what a masochistic thing life is.

Taking one step, then two, I move until my feet are in line with the dock's edge. Just one more step and all of this could be over. No more pain. Maybe this is what facing my demons is all about. Maybe this is me letting go of…everything.

With that thought in mind, I close my eyes, take a deep breath, and I…let go.

The icy water is like a thousand needles piercing my body. I sink further and deeper, the need to resurface and take a much-needed breath doesn't encourage me to swim anytime soon. It's so peaceful down here, so black. No one can touch me.

Things become clearer, which is ironic, considering I'm sinking to a watery grave. My life flashes before my eyes in a kaleidoscope of colors, and suddenly, everything clicks into place. I didn't come this far to give up now. I refuse to surrender.

The noise blaring loudly in my ears breaks my beset state of mind, and my muscles are filled with an unexpected burst of energy because all I want to do is live. Instinct takes over, and I swim to the surface, the feeling of weightlessness salving my soul. The moment I emerge, my lungs are filled with oxygen, which has never felt sweeter. My body is singing—I feel alive.

With my newfound sense of glory, I take to the water like I was born to own it. My arms, which once felt feeble, now feel stout as I power through the water like an unstoppable force. I keep pushing forward because the burn raging throughout my body is a sure sign that no matter my doubts, I will not drown.

Each stroke takes me closer to my goals, and that is enough motivation to keep going. I don't know how far I've swum, but it doesn't matter either way. The fact I tried is enough for today because it gives me the inspiration to try harder and go farther tomorrow.

I stop to catch my breath and take in my surroundings with a new eye. The sunlight bounces off the peaks of the waves, reflecting vibrant rainbows into the crisp atmosphere. As I turn to the left, I see I've come to rest in line with a tall red maple tree.

My eyes are instantly drawn to Jude's house. It looks bigger somehow. I don't know for certain, but I'm guessing I've swum a little over half a mile. A smile stretches across my cheeks, a sense of accomplishment overtaking me. Jude's house will be my finish line. Each day—hail, rain, or shine—I will swim closer and closer, marching forward until I cross that threshold with a sense of pride. The question is, what happens when I get there? What happens once I get to the other side? Deciding to tackle one challenge at a time, I turn and head back for home.

I'm almost at the dock when a flash of color soars through the air. I instantly stop, wondering what it could be. A moment later, I see a kite in the shape of a butterfly with wings painted every color of the rainbow zipping and zagging through the air. The sight is strangely liberating, a reflection of how I currently feel.

Needing to discover who is giving life to this sight, I swim faster, letting out a breath of relief when I reach the dock. I climb the ladder, my heavy muscles relishing in the feel of placing my feet on land. Taking a minute, I zero in on a young boy standing near my back steps. As I take a closer look, I see that the young boy is Angus. His eyes are aimed at the sky, focused on keeping the kite in the air. A jubilant smile kisses his cheeks, displaying his happiness at maneuvering something he obviously enjoys.

Remembering our last encounter, I contemplate leaving him be and not disturbing him. However, when I look down at my fingers and see they resemble prunes, I decide to get out before I shrivel any further. I dry off, never breaking my perusal of Angus even though he still hasn't seen me.

Wrapping the towel around my body, I decide to try again with Angus. Now that I know he's a little shy around strangers, I can approach him a little more cautiously. I wonder if he's visiting Henry. Or maybe he lives close by? I'm assuming he lives with his father, a man I have no clue about.

I try my best to announce my arrival and not sneak up on him. "Hi, Angus. I like your kite," I say, hoping he doesn't see me as the enemy.

He nervously chews his lip.

"You're really good." I continue moving forward, my steps slow and steady, not wanting to chase him away. Angus focuses on my mouth. "Maybe you can teach me?" I almost sing in relief when he nods shyly.

This is progress.

For the next hour, Angus lowers his guard and allows me into his world. This beautiful young boy is smart, funny, and skilled. He's patient enough to teach me how to fly the kite, giggling when I failed but never giving up. He may not speak, but we don't need words because his actions speak volumes. He's just a normal kid living an extraordinary life.

As I'm in the kitchen preparing us something to eat, I can't help but think about Rosemary. I don't claim to understand her circumstances, but leaving behind a remarkable child like Angus doesn't sit right with me. A mother's job is to protect her kin. No matter the situation, there is no excuse. Leaving behind your young just seems so…weak. Henry may not see the error of his daughter's ways and instead blame Angus's father, but at least he stuck around. It takes a real man to be a father. And it takes a coward to leave her son behind.

The back door closing snaps me from my thoughts. Angus strolls into the kitchen, red cheeked and eyes alive. He looks down at the PB&J sandwiches, and his lips almost smack in delight. I can't help but smile. When he walks over to the sink and lathers his tiny hands with soap, I know that his father, regardless of what Henry thinks of him, is a good man.

He climbs the tall stool, smiling as I place his lunch down in front of him. I'm thankful I have a firm hold of the glass of milk because just as I'm about to set it down, Angus looks up. He pulls in his bottom lip, and before I can ask if everything is okay, he mumbles, "Thank...you."

I nod, too stunned to say anything.

And as he happily chews his sandwich, he doesn't realize that I'm the one who should be thanking him.

"Watch out!"

I wake with a start.

Jolting upright, it takes a second for my sleep-clogged brain to realize where I am. I'm in my bedroom in my new home. I'm no longer in that dark alleyway, a pain so sharp tearing through my chest cavity as a bullet rips through my flesh, shattering bone.

The darkness pooling in from the open window reveals it's late. Revisiting my last memory, because the nightmare is too much to face, I smile, because it was of me saying goodbye to Angus. I asked if he wanted me to walk him home, or take him over to the Sands, but he shook his head. He jumped onto his bike and rode off down the road.

I have no idea why he was in my yard flying his kite in the first place, but I told him he's welcome back anytime, and I meant it. I've made my first real friend, someone who has changed my entire outlook on life. Moments before, I was sinking to the bottom of the lake with no real desire to surface ever again. But spending the day with Angus made me appreciate life because I should be thankful for all I have.

My stomach grumbles, something which doesn't happen often. Stretching, I rise from my bed, not as sore as I thought I would be. I have a skip to my step as I bounce down the stairs, wondering if I have any more food in the house.

Just as I walk down the hallway, I hear a light scratching on the front door. Turning my head, I pause, unsure if I heard the noise or not, and wait a few seconds. When it sounds again, I yelp, terrified someone is trying to break in.

No one stands before the frosted glass panel on the front door, but I'm certain the noise is coming from my porch. The moon is full and bright, not exactly an ideal night to be committing a crime, so with that thought in mind, I tiptoe to the front door, determined to stop living in darkness. If I'm going to do this starting over thing, then I need to learn how to depend on myself. I reach for a lava lamp, left behind by the previous owners for obvious reasons.

I continue my slither toward the door, taking a deep breath

when I reach it. Bracing the brass handle, I count to three before yanking open the door, lava lamp in hand. Adrenaline soars through me, and I bellow like Zena the Warrior Princess.

My war cry is completely pointless because no one is there. Looking from left to right, I see that the coast is clear and feel utterly absurd, so I lower the lamp. However, just as I let my guard down, something furry brushes against my leg. I scream bloody murder and jump so far backward I topple into the door and land straight on my ass. Scrambling backward, I'm about to toss the now useful lamp at whatever critter is about to eat me, but stop when I see two emerald eyes watching me closely.

When my brain stops imagining that I'm on the set of *Supernatural*, I squint and see those enormous emerald eyes belong to a gray tabby cat. He saunters into my home, none the wiser that I was seconds away from having a damn heart attack.

"Is everything all right?" I yelp again when Jude comes barreling up my porch stairs and storms into my living room. He looks ready to pounce on anything that stands in the way. However, when he peers down at me, he cocks an amused dark brow. "What are you doing?"

"I think I should be the one asking you that. You lingering around my home is getting rather creepy," I taunt, unable to wipe the smile from my face as I lower the lamp. This entire situation is ridiculous.

"I was hardly lingering," he defends, scoffing playfully.

"What were you doing then?"

He opens his mouth but quickly closes it. Now I'm the one to raise my eyebrow. Has he inadvertently admitted to lurking? I don't know whether to be creeped out or flattered.

The cat works his magic on Jude and rubs against his legs, purring like a lawn mower. He looks down, smirking. "*This* is the reason for you screaming down the neighborhood?"

"I didn't scream," I reply, pulling a face at his dramatics.

"My perforated eardrums beg to differ."

I roll my eyes but can't stop the smile from spreading cheek to cheek.

Realizing I'm still sprawled out on the floor, I attempt to lift myself up, but Jude quickly swoops forward and offers me his hand. I look at it. He appears puzzled by my hesitation, which has me kicking my butt for being so suspicious.

Jude has been nothing but nice to me. He has every right not to even bother being neighborly after the way I've treated him. But here he is, saving the day once again. This time, however, I don't mind.

"Thanks." The moment I slip my hand into his, my entire being is set alight—and not just physically either. My whimsical mind conjures up a scenario of Jude and me meeting in a different lifetime. I'm just a normal girl with no baggage and no problems who just wants to belong to someone who likes me for me. And Jude does. We take long walks along the lake's edge, watching our brown-haired, blue-eyed children running in the summer sun as we reminisce on our life and how perfect things are.

Jude tells me that he loves me each morning and kisses me on the forehead before he leaves for work. I then go about my daily chores being a wife and mom—my dream come true.

But that's not my life.

My life is nothing like that.

I haven't given up on finding true love, but my eyes have been opened, and sadly, reality has ruined the magic.

Returning to the here and now, I stand, thankful my two feet hold me up. My hand sits snuggled in Jude's, resting low between us as we stand inches apart. He makes no secret that he's watching me closely, and funnily enough, I do the same.

He really is remarkable to look at, but there is something more to him than just a pretty face. He has depth, substance, and the constant sadness buried deep within those blue eyes reveals he's something…more.

He knows my story, and I suddenly want to know his.

"Would you like some coffee?"

Jude drops my hand, not hiding his surprise at my sudden hospitality. I hold my breath, not knowing how he'll respond. I let it out when he accepts. "Sure."

Ignoring the unexpected fluttering within my stomach, I turn the hallway light on and make my way into the kitchen. Jude's boots sound along the floorboards as he follows.

"Do you have any milk?"

Spinning around, I can't help but coo when I see the cat

snuggled in Jude's large hands.

"Sure. There should be some in the fridge."

Jude nods and walks over to it. He pulls on the handle, expecting the refrigerator to open because that's what most fridges do. But mine doesn't open without a tug of war. I watch on, hiding my smirk, as he attempts to battle the old steel block, but back in her day, they made them to last. I'm almost certain she could be used for a bomb shelter.

After four attempts, he finally pries the door open. I bite my lip to stop my smile. My smile dies, however, when he sees the measly contents of my fridge. Half a carton of milk, a jar of jelly, and an apple are all that sits before him. In my defense, Angus was one hungry boy.

Now that I can think straight, I realize this is the first time Jude has seen inside my depleted home. It looks better from the outside, but that's not saying much, seeing as the outside looks like it's ready for demolition. He doesn't make a fuss, though, and simply closes the fridge, cat and milk in hand.

After washing out the new crockery set I purchased from the thrift store, I pass Jude a saucer. We work in silence, moving about my small kitchen in sync. He pours a splash of milk on it, then places the cat and his supper in the corner of the room.

"What are you going to call him?" Jude asks, breaking the silence.

With my eyes still focused on the little fur ball, I grin. "He reminds me so much of the cat I had back home. He too had big green eyes and a little fat belly." As if on cue, the cat's tail shakes excitedly.

Jude smirks, a dimple hugging his whiskered cheek. "What was his name?"

"Jäg."

Jude can't contain his laughter. "After Jägermeister?"

I bite my lip. "Yes, he even had an orange collar."

"Then Jäg it is."

Silence fills the room once again.

The stillness isn't uncomfortable, it's merely pensive. I can't help but wonder what Jude is thinking. He answers my query a moment later.

"So, I couldn't help but notice a few things around your home needed fixing up." He rubs the back of his neck, appearing concerned he's overstepped a line.

I don't take offense to his comment because it's the truth. "That they do. I'll get to it eventually."

"I would be more than happy to help. I'm good with my hands."

I choke on air. Thumping on my chest, I wheeze, "It's fine."

He stubbornly shakes his head. "Write out a list, and I'd be happy to help. What are neighbors for?" he adds.

I nod in response as I'm still finding it hard to breathe.

My mind races with so many questions, but I don't want to be rude or overstep any personal boundaries. But I need to know more about him.

"So when you're not offering to help your neighbors, what do you do?"

He smirks. "For the record, I only offer to help the ones I like."

"Well, I'm glad you like me." I bite the inside of my cheek, realizing how that comment could be misconstrued.

But Jude's gruff laughter makes me relax. "I work in town." I look at him, waiting for him to elaborate since that comment is as vague as they come. "I'm a jack-of-all-trades."

And the ambiguity continues.

Moving my mouth from side to side, I don't know if he's being evasive on purpose or just being a typical male. "Jack-of-all-trades is rather broad. Care to be a little more specific?" I smirk, keeping my tone light.

He mounts the barstool and rests his forearms on the counter, leaning forward. "If I tell you, I'll have to kill you."

I gulp.

A threat has never sounded so promising.

"Ah c'mon, you know all my secrets. It's now my turn to know yours." I hope I sound confident because I'm currently a bundle of nerves.

He reads my determination and smiles. "Growing up in this town, you've got one of two options." He holds up one finger. "You can either make something of yourself by leaving." He then raises another. "Or you can stay here and watch your life pass you by because you don't know any better."

I can't help but pry. "But you're still here, and you seem to know better."

"The fact that I'm still here shows you that I don't," he gently argues.

I ponder on his comment. It appears he doesn't want to be here, so why does he stay? There must be a reason he doesn't leave. What's holding him here?

I don't have time to ask what or *whom*.

"Growing up, my mom told me I was special. That I would amount to something. She said I was destined for big things." He appears to be lost in the past.

"Well, they do say mothers know best," I encourage.

His lips tilt into a bittersweet smile. "They also say parents are blind to their children's faults."

Thinking to how my mother behaved when I told her about Matilda and Bryan—and the fact it took her a week to believe me—has his comment ringing true.

The sorrow must reflect on my face because the mood suddenly turns still.

"Can I ask you a question?"

Meeting his eyes, I nod. "Sure."

He hesitates before he inquires, "What happened on the night you got shot?"

The sound of the kettle blaring reflects my inner scream.

My face instantly drops as that was the *last* question I thought he'd ask. "Shit, I'm sorry," he quickly apologizes, scrunching up his face. "I'm an idiot. I shouldn't have asked. Never mind."

His sincere regret has me shaking my head. "No, it's fine. I'm happy to talk about it." I suddenly realize that I *am* okay to discuss this.

Needing some caffeine before I make my confession, I quickly prepare us some coffee. Jude sips his while I gaze into the blackness of my mug and lose myself in the past. "Bryan and I were out celebrating my birthday. I was so happy back then, so in love with my fiancé who could do no wrong. I was an idiot.

"Bryan proposed. After ten years of dating, he finally decided to make an honest woman out of me. After celebrating right there on the sidewalk, we walked to our car. I ran into a man." I take a deep breath. "This wasn't supposed to happen. I was twenty-seven, fit, healthy, and on top of the world."

Jude reaches across the counter and squeezes my fingers, encouraging me to continue.

"He asked for our keys, and I thought that was it. But he was playing with us, taunting us because what he really wanted was to hurt me. He dragged me into an alleyway. He had a gun. I thought he was going to r-rape me, but when he reached for my ring, as if taking my integrity wasn't enough, I snapped.

"I fought him, fought harder than I had ever before. Then…" My palms begin to sweat as I wipe them on my jeans. "Then I saw a man. I couldn't make out his face. It was dark. But he was running to my rescue while Bryan was straggling behind. I understand he was in shock and terrified by what he saw, but I was, too. I expected Bryan not to let it get that far. Stupid, right? The man had a gun. But I felt safer with my rescuer than I did with Bryan. A complete stranger was running to my aid while my fiancé looked moments away from running in the opposite direction. He was supposed to protect me."

I sniff.

Jude runs his thumb over my knuckles. "Did you see who the man was?"

"No," I whisper, looking down at my bare feet. "But every night, I know he's in my dreams…I just can't see who he is. I only remember bits and pieces, but I feel safe."

We're silent, and Jude most likely wishes he'd kept his mouth shut.

"I got shot. Two bullets were fired. One tore through my chest, and the other was a stray. The doctors said I was lucky, that I was a fighter, but I don't feel like either." I rub my temple, squeezing my eyes shut. "I thought there is no way something so small could cause me such great harm. But that's the thing about a wound—it's not about what you can see, it's about what you *can't* see that hurts you the most.

"With all the bandaging, I still felt the same. But when the bandages unraveled, I saw I wasn't the same." Tears fall down my cheeks, the betrayal still so raw. "Bryan was repulsed by me. I could see it every time he looked at me. For the first few months, I couldn't taste, feel, smell. Love. I felt dead inside. Bryan stayed away, treating me like a leper. That's why he cheated on me with my sister. Because…I'm incomplete. I'm nothing." I'm sobbing by this stage, unable to see anything but my watery regrets. The tears are streaming down my face, the betrayal still so real.

"Victoria. I'm so sorry." Jude clenches my fingers, the weight comforting. "You're wrong. You're everything. You're so much and more. He's a goddamn coward."

His words only make me cry harder.

"I'm sorry I've made you cry." His apology is filled with nothing but pain and regret.

His warmth touches me. Wiping the tears from my eyes, I shake my head. "You didn't."

His jaw clenches as he spits, "I'm so sorry you went through that." I can see he has one final question to ask. "And the man? Did you ever find out who he was?"

"No," I whisper, "but I wish I did. I'd throw my arms around him and thank him for saving my life."

"Do you want to remember?" he asks apprehensively.

"Remember?"

He nods. "Yes, that night. There are holes in your memory for a reason."

I begin to tremble. "I've got PTSD. It's normal."

Jude doesn't look convinced. "The answers are right there at your fingertips…" He brushes his finger along mine. "You just have to let them in."

I don't know what that means, but I allow him to comfort me because it feels nice to let my guard down.

"How about we finish our coffee another night?" he suggests, his thumb rubbing wide circles over my inner wrist.

"Sorry for being such a mess. I promise I'll pull it together and have a normal conversation with you one day."

Jude smiles, and the sight warms my heart. "This is the most normal I've had all day."

I can't help but smile also. "Me too."

Jäg weaves himself between my legs, purring loudly. The sound soothes me. Bending to pick him up, I meet Jude's stare. The air sizzles and pops around us, a tangible static overwhelming me.

"Okay, then." He clears his throat. "Good night."

"Good night."

His words are that of departure, but his actions reflect a desire to stay. A whisper of a butterfly's wings flutter within, but I squash it down. "Night," I repeat, turning my back and making my way down the hall. I don't hear the back door close until I reach the top of the stairs. I can't help but smile at Jude's chivalry.

It's not until I strip off do I realize that not once today did I attempt to cover something that isn't and will never be there. When flying that kite with Angus and allowing myself to grieve with Jude, I grasp that I finally felt like…me.

I've transformed and grown into something inexplicable, and I can't wait to find out what that is.

*Caterpillar: The **Feeding** Stage*
The larva stage is a time for growth.

The Second Stage: Larva

Seven

The sound of banging disturbs my peaceful slumber, which is a shame, as it's the first one I've had in months. Stretching the sleep from my bones, I laugh when my new friend does the same.

I seem to be acquiring a lot of them lately.

For someone who wanted to be left alone, I sure as hell have managed to do the opposite.

Jäg meows, hinting he's probably starved. After I find out what that banging is, I'll head down to the store and fill my empty cupboards.

Slipping on an oversized sweater, I pad down the stairs, chuckling at Jäg as he tries to keep up. "No point in you running. There is absolutely no food"—I pause, my eyes feasting on the unbelievable sight before them—"in the house," I conclude, looking at the array of food spread out on my countertop, making a liar of me.

When did this happen? One usually finds their home barren when an intruder enters, not the other way around. Fruit sits overflowing in a bowl which I didn't even know I owned. Next to it are bags stocked full of everyday household items that my home lacks. Standing on my tippy toes, I see I'm now equipped with all the essentials to bake a cake if I felt the need.

Who on earth bought all this? And more importantly, how did they get in?

The banging is no doubt the key to whoever my intruder is, so I peek out the back door, unsure of whom or what I'll find. I do a double take when I see Jude hammering away at my staircase, shirtless. I knew he was big, but seeing him in the flesh, literally, makes me realize I've underestimated him.

His shoulders are broad; his skin tanned. The valley between his firm pectorals is defined, leading down to rock-hard abs. I've never appreciated the term "six-pack" before, but now that I'm confronted with the epitome of the word, I'm a complete convert. A light dusting of dark hair paints his navel, slithering down...down. His V muscles are like a giant arrow pointing, well...downstairs.

I need to stop staring, but dear god, what does this man eat?

His biceps are the size of my head, and I won't even touch on his muscled flank. Tilting my head to the side, I faintly see a hint of ink running across his obliques. I have no idea what it says, but I suddenly have the urge to find out.

But first things first, I need to stop staring like a creeper and ask why the contents of the corner store are in my kitchen. Attempting a calm demeanor, I open the door and stand at the top of the stairs with my arms crossed. Jude looks up, a smirk playing at the corner of his lips. "What are you doing?" I decide to ask the obvious.

Jude removes his baseball cap, wiping the sweat from his brow with the back of his hand. "Fixing your step. It's a hazard."

"I've managed just fine," I state.

His smirk grows wider. "I was talking about it being a hazard to Jäg. I doubt his little legs could make the jump from step to step."

"Oh." Now I feel completely stupid.

"Your legs, however"—his eyes drop to my bare thighs— "I'm sure they can manage just fine."

My hand flutters to my face to ensure my cheeks haven't set alight because I'm quite certain I'm on fire. He smirks, making me blush even harder.

"I…you…thanks." I fumble over my words, not even sure what I want to say. Pulling it together, I amend, "Thanks for the food. I'll pay you back as soon as I get to a bank. It might take a day or two, as I need to figure out if any buses run this far out." I hate not having a car. One of the many reasons I need to find a job asap.

"It's fine. Don't worry about it," Jude says, waving me off. The movement highlights the fact he's still topless. The chain which caught my eye when we first met still hangs between his collarbones. The shine emphasizes his broad upper body.

I force my eyes to stay affixed to his face and not drop to the forbidden land of bulging muscles and washboard abs. "I do worry. It's too much. I can't accept it for free."

He shakes his head playfully. "Well, how about you make me dinner one night, and we can call it even?"

Seems like a fair trade, so why are my hands suddenly shaking?

"Sounds fair, although, I think you've got the raw end of the deal here because the food you bought amounts to a lot of dinners."

"I'm a growing boy. I could always eat two." He accentuates his comment with a wink.

His entire being this morning is too much. "I'm going to take a shower. Help yourself to some coffee." I'm surprised at how natural that sounded. "By the way, how did you get inside?"

He replaces his baseball cap with a smile. "Your back door doesn't lock."

"What? Yes, it does," I argue, not believing him.

"No, it doesn't," he presses. "Last night, I tried to lock it, but it wouldn't lock."

"That's impossible." He shrugs, smirking. I have locked the door numerous times. Deciding to test his theory out, I walk inside and close and lock the door. Turning the handle, I pull at the locked door. Just as I'm about to gloat, the door opens, and I yelp, jumping backward. "What in the hell?"

"Told ya," he singsongs from the doorway.

"I don't understand."

"It locks from the inside, but not the outside," he explains. "I've bought a replacement, so it'll be fixed today." Taking a step toward me, his commanding presence fills my small kitchen. "You can trust me."

I lick my lips, my mouth suddenly going dry. "T-thanks." I can't help but draw in his masculine fragrance. It's deep, earth peppered with an undercurrent of fresh cologne. My mouth waters at the perfume.

Peering up at him, I see he's watching me as closely as I'm watching him. He keeps his cards close to his chest, though—the perfect poker face. My heart begins to gallop, and something stirs within. Am I...turned on? No, that's impossible. My lack of feeling pulverized my libido, and it hasn't surfaced since. But this fire building low in my belly is a feeling I once knew.

His magnificent body is all too tempting, a true beauty that needs appreciating. My gaze drops low, focusing on the cursive font wrapped around his flank.

Imperfect.

The irony of this tattoo is not lost on me because what stands before me is anything but imperfect.

Thoughts of imperfection have me thinking about what

true imperfection is, and I absentmindedly wrap my arms around my chest. "I better take that shower." My voice is low, my high soon fading.

Jude nods, able to read my retreat. He doesn't press—another thing I like about him.

Just as I turn my back, Jude's voice falters as he unnervingly confesses, "By the way, the answer to your question is…I work at Pop's Hardware Store. I also do handyman jobs for the old man around town." I don't understand why he would be embarrassed, but he soon clarifies. "It's not great money, and it doesn't require a college education, but it's a job."

I want to say so many things, but I don't. I can sense his discomfort at working a job he obviously doesn't think too highly of, so just as he did for me, I don't press. Jude has his skeletons, and I have mine.

In the shower, I lather up some soap and commence my washing routine, leaving my chest to last. I hate that I feel this way about myself. I feel ungrateful and undeserving of my life because I'm one of the lucky ones.

I survived.

I may have come out of this a different person, both physically and emotionally, but I walked out of it with my life intact. The same can't be said for the dozens of people I saw one day and not the next because luck wasn't on their side. It wasn't in the cards for them to embrace another sunset and experience a new dawn. But it was in mine. I need to remember that.

I wash over my jagged scar, tears pricking my eyes as I refuse to look down. I may be able to appreciate my survival, but one step at a time.

Once clean, I dry off and dress in jean shorts and a baggy tee. The good thing about having short hair is that it takes no time to style. I run some product through it to tame the flyaways, and then I'm good to go. As I walk past my cosmetic case, some ChapStick catches my eye. I decide to apply some and maybe just a light dusting of powder, too. Once it's on, I look at myself in the mirror and am surprised to find I look half human.

Voices from downstairs have me wondering who else decided to drop in. The moment I reach the bottom step, I can't help but smile. "Good morning, Charley," I say as I enter the kitchen.

"Good morning," she replies in her usual merry voice. A cup of coffee sits in front of her while Jude is leaning against the counter drinking his. I'm thankful he's now wearing a T-shirt. "Where's your car?"

I groan. "Probably still sitting in the ditch I left her in."

Charley's eyes grow wide. "What happened? Are you all right?"

"I'm fine. The same can't be said for my car, though. I really need to find a job."

Charley reaches into her bag and pulls out a newspaper. "I can help you job hunt."

"Thanks. I really appreciate that."

As I reach for the paper, Charley's true motives surface. "And while we're doing that, I thought maybe we could discuss the guest list for your housewarming this weekend."

Ignoring her, I unfold the paper and flip to the classifieds. Jude mutes his chuckle into his coffee cup.

"C'mon, Tori, it'll be fun." Spreading the newspaper onto the counter, I steal her coffee and begin my search. "I promise not to invite anyone you don't want me to," she offers as a bargaining chip.

Sipping my coffee, I reply, "Well, that's easy, then. I don't want anyone here, so that solves that issue." She sighs while I continue perusing the paper.

I know I'm being difficult, but the thought of having strangers in my home is as appealing as having another dinner date with the Sands. Speaking of. "Please feel free to leave Henry Sands off your list."

I'm surprised when Jude asks, "Why's that?"

Peering up, I see his curiosity is piqued. "Because I had the pleasure of meeting him and his wife the other day, and it was nothing short of awkward. She was lovely, but he was—"

"A jackass?" Jude answers for me.

"Something like that," I reply, sensing our mutual dislike for the man. I wait for him to elaborate and maybe share some dirt on the sheriff, but he doesn't. He throws back his coffee before rinsing his cup in the sink.

"I better get back out there. Your step is fixed. I'll just grab some tools from my truck, then fix your door." He doesn't give me a chance to thank him, as he's out the door in seconds.

My mind runs in circles, and I wonder why the room dropped ten degrees. Henry doesn't appear to be a people person, and Jude doesn't appear to take shit from non-people persons. They are neighbors, so it wouldn't surprise me if Henry has rubbed Jude the wrong way. Yet another mystery to add to the list.

"So when did you and Mr. Handyman get so friendly? Last I heard, you were volunteering at the local cat shelter."

I can't help but laugh at Charley's humor. "Very funny. I don't know, he's just been hanging around. He seems nice enough."

"So what's his story?"

I shrug. "I don't know. He knows everything about me, but he doesn't talk about himself, so I know the bare minimum. And I'm not sure how that happened," I add, thinking back to the numerous times I've purged.

"Everything?" she asks, incredulous.

"Everything," I confirm with a nod.

"Wow, Tori, that's great. See, this living isn't so hard, right?"

"Ask me that after I get my life back on track," I reply, focusing on the paper in front of me.

"So…" Peering up, I know nothing good can come from her next comment. "Do you think he's cute?"

"Who?" I reply, playing dumb.

"You know who." She emphasizes her point by wiggling her eyebrows up and down.

"We are so not having this conversation. Ever. I have no intention of hooking up with anyone. Especially someone whose surname or age or history I don't even know. He could be a serial killer for all I know. He does an awful lot of skulking around," I add while Charley cackles. It's nice to have this conversation, even if I'm not ready to face it.

As much as I don't want to have this housewarming, I know it's probably a good excuse to get to know my neighbors. If I'm looking at getting back into teaching, then odds are I'll be teaching my neighbors' kids. It wouldn't hurt to get my foot in the door.

Just as I'm about to tell Charley I've caved, I hear a car drive down the road. We both look at one another and decide to find out who it is. Walking into the living room and looking out the window, I see a blonde get out of her white station wagon with her cell pressed to her ear.

Jude appears a moment later and approaches her. There doesn't appear to be any confusion or animosity, so he obviously knows her. Charley doesn't say a word; she stands beside me, silently watching the scene unfold.

The girl looks young, barely twenty-one. Although I can't see her up close, she looks quite attractive from afar. Her blue summer dress, gold sandals, and long braided blonde hair give her a bohemian vibe. I wonder who she is. She looks like a magical nymph out here in the greenery.

They appear to talk for a few moments before she gets back into her car. He watches the car drive down the road, waving goodbye. He only turns back around when the car is no longer in view. Charley and I are still standing by the window when Jude's gaze lands our way. We both yelp and jump backward. The heavy lace curtain shrouds us from his eyes, but we still scamper off, afraid we've been caught.

"Who was that?" Charley whispers as we scurry into the kitchen.

"No idea. Probably his girlfriend," I offer, opening the fridge as I need some water for my suddenly dry mouth.

"You're jealous," Charley teases, pointing an accusing finger at me.

"Am not." But am I?

Not wishing to discuss this further, I snatch the newspaper off the counter and look around the room for my bag.

"What are you doing?" Charley asks, curiosity lacing her tone.

Holding up the paper, I say, "It's time to start living."

"This was a bad idea," I mumble under my breath as I shuffle in the creaky plastic seat. The receptionist glares down at me from behind her desk, her glasses sliding down her narrow nose.

"Too late now," Charley says unsympathetically.

Looking at my resume, I go over each point methodically. There isn't anything more I can add, but I want to ensure it sells me for the wonderful teacher I am. Or was. Who am I kidding? I don't even know if I want to teach anymore.

"You look great," Charley whispers, bumping me with her elbow.

Thanks to borrowing a gray tunic, a pair of heels, and some pearls, I look the part of an upstanding, dedicated elementary teacher. Too bad I'm searching for the nearest exit.

Jude and the mystery blonde play over and over in my mind. Who was she? Although they looked close, I didn't really get the girlfriend vibe. Surely if she was, he'd maybe greet her a little more intimately? Either way, I need to stop thinking about this because it's none of my business.

Someone clears their throat. "Ms. Armstrong?"

Charley nudges me in the ribs.

Glancing up, I see a plump, balding, middle-aged man standing in the doorway of his office. He is holding a notepad, most likely using it as a shield. His stained, crinkled white shirt sits half tucked into his brown pants, which are two sizes too small. I'm surprised he hasn't died of a heart attack by now.

Gathering my wits, I remember why I'm here and stand. "Yes, that's me."

A strained smile pulls at his thin lips. "I'm Principal Washman. Please, come in." He stands out of the doorway so I can squeeze past. Charley gives me an encouraging nod. I take a deep breath before walking toward my future.

Henry mentioned Pinewood was looking for a teacher, so I decided to start here. I called up and was pleasantly surprised when Principal Washman agreed to see me. The door closes behind me, sealing my fate.

When Principal Washman sits behind his oak desk, the worn leather seat whines in agony. "Is that your resume, Ms. Armstrong?" He gestures to the paper I'm holding onto for dear life.

"Oh, yes." I pass him my credentials.

Slipping the silver glasses from his head, he places them onto his splotchy face, perching them on the bridge of his round nose. I look around the office while he reads over my resume. It appears Principal Washman attended Yale and has been teaching for twenty years. A photograph of a woman and two little girls sits on his cluttered desk. From the layer of dust on the glass, I imagine it's not a picture he gazes upon often.

He asks the dreaded question. "Why did you move?"

"I just needed a change of scenery," I reply, nervously crossing my ankles.

He peers up from examining my paper, his beady eyes focused on me. "And why did you stop teaching? It says here you've been out of work for over nine months." He jabs his chubby finger at my resume.

My foot begins to jiggle on its own accord. "I was ill." When he makes it clear this response isn't adequate, I add, "I had PTSD." His face falls, filled with pity. "But I'm okay now." That's not completely the truth, but I'm getting there.

He nods.

I exhale softly, thankful he doesn't pry.

He flips to the back page and reads over my references. "You can call any of my references. They'll tell you what a hard worker I am."

"That won't be necessary," he replies, turning the page over.

My heart sinks.

What he says next, however, makes my heart sink even further. "Sheriff Sands has already spoken to me about you. That's the only reference I need."

"*What?*" I don't keep the surprise from my voice. "Is that why you agreed to see me?"

He nods like I'm slow to have not pieced this together the moment I walked through the door. "Congratulations, Ms. Armstrong. Welcome to Pinewood."

My head is spinning. I feel an impending headache.

Principal Washman details what's expected of me, but I'm not listening. I'm indebted to someone who I sure as hell don't want to be beholden to.

I accept all the paperwork, desperate to flee before I change my mind. If Principal Washman can read my anguish, he hides it well. "See you soon, Ms. Armstrong."

"Thank you again for this opportunity." I'm out the door before he can say another word.

Charley stands, the anticipation painting her face. "How'd it—" But I don't allow her to finish. I latch onto her forearm and drag her out the door, not even bothering to say goodbye to the receptionist.

Once outside, I take a much-needed deep breath while Charley stands off the side, watching me closely. "What happened in there?"

"I got the job," I reveal, placing my hands on my hips and raising my face to the sky. The fresh air cools my skin.

"That's great!" When I close my eyes and inhale deeply, she questions, "Isn't it?"

"Yes, it's awesome news."

"So why do you look like you've been told you've got jury duty?"

Taking one last breath, I look at her and sigh. "I only got the job because Sheriff Sands put in a good word for me."

"Oh," she replies, understanding my frustration. "That's not so bad, though."

"I know, it's just…I don't want to owe anyone anything, especially not Henry Sands. He gives me the creeps, Charley. I don't know why, he just does."

She rubs my arm. "I understand, Tori, but look on the bright side, you have a job. I'm sure Principal *Dillweed* wouldn't have hired you if he didn't think you were capable."

"I don't know." I shake my head. "I have a feeling Henry Sands has a firm hold on this town."

"No wonder his daughter left."

I nod.

Although I don't agree with her leaving Angus behind, I have a feeling that maybe there's more to this story than I originally thought.

By the time Charley drops me off at home, it's dark outside.

Jäg is curled on my bed when I stagger to my bedroom, so ready to call it a night. I realize I haven't fed him since this morning, so he's probably starved.

Opening the fridge, I ignore the bright colors and reach for the milk, choosing to just accept the situation for what it is, as I don't believe in wasting food. Although Jude said I didn't owe him anything for his kindness, I still feel like I'm now indebted to yet another person.

As I open the pantry, a note on the counter catches my eye. Reaching for it, I sigh.

Jäg has been fed. I went to the store and got some things for him. It's all in the laundry. I hope that's okay.

The lock on your door has been replaced. So has the bulb on the back porch.

J

Leaving the letter on the counter, I switch off the light and trudge up the stairs.

Eight

The next day, I'm sitting on my back porch enjoying a coffee and some sunshine when Jude's green pickup drives around back. Like the customary nightmares weren't enough, I'm now graced with dreams of Jude and the mysterious blonde. Why can't I stop thinking about who she is to Jude?

I don't like feeling conflicted, but that's how I suddenly feel around Jude. I think we need to cool it.

Standing, I straighten out my dress and lean on the railing, making no attempt to greet him downstairs. He jumps from the pickup and reaches for a toolbox in the back. He waves when he sees me watching him. "Good morning."

"Morning," I reply. Images of the nymph float to the surface, and I can't help but scowl. "Whatcha doing?"

He holds up his toolbox with a slanted grin. "I'm here to fix your pipes. I heard them whining yesterday. Should be an easy fix."

The thought of my groaning pipes no longer whining is almost enough for me to give in—as I'm convinced a water poltergeist haunts my home—but memories of the blonde float to the surface, and I stand my ground. "It's okay. You don't have to do that."

"I don't mind," he says, climbing the stairs.

Pushing off the railing, I stand at the top of the stairs, blocking the back door. Jude looks up at me, nothing but confusion swimming in his blue depths. "Everything all right?" he asks, stopping on the second step.

"Yes, everything's fine."

He cocks his head to the side. "Why do I get the feeling you're not telling me something?"

I shrug and avert my gaze. "I really appreciate everything you've done for me, but I think I've got it from here. Thanks for fixing my house and buying my groceries, which I'll pay you back for this week."

His face pulls into a tight scowl. "I told you I didn't want your money. Consider it a gift."

"And now I'm telling you I can't accept it and would feel better if you let me pay for them," I counter.

"What's going on? What's happened?" He braces his foot on the step above him, narrowing his eyes at me.

"Nothing. I just don't like owing anyone anything." Henry's stunt yesterday grates me raw.

"You don't owe me anything, Victoria." Disappointment fills his tone, which makes me feel guilty for saying anything.

"I know, but I'd feel better if you just accepted the money, and then we'll call it even." Why is he being so stubborn?

"No one is keeping score. What's wrong with someone doing something nice for someone else?"

"Because in my experience, that only lasts for so long before favors are called in and that nice gesture gets thrown in one's face." I hate to sound so negative, but Jude hardly knows me.

"Favors?" he asks, puzzled.

"Yes." I shuffle my feet.

He scoffs, shaking his head. "Don't worry, your virtue is safe with me."

I pull back, offended. That's not what I was insinuating. "Well, that's great to know. Thanks."

He reads my offense and quickly backtracks. "I didn't mean…"

But it's too late. "I know what you meant. I'm not perky, blonde, and perfect." I fold my arms over my chest, daring him to challenge me.

He scrunches up his face. "What are you talking about?"

"I'm not interested in being indebted to you or becoming one of your floozies! I saw you yesterday," I state, heatedly. He wasn't doing anything wrong, but the thought of him and another woman sends me into bitch mode in point two seconds.

He processes my comment and then has the gall to laugh a moment later. "Floozies? Oh. That's funny. She'd love that."

I grimace. I need to calm the hell down, but I can't. I'm so bloody jealous my vision has turned green and completely irrational. "Glad you find this funny. How many other women have you *helped*?" The word "helped" has never sounded so dirty.

Now he's the one to look offended. "I think it's best I leave. I've reached my insult quota for the day." He rushes down the steps, shaking his head, while I follow in hot pursuit.

"You're offended? I'm the one who should be offended!"

"Why? What have I done to offend you?" he asks, spinning around.

He appears incensed, but so am I. "I'm not some charity case, Jude."

He throws his arms out to the side. "I never said you were. If it makes you feel better, then pay for the fucking groceries! The lock and globe were $24.97," he exclaims, closing the space between us.

But I won't allow him to make me feel guilty for standing by my beliefs. I charge forward, only stopping when we're inches apart. "Now you're really insulting me," I roar into his face. "I don't know what's worse, the fact you insinuated you were in no way attracted to me because I'm some bush pig, or that you're implying I'm being petty!"

Jude doesn't confirm or deny either way and stampedes over to his truck, throwing his toolbox into the back. The contents spill out, decorating the bed with numerous tools. The hinges whine in protest as he yanks open the door. I'm surprised he didn't rip it from the frame.

This escalated rather quickly, but he hasn't exactly denied any of my claims. I rub my temples, feeling my day slowly turning to shit. Just as I climb the first step, I hear Jude's boots tear through the grass. Turning, I see him come to a stop a few feet away.

He runs a hand over his heavier scruff. "For the record, I don't think you're being petty. I understand why you find it so hard to believe that a stranger could do something nice, no strings attached. I mean, the two people you trusted most in this world completely screwed you over. It makes sense you're apprehensive and suspect I have an ulterior motive. But let me assure you, I don't. I told you, you can trust me, and I mean it. I'm...drawn to you, Victoria," he confesses, appearing baffled, "and I don't know why."

I gasp, my mouth parting. What does that mean?

"It could be because I see something in you that you don't see in yourself," he adds before returning to his truck. I'm still standing motionless when he looks at me over the roof. "And by the way, I don't think you're a bush pig...whatever that is." A ghost of a smile plays at his lips before he jumps into the truck, and I hear the engine roaring to life.

Standing with my mouth hanging open, I watch his truck speed down my driveway and disappear along the dirt road.

I don't know how long I stand, watching the empty driveway and the plumes of dust catching the light, balmy breeze, but when the air clears, I finally see what an idiot I am.

My iPhone and glass of red sit within reach, and I contemplate which to reach for first.

I feel beyond humiliated for behaving the way I did today. I don't know what it is about Jude, but he pushes my buttons. A little voice inside me whispers not so quietly that he stirs something in me I don't want to face. My plan was to move here and have no complications, but I haven't even been here a week, and already, I'm exhausted.

With that thought in mind, I reach for my wine.

My thoughts wander to Jude and how I should call and apologize to him for being such an idiot. I still have no idea who the blonde was, and honestly, it's none of my business. I tend to believe Jude when he says he has no ulterior motives. I need to accept that some people are genuinely good. I used to think that way, but that thought process changed some time ago.

I've become this bitter, cynical person, and I hate it. When I look into the mirror, the person staring back is someone I hardly recognize. I'm forgetting my smile, my love for life, but most of all, I'm forgetting my ability to see the sun through the clouds. I always looked on the bright side, but now, I feel trapped in a cocoon. I'm losing who I am, and it's killing me.

Gulping down my wine, I tuck my feet beneath me as I lean against the sofa cushions. Jäg snuggles up against my legs, loving me no matter my flaws.

My phone rings, a thankful distraction from the clutter inside my head. The caller is private. Against my better judgment, I answer the phone.

"Hello?"

"Victoria?"

That deep voice, the voice which used to tell me how much he loved me, brings home many memories, one of which is him telling my sister how much he loved being inside her.

I can't breathe.

"Tori…it's me. Can you hear me?"

"W-what do you want?" I don't fail to hide my contempt.

"I…" He appears taken aback by my hostility. "How are you?" he says as if talking to an old friend.

"How am I?" I scoff. "How do you think I am?" I sit up tall, my entire body trembling.

"Baby, I want to talk."

"I am *not* your baby. I have nothing I want to talk to you about."

"I miss you."

I've heard some ridiculous things in my life, but this tops the list. "You miss me? What, my sister's vagina not keeping you company? Do not call me again," I warn.

"I'm sorry," he cries on a rushed breath. When I remain silent but stay on the line, he sighs. "I fucked up. I'm so sorry."

But I've heard it all before. This speech has been on a loop, and sadly, the effect is still the same. "It's too late, Bryan. We're over. Nothing will ever change that."

"Give me another chance."

I shake my head, incredulous to his bullshit. "Are you high? You slept with my sister because you lacked the balls to be the husband you promised to be. And not only that, you left me to fend for myself. I needed you. I do remember you wanting to take our vows, promising in sickness and in health. You lied."

"I'll never forgive myself for what I did. Please, come back to me. I'll make it up to you if you do."

"No!" I gulp, suddenly feeling hot and as though the walls were closing in on me. I can't breathe.

"I love you."

I close my eyes, wishing his declaration would make this all go away. It would be easy. I could go back to the way things were and stop hurting. But going back to Bryan would hurt me more.

"I'm sorry I slept with Matilda. But I…I just missed you."

"Missed me? Funny way of showing someone you miss them by sleeping with their sister."

"I didn't save you. I'm sorry. You needed me, and I let that bastard take you. I should have fought harder."

He's forcing old feelings and memories to resurface, ones I never wanted to relive.

My heart rate begins climbing. My pulse flutters wildly in my neck. I gasp.

"Tori, baby...can you hear me?"

A deafening ringing sounds loudly in my ears. I rock forward, cradling my head, desperate to make it stop.

"I'm sorry."

His voice fades into nothingness, and it's the last thing I hear before my mind switches off, and I go numb.

"Watch out!"

I scream. My vocal cords are raw.

I'm lost in a dream world and reality, actually, no, I'm between.

"C'mon, wake up, please, wake up." Jude's soothing voice is the beacon of light, my anchor to which plane I belong in.

My eyes flutter open, gradually taking in my surroundings. I'm safe, nestled in Jude's arms. He brushes the sweaty hair from my brow, his deep blue gaze settling my racing heart. "Oh, thank god! I thought you were dead."

I chuckle, the sound strained. "That's a little overdramatic, don't you think?" Jude's lips pull into a thin line. "How did you get in here?"

"You really need to learn to lock your doors." His warm arms envelop me tighter, and I sink into the embrace, needing this comfort, needing his care. I lose myself in him, wrapping my arms around him and resting my forehead against his heart. He rubs my back, resting his cheek atop my head.

"Was it Bryan?"

Am I that obvious? "Yes. He called me."

"What did he want?"

He's trampled on my new beginnings and brought me back to the past—a place I rarely leave. I can't believe he thought I'd even be remotely interested in giving him a second chance. He blew all his chances by blowing into my sister. "To talk about how sorry he is. I can't forgive him, Jude. Does that make me a bad person?"

Jude's silence has me worried. "No, it doesn't. It makes you...human."

His words have an unexpected effect on me, and before I know it, I'm crying against his chest.

"Shh, it's okay. You'll get through this."

"I'm glad you're so certain because right now, I feel like I'm drowning. I don't know which way I should go."

A heavy silence fills the small space between us. I haven't been in someone's arms this way since Bryan, but Jude doesn't feel like a stranger. "Life is complicated, Tori. No matter what decisions we make, there are always going to be consequences."

Still cocooned in his arms, I rearrange myself and meet his stare. With shaky fingers, I caress the corner of Jude's bow lips. It's the first time in a long time I've felt warm. The tremble to his lower lip alerts me that he is as affected by this moment as I am. He gasps, appearing stunned by my touch.

I don't know where this surge of confidence has come from, but I trace his lips, the moisture coating my finger. He doesn't move. He doesn't breathe. He allows me to paint his face with my finger, leaving an invisible smear the color of desire behind.

He clenches his angular jaw when I place my palm against his whiskered chin. I run three fingers along the apple of his cheek, mesmerized by how contoured, how strong yet supple he feels. I need to stop this now, but stopping would feel like a crime.

His deep blue eyes widen, and I get lost in the stormy depths. I can see into his soul, and what I see is beautiful.

His lips part, and I gasp. The spark, the invisible current is charging between us, and now, all I can think about is wanting to kiss him. It's been so long since I've been kissed by anyone. Maybe I'm mistaking the feelings for something that isn't there. But I don't think I am.

"If I kissed you, would you feel anything?" He is a beautiful, contradictory creature, so certain, yet so unsure.

I don't know how to respond. I avert my eyes, suddenly losing my confidence.

His imposing presence engulfs the room as he leans forward, leaving mere inches between our lips. "Because I think you would." His masculine fragrance takes flight, and I inhale.

The air whooshes from my lungs when he presses his forehead to mine and traps me both physically and emotionally. I lick my dry lips while Jude follows the movement hungrily. "I-I don't know." My voice is high and breathless.

The moment he places his hands around my waist, I feel alive. Finally. I can breathe again. He settles me onto his lap, encaging me in a muscled prison as he positions my knees on either side of him to straddle him. The warmth from his body heats my skin, and it takes all my willpower not to close the distance between us.

"Deny it all you want, but I know you feel it."

"Feel what?" I whisper, feeling vulnerable and at his mercy in this position.

When he lowers an arm and seizes my wrist, I gasp at the blistering contact. He gently places my hand over my belly. "The butterflies. I know you felt them."

My mouth falls open. How did he know?

As if he can read my mind, he raises my hand and places it over his hammering heart. "I know you felt them...because I felt them, too."

I don't know what to say. No man has ever said something so beautiful and honest to me before. Tears fill my eyes because it's not fair that I'm so torn. I can't drag Jude through my emotional baggage. I won't do that to him. He's too good.

"Tori, I need to tell you—"

But I place my finger over his lips. He can't finish that sentence because it makes this too real. It makes this a two-way street, and I can't deal with that. I'm trying to do what's right even though it feels so wrong.

"I'm sorry. I really am. But I moved here to get away from drama and complications. Us being anything but neighbors is a huge complication."

He closes those intelligent eyes for the briefest of seconds and then exhales. "We're more than neighbors…and you know it." I open my mouth but close it when he bends forward and kisses me lightly on the forehead. "I know none of this makes any sense, but it will. You're strong. You just have to believe in yourself."

There are no words to follow, so I rest my head against his shoulder, hoping that belief comes one day soon.

Nine

Over the next few days, I come to realize that I haven't grieved. With the physical attack, then the affair, my body shut down to any emotion and locked down into survival mode. I feel like I'm only just now going through the five stages of grief—denial, anger, bargaining, depression, and acceptance. I sometimes experience one or all of these emotions on any day. No wonder I'm a mess.

As I walk down the stairs, I pause in awe. Charley has done a wonderful job of decorating. She's used the bare minimum to transform my house into a cozy little home. "So how long does this go for?" I inquire, looking at my garlanded surroundings.

"I didn't really put an end time on the invite, Tori. That would be kind of un-neighborly," she explains, adjusting the scented candles on the mantel.

"So I guess flicking the lights on and off at midnight would be kind of rude, then?"

She giggles, but who said I was joking?

"C'mon, it'll be fun."

A night with a bottle of wine, my pjs, and Bradley Cooper is my idea of fun. But I put my happy face on.

When the doorbell chimes, Charley smooths out her stunning red cocktail dress. "Go answer the door. I've got to check on the hors d'oeuvres." She dashes to the kitchen before I can object.

Sighing, I put on my big girl panties and inhale deeply, hoping to fill my lungs with enthusiasm. Forcing a smile, I tell myself this is what I need to do to move on.

I continue with that frame of mind as I open the door to a group of strangers who yell, "Happy housewarming!" I take a step backward, afraid they're going to tell me about Jesus.

"Welcome, we're the Andersons. We hope you like lobster tail." Before I have a chance to tell her I'm allergic, she thrusts the colossal plate into my hands.

A convoy proceeds for the next five minutes, and by couple number seven, I've forgotten who everybody is. Thank god for Charley and Mrs. Anderson, who are nice enough to stand by my side and help with introductions. I stick to both like glue, happy to blend into the background. I barely speak a word.

The moment Charley ducks into the kitchen, Debra Higgins, my neighbor from two doors down, makes a beeline for me while I throw back my wine.

"How do you like it here?" Debra asks. She's a middle-aged woman who looks friendly enough, but she definitely isn't someone I'd share my deepest, darkest secrets with. During the evening, I've seen her eavesdrop on almost every conversation within earshot.

"It's great," I reply, stealing a glass of champagne from a waiter.

"Have you met Henry Sands yet?"

That name has me almost choking on my drink. "Yes, I have." I don't go into further detail.

"Well, he and my husband are best friends. They have been for years," she reveals, reaching for a mini quiche from a passing waiter.

I nod, sipping my champagne and scanning the room for a familiar face, like Jude's.

Her brown eyes widen in excitement at the prospect of gossip. Leaning in close, she whispers from behind her hand, "Just awful what happened to Rose." Her omission has me stopping mid-sip. She tucks a lock of brown hair behind her ear. "I've said too much." Even though she has, I know she won't stop.

I don't want to know, but my curiosity gets the better of me. "What happened?"

She moves in closer. "Poor Henry... not only did his only daughter up and leave without a trace over twelve months ago, but he's now been restricted on how often he sees his grandson. It's such a shame. He loves that little boy. But I don't know why he's so intent on gaining full custody. The child looks so much like his father. You'd think he'd want nothing to do with him as there is no blood lost between him and Rose's husband."

"She was married?" I ask, voicing my thoughts aloud.

She nods.

This makes the betrayal so much worse. She not only left her son behind, but she left her husband, too. Why?

"Who is Angus's father?"

Her eyes feast around the room. They widen once they land on the front door. "Him."

I follow her finger's path, almost falling over my feet when I see who she's pointing at. My brain can't process the information fast enough. "*Jude?* Jude is Angus's father? Rose's *husband*?"

"Yes. You know him?" she queries, her tone filled with interest.

"Yes. I do." I'm surprised I can construct a coherent sentence right now.

"We all know Henry blames Jude for what happened to Rose."

My head snaps up. "What? Why?"

"Because it's his fault Angus is deaf. If he hadn't been MIA the night Angus was born, Rose wouldn't have ended up running off that embankment while driving herself to the hospital."

I cover my gaping mouth with a trembling hand.

"Poor Rose was unconscious for god knows how many minutes, her and Angus suffering. Henry was the one who found her. He rushed her to the hospital and almost lost both of them. They both pulled through, but Angus was born with his defect."

I blindly reach for two champagne glasses as the waiter passes us by. Debra smiles, extending her hand out to reach for one, but these are both mine. I gulp down the contents of one, then down the other. This is too horrible to digest. My heart bleeds for Angus. And for Henry to find his daughter that way—I can't even begin to imagine his pain.

But to say it was Jude's fault is nothing short of unfair.

No one can say that. Fate doesn't work that way.

The truth is, everything happens for a reason, and even though that reason may be completely unfair, it's part of your life's plan—part of your stepping-stones in living. So what doesn't happen today will probably happen tomorrow. It's all mapped out because no one can change destiny.

"It's unfair to blame Jude," I whisper, watching him as his eyes land my way.

"That child was premature, hardly developed," she argues. "He was starved for oxygen. He'll never be able to function properly. It probably would have been best if he died. What kind of life can he lead? He'll never marry."

My blood boils, and I feel my cheeks heat to the flames of

hell. Just as I'm about to throw her ignorant ass out, I hear a gruff voice to my left.

"Sorry, I'm late." The familiar, rough voice has Debra turning around nervously and smiling innocently.

Peering over at the clock on the mantel, I see that Henry's not overly tardy.

"Out saving the day again, were you?" teases Debra.

Henry doesn't crack a smile. All vigilante talks are over when he clears his throat. "Thanks for inviting me, Victoria."

Thankful to change the subject, I smile. "My pleasure, Henry. Although I can't take credit for any of this." I see Charley mingling with Jude and point her out. "That amazing woman did all the hard work." Henry follows my line of sight. His face instantly hardens when he sees who she's talking to.

Debra doesn't look a tad guilty while I'm almost certain Henry knows we were talking about him seconds ago. "Is Jillian with you?" I ask, needing to fill the silence.

Henry shakes his head. "No, she said to pass on her apologies. She has a migraine."

Debra's eyebrows rise into her hairline, and I wonder why. This entire situation is giving me heartburn.

I'm about to excuse myself when I hear a familiar smug voice. "Good evening, neighbors."

The incensed lines etched between Henry's brow, and the way his mouth is pulled into a thin, angry line can only mean one thing. He's seconds away from starting World War III in my living room.

"Hi, Jude." When I turn to face him, he doesn't take his eyes off me. The room is crackling with tension, and an unseen anger hums close to boiling point.

"Hi, Victoria. Great party. Thanks for inviting me." When he gazes over my shoulder to where Henry stands, I hear teeth grinding.

I nod. "No problem. Thanks for coming." Both men make no secret of their mutual hate for one another.

"Hey, Henry?" I bite the inside of my cheek when Jude addresses Henry. He gets a grunt in response. "Have you tried the pigs in blankets? They're to die for." Debra clears her throat, tugging at her gold chain. "The house looks good, Victoria." It's the first thing he's said that isn't dripping with sarcasm. He peers over at the red chair, his lips pulling into a tight smile. He's the only person who understands the significance of it, and for that, I'm unexpectedly glad.

"T-thanks," I reply when I finally find my voice.

Those piercing blue eyes soften, making me forget everything I've just heard.

I knew from the moment I met him that he was different, but I just didn't know how much. His tattoo now takes on a whole different meaning as it could denote so many different things. No matter if he were MIA, he can't be held responsible for Rose jumping into her car and ending up off the road. He also can't be held accountable for Angus's condition.

Bad things happen as often as good things—that's the balance of life.

"Hey, everyone." The moment Charley walks over, I exhale in relief. "Tori, can you spare five minutes? There's someone who wants to talk to you."

I steal a glance at Jude, admiring the guts it took for him to be here tonight. He knew Henry and the mass of judgmental neighbors would be here, yet he still came. "Save me a dance?"

"Sure," he replies, a genuine smile spreading across his full lips.

I loop my arm through Charley's, hinting she lead the way. When we're a safe distance away, she whispers from the side of her mouth, "What's going on?"

"I'll tell you later." When she's about to object, I add, "You'll need to be sitting down for the bombshell I'm about to drop."

She thankfully doesn't argue.

"So who wants to see me? Or was that a genius ploy to get me away from the mob of neighbors and their pitchforks?"

I expect her to laugh, but when her lips pull into a tight, thin line, I know something is wrong. Before I have a chance to ask what's going on, a set of familiar eyes come into view. "Mom?" I almost choke on the word.

My mother, Annabel, looks exactly how I remember. Large hazel eyes, long brown hair, and freckle-kissed skin. She looks exactly like me. And *her*. I can't exactly remember the last time I saw my mom, but I know it's been months. All my days since the accident have blended into one.

"I miss you, honey," she coos, her voice bringing back so many happy memories. Those memories get shit on, however, when she adds, "We all do."

This is the reason I don't answer her calls. She doesn't know when to stop. I have told her until I'm blue in the face that I will talk to Matilda when I'm ready. But when she insists on pressing, I retreat.

"Your sister—" And that's my cue to tune out. I go to another place, a place where there is no sorrow, just stillness. I find myself going to this place often because it's better than facing the nightmares.

"I just wish you'd come home. If you did, all of this would be over." Her voice grows softer and softer. "Bryan and Matilda, they both miss you. Your father, too. Months ago, your life was ripped out from under you, and now here you are in—"

Just as I sink deeper into despair, a warmth spreads through me, and I'm yanked into the now. I don't even need to open my eyes because I know it's Jude. "You let her in?" he scolds as he wraps me in his arms. I bury my nose into his soft sweater.

"I-I'm sorry. I thought it'd help her," Charley quickly apologizes.

"Help her how?" He tightens his hold around me, not disguising his anger.

"I don't know. We need to do something. If we don't, she'll fade away."

Although I'm standing right here, I feel so detached from the conversation. I hate feeling this way. I just want to get better. Charley is right. I am fading away. Each day, I'm losing who I am.

Unwrapping myself from the comfort of Jude's arms, I wipe my nose, determined not to cry. His inky blue stare contains nothing but concern. How I've come to rely on him so quickly scares me. "I'm fine, Jude." When he lifts an unbelieving brow, I affirm, "Promise."

With a sense of hesitancy, he reaches out and brushes a strand of fallen hair from my brow. He always appears so affected when we touch. "Okay, as long as you're sure."

I nod. "Thanks for coming to my rescue. You seem to be doing that a lot lately."

Something changes in his face, but it's gone a second later. "Did you want me to kick everybody out?" A ghost of a smile tugs at his lips.

I can't help but laugh. "As tempting as that sounds, I think I better see this through. This is all part of moving on, right?" Both he and Charley nod, smiling sadly.

Taking a deep breath, I turn to look at my mom, who has tears welling in her eyes. I wish I was the daughter she remembers, but I'm not. Something has changed inside me.

"Goodbye, Mom."

A single tear slips down her cheek, and just like that, she

accepts my need for space. She turns her back and walks out the door.

When the night comes to an end, and we're cleaning up, I fill Charley in on all the gossip. She's as surprised as I am. She can't believe Jude has an eight-year-old son since we're guessing he can be no older than thirty. After discovering Henry's past, I must admit I do feel for him, but there is something I can't quite put my finger on. I get a sense that under his cool, calm composure lays a ticking time bomb, waiting to explode.

Thankfully, both Henry and Jude stayed away from one another as I didn't fancy cleaning blood from my walls.

Debra's comment about Henry wanting full custody has me thinking that Jude is trying everything in his power to keep Henry away from his grandson. I can't help but speculate. Is he the reason Rose left?

"I think my ovaries exploded tonight."

I turn to look at Charley, snapping out from my Jude bubble. "What are you talking about?"

"Those subtle looks between you and Mr. Hot Pants." She wiggles her eyebrows.

I scrunch up my nose as I have no idea what she's talking about.

"Jude was so eye flirting with you," she states animatedly.

"What is that? Is that even a thing?"

"It is when Jude Montgomery is involved."

"Oh, you found out his surname." I decide to comment on that rather than address her ridiculous claims.

"I found out a lot of things," she says in a singsong voice.

So did I.

After everything I've found out about him, you'd think I'd want to stay away. But the funny thing is, I'm now even more intrigued.

"Goddamn, he may be a cocky son of a gun, but did you *see* that ass?"

I roll my eyes, but yes…yes, I did.

Needing to change the subject, I ask, "Did you see Mrs. Anderson? She was carrying on like she owned the place. I was certain she was going to make a 'welcome to the neighborhood' speech."

Charley nods but doesn't comment. She drops her half-filled garbage bag and stifles a yawn behind her hand. "I'm beat. See you tomorrow?" I nod, her yawn contagious. "Happy housewarming. Your gift is upstairs," she sweetly states before making a beeline for the door.

"My what?"

"Don't be mad." She hugs me quickly before sprinting down the driveway.

I watch with curiosity as she gets into a hybrid. "What

happened to the Fiat?" I call out, but she doesn't reply. She waves with a grin as she drives away. What is she up to now?

Just as I'm about to turn out the lights, there's a knock on my front door. Wishing I could ignore it, I lumber down the hallway, wondering if Charley left something behind. However, it's not Charley standing before me, but rather, Henry. I don't know why he's here.

"Sorry to turn up announced."

"That's okay. Did you leave something behind?" I ask. That's the only reason I can think to why he's here.

He clears his throat, the sound so somber like his appearance. "I'm going to be brief. I couldn't help but notice that you and Jude Montgomery looked…acquainted."

I fold my arms over my chest defensively, blocking the doorway, as I'm not inviting him inside after that remark. "Yes, he's been kind enough to fix a few things around my home."

He clenches his jaw. "I know you're new in town, so I'm going to give you a friendly piece of advice—stay away from him. Jude Montgomery is bad news. Nothing but trouble follows him."

There was absolutely nothing friendly about that statement. Not to mention, something similar was said about him hours ago.

This guy has some nerve coming into my home and telling me who I can or can't be friends with. He may have control over this town, but he certainly doesn't have control over me.

Nevertheless, for argument's sake, I nod. "Thanks for the tip, Henry."

As I attempt to shut the door, he wedges his foot into the way. His anger is almost blinding. "I'm not sure if you're aware, but Jude is my son-in-law." I continue staring at him, indicating that if he has a point, then to make it. "I've known that boy for years, and he's never changed. He's a thug, a lowlife. If you're seen with the likes of him, well…"

I blink, getting more pissed off by the minute. "As I said, thank you for the *friendly* tip," I quip, "but I'm a big girl. I'm also a good judge of character." I don't conceal the fact that my original thought of him being an asshole was completely correct. "Your son-in-law is also Angus's father, and from what I can see, he's doing a damn good job at being a single parent."

Henry's face pales, then reddens to a blistering rage. The jibe had a lot more bite than I intended, but it's exactly how I feel. "Now if you'll excuse me, I'm tired and want to go to bed. Good night." I don't give him time to respond as I shut the door in his face.

The nerve of some people.

I'm left in a bad mood thanks to Henry's assholeness, so when I flick on my bedroom light, and a bright pink box sitting in the center of my bed catches my eye, I thank the heavens for my best friend.

Tucking my weary feet underneath me as I sit at the foot of the bed, I drag the box toward me. Reaching for the card, I can't help but smile at the picture of two elderly ladies in prison stripes, sipping coffee. On the bottom, it says, "Friends for life."

When I open it up, my smile grows even bigger.

Dearest Tori,

This gift is <u>non-refundable</u>, so don't even think about returning it.

I'm so proud of you. Here's to new beginnings!

C x

The mystery as to where Charley's Fiat is has been solved— it's in my palm. Not literally, but the car key is an indicator that it'll be in the driveway come tomorrow.

Reaching for the cell off my dresser, I shoot her a quick text.

You are the best xx

Charley makes life so much better. She makes me feel normal…well, almost.

I stand and hunt through my dresser, pulling out my pajamas. Just as I shut the drawer, I hear a faint whisper catch on the warm breeze. I turn my ear to the open window, quite certain I heard that titter float in from that direction. I wait, my breathless anticipation filling the still room.

Just as I believe I'm hearing things, the sound hums once again. The contents of my stomach drop, and I suddenly feel hot. I act before I can think and dash across my floorboards to switch off the light. The room is shrouded in instant darkness, making what I intend to do all the more devious. I creep through my room, keeping to the shadows, using that whisper as my beacon of light. I stop, quite certain I'm cloaked, and hold my breath as I allow myself to peek across my yard.

I see Jude standing at the end of my dock. He gave me a warm hug goodbye hours ago, so why is he still here?

He's standing with his back to me, so I can't see his face. But his downturned shoulders hint that something is wrong.

Why do I feel like I've just swallowed lead?

Wiping my sweaty palms onto my dress, I know I have two options: I can either ignore him, or I can go to his aid. Sighing, I know there wasn't really a choice.

I stride through my home, silently closing the back door and walking down the steps. The porch light, the same light Jude fixed for me, suddenly flicks off. Great, this makes the mood even bleaker.

My bare feet whistle through the long blades of grass as I make my way toward Jude. I know he can hear me, but he doesn't turn around. He looks so lost, broken, and I don't know why. Could it be seeing Henry brought back memories of all that he's lost? It makes sense.

"If you knew something that would change someone's life forever, would you tell them?" It's a poignant question. I have an inkling we're not talking in the rhetorical sense.

Stopping just before the dock's edge, I take a minute to reply. "Yes, I think that I would."

Jude's sigh is heavy. He places his hands into his jeans pockets. "You're brave and honorable, Victoria."

And there's that word again. Brave. I don't feel brave. Each day, I seem to lose sight of what courage looks like. "Since the incident, seconds seem to morph into minutes, hours, days, weeks." I leave a long pause between each word, wanting to give recognition to all the time lost. "I don't know what reality is, and what a dream is anymore. I feel neither here nor there. I'm in limbo."

Jude lowers his head. The sight is moving.

"Everyone wants to help me, but most days, I just want to be left alone. My parents thought Matilda moving in would help me get over what I'm dealing with, but it didn't. Nothing has helped. Each day is the same as the next." Clutching at my chest, I confess, "There is no light at the end of my tunnel. I feel like I'm losing it. Like I'm losing my mind."

My words are the fire under Jude as he spins around, shaking his head furiously. "Don't say that. Never give up hope."

"It's hard not to when all hope is gone. I feel so lost. Alone."

The pause before he speaks betrays Jude's fear of expressing his thoughts. "You've got me."

The space between us fills with tenderness. "You're the only thing keeping me anchored. Each day, I forget who I used to be. I feel like I'm slipping away, and if I blink, I'll be gone." My lower lip trembles, but I refuse to cry.

The night is dark—pitch black, in fact. The stars stay hidden behind the lingering storm clouds, but regardless of the darkness, I can see the shine in Jude's eyes. His heavy footsteps sound along the weathered dock as he walks toward me. A coil within draws me closer and closer, needing to touch him, feel him near. He is the only thing that has made me feel alive. The revelation is a heady sensation. Maybe I'm not dead inside. Maybe there is hope for me after all.

There is always a look of surprise on Jude's face when we touch. Two fingertips caress my cheek as he reaches out softly, akin to the flutter of butterfly wings. "Maybe we can ground one another?" His reply is cloaked with so much emotion, and I find it hard to breathe. Leaning into his touch, I close my eyes.

The reason I feel so unguarded around Jude is because he understands. Don't ask me how I know, but I just know he understands what it's like to hit rock bottom. He knows how hard it is to try to climb your way back up because you refuse to be beaten. Refuse to give up because the fight, the fire in you drives you to never back down. To never stop believing that you…are…worth…it.

Rose was an idiot for leaving behind such an extraordinary man.

"I think that's the only way I'll survive."

Jude runs his thumb down the center of my lips. "Storms don't last forever." He always knows what to say.

My voice is a mere whisper. It's also a voice laced with…
hope. "But when they do…I'll just adjust my sails."

His reply has tears stinging my eyes. "I never doubted
anything less."

Ten

Three Weeks Later

It's Friday afternoon, and to celebrate my first week of teaching, I've decided to treat myself to dinner in town tonight.

I thought I'd lost my passion for it, but the moment I stepped into the classroom, it was like I returned home. The kids are great and so well behaved, it's like they're not even in the room.

This town is slowly becoming my home, and I can see myself being here for a while. I still wake up every night screaming, but now I settle as soon as I realize where I am. I also get a sense of peace from the hushed voices which catch on the cool breeze and drift across the lake and into my open window. It's nice to know I'm not alone.

A fact which upsets me more than I care to admit is that

after the night of the housewarming, Jude has kept himself scarce. I know he has his own life to lead, but I've come to rely on him, and I'm woman enough to admit that I miss him.

As I pull into the driveway, I see Angus is standing on my dock with a remote control in hand. I park the car and reach for the bag of groceries on the passenger seat. I watch him closely, not wanting to sneak up on him, seeing as he's so close to the dock's edge. The moment I step onto the wooden rafters, he spins around. He's so in tune with his surroundings, but I suppose he has to be. What we take for granted, he would embrace with both hands.

"Hi, Angus." I hold up my free hand.

He smirks, his lopsided grin so much like Jude's. Now that I know he's Jude's son, I can definitely see the resemblance. Expressive blue eyes, tousled brown hair, and a gentle, kind soul. He waves happily, holding up his remote.

"What you got there?" I ask, walking closer.

When I'm standing close enough, I chuckle. "Are you the captain?" I query, looking at his little blue sailor hat.

He nods, his tongue poking out the side of his mouth as he turns back around to steer his mechanical sailboat. The light wind pushes it along, the white sails catching in the breeze. The momentum has the red boat sailing across the water effortlessly.

Angus cheers in delight, turning to me and pointing at his toy.

His energy and love for life have me questioning how anyone

could leave him behind. I have no doubt Jude is a good dad, but his choice in spouse is a mystery to me. Our circumstances are so similar yet so different. We both don't know where our partners are, or what they're doing, but the difference is I don't care. I have a feeling Jude is also grieving. I wonder what stage he's at.

A little finger poking into my side makes me look down and smile. Angus holds out the remote, gesturing it's my turn. Unable to turn down such an offer, I accept his request. The buttons taunt me with their cleverness, and I move my lips from side to side.

Angus must be able to read my prehistoric take on technology because he smirks. He raises his hands and hurriedly signs, but I have no idea what he just said. He reads my confusion and reaches for the control, teaching me how it works.

Just as I'm about to take over, Angus tugs on my arm. As I look down, my heart fills with adoration—a feeling I haven't experienced in a long time. His little fingers are extended upward, offering me his sailor hat.

I spend the next twenty minutes, hat happily perched on my head, steering the boat across the lake. Being around Angus brings me a sense of peace, but I don't know why. I remember Jude's words to me. *"I'm drawn to you."* At the time, I didn't fully understand what he meant, but now, I feel exactly the same way about his son.

Angus's excited shrill has me turning to see what the commotion is all about. When I see Jäg sauntering toward us, not at all afraid, I can't help but smile.

Angus runs toward Jäg, who sits and licks himself, relishing in the attention. As I watch on, I can't help but think about Jude. Slipping the phone from my back pocket, I scroll through my contacts until I land on J. I could send him a friendly text, and say what? I miss you? Where have you been?

All thoughts of being poetic are put on hold when Angus yelps and laughs. It appears Jäg has worked his magic on him, too. Lost in the moment, Angus begins to sign to the cat. He smiles, a dimple expressing how contented he is.

An idea strikes and I quickly search my phone for a quick tutorial on sign language. After a few attempts, I finally decode what Angus is saying. It's simple and straightforward, but it whets my appetite for more.

Cat.

He is signing the word cat.

This extraordinary boy is my teacher, and I'm his pupil, wanting to learn. Wishing to express to Angus how much his friendship means to me, I sign my first and most important word. When he watches me with nothing but interest, I interlock my index fingers twice.

Just when I think I've misunderstood what I've read, he runs over to me, stopping a few feet away. This moment is filled with purity, the enchantment of something as simple as language—

something as simple as friends, the word I just signed.

Friends.

Angus bites his pouty bottom lip before linking his index fingers together and pulling twice. I don't know what that means, and I'm about to google it but am thrown off guard when he wraps his arms around my waist and holds on tight. I simply stand and store this moment into my memory bank as I gently run my fingers through his soft hair.

The moment only lasts for a few seconds, but it's enough to touch something inside me I thought I'd lost. Angus has shown me that we won't live in the dark forever.

Before I can say another word, Angus lets go and is waving goodbye.

Remembering what he signed, I search my phone once again. Once I find the meaning, I can't help but smile.

Good friends.

Angus has corrected me. We're not just friends, we're good friends…and for that, I'm glad.

I can't help but smile at Angus's sailor hat sitting on my passenger seat. I completely forgot to give it back to him, which I interpret as the universe's way of telling me that I'm supposed to see Jude. I'm suddenly hungry for life. I'm hungry to start anew. But right now, I'm hungry for Outback Steakhouse.

As I'm hacking into my steak, for some unknown reason, I gaze to the left and am greeted with a sight which has me almost inhaling my dinner. A person who I'm almost certain is Jude, steps from a black BMW, which is idling near the curb. The driver, an older woman wearing large, dark shades, appears awfully suspicious as she glances around, scoping out her surroundings. She reeks of money and control. Her flashy diamond necklace and car confirm my assumption.

I'm completely intrigued when the person who is most definitely Jude, slips the hood over his head, cloaking his appearance, and walks to the driver's side. I sink low, afraid he'll see me, but crane my neck and watch in horror as he tosses a huge wad of cash at the woman. He couldn't care less that he's just thrown the equivalent of my life savings at her while she grins, pressing her full, ruby lips together and blowing him a seductive, well-sated kiss.

The transaction is subtle, and if you'd blinked, you'd miss it, but I've seen it all. In one fluid motion, he jogs across the road and disappears into the night. The car takes off, the population none the wiser, except me. My brain short-circuits, not understanding what I just saw. If I'd seen this particular scenario take place in a movie, I'd without a doubt assume that what I just saw was incredibly...dodgy.

All the pieces are there. I just don't want to put them together.

With my appetite totally shot, I pay the bill and make my

way home, my mind processing everything I just saw.

I know Jude has secrets, we all do, but his secret is one that rules him.

I can't help but wonder how Jude keeps Angus enrolled in the school that he does, as Henry hinted the cost wasn't cheap. He confessed his job at Pop's wasn't raking in the big bucks, so how could he afford handing over that huge wad of cash? There's no way he could have those kinds of funds just lying around.

I think about the bullies mentioning that Angus's dad was a deadbeat. Is this the reason Henry dislikes Jude so? The reason Rosemary left? Is Jude involved in something so sinister, so crooked, his wife couldn't stick around? But her leaving Angus behind doesn't make any sense.

None of this does.

Pacing my kitchen doesn't help, so I decide I need fresh air. Storming over to the back door, I yank it open and take a much-needed deep breath. My head is bowed, so I don't notice a figure in my yard until I hear a thud and a curse. Using the moonlight as my conductor, I catch sight of someone face planted on my lawn. I know without really looking who it is.

At first sight, it appears Jude is drunk and passed out. But when I see his left hand extended above his head pull at blades of grass; I know I'm wrong. My gut churns as I race down the stairs.

"What happened?" I call out shrilly. Jude groans.

He doesn't answer; instead, he attempts to crawl toward me. He moves an inch before giving up. I gasp, quickening my step. The moment I reach him, I cover my gaping mouth. Jude has rolled to his side, his gray sweater stained in bright red.

All thoughts of what I saw tonight are put on the backburner. "Oh my god!" I screech, crouching beside him, and quickly unzipping his hoodie as I roll him onto his back. Without a second thought, I tear off my shirt and scrunch it into a ball. I press it over the bleeding wound to his abdomen.

His cool fingers unexpectedly fly up, clasping my wrist. I yelp in surprise but also fear for his safety. "Inside," he forces out between staggered breaths. His face is a complete mess.

Squeezing both eyes shut, I inhale through my nose, centering myself before I pass out. "No." My voice is choppy. "Y-you need to go to the hospital!" I press, as I think he's been… shot.

"No." His head lolls as he attempts to shake it. "You."

"Me?"

He nods, his eyes pleading with me.

I don't know what to do. I know first aid, but that does not include treating a bleeding, half-conscious man.

"Please," he begs, squeezing my wrist. "I can't go to the hospital…please, Victoria." His desperate plea is my final undoing. I squash down all my personal demons because Jude needs me.

Brushing the sweaty hair off his brow, I nod. "Can you

stand?"

He makes a pained face but manages to sit up, hunched over.

"Hold onto me," I instruct, still pressing the shirt firmly over his wound.

Jude grins a pained smile. "That won't be a problem." He wraps a shaky arm around me while leaning against me.

"Okay. One…two…three." Jude groans but tries his best to lift his weight, making it easier for me to stand him up. When he's upright, we commence a slow, unsteady walk toward my home. He stumbles and almost falls along the way, but we manage after three attempts to get him up the stairs and inside.

"I'm sorry," he gasps, sagging against me as we stagger into the kitchen.

"It's okay. Just don't die on me." He lets out a pained laugh.

I lead him over to a dining chair, which he slumps into, letting out a braying grunt. He clutches his side, winded.

"Can you take your sweater o-off?" I ask, endeavoring to help him with one hand as I'm still pressing the shirt to his side. He nods, hissing as he attempts to slip out of his hoodie. At this rate, he'll bleed all over my kitchen floor. "I never thought I'd say this, but let me help you…u-undress." I gently touch his shoulder.

Jude laughs at my coyness but chokes on a strangled gasp. "Thanks."

I go into survival mode as I carefully remove his sweater

and soiled white T-shirt. I've spent enough time in hospitals to know what this is. I only have to look down at the scar on my chest to see the likeness.

"I've got to go upstairs and get my first-aid kit. I'll be right back. Press this to your side until I get back, okay?"

He nods, gritting his teeth together as he presses over the wound.

Flying up the stairs, I head into the bathroom and yank open the medicine cabinet. I grab whatever supplies I think I'll need and reach for the first-aid kit under the sink. Rushing into my room, I throw on a T-shirt, as I'm only in a camisole, then I google *bullet wounds for dummies*. I still have no idea what I'm doing, but I'm back downstairs in less than two minutes. I make a beeline for the freezer and pull out a bottle of vodka.

Jude has his head thrown back, blood staining his hand, but the flow has thankfully subsided.

"You're not going to pass out, are you?" I ask, rushing over to his side and placing my supplies on the table.

His head snaps forward, his eyes blurred, but he shakes his head. "No, I'm good."

I stop rifling through the kit, concerned at how pale he's becoming. "Are you sure you don't want me to call an ambulance?"

"No," he stubbornly replies.

Slipping on a pair of gloves, I grab the peroxide and some gauze. I crouch down in front of him and gently remove the makeshift bandage from his flesh. I breathe out a sigh of relief when I see the wound has stopped bleeding. It appears superficial. The bullet only grazed his skin, and thankfully won't need any stitches. But it's still deep and large enough to have caused some substantial bleeding.

"This is going to hurt. A lot." I pull an apologetic face as I look up at him from under my lashes.

He sits upright bravely, radiating strength and trust as he pins me with a confident stare. "I'm used to pain." His comment has me clucking my tongue.

"What happened?" I unscrew the lid of the solution, dampening the gauze.

He chooses to ignore me. "How bad is it, doc?" The fact that he's joking and not moaning in pain is a good sign.

"You'll live. Now stop avoiding the question." I can feel him watching me closely as I gently apply the gauze to his side.

"Why does anyone do anything? To better their life."

I know talking is difficult right now, but I need answers, especially after what I saw tonight. "Unless you're a glutton for punishment, getting shot and beaten to a pulp is not bettering anyone's life." He hisses as I jab a little too roughly at the wound, annoyed by his aloofness. "Sorry. I just…help me understand."

Jude sighs, leaning his head back. "I'm sorry. I didn't mean to bring my shit to your doorstep. I just didn't…I didn't know where else to go."

"It's okay." I tend to his wound as gently and as quickly as

I can.

"If I didn't know any better, I'd say you were worried about me," he quips.

My fingers shake—not because I'm queasy, but because I can feel Jude watching my every move. Once I'm happy that the wound is clean, I stand between his spread legs and hunt through the kit over his shoulder. I also grab the vodka.

"Should I be concerned that you've got all this stuff on hand?"

I'm thankful he's making jokes. "At the moment, you should be grateful. PTSD makes you a little over cautious at the stuff you have in your first-aid kit," I add. "It also prepares you to deal with the unexpected and to keep your cool and use your smarts when your bleeding, beaten neighbor is passed out on your lawn."

As I slip on a new pair of gloves, I peer down and see Jude looking up at me. A dark circle is beginning to form around his right eye, his swollen upper lip is caked in dried blood, and coagulated blood is seeping from his nose. But I'll deal with one drama at a time.

Taking a swig of vodka, I pass him the bottle. "Ready?"

He accepts gratefully and nods. "No." I can't help but grin.

As I bend back down and ensure the wound is dry, I know the only way he'll get through this is by being distracted. "I wanted to apologize for being so awful to you when we first met. I was a little…unhinged," I say, unscrewing the lid from the liquid bandage.

"You weren't awful."

"Yes. I was." Applying the liquid to the edges of skin around the wound, I tear off small pieces of tape with my teeth. This is the easy part. Now comes the part that'll hurt like a bitch. Fastening a strip of the tape to one edge of the wound, I squeeze the flesh together and quickly apply the other side of the tape.

"Motherfucker!" Jude roars, stomping his foot.

"I'm sorry." I flinch, as I can only imagine how painful this would be.

"It's not your fault. How many more of them are there?" Matted hair sticks to his face, pushing off his cheeks as he exhales forcefully.

Looking at the size of the wound, I shrink back. "Maybe four."

"Fuck me." Another deep breath, then another shot of vodka.

As I reach for another strip of tape, I think on my feet as I can't bear to see him in pain. "I wasn't…I'm still not in a good headspace. But I'm getting better."

"After everything you've been through, it's natural for you to be a little…hostile." He grunts as I attach the tape a little too firmly as I'm caught off guard by his comment.

"I thought you said I wasn't awful?"

"I did…I never said you weren't vicious, though. You're like a koala bear. Cute yet vicious."

I chew the inside of my cheek to stop my smile. "It's just koala, not bear. Koalas are marsupials, not that it matters." This playful banter is taking my mind off the situation at hand, and I'm not just talking about his wounds.

"Do I make you nervous?" he suddenly asks. His eyes are on me; I can feel them.

"Yes," I whisper, my hands trembling

"Don't be," he replies in a tone akin to mine.

We're silent until his abs ripple. I know he's in horrible pain. "Do you want me to stop?"

He throws back another large mouthful of vodka. "No. Keep going."

I do.

If I distract him, then things might go quicker. So, deciding to be honest, I confess, "I met your son. In town." I'm certain he stops breathing as his body turns rigid. I don't have the courage to meet his eyes, so I continue. "Then he was flying a kite in my yard. And then, just today, he taught me how to sail a boat. Well, a motorized sailboat."

Jude's response has me sucking in a deep breath. I halt from nursing his wounds. "*You're* the pretty lady?" He flicks the hair from his face, his eyes soft, almost poignant.

"I…um…I…don't know?" I shrug, embarrassed.

"Angus mentioned a pretty lady," he explains in awe. "I told him not to talk to strangers, but he said you're not." He smiles, the sight almost bittersweet, considering his face is a mess. "I now know what he means. Seems we're both…" But he pauses, leaving me guessing what he was going to say.

I don't press and continue stitching him up, but his words keep swimming around my head.

He notices the tremble in my hands. "So I guess you know all the details then?"

He doesn't need to clarify, so I nod. "Yes. I'm really sorry about what happened to her…your wife. I didn't pry, I promise. Angus is a remarkable young boy."

"Thank you."

"Do you know where…Rosemary is?" I sneak a glance at him, witnessing his lip curl in anger.

He shakes his head, his jaw clenched. "No, I don't. All she left me was a Dear John note that read *'Don't try to find me.'* I knew she'd leave one day. Rose and I met in high school. I was smitten by her, everyone was. She had a way of getting what she wanted, and for some reason, she wanted me. Everyone said she was bad news, but I didn't listen. I was a punk, a kid who got into trouble any chance I got, and she was…she was the sheriff's baby girl.

"I know she only dated me to get under Henry's skin. He was overbearing, telling her to act and think a certain way. I was outside that mold; therefore, I was everything she wanted. Rose was…" He pauses, searching for the right word. "Wild. She was the perfect daughter to the outside world, but behind closed doors…I've never met someone like her."

I'm done stitching him up, but I let him continue as I apply an antibiotic spray.

"She always wanted to leave," he reveals, lost in the memories. "But no matter what a total douchebag Henry was, Rose loved Jill."

"You don't think he's got something to do with Rose's disappearance, do you?"

Jude's face falls. No matter what she's done, he's still worried about her. I can see it in his eyes. "No, I don't, and that's why he hates me. This entire thing is apparently my fault. Rose did the one thing that no one in this town has ever done. She left. Generations of families stay here, content with living the norm, but not Rose. She was always destined to leave; I was just too blind to think she'd ever take me with her."

I don't even know what to say, so I stay quiet, allowing him to purge.

"She fell pregnant when she was nineteen. I had just turned twenty. She never wanted Angus, but I did. In the perfect role reversal, *I* was the one talking her out of having an abortion. I thought a child would change her, but it didn't. When Henry found out, after he promised to have me neutered, he said we had to get married. He couldn't have a scandal such as this tarnishing the Sands name.

"Things were okay for a little while, but when Angus was born, Rose fell out of love with us both. I loved him regardless of his...limitations, but she saw him as a punishment. I knew he was special. But for the first time in her life, she and Henry agreed on something—her misfortunes were my fault. I stayed for so long because I didn't want Angus growing up without both parents. I never knew my dad, and I would never do the same to my kid. But for Rose, the only way to deal with such misfortunes was to find her luck elsewhere." The last sentence is spat with such venom; it can only amount to one thing.

"I-I'm so sorry."

He nods, snickering. "It appears neither you nor I was enough."

Tears prick my eyes. Being cheated on is one of the worst feelings in the world. "You're more than enough...she was the one who became self-centered and selfish. Although I think she always was." Suddenly, the patter, the flutter of butterfly wings returns. I try to squash them down, but I can't.

Reaching down, he brushes away my fallen tears. "After Rose left, I was broken. I no longer recognized the person I was. She changed me. She tore out my heart and took it with her. I hate the cynical, bitter person I have become because of it."

"So she left without a trace?"

Jude nods, his finger still tracing my cheek. "Yes. Looks like the sheriff isn't such a good detective after all."

"Why did she stay for so long? She didn't sound happy." My lower lip trembles as his finger skims across it.

He watches our connection intimately, opening up like never before. "Because no matter what, I take care of what's mine. She loved being the center of my world, but when things got too tough, and she grew tired of our life together, she took everything she could, leaving me broke and broken. I should have left years ago." He swallows harshly, his Adam's apple bobbing. "But everything I do, everything that I am, I do for my son."

Is he confessing to a life most would consider unorthodox? Maybe even immoral? No matter what life he chooses to live, he's a survivor, a fact which makes me admire him even more.

Unaccustomed to these feelings, I clear my throat and stand, removing my bloodied gloves. "It'll probably scar. I'm sorry."

Jude reaches out and snares my wrist. "I'm used to scars." His eyes drop to his tattooed side before meeting mine. "It's the unseen scarring that hurts the most." Tears prick my eyes once again because his comment means so much more to me than he'll ever know.

I stretch around his huge frame with one hand to rifle through the first-aid kit for supplies to clean his face, not bothering to remove the other from his grip. I should, but I can't. God strike me down, but I don't want to, and that feeling is shockingly healing.

Soaking a pad, I gently clean his eye.

With his finger still running over my pulse, he states, "Every scar tells a story. It's a stepping-stone in one's journey. Maybe one day…you could show me yours."

He doesn't know what he's saying. He doesn't want to see my scars—both inside and out.

He senses my retreat and slides his hand into mine. "Never be ashamed of your scars. They simply mean you were stronger than whatever tried to tear you down. You're a fighter, just like me. Never forget that." His comment rings true, and just like that, I know I've passed the point of no return.

Reaching up, I gently finger the pendant hanging from his neck. Turning it, I see it's a medallion of Saint Jude. "It's beautiful."

He appears poignant for a moment, before finally revealing, "He's the patron of hope."

Peering up at him from under my lashes, I say the unsaid through a look alone—we have hope that tomorrow will be better than today and the day before it.

One can only hope.

Eleven

The sunlight streaming in through my open window alerts me that it's morning. The time, however, remains unknown.

I rub the sleep from my eyes, my foggy brain churning through the unbelievable events of last night. I cleaned up Jude as best I could and told him he could stay the night—on the couch, of course. After I grabbed him a pillow and blanket and said good night, he got comfortable and was out like a light. I'm surprised he didn't pass out sooner, considering his injuries. But last night proved Jude is a survivor—another quality I like about him.

And that's the problem; I like a lot of things about him. When did that happen?

His quest to better his son's life is admirable. Regardless of his past, he refuses to give up. He refuses to dwell on what could have been because hindsight doesn't help anyone.

Groaning, I kick off my sheet and decide to take a shower. Once I'm dressed, I run my fingers through my damp hair and bounce down the stairs, excited to have a guest sleeping on my couch. I've become accustomed to living alone, but it's nice to have someone to wake up to.

With that thought in mind, I round the corner, ready to bid Jude a good morning, but as I walk into the living room, I see he's still sound asleep. The knitted blanket has fallen to the floor, along with the throw cushions. His gigantic body barely fits on my sofa, his arms and legs contorted at extremely odd angles. I instantly feel guilty for not offering him my bed. His face looks better than when I saw it last, but by the twisted scowl, I dare say he's still in a lot of pain.

I tiptoe into the kitchen, silently moving around as I make a pot of coffee.

Waiting for it to percolate, I think about whether I should tell Jude about what I saw. Would the truth change the way I act around him? The way I feel about him?

This entire time I backed away, closing myself off to a friendship with this man because I...like him. Yes, he's incredibly attractive, but I actually find myself being drawn to what's inside. There's that word again—drawn. It appears we're both drawn to one another.

"Coffee smells good." I jolt, Jude's gruff voice startling me from my thoughts. "Sorry. I didn't mean to frighten you."

I peer up, almost gagging on my tongue when I see him standing in my kitchen, topless and slumber kissed. The sunlight flooding in licks the blond strands of his messy locks, which are sleep tousled and rebellious. His lips are exceptionally pink and full, the color underlying his dark scruff.

He is absolutely incredible, and I can't stop staring—so much for being primarily drawn to what's on the inside.

"Thanks for letting me crash," he says as he hobbles over to my kitchen counter.

His limp is the mental slap I need. I instantly revert to protector mode. "How are you feeling?"

He shrugs, running a hand over his bloodied bandage. "Not too bad, thanks to you."

"It was nothing. After we're done, I can change your bandage, if you like."

He nods with a smile.

"How do you take your coffee?"

"Black."

Pulling out two coffee mugs, I pour us a decent helping of the exotic smelling goodness and slide one cup along the counter. He gratefully accepts as he takes a seat on a stool.

I nurse my mug, his silence making me uncomfortable, because what he lacks in the vocabulary department, he's sure making up for by staring a hole straight through me. It's not fair. He looks so composed while I feel as though I'm the one who got shot last night—straight through the heart.

I need to say something, anything, because I'm seconds away from drooling into my mug. "So, are you going to press charges?" I cringe at my bluntness. What the hell is the matter with my brain?

He thankfully laughs. "No, I'm not. To do that, I would have to talk to Henry, and that thought is as appealing as getting shot."

"You almost died last night." I can't keep the bite from my tone as I'm still angered by what happened to him. I know it's a tad overdramatic, but he could have if it had been any worse.

"Tori." Sliding his hand across the counter, he reaches out and grabs mine. I should shy away, but I don't. "I've lived through worse."

I blink. "What?"

He knows he's said too much.

"Hold up." I raise my finger. "What's that mean? What's worse than almost losing your life?"

When he looks away guiltily, my stomach sinks to the bottom of my coffee. I need to know the truth; otherwise, this will eat away at me, and I'm bound to get indigestion from it.

Swallowing down my humiliation, I scratch the countertop with my nail, avoiding his stare. "I…saw…you."

"Saw me?" His confusion is clear.

Pushing myself to continue, I take a deep breath. "Yes, last night. I was at the Outback Steakhouse, and I saw you…getting out of a car." My confidence takes a nosedive, and the words get lost in my larynx. The silence is killing me, so I raise my eyes, afraid of what I'll see.

Jude's head is tilted to the side, waiting for me to continue. But I can't.

"So what time should I pick you up? The movie starts at four."

"What are you talking about?" I ask, as he completely ignored my question.

"I promised Angus I'd take him to a *Harry Potter* movie marathon. He's going with a bunch of moms and kids from his school. I think he's trying to impress a girl." He smirks proudly. "I promised him I wouldn't embarrass him and keep a low profile. You're welcome to come." But that's not the issue. I bite my lip. Why did he just ignore me?

"C'mon. It won't have the awkward, first date vibe. Not that this is a first date," he quickly backtracks.

I suddenly feel hot.

"'Cause we're past that. I mean, as far as first daters go, we're totally backward," he rambles, rubbing a hand over his fuller beard.

Is he at a loss for words? Jude "the smooth talker" Montgomery is tongue-tied. Now I've seen it all.

"We missed all the getting to know you part and jumped straight into the deep end." He's right. Our first meeting wasn't exactly conventional. None of our encounters have been, and for that, I'm glad.

Jude has proven that he's a loyal, thoughtful friend, and I'm going to do the same. Regardless of the fact I caught him throwing wads of cash at an older lady, it won't change the fact that I like being his friend.

"I mean, you got to know my son before really knowing me—"

"I like being your friend, too." I cut him off. His eyebrows shoot up into his hairline, not expecting my admission. "I'll meet you there around three. I want to get there early to check out the candy selection. Oh, by the way, I'm paying. And that isn't up for discussion because that's what friends do. They do nice things for their friends."

He smirks, knowing this is an argument he can't win since it's a line he's used on me before.

Touché.

I park my car a few blocks from the cinema, wanting to walk and feel the crisp breeze against my cheeks. It's a good day to be alive as the universe and I are somewhat in sync. It's a nice sensation, beginning to feel like me again—version 2.0.

For some unknown reason, I begin thinking about my family and my sister, in particular. I wonder if she's found a sense of peace with what happened. There was no doubt she felt guilty, but was that guilt because of the act itself or because she got caught? I hate that I believe it's the latter. I've missed several calls from my mom, and yes, I guess I've been avoiding her in a way. I just can't deal with the "it's time to forgive your sister" speech. That won't happen. One day, I may be able to sit in the same room as her, but forgiveness…I don't think I can.

Jude is certainly more forgiving than I am because when I think about Bryan, all I can envision is running him over with my car. In a way, I envy Jude's ability not to hold a grudge against his wife. I sense he still cares for her, but I know the love is gone. Nevertheless, it must be nice not to visualize your ex getting trampled by African elephants daily.

As I round the corner, I'm pleased I'm not huffing and puffing like an eighty-year-old man. The daily swims have been doing me good. Each day, I'm swimming farther and farther, and before long, I have no doubt I'll reach the other side. I wonder what will happen when I do.

The sidewalk is surprisingly busy, but as the crowd clears, my heart does a tiny flip flop when I see two boys who look so alike, standing side by side.

Angus is holding Jude's hand tightly, his tiny frame only reaching below Jude's waist. Trademark *Harry Potter* glasses sit loosely on his face, and in his left hand, he's clutching a plastic wand. He looks excited and full of pride to be holding his father's hand. Jude's injuries are masked by a baseball cap perched low. He pulls a goofy face at Angus, who laughs happily. There is nothing but love reflected in this image—it's innocent and pure.

A father, his son, and…me.

The moment Angus sees me, he lets go of Jude's hand and runs my way. I laugh, elated he's as delighted to see me as I am him. The moment he reaches me, I kneel, and he throws himself into my arms. The gesture is so genuine, I can't help but smile.

I look over his shoulder to see Jude walking toward us, smiling happily. His motorcycle boots pound against the asphalt, setting off his ripped jeans and a black fitted tee. "As you can see, my son is so shy," he comments, tongue in cheek.

I giggle. "Your son is amazing."

Angus pulls away, showing me his wand. He bops me over the head with it, his lens-free glasses sliding down his nose. "Are you turning me into a princess?" I ask.

He looks at Jude over his shoulder and signs. I watch in interest, wondering why Jude is laughing. He explains why a second later. "He said you already are."

"Watch out, you've got a sweet talker on your hands." I refrain from adding like father like son.

"Don't I know it."

When I stand, Angus looks up at me, then at Jude, and smiles. I wonder what he's thinking. "You ready, buddy?" Jude says, signing and speaking aloud. It's the first time I've seen Jude sign, and it's impressive, to say the least.

Angus nods, his smile broad and euphoric.

A group of about twenty moms and teachers and a large

number of kids begin walking into the cinema. A young girl with blonde pigtails and braces waves for Angus to come join them. He reaches for my hand and drags me inside, leaving Jude to follow.

As we wait in line for tickets, I soak up the excitement around me. Kids run around madly, screaming *Harry Potter* spells to their siblings or friends. Angus watches them closely. He's always so in tune with his surroundings.

He looks up at me and begins signing quickly while Jude laughs. I really need to learn sign language. I'm fascinated with the way they communicate. It's like their secret language.

Jude messes up Angus's hair before meeting my curious eyes. "Angus just asked how old you are because he'd like you to be his date for the annual dance at school. But he understands if you don't want to come because he's not a very good dancer. You don't have to go," he adds, and I suddenly get the feeling he doesn't want me to attend.

Without a second thought, I bend low and use one of the few words I've learned in sign.

Yes.

Angus's smile lights up the room, but I frown as I watch Jude grow pale. I wonder why.

"I wouldn't miss it for the world," I confirm quickly. "There's no place I'd rather be." Jude's face falls sentimental.

The space around us abruptly turns silent, and I'm lost in those blue, expressive eyes. I can feel that something has shifted between us. There's always been an undercurrent lapping at the surface, but now, I feel like I'm drowning.

Suddenly, he breaks our heated exchange, appearing embarrassed. He doesn't usually look away first, so what's changed? I can't deny that there has always been a pull between us, but something feels different this time. Jude has been cocky, flirty, but now, he seems...torn.

I don't have time to process his response because the doors open to cinema five, allowing everyone in to see their favorite wizard. "Did you want any candy?" Jude asks, clearing his throat.

"No, I'm okay," I reply, suddenly losing my appetite.

When we silently make our way inside, we see that Shelley, the little blonde, has left three free seats next to her. Angus sits beside her, bouncing happily in his seat when Shelley offers him her popcorn. Jude and I take the end two seats. He shifts to the left to avoid touching me, but I don't know why.

When the previews start, it dawns on me that without subtitles, Angus may get a little lost. I'm assuming he'll lip read and get the general gist of what's happening through the very animated acting, but it's simple things we take for granted that Angus struggles with daily.

Peering down at him, he looks up at me, his cheeks pushed out as he chews a mouthful of popcorn. He doesn't have a care in the world. I smile, wishing I viewed the world through rose-tinted glasses too.

Two *Harry Potter* movies later, Angus's head lies nestled in my lap.

Even though we're in a dark room, I know Jude has been avoiding me. His body language displays his coldness—his arms are folded tight, a sure sign he doesn't want to let me in. I'm racking my brain, desperately attempting to piece together what would have caused the sudden change of mood. Maybe he really doesn't want me to go to the dance. I guess that's understandable, as it's a mommy thing to do, and I'm not Angus's mom.

Once we're outside, I'll let him know that I won't go if it bothers him. I don't want to overstep any boundaries or make Jude uncomfortable. As the credits roll, Jude *finally* meets my eyes. "I better get him home."

I nod, as I wasn't expecting to stay for the entire marathon.

He looks apprehensive to lift Angus from my lap, so I scoop an arm underneath him and cradle him against me. Jude then wraps an arm around him and lifts him like he weighs nothing at all. I instantly miss his warmth.

It turns cold when we step outside, but I don't know if that's just the stale mood between us. "Where did you park?" Jude asks, holding up Angus as he's asleep on his feet. Shelley's mom steps out also, holding a sleeping child to her chest.

"Just down the road."

"I'll walk you to your car."

I can sense he's only saying this to be polite, not because he wants to. "No, it's fine. You better get Angus home." He looks thankful I've refused.

I don't understand what I've done wrong. Things were great, and now they're...this. It seems Jude is as confusing as I am. "Well, thanks for inviting me. I had a great time."

"Me too."

Lies.

He shuffles his feet. "I guess I'll see you around." His comment sounds like a dismissal. A final farewell.

When he makes it quite clear that he has nothing left to say, I pull back my shoulders and turn to leave. A part of me hopes he'll stop me and apologize for being so confusing, but he doesn't, so I walk down the sidewalk, refusing to look back.

The walk here was refreshing, my mood so different than now. I suppose Jude has several hall passes to act a little strange from time to time, seeing as I've had my fair share of irrational episodes since we've met. But most of the time, he knew why I was acting like a complete basket case. I have no clue what's caused this sudden change in his mood.

All of the stores have closed for the night, leaving the street virtually deserted. The sound of my car unlocking echoes off the vacant buildings, amplifying that I'm out here alone. I toss my bag onto the passenger seat and lock the door as I slam it shut behind me. Exhaling loudly, I'm proud of myself for walking to my car and not freaking out.

The drive home gives me ample time to think about Jude.

I have no idea why his strange behavior bothers me so much. He's just a friend, and if he wants to be a grumpy pants, then good luck to him. However, the longer I drive, the more annoyed I become.

Since the moment we met, he's come on strong—not in a romantic way, but he's wedged himself into my life and made every effort to get to know more about me. Now that I've finally opened up, I feel like he's disregarded something which was quite difficult for me to do. I actually had a good time tonight, but now I'm just pissed off.

I've stewed for too many minutes and can't be held accountable for my actions when I race down my street, past my house, and end up pulling up by Jude's house. I don't hesitate to kill the engine and attempt to fly out of my seat and ask him what's going on. I give myself whiplash, though, as my seat belt is still fastened. That should be a big, fat warning that I'm being absolutely irrational and should turn around and go home, but I don't.

I don't mask my annoyance as I slam the door shut and charge up his front stairs. The lights are on downstairs, so I know he's still awake. When I climb the top step, the reality of what I'm doing kicks me in the guts, and I freeze, ashamed that I was coming here all gung-ho to ask Jude what's going on.

He had the decency to leave me be when I freaked out for no apparent reason, and now, I owe him that same respect. I can't remember the last time I felt this passionate over something... *someone*...and it suddenly scares me.

I care about Jude and Angus—that much is clear. But why am I so...upset? I feel like he's broken up with me or something. A husk of horror cocoons around me when I digest that thought, and I almost face plant as I run down the steps, two at a time.

My focus on getting to the car has me shut off to my surroundings, so when a hoarse, familiar voice says my name, I scream and trip down the last step. Thankfully, I manage to stay upright. Although, when Jude comes rushing down the stairs, I wish I'd knocked myself unconscious, so I don't have to explain why I'm loitering in his yard.

A cigarette hangs from his lips, explaining why he's outside. He doesn't hide his surprise. "What are you doing here?"

I could lie and pretend I locked myself out, but I'm done hiding in the shadows. Charley once said this thing called living isn't so hard, and she was right. I was afraid once, but now, I'm just annoyed.

"I-I..." The words die in my throat as my confidence suddenly takes a nosedive. After a deep breath, I steady myself and remember how liberated I felt when setting that infernal chair alight. "Did I do something wrong?"

Jude takes a drag from his smoke, obviously needing a nicotine hit to reply. "No, Victoria, you did nothing wrong."

"Then why did you run away like I was foaming at the mouth and groaning for your brains?"

His lips twitch, but he quickly turns serious. "I needed to get Angus home."

"Jude, there is one thing I like most about you." He knits his eyebrows together in intrigue, so I go on to explain. "You've been nothing but honest with me. Since the first moment we met, there's been no bullshit. You've still wanted to be my friend, regardless of the fact I almost set you on fire and insulted you more than I care to admit. So please, don't start lying to me now."

He blows out a cloud of smoke before butting out his Marlboro with his boot. Running a hand through his snarled hair, he replies, "There are things about me that you don't know." I open my mouth, ready to protest, but am interrupted without a second thought. "And before you go on to say that those things don't matter, save your breath, because they do."

I want to tell him that it doesn't matter, but he won't let me speak.

"I can't have you in my life. In Angus's life," he adds. The words are like a slice to my heart. "It's too confusing for him."

"Confusing? How?" My voice breaks.

"He likes you, Victoria. I can't allow him to get attached. What happens—"

"What happens what?"

He sighs. "What happens when you find out this place isn't

real? You leave. You go back to where you came from. To what you know. To *whom* you know." He's implying I'll eventually reconcile with Bryan. "It may seem like home now, but you'll soon discover this town is teeming with people's broken dreams. We're all just too afraid to leave." How incredibly sad. Do dreams seek this town out to die? I thought it was my new beginning, but Jude seems to think it's the equivalent to doing life without parole.

"I will do anything to protect my son, and I know your intentions are good, but I can't have…complications."

"You think I'm a complication?" I whisper, lowering my eyes.

With two fingers, he gestures back and forth between us. "This…it's complicated," is his ambiguous response.

I should be offended, but instead, I'm hurt. I'm hurt that Jude is ending something I didn't even know I needed. Without knowing it, he has pulled me through the toughest time of my life. I was just too blinded; wallowing in my self-pity to appreciate what was standing before me. And now that it's being taken away, I want it more than I need air to breathe.

What's the point of feeding your heart if there's no room to grow?

"I-I should go."

"Victoria…wait."

But I can't.

I race to my car, needing to separate myself from Jude and

his words, but halt when I hear the only sound that makes a lick of sense. "Stop."

Spinning around, I see Angus standing next to Jude, sleep-laden hair and heavy-eyed. I don't dare move. Jude closes his eyes for the briefest of seconds before running a hand down his face.

His love for Angus is immeasurable, and I know without a doubt he'd happily lay his life down for that little boy. My intentions are good, but Jude is right; I *am* a complication. I'm a complication because I don't know what I feel for Jude. All I know is that it's something *more*.

Until I figure out who I am and what I want, then I have to stay away. If this is what sacrifice feels like, then I hope it's worth the pain.

I walk toward Angus, smiling and feigning that everything is okay. Jude places a hand on his son's shoulder, expressing that sacrifices are actually rewards if the person is worth sacrificing for. "Hey, little wombat. You should be in bed."

He signs, looking up at Jude to ask him to translate. "He said he was up getting a glass of water and saw you through the window. He wanted to say good night."

How can someone be so innocent, so pure? Staring up at Jude, I know the answer lies before me. "Well, good night, sleep tight, don't let the bed bugs bite." I tickle his sides, and he giggles uncontrollably.

He signs, nodding.

"He asked if you'd tuck him in."

I ache because I know this is probably one of the only chances I'll get to tuck anyone in. Kneeling on one knee, I say, "I'm sure Daddy is better at that than me. Besides, I have to get home and feed my cat."

He nods. A yawn following soon after.

"Goodbye, Angus. I'll see you soon." I sniff back my tears, staying strong. Just as I attempt to stand, he reaches out and interlaces his fingers through my hand. Looking down at our connection, I smile.

He breaks our union, only to sign, before bending forward and kissing me on the cheek. He waves and lumbers up the stairs before I can reply. I'm still on one knee when I glance up, watching Jude swallow with regret.

"He said it's not goodbye…it's good night."

Blinking back my tears, I stand with a bittersweet smile. "Well, good night, Jude." I wish Angus was right, but this feels like goodbye.

He interlaces both hands behind his neck and sighs. "Good night, Victoria."

I want to say so many things, but I don't. Regardless of the butterflies, the tiny flutter of wings, I need to stay away because those butterflies are what led me astray.

Twelve

One Month Later

I'm sitting at home on a Saturday night, alone and cross-legged on my red seat, attempting to learn sign language from a book I purchased online. Surprisingly, it's the only thing that makes me feel better. I've given up on grading papers as my mind is elsewhere, or more accurately, it's across the lake at Jude's.

Over the past month, I've done some soul searching. It wasn't easy, but finally, *finally* I'm on the right path. I had taken a major detour, but now things have never looked clearer. Work, friends, and focusing on my new life have kept me busy. It's kept me from wondering about my neighbor.

But I have no other choice but to accept what it is.

Acceptance.

I accept what life is and let go of what was. I have faith in what it will be.

Jude is someone special. He crept up on me when I least expected anyone to. He showed me kindness. He also showed me I was stronger than I believed myself to be. He pushed me to better my situation, and all I did was push him away.

Acceptance.

I accept that for the first few weeks of living here, I was a stark raving lunatic.

My ribs still ache from my acceptance. Missing Jude and Angus more than I thought possible, I did something impulsive—I got a tattoo. There was no question on where I was going to get it. And what I wanted the word to be. Jude bears his scarlet letter, and now, I wear mine.

I remember thinking my feelings for Jude were *more.* I didn't know what it meant then, but now I've come to realize that what I feel for him is more than friendship, but not enough for…love? That word still scares me. I think it always will. But right now, the only person I want to feel more for is myself.

My cell sits near me, taunting me with its ability to contact Jude. Groaning, I slump back into my chair. By texting him, I could demonstrate that I'm slowly becoming uncomplicated and accepting that I…what? Have feelings for him? *Do* I?

Rubbing my temples, I feel a headache approaching, as all of this thinking has given me a serious case of needing a stiff drink. Just as I rise, my cell rings, scaring the living bejesus out of me. My frayed nerves are already shot, so when I see who the caller is, I think I'm going to need a Valium.

"Jude?" I don't mask my shock at him calling me. "What—"

But he doesn't allow me to finish. "Have you seen Angus?" He sounds panicked.

"No, I haven't. Is everything all right?" His exasperated sigh is all the answer I need. "When did you see him last?"

"Around six," he replies, his heavy footsteps pounding on floorboards. "I've looked everywhere."

The clock on my mantel reveals it's now bordering on eleven o'clock. "Have you called Henry? Maybe he's gone over there?"

"I'm not calling him. I can't."

I understand why he's so apprehensive. This is just another excuse to blame Jude for Henry's bleak view of the world. "I'll help you look. He couldn't have gone far."

"I'll be right over." He hangs up, and I could swear I hear his truck roar to life seconds later.

My body trembles, and I know it's got nothing to do with the cool night. If anything happens to Angus…I simply can't finish that thought. There is a sharp banging on my front door; it thumps in time with my hammering heart.

I race toward the door, hurling it open. Jude is standing before me, appearing seconds away from losing it. His hair is snarled, his usual healthy complexion is now washed out, and his eyes are haunted with the unknown. I don't say a word and slip into my coat, locking the door behind me as he charges down the stairs.

I'm troubled with images of Angus lost and alone, but I don't dare express these thoughts to Jude, as one of us needs to keep it together. Just as I'm about to call out, I seal my mouth shut as I realize that won't do a lick of good. He won't be able to hear me.

"Where have you looked?" I ask, my shaky legs barely able to keep up with Jude as he races down the road.

"Everywhere," he replies, not bothering to look at me. The ray of the flashlight flicks from left to right, its jerky movement reflecting Jude's mood. "I should have known he'd do something like this."

"You couldn't have known. You can't blame yourself." I'm chasing after him, certain I'll have to run to keep up.

"Tonight is the stupid dance at Angus's school!" he rebukes, his shoulders slumped.

"Oh." That changes everything.

"Yes, exactly." He spins around so quickly, I run straight into the solid wall of his chest. His arms shoot out, and he secures a firm hold around my biceps. He's a live wire, and I feel the electricity humming through his fingertips.

With Jude telling me to keep away, I had totally forgotten about my promise to attend the dance with Angus. If this is anyone's fault, it's mine. "This is my fault." My eyes fill with tears. "I've let Angus down. I promised I would go, and I didn't even remember! I'm so sorry, Jude."

His grip becomes almost punishing as he squeezes tighter,

before letting go. "Stop it. It's not your fault. I know you would have. By trying to protect myself, I've inadvertently hurt my son." Tugging at his hair, he exclaims, "If I had a better hold on my feelings for you, none of this would have happened!"

I can see the regret the moment the confession leaves his lips, while I'm having problems breathing. Feelings? For me? There must be some mistake. But when he gnaws on his bottom lip so hard I'm certain he's drawn blood, I know there's no mistaking what I heard.

Jude has feelings for me, and I have feelings...for Jude? *When* did this happen? But more importantly, what happens now? My tattoo itches, and I suddenly feel high as a kite.

Kite.

Of course.

Focusing on what's important, I step away from Jude. He appears hurt by the detachment but soon understands why. "I think I know where Angus is." I don't wait for him to reply.

I spin and run faster than I've ever run before. Jude's heavy footsteps follow in hot pursuit. I'm running toward finding Angus, but I'm running away from what weighs heavily within.

As I sprint down my driveway and turn left toward the dock, my heart explodes in my chest when I see a small figure standing by the lake's edge. It's without a doubt Angus, as the butterfly kite he's holding confirms what I thought to be true.

After Jude revealed tonight's significance, I figured Angus running away had something to do with me. Jude rushes past me, and I pull back, giving him a minute to reunite with his son. He scoops Angus up, almost crushing the little boy with the force of his relief. He doesn't let go and simply hugs Angus, enfolding him tightly. The sight is truly beautiful. The butterfly floats in the sky, trailing behind and watching this reunion unfold.

Jude finally lets Angus go and sets him to his feet. "You can't run off like that," he says, signing. "I was so scared something happened to you."

Angus replies, but Jude shakes his head. "No, buddy, you can't do that. You have to ask."

Walking closer, I narrow my eyes, reverting to the little sign language I've learned over the past month. I'm not certain, but I think Angus just said he wanted to see Jäg.

Jude reprimands Angus, but underneath his scolding is relief. "I looked everywhere. I even came past here once or twice. Where were you?"

Angus replies with Jude explaining aloud what he's saying. "I was here for a little bit. Then I rode my bike to catch fireflies."

"You're like the damn Flash when you want to be."

Angus's eyes rivet on me as I walk closer, and a smile spreads from cheek to cheek. He ignores Jude, who is still chiding him, and runs over to me. I crouch down and welcome him into my embrace. His tiny arms wrap around my neck, holding on so tight I can barely breathe. But who needs air when I've got this?

When he finally lets go, he signs hello. He also asks if I

saw him fly his kite. He's completely oblivious to the worry he's caused because he never thought he was missing. He was at my home, a place that isn't foreign land.

Just as Jude is about to explain what Angus said, I sign back. "I did, wombat. You're very good." Both Jude's and Angus's jaws drop to the ground. However, Angus grins a second later, signing so speedily, I can't help but laugh at his excitement.

"I'm still learning," I reply, messing up his hair as he grins.

Standing, I brush off my hands, embarrassed that Jude's looking at me like I'm a stalker. "He either said he's happy that I'm learning, or that he's a yellow Martian who likes pie."

Jude chuckles, the sound breaking through any tension I feel. "You're right. He did say he was happy. The last part was him asking what a wombat was." Now I'm the one to chuckle.

Lowering my eyes, I chew on my lower lip, wondering what to say. Jude speaks for me. "So, you learned sign language?"

"Um, yeah. Weird, right?" I roll a stone under my shoe, needing to do something other than squirm.

"No, it's not weird, Victoria. I think it's pretty cool. And considerate."

My stomach does a tiny flip flop as I meet his heated stare. "Oh, okay, awesome. I just thought on the off chance I'd see Angus again, I wanted to be able to say hello." Jude nods, his soft hair blowing in the gentle breeze. He takes one step, and then two, while I continue rambling, that electricity zapping between us. "I'm not very good, and honestly, half the time I think I'm signing the wrong thing, but...I...um...I missed him and..." I can't finish my sentence because one minute I'm standing still, and then the next I'm engulfed into Jude's arms.

I'm rigid, afraid of what happens when I move, but when Jude tightens his hold and moans softly into my ear, I let go of all reservations and just feel. Everything about him feels so right—his hardness complements his softness, and his shallow breathing amplifies the galloping of his heart. I've already forgotten what being in Bryan's arms feels like, but this, this I can never forget. I'm addicted to Jude's smell, the touch of him, and the way my body responds to him.

Whether it's temporary insanity or the fact I suddenly want Jude more than I need air to breathe, I'll never know, but pulling away, I raise my wavering hand and draw it to his face. He doesn't hide his shock that I'm openly touching him.

With the tips of my fingers, I trace over his furrowed brow, then stroke across the line of his forehead, appreciating the soulfulness to his eyes. I descend over his stubbled cheek, his whiskers tickling my skin. His lips, even though they're trembling, are still the softest, most kissable lips I've ever seen. And...I want to...kiss them...so badly. I can scarcely think of anything else but losing myself in him.

His mouth parts, his breath is warm, and his irises are swallowed up with black pools of wanting. I inch forward, forgetting who I am and forgetting that this shouldn't be happening. With eyes locked, Jude edges forward, his tongue sweeping over my finger, which is familiarizing itself with every contour of his lips.

I ride this wave of impulsiveness because it feels so right. Sadly, that rightness comes to a screeching halt when I hear a sweet voice sound from behind us. "Angus, thank god I found you."

Looking over Jude's shoulder, I see the blonde nymph who stood in my yard weeks ago, here, in the flesh, standing in my yard once again. A cold bucket of "what the hell are you doing?" douses my flames, and I shrink backward, suddenly feeling a fool.

Jude looks as surprised as me, but not by the nymph, but rather, my reaction to the harpy in my back garden. Once he regains his composure, he clears his throat and turns around. "Hey, Grace. It's fine. Crisis diverted. We found him."

"Ready to go?" she says, smiling at Angus and ignoring Jude. Seems he has a knack for pissing everyone off.

Go where exactly? Do they live together? My stomach goes into meltdown mode, and I'm certain I'm going to be sick. I knew Jude had secrets, but this is more than I can handle.

He shakes his head. "I might stay..."

But I butt in, as I have no intention of being the third, fifth, or god knows how many, wheel. "No, I think it's best you leave."

Jude turns around slowly, not bothering to mask his annoyance. His eyebrows are knitted together as he tongues his upper lip. The space between us seconds ago was filled with desire, but now it's filled with a desire of a different kind—my desire to strangle him. He may have Grace wrapped around his little finger, but my little finger is about to poke out his eyes.

Angus appeases my need for violence when he waves goodbye. Jude signs to Angus good night, and that he'll see him in the morning. It appears he intends on staying for a while.

I don't want to make a scene in front of him, so I stand off to the side, arms behind my back, wringing my hands together. "I'll leave the porch light on for you." Grace is just twisting the knife. Jude doesn't reply; instead, he continues watching me closely with a stiff upper lip.

Jude folds his arms across his chest, daring me to speak. But he's the one who insisted he stay, so he can explain what's going on. "What's the matter?"

I scoff. "Nothing is the matter."

"Obviously, something is up because you look like you're seconds away from murdering me," he smartly replies, which infuriates me further.

Stalking toward him, I jab my finger into his chest. I ignore how good he feels. "I'm not interested in being one of your floozies!"

His jaw clenches, his nostrils flare. "Let me assure you, Grace isn't a floozy. Although I'm flattered, there's no need for you to be jealous."

I ignore his jibe, and demand, "Then who is she?"

His cheeks puff as he blows out an exasperated breath. "Just trust me."

"Trust you?" I laugh sarcastically. "I saw you, Jude. The night you got shot." I swallow, the memory still too raw. "I saw you with that older lady in the car. You gave her money." He pales, cementing his guilt. "What, are you her boy toy or something?"

I'm so mad I'm shaking.

He runs a hand down his face, exhaling forcefully. "L-Let me explain." His falter is enough.

"There's nothing to explain because, the truth is, I don't know what to believe."

Jude's face softens, and the anger between us dissipates.

A dull knocking taps at the back of my head, not loud enough to be painful, but constant enough to be annoying. I rub my temples with my fingertips.

"Are you all right?" Jude asks, swallowing.

"No, I'm not." I'm sick of the lies. "I don't think I ever will be again."

My honesty seems to trigger something in Jude. "Victoria, I need to…I need to tell you something…" The pause reveals his "something" is big. Do I have the strength to hear what it is? The sliver of moon hides behind the looming clouds, setting an ominous mood around us.

I wait, unsure if I want to hear his confession, but I'm sick of not knowing, of constantly feeling lost. Deep down, I know that Jude has the answers I so desperately seek. I don't know how I know; I just know that I do. It could be the fact that we're both lost souls, trying to find our way home.

"I…" His wavering makes me nervous, and I lick my dry lips. I feel parched as if I haven't drunk in days. "I want to tell you, but I'm afraid. I'm not brave like you."

"Afraid of what?" I whisper.

"Afraid of losing…this." He sweeps two fingers back and forth between us. "You're the only person who makes me feel whole again."

His confession touches me because I feel the same way about him. "You know, telling someone your secret lifts the burden of having a secret to tell. I had secrets, but once you tell someone, they're not secrets anymore." It's my way of expressing my gratitude to him.

He peers down at his boots, jaw clenched. "It's not that simple. Some secrets are best left unspoken."

A shiver runs through me, and I turn, certain someone is behind me, watching, breathing down my neck. "Jude…"

"I have to go." The ambiance turns stale, losing all warmth.

I could beg him to tell me what's wrong, but just as he did for me, I don't push. Jude was my safety net when I was afraid I'd fall, and I owe him the same respect. "Okay."

Jude and I share a connection, but where that connection stems from, I still don't know. I can't shake the feeling the answer is right there. I just don't know where to look. Not yet anyway. The ache grows stronger as if my mind is telling me to stop searching for something I'm not ready to find.

Stepping forward, he presses his palm to my cheek. "One day, I promise this will all make sense." I stand numbly and nod. His eyes search mine before he bends forward and kisses me on the forehead. "Good night."

"Night."

As he turns, a panic surrounds me. "Jude?" He stops in his tracks but keeps his back turned. "Promise me this isn't g-goodbye. I couldn't take it if it were."

With shoulders hunched, he whispers, "I promise. I can't say goodbye, and that's the problem. I should let you go, but I can't." I don't know what he means, but he's gone before I can ask.

A tenacious knot begins unraveling in my belly. I feel hot, breathless, as though I'm seconds away from passing out. My vision clouds over, and a bitter nostalgia swarms around me.

"Watch out!"

Fading between the past and now, I seize reality, refusing to let these nightmares rule me.

Jumping to life, I strip off my clothes, the weightlessness instantly making me feel lighter. My bare feet pound against the grass as I run at full speed, needing to be reborn. I don't think twice. I sprint down the dock and jump into the murky water, the iciness like needles stabbing at my foundation.

My body takes over, and I begin swimming. The daily swims have helped me build up strength. I push myself until I'm unable to take any more. But this is different. Each stroke, each kick, each breath, I feel like they're the last I'll ever undertake.

Peering to the left, I see I'm way past the enormous tree, which is my marker to how far I've swum. Usually, by this stage, my body is aching and my arms exhausted, but today, I have to go on.

All I focus on is kicking my legs and sweeping my arms to propel me farther and farther. I was so curious to know what happens when I reach the other side. That curiosity will soon be put to rest because I'm only a mile from the shore. I push harder, faster, my heart violently thrashing about in my chest. Jude's home rises from the darkness, the porch light my beacon of direction.

Grace's words, however, stab at my fragile mind, and I suddenly realize that nothing waits for me on the other side. This entire time, I thought once I swam through my nightmares, I'd get better, and everything would be clearer. But now, everything feels worse.

I immediately stop swimming, swaying with the water as I remain motionless, attempting to catch my breath. My teeth chatter when the breeze picks up, but the wintriness is a reminder I'm still alive. As I continue staring at Jude's house, I begin to wonder if that's what I want. What I'm doing now, is this really living? I've lived before, and this right now, this feels like a death sentence.

Accepting my fate, I don't fight it. I'm so tired. I sink to the bottom and stay submerged as if I can escape my life beneath the darkness. I tuck myself into a small ball and close my eyes because the moment I surface, I'll have to face tomorrow, and I'm not ready to deal with that just yet.

However, I'm running out of oxygen. But what would happen if I stayed down here? I would die, that's what. And would that be so bad? I mean, who would miss me?

Just as I'm about to sink lower and accept my fate, a pair of lips press softly against mine. My eyes open in alarm as my underwater fantasy has come crashing down, and I realize I'm gasping for breath. But suddenly, my lungs are filled with air, as Jude is my life source. His steady breaths are feeding my starving lungs, and I relax, allowing him to bring me back to life.

With one last breath, he seals his lips around mine, and our exhalations become one as we kiss, becoming each other's lifeline. I never want it to end, but Jude quickly swims us up to the surface as our lips move in unison.

As we break the surface, we are panting and breathless, but our lips never break contact as Jude presses my naked form to his. Wrapping my legs around his waist, I latch on tight with no intention of ever letting go. The kiss isn't slow or gentle; it's heated, and reckless, and passionate. It's everything I've been missing. Everything I've craved. His tongue duels with mine, but it's a fight I'm happy to lose. His unreserved dominance has a flutter coiling in my belly. A gentle flight of butterfly wings soars high, and I suddenly feel weightless—I feel alive.

His mouth is wet and warm, and everything I need. He's aggressive and soft at the same time, and I can't get enough. I press further into his chest, his heart racing in song with mine. His hand is draped around my nape, he's driving the tempo, and I like it. I'm ashamed and embarrassed when my hips want to rock against him, needing some kind of release—a feeling I haven't experienced in so very long.

His whiskers score my skin, and the sensation heightens my already aroused state. I whimper when he bites my bottom lip, pulling it into the warm cavern of his mouth in a deliberate, calculated, unhurried speed.

I clutch at his wet hair, the soft strands gliding between my fingertips. His breathless growls and my impassioned moans fill the night air, expressing to the universe that we were always fated to end up this way.

His fingers dig into my waist, his touch desperate, his need for me depriving me of breath. I gasp into his mouth, unable to get enough of him as his touch is like my own personal drug. I should be ashamed that I'm in his arms naked, but I'm not. I feel vulnerable, wanted, desired. I also feel like I've been reborn.

His tongue rolls in my mouth, stoking my inner fire, leaving me needy and writhing in desire. When he breaks the kiss, I hiss, inhaling a series of much-needed breaths. The moon slips out from behind a cloud, illuminating the emotion behind his inky eyes.

"Let's go inside." His voice is heavy and filled with passion. I hold on tight as he swims us to the bank effortlessly. I feel so safe in his arms.

My chest is pressed to his as he emerges from the water, walking us toward the safety of his home. He enters the back door as quiet as a mouse and climbs the stairs to what I presume is his room. The door shuts softly behind us, sealing us in, but I'm prepared to accept my fate.

His strong arms are wrapped around my middle, and although we're now inside, I feel like he's holding on tighter, refusing to let go. I slowly pull away, my eyes searching his, desperate to know what he's thinking. His supple bowed lips part, and I whimper, the sight sending a thunderbolt straight to my core.

Without a single word, he walks us through the room, his footsteps ricocheting in time with the throb humming through my body. The blankets are soft underneath me as he lays me on the bed. I shift backward, resting up on elbows without ever breaking eye contact.

His jaw is clenched, and his body is wound tight, but he refuses to look past my face. The realization that I'm naked, and proof of my imperfection is showing hits home. I quickly wrap an arm around my chest. But Jude shakes his head, the wet strands sticking to his corded neck. "Don't hide who you are, butterfly."

"Butterfly?" His term of endearment is one I suddenly

adore.

"Yes." He prowls forward. His belt buckle hits the ground as he steps out of his wet jeans. Placing one knee on the bed between my parted legs, he slips off his T-shirt. I gulp. His skin is tanned, his flesh so firm; he really is a work of art. The bullet wound has scarred, but it adds to the magnum opus.

"Why butterfly?" I gasp as he rests both palms on either side of my hips, leaning forward, so we're inches apart.

His breath is warm against my cheeks. "Because I can't wait to watch you spread your wings and fly." He doesn't give me time to respond. He lightly runs his fingertips over my knuckles, before removing my hand and uncovering my breasts to him.

Our eyes are still locked, but I avert my gaze, suddenly embarrassed. "I-I'm sorry I don't have something nicer to offer you."

Two fingers rest under my chin, coaxing me to meet my fears. "I don't see your scars…I see you." Jude lowers himself so we're pressed chest to chest.

His skin is warm, heating my trembling body with his. I fall backward, my head hitting the pillow, and Jude tumbles with me. He's suspended above me, and the sight is too much.

I lie still, unbreathing, too afraid to move.

Jude's eyes search every plane of my face. It appears he's cataloging me to memory, and I don't know why. All thoughts are forgotten when he lowers his lips to the corner of my mouth. I stay still as he kisses my chin, my neck, unhurried to discover every part of me.

His tongue swirls in the divot of my collarbone, spreading goose bumps to the tips of my toes. "You smell incredible," he hums against my flesh. He continues his downward journey while I try my hardest to relax.

No one has seen me this way since the accident. I was too ashamed. But as Jude gets closer and closer to my scar, my worries begin to ebb away. I settle into the mattress as his kisses are inches away from my fears. Just as he's about to descend lower, I wrap my arm around me, unable to take the final step.

I press my eyes shut, a tear slipping from the corner of my left. "I'm sorry, Jude."

"We don't have to do anything you don't want to," he softly states, kissing the end of my nose. I believe him.

"I do want to…" I confess. "But I'm scared."

With the softest of kisses, he presses his lips to mine. "I'm scared, too." His declaration floats over my flesh. My eyes snap open, surprised by his admission. "I never thought I'd be able to make anyone feel this way ever again."

"Because of Rose?"

He turns his cheek, his reaction enough of a response. "I'd be happy to just lie with you forever and feel this."

"Feel what?"

He presses his palm on my chest above my heart. "Alive."

There is nothing but sincerity in Jude's eyes; it's the same look I've seen since the moment we met. This man has an unexplained need to protect me, he always has. With that thought in mind, I slowly remove my arm, baring all that I am to him.

He hisses a sharp breath through clenched teeth as his gaze falls to my chest. My breaths are mounting, my pulse spiking, and I think I'm seconds from passing out. When he remains motionless, simply staring, I'm frightened he's changed his mind, and my nakedness has repulsed him somehow.

He arches up, gaining full frontal access to my body. His fingers reach out, and with a steady, passionate touch, he traces over my scar in awe. The look is not one I'm accustomed to because when I look upon it, all I want to do is turn away.

His finger runs down the jagged length, outlining the area with nothing but admiration in his inky depths. These feelings are too much, and tears sting my eyes.

"I'm sorry." He lifts his hand away quickly, his face blanketed in pain. "This is too much for you. I understand."

But he *doesn't* understand. The tears I shed are of the happy kind. "No, Jude, don't stop. I'm crying because I'm happy. This is the first time in a long time that I feel…human."

Reaching for him, I wrap my hand around his nape and draw his face toward mine. Our mouths crash together, the feeling surreal, almost out of this world. This kiss is different than the first one we shared; it's filled with yearning, and also a sense of belonging. The way I feel underneath him is nothing like I've ever experienced before.

He sucks my bottom lip, groaning into my mouth as I bow into his body. He severs our connection and trails kisses down my neck, sucking over my pulse. My legs scissor beneath him, a scorching heat setting me on fire. He descends lower, his lips everywhere, his hands touching every part of my body. A primeval urge seizes me, and I shamefully buck my hips, needing a deeper connection.

Jude reads my desperation and sinks lower, his hot mouth blistering my skin. When he reaches my chest, he pauses in a silent question if he's okay to continue. I reply by enfolding my arms around him and pressing him into my body.

The need to be wanted, to be loved, can be undoubtedly felt in our passion, and I come to understand that we're both desperate to find someone who makes us feel worthwhile. Our paths are marred with scars, both inside and out, but those scars are our badges to show the world we survived.

He continues kissing downward, his lips brushing the tops of my breasts. He doesn't hesitate or recoil and shows the same passion as he kisses over my scar. Every touch has me mewling, not believing how good it feels. He continues kissing my scar, making me feel beautiful and changing my imperfection to perfection. He doesn't make me feel different—he makes me feel special.

His large hand cups my breast, his deft fingers rolling my nipple. I moan, the feeling too good to be true. However, when he licks the side of my breast and takes the pearled bud into his mouth, I know this is extraordinarily true.

All shyness is long forgotten when he slides a hand between us. My stomach roils, and I arch my hips, needing more. With his lips still locked around me, he walks his fingers down, brushing over my sex. His simple touch is electric. I want more, so much more, but I'm too afraid to ask. He shifts over to my other breast, kissing the scar along the way. I no longer feel self-conscious; instead, I feel adored.

A knot begins building and building. I feel Jude in every pore. He's being a gentleman, skating around the rim, but it's not enough. I shyly open my legs, hinting at what I need. He stops, peering up at me with uncertainty in his blue eyes. "Are you sure?" His lips are red, swollen, the sight cementing my response.

"Yes." I arch forward, licking a bead of water from the slope of his neck. He growls, and without delay, he presses his lips to mine, consuming me with a ferocious need. The mood shifts, things turn needier, and before I know it, Jude slips a finger inside me. We both gasp; the contact feels incredible.

He dives in slow, which I'm thankful for, as my muscles are unaccustomed to such a delicious intrusion. It doesn't take me long to catch up and find the rhythm that has me moaning in bliss. He works with my body, adding another finger while I bite down on my lip.

Tossing my head back, I squeeze my eyes shut as everything is too much. Jude breaks our kiss and slides down my body, detouring to the junction of my thighs.

In half a second, his mouth, that sinful, skillful mouth replaces his fingers, and he's lapping at my entrance. I rocket off the bed, unable to hold back my screams, but I chew the inside of my cheek, realizing Angus is sleeping down the hall.

Needing to touch him, I place my hands on his muscled back. His flesh is on fire. I clench his broad shoulder and fist his wet hair, shamefully bucking my hips. He growls, the sound possessive as he buries his face further into my core.

I let go of reservations and allow him to command my body, and command he does. He raises one leg over his shoulder while the other he pushes out to the side. I'm opened up to him, my shame long forgotten. He devours me, leaving no part undiscovered. Both hands are now threaded through his hair, using the longer strands as reins as I hold on tight and jerk my hips.

The fire in my belly is mounting, each flick of his tongue spirals the flames higher and higher. His animalistic grunts mirror his actions, and when he sucks over my center, I cry out. I'm so close. But then realization hits me about how I'm being incredibly selfish. So I paw at him, hinting to come up for air. He doesn't rise but merely buries himself further. His heavy scruff adds to the sensation. I think I'm going to explode.

His need to consume me is too much. My body undulates, my heart explodes, and stars flash before my eyes. Digging my heel into his broad back, I arch my hips, focusing on his tongue, lips, mouth, hands. He's everywhere, I'm lost in him, and for the first time in months, I…let…go.

Sparks flash before my eyes. I half cry, half moan, feeling too many emotions mixed in at once. Everything I've endured to get here, to feel this with Jude, I realize it was all worth it.

I'm breathless, my body totally spent. That was the most powerful orgasm I've experienced. Ever. Everything is heightened.

Jude lazily kisses my sensitive flesh before unhooking my leg from his shoulder. Laying a kiss on my inner thigh, he then skims up my body.

My eyes are still sealed shut, my head thrown back as I attempt to catch my breath. The pillow divots, and I sense Jude. Prying one eye open, I instantly turn a beet red. Jude smirks, adding to my embarrassment.

"That was incredible," he says, brushing the matted hair from my brow.

My voice is hoarse. "Yes, it was."

"I didn't hurt you?"

I shake my head as my cheeks blister. "It felt good." Thinking back to weeks ago, I can't help but say, "I thought I was a complication."

"You are…" Just as I'm about to object, Jude adds, "But I don't care."

Shifting closer so our bodies are pressed front on, I bite my lip when I feel something nudge me below. He peers down with a smirk. His lips are slathered with my arousal. "Wow. I haven't felt that in a long time."

I shyly reach between us and brush over his swell, but he seizes my hand in his. "But I want to," I whisper, hating how desperate I sound.

He blows out a shallow breath. "I do, too."

"But…" I wait for him to fill in the blanks.

"But not now. Let's not push our luck."

"Luck? What's luck got to do with it? Right now, you're refusing to get lucky."

His mouth twitches, but I know he's serious.

"Good night." He tucks me into his arms and sighs contently.

As he drifts off to sleep, I lie wide-awake, envious, as my mind pings at a million miles an hour.

I lie in the darkness for hours, listening to Jude's steady breaths. Peeling myself from his vise-like grip, I stare at his striking face, wondering what secrets lie behind those conflicted eyes. I trace the hill of his strong nose. Caress the whiskers on his angular cheeks. Why did he get shot? I outline the curve of his bow lips. Stroke his chiseled jaw. Did it have something to do with the mysterious woman? As I run a finger across his pinched brow, the most important question plagues me…why do I feel like we've met before?

Thirteen

I wake the next morning feeling like someone other than me. I don't know how many hours I've slept, but regardless, I slept...straight through. Not a single nightmare plagued my slumber. Nor did I wake up in a cold sweat.

Stretching, I crack open one eye, freezing suddenly when my impaired vision reveals I'm in a foreign room. The walls are painted an eggshell white, accenting the beige and brown tones. Snapping my head from left to right, both eyes are now open as I observe the simple, yet stylishly furnished room.

Where the hell am I?

"Morning."

I shoot up in bed, pressing the sheet to my thumping chest. Jude stands in the doorway, sheepishly holding a cup of coffee. He's dressed in the same T-shirt I remember seeing him in, but now he's wearing black sweats instead of jeans. The sun filtering in from the open window reveals it's morning. The last thing I remember was…shit.

"How'd you sleep?"

"F-fine," I stutter, sitting up higher. Memories of what we did, what *he* did to my body assault my brain, and I almost gag on air.

His bare feet sound against the floorboards as he pads across the room. "I'm glad you're awake. You were dead to the world when I got up. I had to check your pulse a couple of times to make sure you were still alive," he jokes. The coffee smells delicious as he passes me the steaming cup.

I smile, but it's small, afraid. Now that I'm no longer shrouded in darkness, I wonder what happens next.

Cradling the cup, I lean back against the headboard, waiting for Jude to speak. He's standing awkwardly by the edge of the bed with his lips dipped into half a frown. "Once you're done, I can take you home."

It's my turn to frown. Is he blowing me off? "Oh. Right. You probably have a million things to do." I throw back my coffee, a pained scowl touching my cheeks as the scalding liquid burns my throat.

"No, I didn't mean it that way," he amends, stepping forward.

"Oh?" I say with a lisp as my tongue has third degree burns.

"I meant, you probably want to think about last night or something?" He rubs the back of his neck, expressing his discomfort.

His uncertainty makes me smirk. "No, actually, I was going to suggest I take you and Angus out for breakfast. I still owe you." I refer to our pact of me making him dinner. Well, in this case, breakfast for all the groceries he bought.

His smile fills the room. "Okay. Sounds good. Angus is still asleep." He pauses. "Would it be okay if I dropped you home, got Angus ready, and then came to pick you up? I don't want to…"

"Of course," I interject, understanding he doesn't want to confuse him with my impromptu sleepover. "Can I use the bathroom first?"

"Of course. It's just down the hall, last door on the left. There's a T-shirt in the bedside dresser."

His comment reminds me that I'm very naked.

"Thanks." I open the drawer and reach for a faded Metallica T-shirt. I slip it over my head quickly and stand, gulping when Jude doesn't move. He's so much taller than me. My mouth waters, and it's sensory overload when his lips curve into a sexy promise. I can't believe I'm reacting to him this way. It appears with honesty comes an even stronger attraction.

He moves aside, a dimple kissing his whiskered cheek. I stand frozen, my breath choppy as he reaches down with an unhurried speed to slip the cup from my fingers. He draws it to his lips and takes a sip. His Adam's apple bobs as he swallows, eyes pinned to mine as he watches me over the rim.

I run for the door, charging out it and sprinting down the hallway. I'm not looking where I'm going as obsession clouds my vision, and I almost bump straight into someone I was not expecting to see.

Grace.

Her long hair is a dirty blonde when it's wet. Droplets run down her long neck, highlighting she's just stepped out of the shower. A Yankees T-shirt stops mid-thigh, and I'm guessing that's all she's wearing.

Just like when we first met, she ignores me. Thankfully, Angus comes out from his room, rubbing the sleep from his eyes. When he sees me, he smiles.

"Good morning, little monkey," Grace says sweetly.

Angus signs good morning.

"What do you want for breakfast?"

Just as I'm about to interject and inform her of our plans, Jude's voice booms from behind me. "Tell your aunt we're going out for breakfast."

The word doesn't register for a nanosecond, but when it does, I almost topple on my ass as I spin around. "She's your *sister*?"

Running a hand through his tousled hair, he replies, "Unfortunately, yes."

Holy shit. Don't I feel ridiculous?

No wonder Jude played off her relationship to him. "Oh my god, I'm so sorry I implied she was a...floozy," I whisper, not wanting her to overhear me, as I'm quite certain she hates me already.

"Don't sweat it." Jude shrugs it off. He steps closer while my heart skips a beat. "It was nice seeing you all green-eyed." I don't even bother defending myself because I'm too preoccupied trying to breathe.

Angus signs that we're all going out for breakfast. When he adds Daddy is bringing a friend, she scoffs, rolling her sapphire eyes. "Typical. He was always bringing home strays."

All bets are now off. "*Excuse me*?" I reply, ready to claw out her eyes. I don't appreciate that she's ignoring me, but I suppose us talking could be explosive.

Angus looks at my unruly appearance, and I forget my need to give her a piece of my mind.

"Okay, I'm going to get dressed. You need a hand getting ready, you shout out." He nods with a smile. There is no doubt he loves her, which makes me think she can't be all bad.

When I think I can speak without cursing, I state, "So, sister?"

"Yeah. She takes care of Angus. It's always been the two of us. Dad split when we were young, and my mom remarried. She has a new family now. Grace is all the family I know." His words aren't laced with spite, just fact.

"Is she mad at you?" I ask as she didn't acknowledge either of us.

He sighs. "She's always mad at me. Actually, I think she's

mad at the world."

Although I'm not angry, I want him to know I don't want any more secrets between us. "You should have told me. You should have told me a lot of things," I add, realizing there's so much more I still need to know.

He nods, chewing his bottom lip. "I should have, but I never thought we'd get to—"

"To what?" I ask when he pauses.

Stepping forward, he intertwines our fingers. "This." He stares at me with a look I haven't seen in quite some time. Well, last night, in fact.

Heat licks at my neck, and I smile because *this* feels pretty incredible.

By the time Jude drops me off, I'm surprisingly exhausted. It could be because I had a side order of awkward with breakfast as Grace continued to ignore me. I don't know what her problem is. I understand she may be protective when it comes to her brother, especially after Rose, but she's sentenced me before I've even gone to trial.

"Jäg!" I call out, looking over the railing and searching my yard. Poor little man is probably starved.

I see a figure from the corner of my eye. It's Mrs. Anderson. In one hand, she holds a small pair of garden shears and in the other, a rake. I haven't had time to tend to my yard, so I appreciate the fact she's tending to my roses late in the afternoon. Although this is extremely odd, I'm grateful, nonetheless. "Thank you, Mrs. Anderson," I call out, but she doesn't hear me with her earbuds in.

"Lost Jäg?"

I yelp, placing a hand over my racing heart. "Holy shit, Charley, you damn near gave me a heart attack."

Leaning against the banister, she smirks. "Sorry, your door was unlocked."

She looks stunning in the same flowing red gown she wore at the housewarming. It's a little dressy for a Sunday afternoon, but it's Charley, so nothing surprises me.

"Why are you all dressed up?"

Her mood turns poignant as she shrugs, picking at invisible fluff. "No reason. How was your night?"

When my cheeks rival the color of her dress, Charley latches onto my forearm. "What happened?"

"Well, where do I start?" I can't keep the excitement from my voice.

"From the very beginning. I want details."

I can't help but smile. I decide to leave out the part involving my midnight swim because I know Charley will worry and I think I'm okay. "Jude and I kissed."

"A-ha," she says dreamily, cupping her chin in her palms.

"He took me into his room. We kissed some more." She

nods quickly. "Then he went down…on me."

Charley's eyes pop from her head. "Oh my god. And it felt okay?"

My cheeks burst into flames. "It felt more than okay."

"Wow." Her mouth is hanging open. "This is unbelievable."

"I know."

"Did you…?" She doesn't need to elaborate as I know her train of thought.

"No. I wanted to, but well, he said let's not push our luck."

"Good thinking."

I pull back, a touch offended. "What's that supposed to mean?"

She quickly backtracks. "I meant, take things slow. What's the rush?"

Examining her closely, I see that she's lying. "That's not what you meant. What's wrong? Between your and Jude's odd behavior, you'd think me sleeping with him was the be-all and end-all."

She lowers her eyes.

A relentless knocking scratches at my temple.

"Are you all right?" Charley's voice is suddenly echoing as if she's standing miles away.

My head feels like it weighs a thousand pounds as I blink twice. On the second flutter, I see blood. "Charley! Oh my god! Your nose, it's bleeding." Her hand shoots up to her face, bright red blood smearing her fingers. The flow is heavy, and it doesn't look like it'll stop. "Come inside."

I grab her arm, but she jars backward, shaking her head. "I'm okay, Tori. It'll stop. It always does."

"Stop? You're gushing blood. It looks like you're seconds away from bleeding out on my deck."

"I said I'm fine." Her voice turns desolate. "I'm used to it."

Used to it? This is the first time I've seen her bleed out half her body weight, so I don't know what to make of her comment.

"I better go." Her hands are cupped over her nose. Bright red blood slips through her fingers, each droplet hitting the deck with a sharp splat.

"Go? Charley, don't be silly. You're bleeding. You can't go. Let me take care of you."

"You were always such a good friend. Thank you. Even though we drifted apart after high school, I always thought about you." Tears prick her eyes before she runs down the stairs.

Is the world on crazy pills? What's going on?

I chase after her, but she's exceptionally fast and gone before I can catch up. I bend at the waist, suddenly breathless, which shouldn't be happening seeing as I've built up my cardio with the daily swims. My chest aches right over my wound. I rub at it, standing upright slowly, afraid I'm going to faint.

From the corner of my eye, I see a flash of gray. Jäg. The air returns to my lungs, and I take off, pushing through the pain. He darts off to the left, headed for a wooded area lined with tall, bottle green trees. I continue chasing him, calling out, but my voice seems to ricochet through the stillness.

As I sprint into the forest, he's nowhere to be found. I halt, looking from left to right. "Jäg?" My screams are drowned out by the foliage.

Where did he go? I saw him only seconds ago.

A menacing flash unexpectedly overtakes me, and I feel the need to flee. A branch snaps underneath my sneakers as I take a step forward. I yelp, and the sound bounces around me. Suddenly, the forest closes in on me, and the hair on my arms stands on end. Spinning around, my nightmares have come to life when I see my attacker standing feet away. *He's* the person who's been looking over my shoulder for months.

My throat goes dry. "W-what do you want from me?" I back away slowly in fear.

Light suddenly turns to dark, and the earth beneath me turns to mud. Peering up at the starless sky, I see two crows with feathered wings the color of a blackened night soar through the shadows, frantic to fly away. However, I watch in horror as they abruptly change direction and dive toward the ground. Their eyes are the color of blood, there is no heart behind them.

My screams are hollow as I attempt to run, but I'm ankle deep in sludge. My muscles burn as I push through the mud, desperate to flee from the feathered projectiles that seem intent on causing me harm. The woods turn evil when overgrown vines wrap around my ankles and wrists. A malevolent snicker fills the night, transporting fear into dread. Not again. No, not again.

Unable to move, I do the only thing I can. I drop to a squat and curl myself into a ball. Shielding my head with my arms, I tuck my chin to my chest, squeezing my eyes shut. "This is only a dream," I repeat over and over while the cawing shoots terror straight to my core. I must have fallen asleep after Jude dropped me off at home. That's the only explanation.

Mud sloshes as his footsteps get closer and closer. This nightmare feels a lot more lifelike than any others before it. I can smell his rancidity. Taste my fear. The cawing gets louder, in sync with his footsteps. I'm rooted to the spot. My chest aches, and I'm so frightened.

"That's it, princess. This will hurt a lot less if you don't fight me."

"No!" I screech. "Leave me alone!" I cover my ears, desperate to mute my pain. I can't stomach these words a second time around.

I'm convinced this is it. I've officially lost my mind. I've skated so close to the edge, and now I've finally fallen off—I've succumbed to PTSD.

His rancid breath fans down my neck, alerting me that he's close. "Scream all you want. I like it when they scream."

This is it—the point of no return. I accept my fate, and I know I'm going to lose. Unlike a lifetime ago, there is no one to protect me. I can't breathe. *I can't breathe.* And I'm going to die.

"Watch out!"

Those words are my salvation. Suddenly, the cawing stops, the air turns clean, and the mud turns to dust. Safety overrides the fear, and I know he's here.

Unshielding my face, I blink twice, unbelieving that I'm free. Lightness has overthrown the dark because of him. He stands before me, his face cloaked, his eyes downturned. With a whisper, he offers me his hand. It's the key to drag me from this delicate hell.

I know once I take hold, all my questions will be answered. But now that I've been offered this lifeline, do I want to take it?

I know there was never a choice.

With trembling fingers, I slip my hand into his. The feel of him is warming, non-threatening. The sun takes cover behind the slow-moving clouds, shrouding us in partial darkness. It appears he is also too frightened to behold the next step.

His height is towering, his shoulders broad, but although he's twice my size, I know he won't harm me. He's protected me from the very first moment I met him.

The space between us is blistering; the intensity of this moment steals my breath away. I look up at my protector. I'm ready for this to end. The wind howls around us, fallen leaves scuttle along the ground. Our surroundings are beautifully haunted, just like me.

Swallowing down my fears, I reach up and clasp his hood's edge. I still can't see his eyes. With a movement no faster than a swallowtail butterfly's wings, I slip back the veil protecting my rescuer's identity. He doesn't fight me. He submits to me completely.

Inch by inch, the curtain falls away, uncloaking my secrets. But just as the final piece is about to slip away, I stop, unsure if I want to know. What happens when I find out? What will change? The choice is taken away from me because long fingers overlap mine, staging the final act.

I gasp, tears stinging my eyes, as piece by piece, I can finally decipher what has plagued me for months. His dark brown hair slashes forward, and his chin is still downturned, but I would recognize this face from the other side of the world. He's finally unmasked, and all has been revealed. But nothing prepares me for the reality.

When he lifts his chin painstakingly slow, there is nothing but regret, sorrow, but most of all, pain in his stormy eyes. My hand unsteadily covers my mouth, unbelieving. A tear hacks at my flesh because the truth hasn't set me free. It's made everything so much worse.

I'm trapped, a prisoner to denial because I cannot believe that standing before me is my protector, my rescuer. I've finally seen his face. But unlike all the other times I've looked upon it and touched it, I just want to turn away this time.

The answers were there all along, I just didn't know where to look. Jude Montgomery is my champion, my knight in shining armor, but now, the question is…why.

*The pupa stage of the butterfly's life cycle is a time for complete **change**.*

The Third Stage: Pupa

Fourteen

I awake in my room, rousing from my vivid nightmare. My chest aches. I spring from my bed, the devil on my heels; there is only one place I need to go. Jude isn't home, so I speed downtown. I need answers, and the only person who can give them to me is Jude.

I pull my car up by the curb, the quietness of the afternoon exactly what I need as I can't deal with clatter today. Pop's Hardware Store is small but stocked well. There is a single register up front which could have been updated about ten years ago. Looking around, I realize the same could be said for the entire store. A faded photograph hangs against the far wall, depicting a young man standing proudly in front of the same red sign which sits out front. I'm assuming this is Pop on the day he opened his store.

"Can I help you, Miss?" asks an elderly gentleman. This is, without a doubt, Pop.

"Hi. I'm Victoria Armstrong. I live on Maple. Jude Montgomery is my neighbor." I reveal the reason I'm here. I'm surprised I can construct a sentence right now. I figured Jude might have ducked into work because I can't find him anywhere else.

Pop smiles a toothless grin. "Oh, yes. Lovely neighborhood, that one."

Too edgy to make small talk, I ask, "I was wondering if Jude was working today."

The moment Pop frowns, I get a heavy feeling in the pit of my stomach. "Sorry, Miss, but Jude doesn't work here anymore."

"Oh?" I feel like I've swallowed lead. Has he lost his job?

Pop appears to be thinking, tracking back to the past. "He hasn't worked here for…well over nine months."

The hair on the back of my neck stands on end. Nine months? "There must be some m-mistake."

"No mistake," he firmly states.

I'm trying not to be rude by acknowledging everything he's saying, but a blaring siren is flashing red inside my head. What am I missing? Jude lied to me about where he worked. Why? My gut sinks.

"I don't understand why he would lie."

He rubs his chin, shaking his head. "I'm not sure. It's unlike Jude. He's worked here for years, but one day, he just didn't show up. If you ask me, it's got to do with Rose going missing. That cut him real deep. He never was the same. He looked at life differently after she left."

I'm so sick of hearing her name. Why do they care when she clearly doesn't?

I need to get to the bottom of this. "Thank you for your time. Sorry to have bothered you."

"No bother. I'm sorry I wasn't much help." I turn around to leave but am stopped as I push open the door. "Oh, Miss? Jude is a good man. I don't know why he lied to you, but I'd guess it was to protect you." My throat closes over as I nod a thank you to Pop.

On the way home, I can't stop thinking about what Pop said. Jude is protecting me, but protecting me from what? Thoughts are rolling around my head like loose marbles. All the pieces are in front of me, but I don't know what the puzzle is to complete the final picture.

I don't understand any of this.

I catalog every word spoken between us and every small confession he made. But I'm more confused today than I was yesterday or the day before. I now know his secrets. I just don't understand why he didn't tell me sooner. Rubbing over my chest, I sniff back my tears. I'm suddenly so angry. I feel like he played me for a fool.

Pulling into my drive, I switch off the engine and make my way to the front door. I'm exhausted both physically and mentally, and I feel like I could sleep for a week. Just as I walk up the steps, a familiar soothing consciousness cocoons me, and I know without looking who is standing behind me.

"Hi."

Sighing, I close my eyes. "Hi." I don't bother turning around. Now that he's here, I can't help but feel cheated somehow.

With my head bowed, I decide to lay my cards out on the table. I've got nothing to lose. "Why did you lie about where you work?"

The silence is heavy. "*What*? You're checking up on me?"

Annoyance passes over me because if anyone has the right to be angry, it's me. Spinning around, I narrow my eyes, ignoring how my insides are happy to see him. "No, I wasn't checking up on you. I needed to see you. I needed you to explain to me why you didn't tell me…who you are. You lied, Jude. You've lied to me over and over again."

The look on his face haunts me. He's silent for a moment, and I can see him measuring up what to say next. His reply is not one I was expecting. "Yes…I lied. And I'm sorry. But I did it…I've done all of this to protect you." He spreads his arms out wide.

I'm enraged and confused. "How does that make any sense? How does any of this make any sense? You know how I figured out who you are?" He digs his hands into his pockets and shrugs. "It's like you were inside my head." I tap at my temple. "How is that even possible? Have I lost my mind? I still don't know if I was dreaming, or what I was seeing was actually true. Do you know how scary that is? To be lost in what you think is a dream, but deep down, you know that it's actually the truth." Tears fill my eyes, tears I never wanted to cry. "Why were you so afraid to tell me you rescued me? Do you regret it? Was saving my life the wrong thing to do?"

His tongue sweeps along his bottom lip, leaving behind a wet glisten in its wake. When I glare at him, challenging him to answer me, he commands, "Get in my truck."

"*Excuse me?*" I stand my ground, refusing to be intimidated. "We're having a conversation, and I'm not going anywhere until you tell me what's going on."

He runs a hand through his hair. The tremble in his fingers tells me this is the beginning of the end. "I can't tell you…" Just as I open my mouth to protest, he continues, "Because you won't believe me. I need to show you."

"Show me?" My voice is small.

He nods. "Yes, Victoria, I was going to tell you everything tonight, but I think we're running out of time." He takes a step forward, his eyes pleading. "Please, just trust me. I know you have every right not to, but please believe me when I tell you everything I did, I did for you."

I don't know why because God knows I shouldn't, but I trust Jude. "Okay, fine. I'll need to grab my coat."

"You won't need your coat," he mysteriously states. I don't bother arguing as I have a feeling I'll need to conserve my energy.

"Lead the way." I sweep my hand outward, indicating I need space. Jude doesn't conceal his despair as he frowns, but he doesn't say another word as he makes his way to the truck.

I'm thankful when he doesn't open the door for me because I've reached my quota of his chivalry. I just need to know what's going on. A loud exhalation leaves me when I shut the door. I survey him through the windshield as he walks around the car, looking like a broken man.

The engine roars to life a few moments later, and we're on our way to god knows where. Honestly, I'm a little scared, and now that I'm in the truck, traveling along this shadowy, quiet road, my brain begins conjuring up possible scenarios of where we're headed.

"So where are we going?"

He grips the steering wheel, his fingers turning a bright white. "To a place I should have taken you weeks ago."

"Why didn't you?"

His profound sigh fills the truck. "Because I wanted to avoid this."

I know exactly what "this" means. It's that stale, uncomfortable static between us that seems to outweigh all the good times we've shared.

We remain silent for the rest of the short car ride as I stare out the passenger window, wondering what happens next. Even though I'm afraid, I know this is the next step because somehow, I feel a kinship to Jude's words—I do feel like we're running out of time.

As we pull down a dirt road, Jude breaks the silence. "Will it make a difference when you find out the truth?"

He doesn't need to clarify that he's talking about my feelings for him. I stare out the window, unable to give him an answer. He parks the truck, switching off the engine with a weighty sigh. "You ready?"

Looking around at my surroundings, I cock a brow, completely confused. "What are we doing here?"

He doesn't reply. "Let's go." As he jumps from the truck, he slips the hood over his head, lowering his face as he walks to a paved path.

What's going on?

I quickly follow, and as he weaves through the winding paths, the shrubbery all perfectly groomed and manicured, I know he's been here before—many times before. It's cold, so cold my skin pricks with goose bumps. I rub my arms, but I can't seem to get warm.

A hoot from an owl is a menacing warning that the path I'm on was the one I should have taken when this nightmare began. With Jude's head hung low and his hands dug deep into his pockets, I can't help but feel we're on a death march. Our current surroundings certainly add to the macabre vibe.

I keep my eyes glued to Jude, who is a few feet ahead. He's a man on a mission. We pass through luscious green, open grounds, and the stillness is really beautiful. But the tranquility conceals the fact this place is filled with loss, sadness, and pain. Jude finally stops at a site covered in wilted flowers.

I feel the need to mute my footsteps because the silence amplifies my every sound. Stopping a few feet away, I gasp when he turns around, blocking my view.

"W-what's going on?" I know what I'm seeing, but I still don't know *why* I'm here. How is this meant to absolve Jude of his sins?

"It's funny…" His deep, sad voice carries on the light wind. "I had this whole speech planned. But now that you're here, it all feels like bullshit. It's all excuses." He runs his boot over the blades of grass and looks off into the distance.

I remain silent as I've run out of words.

"You're right. I did save you the night you got shot. I'm your masked rescuer. But I think, deep down, you always knew." His words are laced with mockery, and I don't know why. "This entire time, I've tried to figure out why we met the way we did. It seems so cruel. Two strangers bonding over an act of violence. What was the point of it?"

I wrap my arms around myself, feeling a sudden chill.

"I know I've asked you this before, but I want you to think, real hard. What do you remember from the night you got shot?"

I rub my biceps as the frostiness is slowly beginning to invade every limb. "I-I told you what I remember." Panic sets in. Why is he asking me this?

He shakes his head, angered by my reluctance to divulge more. "The answers are there, Tori. All you have to do is want to see them."

"See what? You don't think I've been trying to see the truth?" I'm hurt, angered that he thinks I'm doing this on purpose.

I know he's hurting, too. I can hear it in his stiff voice. "You've only seen what you've wanted to see. This entire time… we both have." The pieces of the puzzle are slowly joining together, piece by piece, but I still don't know what it means.

Stepping forward, he brushes the fallen hair from my brow, his stormy eyes swimming in utter mourning—a grief so deep, a sob escapes me. "Jude, what's going on?"

He removes the hood from his head and runs a hand through his snarled hair. "Victoria, the night you got shot, I… got shot, too."

My heart begins to beat faster and faster. "What? No, that's impossible." I shake my head fiercely. What is he talking about?

"I'm sorry I didn't…" He swallows, needing a moment to catch his breath. "I'm sorry I didn't tell you sooner."

I'm suddenly finding it harder to breathe. "I'm not following."

Jude exhales as he raises his head to look up into the sky. "I wish we met minutes, seconds before we did because I would give anything to tell you in person that I…love you."

"What?" I gasp, the words trapped in my throat. "I-I don't understand." He loves me? Why is his admission so bittersweet?

He finally meets my eyes, a tear streaming down his whiskered cheek. I know what he's about to say even before he speaks. I shake my head, but a melancholy smile splays on his lips. This is the truth I was so desperate to know. "This—" He steps backward, raising his sweater, the moonlight betraying his grotesque secret "—is the real me. This is why I never told you the truth. How do you—" He pauses, closing his eyes for the briefest of seconds before reopening them slowly "How do you tell someone you...love...that you're...dead?"

"*W-what*?" I blink, tears coating my lashes. "What? *Dead*? That's not...that's not p-possible. I-I d-don't even k-know what to...no. *No*. It's not t-true." I can barely speak, words escaping me. "That's not e-even f-funny."

"It's true, Tori. Think about it." His words are as pained as mine.

I scan through everything, all the secrets, all the odd mishaps, and am suddenly kicked in the guts. "*No*."

The world reels around me, and I drop to both knees, the earth beneath me too shaky to stay afloat. I cover my mouth to hold back the violent sickness festering within. This can't be true. *This* is his secret. I'm not crazy after all? Or am I? His secret is that he's...no, fucking no. I want to reach out and touch him, but I just can't. I'm afraid once I move, all of this will be real.

The bleeding wound gorging on Jude's life, his soul, his essence shreds a guttural scream from my throat. The gunshot wound marring his torso is the same one I tended to all those nights ago, but this wound isn't a graze, it's a wound that took someone's life—Jude's life.

He lowers his shirt and steps aside. He hands over the final piece to this puzzle, and that final piece is his gravestone.

How can he be so...calm? My body begins trembling, and I claw my fingers into the mud, needing an anchor before I sink in despair. "No! No! No!" I cry, spittle running down my chin. "You're not dead! You're not! This isn't true. Please, god, no. None of this makes any sense." I pound my fists into the ground, my eyes unable to read the inscription of who Jude was.

Angry tears well in his eyes. He looks away, wounded. "Do you think I want this to be our reality? Do you think I want to be buried in that grave?" He jabs at the tombstone violently. "This is just as much of a nightmare for me as it is for you."

I pull at the blades of grass beneath my fingertips, tearing at the lawn in horror. "This is just a dream. This is just a dream," I repeat over and over, a ringing knocking loudly against my skull, the air suddenly robbed from my lungs.

"This is real. I'm so sorry I couldn't protect you this one final time." I can't hear this. His words are like gravel in my ears.

I refuse to believe this.

I can't.

"You're fucking insane!" I cry, thumping my fist into the ground. "I knew you were too good to be true. There is no way this is possible!"

Jude's wounded stare says otherwise. "I know how crazy

this sounds, shit you see in the movies, but this is our reality, Tori. It has been since we met."

"No. Take me h-home."

"I can't, Tori, not until you know the rest. If you still don't believe me, then I swear to you, I will take you home, and you'll never have to see me again."

The thought of that certainty is a sad one, but how can I believe this? This is the stuff nightmares are made of. Thinking back to the nightmares I've had, I come to realize that that's what I've been living.

I'm sinking, and this time, there is no lifeline.

He drops to his knees in front of me, pressing me into his chest. I clutch onto him, desperate to feel that this…*he* is real. "If I could save you this heartache, I would, but as I once told you, I was drawn to you. I didn't understand why, but now, I do."

"Is this really happening?" My voice booms in my ears. I think I've slipped into denial, or shock—most likely both.

"Yes, it is. I know it's hard to believe, but this is our world… for now. We're stuck in a place between worlds." For now? Is he planning on leaving? Leaving me?

I push out of his embrace. "If you don't want to be with me, then just tell me. Don't make up some god-awful l-lie." I'm grasping at straws because as the seconds tick by, I know he's telling me the truth.

"Lie?" He shakes his head angrily. "I'm buried six feet under, that gravestone marking where I lay because I want to break up with you? C'mon, Tori! That's more ridiculous than the truth!"

"How can I believe this, Jude? You're telling me you're dead. What in the actual fuck am I supposed to think?" I would stand, but my legs have gone numb.

"I know that, but I'm trying to be honest with you. I would never lie to you, especially about this." His words...they are filled with nothing but the truth.

Oh god. The world comes crashing down around me, and I wrap my arms around my middle. No, this can't be happening. I can't even process a world without Jude living in it. That world surely doesn't exist.

I still can't accept this. How can anyone take this in their stride? Words have obviously failed Jude because he cautiously reaches for my wrist, afraid I'll recoil or tell him to stay away. I do neither, too dazed to do anything but watch in a comatose state as he lifts my hand and places it over his heart. The usual rhythmic step is suddenly out of sync. He presses harder, his face empty, pained.

I wait for the natural cadence, the one which denotes the life source flowing through our veins, but I feel...nothing. There is no thumping, no hammering heart. What lies within Jude's chest is no longer beating.

I cry, pulling from his embrace, and violently press my ear to his chest. I toss back my hair so we're connected, flesh to flesh. But no matter how many seconds I wait or how many seconds I hold my breath, there is no sound of a beating heart. What was once thumping is now an empty vessel.

Ugly tears wrack my body, and I sob harder than I've ever sobbed before. I'm being wounded all over again, but this time, I don't want to wake up. I fall into Jude's chest, weeping. This is really true.

"*No*, please, no. Anything but this. You c-can't be…d-dead."

"I'm sorry, Victoria."

But I'm the one who's sorry—Jude *is* dead.

I sob for minutes, Jude consoling me the entire time. When I can see past my tears, I peer over his shoulder, focusing on a blackbird perched on a branch in a large oak tree. At this moment, I'm envious of that bird. I wish I could spread my wings and fly away from this nightmare. "You c-can't just give up. I mean, you have to fight." I'm still unable to look at him, so I continue gazing at the bird, his freedom giving me the strength to go on.

"Fight for what?" The surrender is clear in his tone.

Taking a deep breath, I collect whatever courage I have left and be the strength Jude needs me to be. This is too incredulous to believe, but I…believe him. "Fight for your life. I don't know what is happening, but there's got to be a reason I can see you, right?"

His silence slashes at my heart once again.

Breaking our embrace, I meet his torn eyes. "I'm tired of fighting a losing battle. I'm just sorry I dragged you into this.

Your strength has made me live again—even if it's on borrowed time."

I can't stop the tears. I want to be strong, but I can't. The man I love is dead. I still cannot believe this reality is mine. "You should have told me."

His warm breath caresses my skin like a lover's touch, and it feels like coming home. "You knowing or not knowing doesn't change the outcome. I'm dead, whether we like it or not. If I lied to you to save you from that reality, then so be it."

I jerk backward, hating how he can refer to death so easily. "Live for me." I can't see past my tears, but I blindly reach down and stroke over his tattoo.

"I have, but it's out of my control now."

"What do you mean?"

"Our time is up, Tori. But I couldn't let all of this…" He swallows, needing time to find his words. "Be for nothing."

He thumbs my quivering bottom lip while I sob, my heart shattering with every single word. "I need you to know that every minute spent with you *was* real. I need you to know I'm the luckiest son of a bitch for meeting someone like you."

His words are so bittersweet, I can't help but cry. "You died protecting me." I weep, still unbelieving of the words I speak.

Never missing a beat, he avows, "Dying to protect you has made me feel alive."

My howls are gut-wrenching and pained because I feel like a piece of me is dying as each minute ticks over. Unable to stay upright, I collapse into Jude's outstretched arms. "Shh. Don't cry. When the time comes, I don't want you to be there. I want you to remember what we had. Who I was."

"You can't decide that for me," I mutter into his shoulder.

"Yes, I can. Let me go with dignity. Remember me as the man who loved you more than anything in this world. Our world."

My snivels become low sniffs when I process what he just said.

He loves me?

With my face a hot, blubbering mess, I pull away, and ask, "You l-love me?"

"I do." He nods, brushing the tears from my eyes with his thumbs.

At that precise moment, I hear freedom. I hear the flap of wings as the blackbird flies from its perch, symbolizing everything I feel. "I love you, too."

He closes his eyes and smiles a victorious smile. "And that, by far, is the craziest thing you've ever said."

With a heavy heart, I wrap my fingers around his nape, his warm flesh never feeling more alive. A tremor passes through him because he can feel our connection too. Pressing our foreheads together, I breathe him into me, filling my lungs with Jude because he's all I need.

"Do you know how insane this is?"

"I know," he whispers, the touch against my cheeks a lover's caress. "You don't believe me?" There is nothing but horror entwined in his question.

But there is nothing to fear because I've never been more certain of anything in my life. "I do."

As hard as this is to believe, I know this is my world now. This unbelievable event is really happening, and for the first time in a long time, I embrace the noise.

I can't keep up with the thoughts racing around my head. Jude nudges my nose with his from side to side. "Jude..." I murmur, not wanting this moment to end.

"Yes."

"Why can I see you?"

He hisses a low breath through his teeth. His reaction has me gulping. I'm brave. I can accept whatever he has to say. So I ask the obvious. "And why can Angus see you?"

A pain slashes at his face. Skimming his finger over the seam of my lips, he replies, "Are you ready for more?"

I melt under his touch. "I don't think I have much of a choice."

Laying a kiss against my mouth, he whispers, "Trust me?"

Again with that word. But this time, I reply without pause. "With my life."

Fifteen

We travel in silence for over an hour, my brain unable to switch off. Although I cannot grasp what Jude revealed, my lateral mind knows that this uncanny reality is really mine. I never believed in goblins, and ghouls, and…

"Jude?"

He peers over at me. I've never seen him look so…peaceful. He hums low, implying that he's listening.

I shift in my seat, embarrassed. "Are you a…ghost?"

Lines etch across his furrowed brow. "I don't know what I am," he replies with a shrug. "This didn't come with an instruction manual."

His gaze lingers long enough that my cheeks heat. He grins, amused by my bashfulness. "Do I feel like a ghost?" He thankfully returns his focus to the road so I can blush in private.

"No," I finally reply once I trust my voice. "You don't. You feel very real." I'm suddenly struck with a thought. "That's why you said my virtue was safe. And why we didn't—" I press my lips shut, blushing all over again.

"I thought best not push our luck," he explains. "Each time we touched, I knew it was by some miracle that you could feel me."

"I always wondered why you looked so surprised when we touched." His thigh stiffens as I shyly reach out and place my hand on his leg.

"I've been unable to feel anything, anyone but you," he reveals, his fingers clenching the wheel. "I can feel Angus. But our touch, it's something else."

I gasp. My flesh suddenly feeling like it's on fire. "What does that mean?"

"It means that whatever I am, I'm somehow connected to you. Logically, none of his should be happening…"

"But it is," I conclude.

We're quiet for the rest of the trip, both needing space and time to try to piece together what all of this means. None of this makes any sense, and when we turn down a deserted road and are outnumbered by the rodents and cockroaches, I have a feeling further uncertainty is about to follow.

This neighborhood looks like the set for a horror movie, but I don't see Hollywood in sight. The farther we drive, the worse the conditions become. We're surrounded by derelict warehouses and decaying buildings covered with layers of graffiti and aged advertisement posters. Most of the windows are smashed in, and I don't even want to think about who or what are using these quarters as their homes.

"Okay, so my original thought of you being a serial killer is quite probable." I lean forward and peer out the windshield, my face reflecting the horror that Jude just may be a mass murderer.

I expect him to laugh, but he doesn't.

Okay, *now* I'm nervous.

The truck is swimming in tension; the only sound is my raspy breathing and Jude's finger rapping against the steering wheel to a silent tune. As he continues driving, the darker and more desolate it becomes. I sit on my hands to stop biting my nails. From the corner of my eye, I notice Jude's knuckles are white from gripping the wheel so hard.

His weird behavior has me exhaling heavily. I suddenly feel like I'm suffocating. However, I'm grounded when Jude reaches out and strokes my upper arm. He turns left, leading us down a short, deserted alleyway. My heart begins to…thump…thump, unlike his. I hold back my tears.

When we come to a blacked-out building that is covered in graffiti tags and has remnants of faded police tape flapping in the wind, I hope I've made the right decision.

This place is obviously deserted, and the only inhabitants are rats and maybe a homeless person or two. Jude kills the engine and squeezes my hand. "This is our stop."

"We're getting out here?"

He nods.

I look at the dilapidated building, wondering if there is a front door. My heart races as I unbuckle my seat belt.

Acceptance.

I gulp. This is it—the moment of truth. I must accept that in minutes I just may die.

Jude jumps out of the truck, scoping out his surroundings before closing the door. I watch as he places the black hood over his head, turning his face down low as he walks around the truck. His behavior is setting me on edge.

He opens the passenger door, stepping close and engulfing me with that smell I associate with protection. I feel safe around Jude…my current situation proves that.

When he reaches over my shoulder, his face inches from mine; I resist the urge to pull back. I stand my ground. His eyes smolder. Producing a black baseball cap, he places it on my head, positioning it so it sits low. It's about two sizes too big and slips down, shrouding my eyes. "Why do I need a hat?"

Jude lifts the bill. "Things may get a little…bright. You ready?"

"No." I nod, wondering what that means. He smiles, but it's bittersweet. He appears regretful for taking me here, but it's too late.

A tingle runs all through my body as he offers me his hand.

He locks the car with my fingers still threaded through his. I know he won't let me go. The air is putrid out here. I raise my wrist to cover my nose. I have no idea what I'm walking into. Our footsteps seem amplified out here in the silence as we commence our march down the alley. The sound, however, alerts whatever critter is watching our every move. We hear a crash and a bottle rolling along the uneven pavement behind us.

I yelp and freeze as I squeeze my eyes shut. Memories overflow me. I wheeze, unable to breathe.

"Tori, do you want to turn around? It only gets…worse from here on in." His voice is my beacon. It gives me the strength to persevere.

"No, I just need a minute." Breathing in through my nose, and out through my mouth, I try my best to stay grounded. Jude gives me all the time I need. Once I'm settled enough to continue, I open my eyes and take another deep breath. We then continue our death march. Jude's with me every step of the way, a silent reassurance that he'll never let go.

The lane is short, and once we're almost at the end, I celebrate prematurely because as I round the corner, a wave of terror drags me under, and I'm gasping for air. What's happening? "Jude!"

His fingers squeeze mine. "I'm sorry, Tori." The heaviness breaks my heart. "This is the only way."

"The only way for what?" The world spirals around me,

blinding me. I'm desperately kicking to the surface, but suddenly, everything explodes in white, and I see the world through eyes that are not my own...

Jude

"Loretta, I don't have time for this shit. Do you have it or not?"

Loretta smirks, putting the Cheshire Cat to shame. "So impatient. You'd think I wasn't doing you a favor."

I snort, shaking my head in disgust. "Favor? Favor would imply you're doing this out of the kindness of your heart." I leave out the fact I doubt she has one underneath that Chanel number she's wearing.

She disregards my attack with a wave of her hand. "Call it what you will. I'm still helping you when no one else would."

She does have a point. "Fine, thank you. Now, have you got it?"

I watch as she leans over and opens the console. She makes sure she touches my leg along the way. When she produces a thick yellow envelope, I sit upright, suppressing the urge to rip it from her hands. "Be careful what you wish for, Jude. It just may come true." She dangles it in front of me, knowing this is what I've been searching for, for over a year.

"Thanks for the warning." I snatch it from her fingers, the

tremor betraying my fears. Inside this envelope lie the answers I have so desperately sought. This envelope contains information on Rosemary's whereabouts.

Loretta Goldbloom may seem like a harmless soccer mom to the unsuspecting, but I know better. She's married to the state, maybe even the country's most elusive private investigator. I didn't ask questions when she promised she could find Rose. All she wanted in return was fifteen thousand dollars. I scoffed, unbelieving at first. I mean, she had just propositioned me at my son's Christmas play. Her daughter, Henrietta, was special just like Angus. That's why I think she offered her services in the first place. She felt sorry for me. Everyone did.

But I didn't need anyone's charity. I would find Rose on my own. However, when one month became two, and both Henry and I failed to come up with a lead, I knew I had no other choice but to pay up. I'm pretty certain Loretta and her husband, whose name I never knew, worked for the entire crime syndicate of the north east. That's why Loretta made me promise not to let Henry in on our agreement. Nothing like the good sheriff to rain on crime's parade.

It took me months of working double shifts and dipping into my measly savings, but I finally had the money. Loretta confirmed she was the real deal and gave me a taste when she showed me a picture of Rose. Her long hair was cut short, and she was wearing a pair of black-framed glasses that were too big for her slender face. But there was no mistaking it was her. She looked different. She looked…happy.

Anger coursed through my veins, and my need to find her changed. My quest was to now locate her and tell her to stay lost. I wanted her to know that when she up and left Angus and me, she gave up all rights, all ownership to her son and also, to my heart. She left us because she was gutless. For that, I would never be able to forgive her. But the sadistic part of me had to see it for myself. I had to see that she'd given up for good because there was no going back, no second chances.

Tearing open the seal, I hesitate for a mere moment before reaching inside and producing a photograph which looks like it was taken via surveillance. The quality isn't great, but there is no mistaking this is Rose. Any small scrap of love I may have had left for her evaporates into the still night air because even though the quality isn't seamless, there is no mistaking her very pregnant belly. She's bearing another man's child. I feel sick. I can't do this with Loretta watching me.

Shoving the photo back into the envelope, I jam the packet into my inner jacket pocket, keeping it safe. I jump out of the car before I stain the leather seats with my disgust. Slipping the hood over my head, I blend into the shadows. I want nothing more than to start my path to redemption.

"Oh, Jude?" Loretta singsongs, hoping to look inconspicuous as she peers around. "Forgetting something?"

Her tone may be light, but I know I'm a dead man if I even think about bailing without coughing up the dough. I walk to her window and don't bother concealing my stash as I toss the rolled-up bills into her lap. "Don't spend it all at once," I quip.

"Nice doing business with you. If you ask me, Rosemary is a fool." She blows me a kiss, a winner's grin slathered on her cheeks.

I don't wait around before I cross the road, desperate to get to my truck. Once inside, I can then deal with the information that's literally in my palm. I have Rose's address. I should feel something, but the god's honest truth is I just feel numb. I've been dead inside since Rose left.

It's deserted this time of night, and that's why I chose this location. It's perfect, as I'm not in the mood for crowds. With my face downturned, my hood covers my ears, so the only sound I hear is my heavy footsteps punishing the concrete with every step I take.

My truck is in sight when a harrowing scream tears through the air. I stop, lifting my head slowly to make sure I heard it, as my nerves are already shot. But when I hear it again, followed by a booming, "No!" I know someone is in trouble.

I could turn the other way, pretend I was never here, but I'm not a coward. I fight for what's right. Unlike my ex-wife. With that thought spurring me on, I take off in a dead sprint, rounding the corner to see a petite girl being dragged down an alleyway while her beau drops like a sack of shit to the ground.

I can hear the girl screaming bloody murder. I have no doubt she has bigger balls than her date, who is sobbing into his palms. Adrenaline pumps through my body as I run toward him, latching onto his bicep and yanking him up. "C'mon!" I shout when he drags his feet. "He's going to kill her."

"I can't!" the pretty boy cries, tearing at his hair with both hands. He's clearly in shock, but his hysteria can wait.

"Call 911!" I command, letting him go and powering after the girl, whose pleas are unexpectedly breaking my heart.

The alley is yards away. I charge forward, desperate to save her, but I don't know why. As I sprint around the corner, I almost get sick when I see him fondling her, her ass bare as she weeps and fights back as best she can.

It all happens in a blink of an eye, but I can see her transform from kitten to tiger in a nanosecond as she strikes her head back and connects with the motherfucker's nose. He screams and jumps backward, cradling his face. "You fucking bitch!" She doesn't waste a second and runs for her life.

Her eyes widen when she sees me sprinting toward her. Footsteps behind me alert me to the fact that the cowardly lion may have found his balls. But I'm faster, and I power forward with all my might. I don't know why, but a need to protect this woman invades every part of my body, and nothing else matters but keeping her safe.

Sheer strength radiates around her because she's determined to live. Her strength suddenly gives me hope. When Rose left, she took a part of me with her, but now, her actions seem so unimportant, so cowardly. This brave, determined woman is fighting for survival, and her resolve gives me a new lease on life. If this young lady can come back from this, then so can I.

I need to protect her. I need to thank her for opening my eyes. She's not running away from her problems; she's tackled them head on. She didn't need saving. She saved herself. "Run!" Her vitality is amplified when *she* attempts to protect *me*. Just *who* is this woman? I need to know her.

She looks at me like I'm someone worth knowing. Someone she needs. Sadly, my newfound rhapsody turns ugly, and my hope is shot down when the assailant pulls a gun, aims, and shoots—twice. One misses, but the other…it doesn't.

A scream shreds my throat raw as I watch in horror as my ray of hope crumples to the ground in a sickening heap. She falls feet away, tangled in a bloodied, crippled mess. The front of her green dress is suddenly stained red as the bullet enters her back and exits through her chest. The exit wound is gruesome. I push forward and reach her in seconds. She's on her back, gasping for breath as she stares up into the starless sky. I drop to my knees beside her, frantically pressing my hands over her wound.

Her dark hair is splayed out around her; one shoe is yards from where she lays. But regardless of her shape, she still radiates that strength which drew me toward her. I can hear crying behind me, useless to us both. "Call 911! Now!" I roar, my gaze never wavering from the angel in my arms.

Her eyes begin to roll into the back of her head. "No! Don't you dare. Stay with me!" I can see the determination as she forces herself to stay awake. "The paramedics are on their way. You stay awake, you hear me?" She nods, her head lolling to the side.

My palms are still pressed to her wound, but there is so much blood. Just as I'm about to yank off my sweater, she raises her arm, and with the softest of touches, slips the hood from my face. Her beautiful hazel eyes focus, and she rewards me with a weak smile. "Thank you." She swallows deeply. "I think…we would have been great friends."

I don't understand what she means until her eyes slip shut, and she stops breathing. She's dying. Every inch of my body howls in anger, and I fiercely attempt to bring her back to life. I perform CPR, breathing my life into her. She has to live. I never thought my heart would work again after Rose left, but now it's breaking for the girl I never knew.

Her beau is finally the man she needs as he pushes me aside so he can take over. But he's minutes too late. I almost pluck out his eyes and strangle him with my bare hands, but stop when I hear sirens wailing. "You got this?" It's not a question, more a threat.

He nods.

Looking down at someone I've only just met but feel an inexplicable connection to, I know there is something I must do. "You live, goddammit. You have to live. You belong in this world." Jumping to my feet, I tear down the alley, ready to take the law into my own hands.

My legs pump beneath me as I run faster than I've ever run before. Nothing else matters but finding the motherfucker who shot her and inflicted a world of pain. I'm blinded by my rage, but follow my gut and turn left, heading into a bad part of town. If I'm going to find this scumbag, it'll be hidden amongst the squalor.

A group of destitute people stands around flaming drums, warming their dirty hands. They don't bat an eyelash as I charge past them. They're most likely used to the drama. I sprint farther and deeper into this foreign land, the smell akin to death. I pull a sharp right, and just when I think I've gone the wrong way, I see him. He's running for his life literally because when I get my hands on him, I'll kill him.

He turns over his shoulder, his eyes widening when he sees me following in hot pursuit. He kicks over a burning barrel, uncaring that he's just destroyed the source of warmth for a lady and her three kids. I jump over it, never losing sight of the asshole. He ducks and weaves, but I'm with him every step of the way. The icy ground gives way, and he clumsily slips, spilling forward onto his front. His ineptness is my advantage, and I pound onward, tackling him as he attempts to stand.

We both tumble forward, but he breaks my fall as he lands onto the pavement face first. He's like a rabid animal as he attempts to fight me, but I'm running on pure rage. Pressing my knee into the small of his back, I fist his mangy, long hair and slam his forehead into the concrete once, twice, celebrating the punishing sound. He tries to scramble away, but the blow has left him disorientated, and he fumbles, allowing me to punch him repeatedly in the flank.

His pained grunts are my reward as all I can see is that bleeding angel dying in my arms. He's still fighting me, attempting to throw me off. He's strong, too strong for someone who is sober. I have no clue what drugs he's on, but they're enough to fuel his adrenaline, and by some miracle, he bucks me off before scampering away.

I fall backward but regain my balance quickly, livid that this asshole is still alive. The words "I think we would have been great friends" play over in my mind, angering me all over again. Because of this motherfucker, I'll never be able to feel her touch again.

I scurry after him, ready to put him down like the dog that he is, but when he rolls over and reaches into his jacket pocket, it's too late to turn away.

The metal from the gun barrel catches the shine of the full moon before I see a spark, hear a thunderous roar, and feel a piercing pain. It takes me a few seconds to realize I've been shot. I drop to my knees, my kneecaps shattering under the weighty force, but who needs kneecaps when you're dead?

I collapse into a heap, attempting to raise my hands to press over my wound, but I've lost the movement in my limbs. Blood seeps out all around me, and all I can do is helplessly watch my substance hemorrhage out of me.

I'm on my back, a position so similar to that of the girl whose name I will never know. The heavens look down at me, shaking their heads at the predicament I find myself in. Maybe I was never destined to find Rose. Or to know who the mystery girl was.

Fuck that.

I'll be damned if I die without at least knowing where Rose is.

Forcing my limbs to obey, I limply reach into my jacket pocket, my fingers brushing over the envelope which is now stained with my blood. I'm on the cusp of unconsciousness, but I push on, determined to see this through to the end. My vision begins to fade as the world veers toward murky shadows. I shake my head, clenching my teeth together, adamant to stay awake.

Just as I slide out the yellow envelope, the only color in my blackened world, a hand seizes my wrist and denies me my last rights. I try to fight him, but I can't. My body is like an overcooked string of spaghetti.

I watch through my right eye, as I've lost the vision in my left when he opens the envelope and simpers a reptilian smile. "I think this lady is my jackpot." He must have seen her info within. No doubt, he's planning on blackmailing Henry with what he knows. Dropping to one knee, he lifts my shirt. "Too bad you'll never find out where she is."

My attempts to fight him are laughable.

"Too bad you'll never have a taste of that apple pie either." His insult toward the girl angers me more than not finding Rose. It's pathetic but defiant, nonetheless. I spit in his face, grinning weakly when my bloodied spittle trickles down his cheek.

He wipes it away with the edge of his sleeve before standing and kicking me sharply in the ribs. For good measure, he adds another two blows to my face. It should hurt, but it doesn't. I refuse to allow his face to be the last thing I see, so I stare into the universe, making peace with the fact that I'll never see my son again. I know Grace will look after him like he's her own. Tears lap at the foreshore, but I refuse to cry.

Footsteps sound in the distance, and I realize that I'm out here all alone. Just as I close my eyes, ready to accept my fate, I'm jarred wide-awake when I'm shaken by both shoulders. "Kid? Can you hear me? Wake up!"

The voice is doubled and slowed down. "For Christ's sake! Jude!" My vision is clouded, but unless I'm hallucinating, I'm almost certain Henry is at my side. "What happened?" he screams, pressing one hand over my wound as he calls in his location to dispatch.

"How…did you know…where…I am?" The breaths between words are drawn out and quite possibly jumbled, but Henry understands what I'm trying to say.

"I followed you. I knew you were up to something when you pulled onto I-90. But I stupidly sat and watched your truck, certain you'd lead me to where you were going. I saw you chasing that scumbag, but I was too...late." For the first time ever, I hear remorse.

Whether it's because I have a newfound forgiveness in my last minutes on this earth, I clutch at Henry's wrist, which is pressed over my faltering heart. "Chase him. He knows...he knows where Rose is."

"*What*?"

I don't have time to explain. I suddenly grow cold. "He has an envelope. It has the information you need. You were right...I was up to something. I always am. But I found your...girl." I can't refer to Rose as mine anymore because she isn't; she hasn't been for a while.

Henry lifts my shirt and hisses. "Jesus Christ, kid. I leave you; you'll die."

My head lolls as I try to shake it. "Go...I'm already...dead." This is what Henry has wanted since Rose left. I don't know why I'm telling him as we're archenemies, but I guess this is what I have to do to make peace. "Go!" I press when he hesitates. "Find her." There's no point in both of us being dead inside.

Henry slowly loosens his hold and gently lays something soft under my head. "Help is on the way. Don't you die. You're a stubborn son of a bitch. Don't let me down now."

I appreciate his concern although it's come about ten years too late. But I suppose better late than never.

As Henry stands, I make my final plea. "There's a girl, she's been shot. Around the corner from where my truck is. Promise me you'll save her first."

"What?"

"Promise me." My heart is failing. I can feel my body shutting down. "Send the paramedics there first. There were sirens but send more."

"Kid…"

"Do it."

With a hesitant sigh, he calls it in. "There's been a shooting at the corner of Appleby and Heights. Send every goddamned ambulance this town has."

My teeth chatter, my vision is virtually gone, but I'm not frightened. I settle into the ground, adjusting myself to be as comfortable as I can. "Sheriff?"

"Yeah?"

"Light me a cigarette, will you? It's not like it's going to kill me." I try to laugh, but all that escapes me is a wheeze.

I hear Henry rifle through his pockets, and then the unmistakable sound of a lighter being lit. Moments later, I feel the smoke being placed between my lips. "Thanks."

"Goodbye, Jude. Your death won't be in vain. I'll find this lowlife and make him pay for what he did to you. And the girl." Henry's parting words are somewhat calming.

Sucking on my cigarette, with my diminishing vision my only friend, I lay alone, staring up into the heavens. I could curse the Gods and beg for mercy, but the truth is, this is the first time in a long time I've felt free. Free from the sadness which took permanent residency inside my soul. Of course, I'll miss Angus, but I know he'll grow into the remarkable man he's destined to become. He's the one and only thing I've done right in my life.

I can no longer feel my body. I'm weightless. This is it—the end.

No one can predict their death, and even if I had a crystal ball and could see into the future, I still wouldn't change a thing. I gave my son the best life I could, taught him what I thought was right to shape him into someone who will do me proud. He's my legacy. The best mark I left on this world. I gave Henry a reason to go on. And lastly, I met someone who, for the briefest of moments, made me have hope for tomorrow.

Before my eyes slip shut, I see a glimmer, a shooting star. A smile cracks my blood-caked lips.

Make a wish.

Henry

"That stupid motherfucker!" I curse, refusing to weep. I don't even like the kid. Why am I sad? I run in the direction I saw that vermin go, desperate to find him because according to Jude, he knows where Rose is.

I don't know how Jude found her, but I don't care. This is

the moment I've been waiting for, for over a year. This will bring my Jillian out of her permanent slumber. We both died the day Rose left, and it's my job to bring her back. She took so much of us when she left. This is the only way I can show Jillian how sorry I am for all that I've done. I'm not proud of my actions, but I'm ready to make amends for the many errors of my ways.

A sense of right overcomes me. I not only need to find this bastard because of Rose, but I also need to find him and make him pay for what he did to Jude.

I take a right, and I see him. This is it—my salvation starts now.

"Stop! This is the police! I said—" Oh fuck, shit.

No.

I wheeze, clawing at my chest, unable to breathe. I'm dying...again...I died twice? Three times? I've lost count. "Jude! No!" A sharp scream rips from my throat, the guttural sound overruled by my harrowing sobs. I attempt to run, but I'm pinned down.

I need to fight for him. I need to save him.

"Victoria!" His voice is my compass, always guiding me when I'm without direction. "Breathe...stay with me." Those words now take on another meaning. They've saved me since the beginning. "Shh, I've got you. You're safe."

"You're here?" I stop struggling.

A kiss is pressed to my temple. "Yes, always."

I don't know how long it takes, but when the room stops spinning, I crack open my eyes, afraid of what I'll see. It shouldn't surprise me that the first thing in my blurred vision is Jude. He's crouched down in front of me, his hair standing on end, his eyes red raw.

"Oh, thank god." He scoops me into his arms, hugging me so tightly I almost can't breathe. That thought leaves me winded as I remember another time when I was left gasping for breath.

Jude kisses my hair, my cheeks, my eyelids, finishing with the seam of my mouth. "Are you all right?" He presses his palms to my cheeks, searching my face for clues.

What I just witnessed tackles me from behind. I slouch against Jude, drowning in fresh tears. A sob escapes me. "I saw you die." My entire being mourns. "You died saving me." I shake my head, unable to accept this as truth. "*No.*" The ache of realizing he's dead rips at my soul once more. "I'm responsible for all of this. I'm the one who deserves to be dead." I gasp. "Henry? He's de…?" I finally manage to half choke out.

Jude nods sadly, lowering his inky eyes. My heart breaks. It gets torn into a million irreparable pieces. Nothing makes any sense. But I know this is only the beginning of things to come.

Jude brushes away my tears with his thumbs. I chew my lip to stop the torrent. His breath is warm like a sunlit summer's day. "Are you ready to see the rest?"

My brain chugs through the darkness, and I slowly process where we are. We're in an elevator.

"There's more?"

Kissing my lips tenderly, he stands, offering me his hand. "There's always more."

The doors slide open as I slip my hand into his. Logically, this shouldn't be happening. But this stopped making sense long ago.

The only thing that makes a lick of sense, however, are three simple words which aren't so simple after all. "I love you."

I'm rendered utterly speechless. This heroic, remarkable man loves *me*? I'm no one special, but he, he is heroic and brave. He is utterly epic. "I was right," I whisper. He cocks his head. "We *are* great friends." I confirm a statement I don't even remember making. It's so unfathomable. But I can't even begin to digest what I just experienced because I know there's so much more to come.

I smooth out the lines between his brows. "But we're even better lovers. I love you, too. In this lifetime and also the next," I add, hoping to express that our connection knows no leaps or bounds.

A victor's grin lights up his face.

I've never felt safer in his arms—arms, hands, heart, and soul, which sacrificed their life for mine. *"Promise me you'll save her first."*

I throw my arms around his nape, burying my face into his

chest. "Thank you."

"Don't thank me just yet." Those words are filled with nothing but remorse.

Regrettably, I untangle myself from his form and look to the right. My eyes abruptly snap to Jude. "What the hell?"

He replies by slipping his hand into mine and leading me into the last place on earth I'd think we'd ever come.

Sixteen

I now understand why Jude suggested I wear a cap. The bright lights hurt my eyes. So do the sorrowing stares of the clusters of people around me. I lower the bill as I huddle closer against Jude's side.

Our shoes squeak along the glossy white floor, disturbing the eerie feel lingering in the air. The staff passes us, talking in a language I can't understand. It's bedlam, but there's also a stroke of stillness. It's a feeling I can't quite explain.

I follow Jude, who seems to know where he's going. I dare say, just like the graveyard, he's been here many times before. We go by countless windows, but the curtains are drawn and the doors sealed tight, so I can't look inside. But the smell, that antiseptic tang, is a vivid reminder of where we are.

As we round a corner, Jude pushes open a double set of

swinging doors. His puckered brow exposes that we're here—wherever here is. I enter slowly, unsure of what I'm about to see. Jude gestures with his chin for me to go onward. I do.

If it weren't for the sound of my footsteps, I'd believe I was frozen solid, but I'm suddenly drawn to a room at the end of the long white corridor. I don't quicken my pace. I take my time. Inhaling a slow, deep breath, I continue my wander, bright lights and voices flickering before me. The closer I get to the room, the more vibrant my surroundings become. I want to cover my ears and black out my eyes, but I don't.

I can feel Jude behind me, but he's lagging feet away, allowing me to process my fate at my own speed. The sterile rooms all have numbers above the frames of the beige doors. They're all counting down.

This is the final countdown.

Ten…

Nine…

Eight…

Seven…

Six…

Five…

Four…

Three…

I stop at door number two. "I'm afraid," I whisper.

"I know, but I promise, it'll be okay." His reassurance offers me the strength I need.

He strokes the length of my neck with two fingers as I peer over at door number one. I wonder what prize lies behind the wooden frame. I force my feet to move, closing the distance on a place I suddenly have recollections of visiting before. My steps become heavy; my breathing harsh.

A memory, one I don't remember making, crashes into me of a doctor flicking open my eyelids, then shining a light from side to side.

"She's non-responsive."

"Blood pressure is sixty over forty. Shit, we're losing her."

Flashback after flashback assaults me.

"Get her into an operating room now!"

I gasp, clutching at my chest, as it feels like a million butterflies are longing to fly free.

"She's flatlining!"

"Clear!"

A pain shreds through my body as I jolt upward, the force breaking two ribs.

"Again!"

I want to scream, to tell them to stop, but I can't. The second shock annihilates my organs. I feel like I'm trapped inside a translucent balloon. The stretchy walls are closing in on me. I push, but the texture snaps back.

"Blood pressure is steady."

"Fuck, that was a close call."

"Tell her family we did all we could. The rest is up to her

now." I pull myself from the memory, my cheeks coated in salted tears.

Night turns into day…seconds into minutes…days into weeks.

"*Tori…it's me. Can you hear me?*"

"*I miss you.*"

"*Give me another chance.*"

"*I'll never forgive myself for what I did. Please, come back to me. I'll make it up to you if you do.*"

"*I love you.*"

I scream. I feel his hand squeezing mine. A deafening ringing sounds loudly in my ears. I rock forward, cradling my head, desperate to make it stop.

"*I'm sorry.*"

I've heard this speech before—every single word. I've felt the exact touch. The only thing missing is my reply.

"*I miss you, honey. We all do.*"

"*I just wish you'd come home. If you did, all of this would be over.*"

Mom?

A sheen of sweat covers my body. She's repeating the same speech, too? What's going on?

"*…Tori, please don't hang up. I…this is hard for me, too. We never meant to hurt you. We both missed you so much. I talk to you every day, even though I know you won't talk back. I'm sorry, please forgive me. I need you. I miss my sister.*"

A storm in a teacup begins to brew, the words, speeches I've heard before all mingle, mesh into one. Their voices, their words, they vibrate in my ears, and no matter how hard I cover my ears, the clamor won't go away.

"Hello, Brittney. Can you call the station? Young Angus has run off into the woods again."

"I ask that you watch over our daughter, Rose. Wherever she may be...please let her be safe and know that we love and miss her so much."

No! Make it stop!

"We hope you like lobster tail."

"Typical. He was always bringing home strays."

I wake, crumpled to the floor, no longer able to distinguish between reality and fiction. I'm cradled in the fetal position, not understanding what I just saw and heard. The fragments from my past are from conversations I've had with people, the only thing missing from each snippet is...me.

I can see the people who I've conversed with loud and clear, but I can't see or hear me. It's like I wasn't there.

I ransack my mind, detailing over every exchange I've had with everyone I've met.

"It's Charley McMann. We went to high school together."

"Retard! Retard! Retard! He doesn't have any money. His dad is a deadbeat."

"Yes, the young boy, Angus...he is my grandson."

"Congratulations, Ms. Armstrong. Welcome to Pinewood."

"I don't know why he lied to you, but I'd guess it was to protect you."

"I will do anything to protect my son, and I know your intentions are good, but I can't have...complications."

I set the final piece down, the puzzle now complete. It was staring me in the face this entire time. I now understand why Grace hated me and ignored me any chance she got. Why all the interactions I had with my family felt forced as if I was being unheard. Why I was ignored time and time again.

It's been said the simple flutter of a butterfly's wing can cause chaos halfway across the world. So, there is one simple difference, a difference which isn't so small after all, and that difference is...life and death. These interactions occurred or didn't occur because *I*...don't...exist.

Peering up at the door, I blink, remembering what lies just beyond it. It was there all along, but I couldn't cope. My fragile mind erected layer upon layer, blaming the holes in my memory on PTSD. But I never suffered from the disorder.

My jelly legs barely hold me up as I stand, but I reach for the doorknob, it whining open as I release the door inch by inch. My view is only a sliver, as I can't process what I'm seeing too quickly, afraid I'll slip back into a place which doesn't exist.

The room is pleasant, a soft peach in color, housing all the essentials that a hospital room would need. The curtains are drawn open, letting in the light, but the mournful faces of the people I love reveal no sunshine will cure their pain.

People come and go, and the room flickers from light to dark to gray. I know what I'm seeing are occurrences which took place days, weeks, maybe even months ago. It's a moving picture of everything I've missed—missed because lying in that hospital bed is me.

"Am I dead?" I whisper, feeling Jude at my back.

"No, you're not dead."

"Then what am I?"

His sigh is heavy. "You're in a coma, Tori. You have been for nine months."

A single tear rolls down my cheek.

"The night of your accident, you almost died. They lost you on the operating table except you pulled through. But you never woke. You've been this way"—he gestures with his hand toward the bed—"since that night."

It's the most disconcerting feeling to look upon you, seeing yourself how others would. Opening the door wider, I step inside, my gaze never leaving the hospital bed where I lay. I'm wrapped in a peaceful slumber. There is no bruising, no blood to indicate I'm hurt. But the machines I'm hooked up to disclose the fact that without them helping me breathe, I wouldn't be alive, if that's what you can call it.

I continue walking until I reach the bed. My body lies still, lost in an everlasting sleep while my spirit and mind are free to wander. "So I really got shot?"

"Yes, you did."

"And you're really dead?"

"Yes, I am." I frown, wishing this was all a dream.

Reaching forward, I gently place my hand over my own. I gasp; I can feel the touch on my skin. I look and feel just how I remember. "Did Bryan and Matilda sleep together?"

"Yes." I'm thankful Jude is giving me the space I need because there is too much, too fast to process. "Those memories you have of what you saw are real."

Thinking of when Bryan said goodbye to me and our home, I now understand why. *"I can't stay here. There's just too many... memories. I can't live in this home any longer. Forgive me. I tried to stay strong, but I just can't. You're so...distant. Cold. You don't want to come back to me."* I thought he was unresponsive, but I was the one who was impassive because I wasn't really there.

The words he spoke take on a whole different meaning now.

There was never an affair of, so to speak, because I wasn't alive in the factual sense. I was lost to Bryan. He never cheated, he was moving on, just as I had in my mind. Matilda and Bryan found comfort in one another, grieving and bonding over an event so horrific, they ended up falling in love.

It makes sense he would sell the house, because as he said, there were too many memories. He couldn't stand to be there anymore because he knew I wasn't coming back. I was so angry with them both; I think I closed myself off to getting better. But there was no need to be hateful or hurt. Wasn't I doing the same in my mind? Moving on and living, the only way I knew how.

All of their apologies were made right here in this room. So was my mother's heartfelt plea at my housewarming. I saw what I wanted to see. I went where I was drawn. Every confession, conversation was made not over the phone, but rather over my hospital bedside talking to the person lying comatose in that bed.

"My home? Does that really exist?" I run my fingertip over my weak pulse.

"Why did you choose the house that you did?" Jude asks gently.

Staring down at my sleeping figure, I lift my shoulders, clueless. "I didn't…it chose me."

Jude takes a step closer, but we don't touch. "Close your eyes and think back to the night of your housewarming."

I don't bother questioning why.

I watch as people enter my home, but it's not really my home. The furnishings are crisp, clean, and modern unlike what currently resides in my house. *"Welcome, we're the Andersons. We hope you like the lobster tail."*

Mrs. Anderson was everywhere that night, playing the perfect host. She was also strangely weeding my backyard. A sense of sadness overcomes me. "Why are the Andersons in my home?"

"Tori…you're in theirs."

A loneliness permeates my soul.

"I've gate crashed the Andersons' home?" I ask, horrified.

"Sort of. You're…suspended… between life and death."

The weird occurrences are suddenly explained. The porch light randomly going off, the back door not locking, the pipes whining for no apparent reason, the fridge being stocked full. I've been *haunting* someone's home.

"I conjured up the housewarming as being mine, but it was theirs, wasn't it?" He nods while I gasp. "And you didn't buy the food in my fridge?" This is implausible.

"No. You saw what you wanted to see."

"And that's why you didn't want to make a big deal about it?" His silence speaks volumes. "You were once again protecting me from the truth." I rub my brow, hoping to ease the looming headache.

"Tori, we all grieve in our own way. This was the only way your mind could heal; deal with what you went through. The housewarming party, you were having an out-of-body experience. You were drawn to the lake house because of me. Your spirit was there, but your body was in a coma. Like astral projection, if you will."

My mouth hinges open. "There is obviously something very wrong with me because who in their right mind creates this fantasy world?" I stab at my form with my finger. "I'm right there, Jude. I can wake up any time, but I choose to stay here. Maybe I really am losing my mind."

My anger is misdirected because I'm not mad at him. I'm incensed at the person lying peacefully and gutlessly in that bed.

"I don't think you have a choice." The room turns cold.

His poignant confession has me spinning around. "What do you mean?"

His shoulders stoop as he brushes past, avoiding making eye contact, which makes my throat go dry. Sitting on the edge of the bed, he wipes his hands along his pant legs before gently stroking two fingers over my inner wrist. The moment he touches me, I whimper, feeling his gentle caress all the way to my toes.

"That's not possible." I shake my head. "How can I feel you?"

Jude continues stroking my flesh, my skin breaking out into goose bumps. "We're connected, Victoria, and I think you're here and not there"—he wretchedly gestures with his head to the bed—"because of me."

The walls begin to converge.

"I should have told you from the very beginning, but I was selfish. You could see what I felt, what I *feel* for you through my eyes. At first, I wanted to understand what this connection meant. But as I got to know you, I didn't care. I just knew I needed to be around you because you made me forget that I was…you made me feel alive."

He doesn't need to finish the sentence. We both know the god-awful truth.

"I don't know for certain, but I thought I was here—didn't pass over or whatever you want to call it—because of Henry. I thought I was here to help him accept that he too no longer had a foot in the land of the living. By doing that, I thought I'd make peace and go wherever people like me are supposed to go, but now, I'm not so sure."

"W-what does that mean?" I lick my dry lips.

Bending down, he lays a tender kiss over my rosy cheek. I raise my hand, rubbing over the spot where I feel his touch linger. "Henry is just as stubborn in death as he was when living. We're both stuck here for a reason." He pauses, brushes the hair from my brow, before revealing, "And that reason is you. It's not *me* who is supposed to help Henry, it's *you*. He won't believe me, but he'll believe you. When he sees your body in a coma, sees Jillian set a dinner place for him and Rose every night as she slowly loses her mind, and when he witnesses the ball is in his honor because he was shot dead in the line of duty, I think only then we can all make peace with our fates.

"You helped me let go of Rose, and I think you need to do the same for Henry. He can't let go, and he's stuck here, just like the rest of us."

"The rest of us" is just so bleak. It brings tears to my eyes. "Henry doesn't remember what you did for him, does he?"

"No, he doesn't remember anything because he doesn't know he's dead." Unable to stand the distance between us, I close the gap, wrapping my arms around him and pressing my chest to his back. "I should hate Rose, but I don't." I try to keep the disappointment from showing. What he says next immediately soothes my worries. "I can't hate her because she led me to you. I now realize she was meant to stay lost because I was meant to find you."

"Jude…" My voice breaks. "By finding me…you died."

He stubbornly shakes his head. "No, Victoria, I was already dead inside. You brought me back to life. You're the reason I'm still here. You're the reason I can't let go."

A tremor of tears racks my body, but I hold it back.

"You were drawn to the house because of us. You're *stuck* here because of us." His last comment is my undoing. "Once we let go, however, you can move on. We all can."

"Move on? You mean…?" I can't finish that sentence as I bite the inside of my cheek to stop the tears. "That's why he blames you. He doesn't want to remember you handing over the information to Rose's whereabouts because that would resurface what happened next. You both died trying to find her. But she never wanted to be found. He thinks you know when, in reality, you both were within reach."

"The dead only recall what they—what *we* want to."

I hate that he falls into such a category.

"That night, when you came to my house, that was you getting shot, wasn't it? And when I saw you after I had dinner at Henry's? You were standing by a car. That was the start of your death…loop? Time warp?" I don't know what to call it, but he knows exactly what I mean.

"Yes."

"Do you relive that often?"

The pause is all the answer I need. "Yes, I die every night. It doesn't matter where I am, I can't escape my death. Sometimes, it happens for seconds. Other times, it feels like it's never going to end. We all deal with our demons our own way. Dying is a reminder that I found you." He turns over his shoulder so our faces are inches apart. "So if anyone is losing their mind, it's fair to say it's me."

"I'm no one special," I whisper, unable to understand his sacrifice. "Not worth dying for."

"Yes, you are. I happily die every night just so I can meet you again." I can't keep the tears at bay any longer and weep uncontrollably.

This is all too much.

Jude embraces me as I fall into his lap. He brushes my hair, whispering that it'll be okay. But it won't. I've just learned that everything I thought was real is actually not, or it's a twisted take on my reality, which doesn't even exist. I'm floating between worlds, and if what Jude says is true, I know what needs to be done to decide which plane is my home.

"So that explains why Grace hates me. She doesn't even know I exist." All the conversations I thought I had, like with the girl in the store when I first met Angus, the reason she ignored me was because she couldn't see me. She's alive, and I'm...I don't know what I am.

"I've heard people call this The Fade. We are haunting earth like a… ghost would, but you, you're different. You've found a loophole. You're suspended."

"The Fade? Like limbo?"

He nods slowly. "Yes. We're between worlds. We're on earth, but we haven't passed over to wherever we're supposed to go yet—heaven or hell, if you believe that they exist. If this were a cheesy movie, I suppose you could say we haven't gone to the light. But you…you're caught in an ethereal realm. Stuck between two worlds. The world of the living where you hear people who are alive and talking to you by your bedside, and the world of those who have died and need to move on—The Fade."

I think back to the conversations I thought I had with my mom, sister, even Bryan; they did occur, but I wasn't really there. It was all happening in the real world. They were by my bedside. The phone calls weren't really phone calls at all but were conversations I overheard.

"We're looking in on the real world, some of us thinking we're really there, able to engage in situations as though we're alive, but sooner or later, we understand that life as we knew it has changed without us. We're here, but we're not really here. Some events are a reflection of what is actually happening in the real world, while other times, it's what we want to see.

"The Fade is the place where lost souls, dead or caught in limbo, roam…waiting, waiting for…" He pauses, the silence heavy.

"So…you *are* a ghost?"

He nods sadly. "I suppose I am."

I gasp, unable to process this. "So…I've fallen in love with a ghost?"

"And I've fallen in love with an anomaly."

It's beyond bizarre to see yourself lifeless while you've never felt more alive. I shiver, understanding why Jude was so reluctant to take me here. If he were to show me this when we first met, I know without a doubt this situation would have turned out so differently. I suddenly understand why he played along with my fire scenario.

"When I thought I was setting that chair on fire, when we first met, you came to my rescue because you knew Henry would come, didn't you? You knew that if I sensed anything was off center, I would start questioning him."

"Yes. You have to understand, it felt like years, not mere weeks before I finally found you. I needed to see how fragile your mind was. You were close to death." He closes his eyes for a moment, pained. "I couldn't let you slip through my fingers again."

I understand why Jude did it. Thinking back to when we first met, I remember how scattered I was. I was lost, wounded from an event which changed my life forever. I felt like I was living in a dream world, and I *was*. The difference is, now I can handle it. I'm stronger.

Looking over at my other self, I ask, "I've died, haven't I?"

He nods. "And you've saved me each and every time?"

"Yes."

I remember Jude's comment when he pulled me from the abyss after I thought I had spoken to Bryan. He said, "Oh, thank god, I thought you were dead." I now know he meant that in the literal sense. "Why did you save me? If you didn't, we could be…"

He hisses an aggrieved breath through his teeth. "No, it won't end that way for you. You need to live. My fate isn't yours."

"Jude…" But he stubbornly clenches his jaw. I leave the matter to rest, not having the energy to fight.

We're both silent, looking over myself. I wonder if I were to jump into my body, would I wake up? Is that how it works? Somehow, I don't think it's that simple.

The heart monitor and breathing apparatus, the machines which are keeping me alive, have me thinking about Jude's comment and how I felt before stepping onto this plane—The Fade. I watch how the pump breathes air into my useless lungs. How the heart rate monitor scrutinizes if my vital signs are stable enough, or if I'm on the way out.

"I'm dying, aren't I?" I felt like time was running out for me, and now I know why. "They want to pull the plug."

Jude doesn't have to reply because I know what his answer will be.

"The longer you stay here…with me…the further away you fade from the world we both know. The stronger our connection, the sicker you become. So you see my dilemma. By saving you in this world, I'm keeping you from the real world where you belong. By defying logic, we're killing you."

"And that's why you didn't bring me here sooner?" I finish for him.

He knows that once this is "over" with, we both lose. Alive or dead.

"Let's get out of here." A staleness infuses the room.

I nod, sadly looking at my other self, knowing that when I return, a decision will be made. We walk through the hallway, both our faces downturned, both plagued with a bottomless brokenness. I suddenly feel hot as the walls start closing in around me.

I need fresh air.

Unable to stomach these hospital walls any longer, I run toward the exit, needing to get outside before I throw up. The door handle doesn't budge, regardless of the fact that I yank at it with all my might. My sweaty palms slip and slide over the brass while tears sting my eyes.

I'm seconds away from losing it, so when Jude pushes the door open for me, I run outside and gulp down three deep breaths of air. It still smells rancid, but better that than me passing out from lack of oxygen, not that that's possible.

Looking around, I see that we're back in the alley where this all started. I have no idea where I am. If I did, I would have hailed a cab and fled a situation which can only amount to trouble. My stomach roils, and I bend at the waist, bracing my hands on my thighs as I steady my breathing and galloping heart.

Jude's heavy footsteps behind me reflect his guilt over bringing me here. Closing my eyes, I take one final calming breath and slowly rise. I'm afraid to face him. He has trusted me with his secrets, and I don't know what to do.

"Here."

Spinning slowly, I see Jude's truck keys in the center of his cupped palm.

"What's that?" I know what they are; I just don't know what he wants me to do with them.

"They're my keys. Drive yourself home, and I'll catch a cab." His snarled hair stands on end, his face mirroring nothing but misery.

"What? Why?"

He turns to the left, appearing like he can't face me. "I'm sure you want to get as far away from me as possible."

I don't reply. This is a shock—a big shock. He's right. I do want to flee and forget this night ever happened.

He reads my thoughts and steps forward, offering me the keys. I lunge for them without a second thought and snatch them from his outstretched hand. He doesn't hide his disappointment as his shoulders drop, and he lowers his chin to his chest.

The sight tears something inside me, but I can't stay here.

After everything I just saw, I need to leave. However, with each step I take, I'm suddenly plagued with a kaleidoscope of emotions. I'm fearful, angry, sad, surprised, hurt, confused, but most of all, I'm torn.

Stopping in the middle of the road, I grasp with both my hands that I'm on the cusp of what's right or wrong. Jude's truck is feet away, and if I were to draw a line down the middle of the hood, this would display the decision I'm faced with.

To the right, I have freedom. I can jump into that truck, start the engine, and drive away, forgetting everything I saw, everything I felt. Or, to the left, I have acceptance—acceptance that fleeing will be the biggest mistake of my life.

Escaping Bridgeport and moving here wasn't running away; it was taking control and refusing to be a slave to regrets. But fleeing now *would* be running away, and it would make my decision to start over be in vain.

There isn't really a choice to be made because fate made it for me.

Without a second thought, I turn to the right, no longer filled with indecision. Once inside, I lean over the middle console and open the driver's door. It's symbolic, as I feel like I'm also opening a door to my heart.

I lounge back in my seat, curling myself into a ball, as I'm suddenly exhausted.

It's minutes before Jude jumps into the truck, and I wordlessly hand him the keys. The engine roars to life, and we drive in dead silence. Twenty minutes in, my eyes begin to droop shut, as I'm too tired to even process everything I've just seen. Tomorrow is a brand-new day—one I plan on seizing.

On the brink of sleep, I'm still alert enough to feel myself being tucked against a soft, manly smelling garment. Remembering the feel of Jude pressed up against me, I know he's cocooned me into his arms.

I know I shouldn't, as my foggy brain is overwhelmed with emotions, but I whisper, "Jude?"

"Yes." His voice is gruff, emotion filled.

Rubbing my cheek against the sweater, I press my nose into the cotton, inhaling deeply. "You asked if it would make a difference once I found out the truth."

The silence is his reply.

And just like that, my uncertainties are no longer. "Well... it doesn't. It should, but it doesn't. It never did."

The silence is almost deafening until I hear a whisper, a *thump...thump...thump.* I gasp, pressing my ear against his chest. "Your heart, it's b-beating again?"

I want to move, to look into his eyes, but his tender words have me wishing we were one body. "My heart beats for you... only you. You breathe life into me, Tori. You always have."

I wish I could say something that expresses how I feel, but all I do is hold on tighter, intent on never letting go.

Seventeen

I'm exhausted, but I know it's all in my head. My body sleeps in a permanent slumber, but my mind defies all logic by even thinking this way.

Jude dropped me home after dropping the bombshell from hell. I cringe, suddenly hating to use that word. I'm not a religious person, but there is no denying some godly happenings are occurring around me.

I've come to realize that I've seen what I want to see. And so do the dead. Some know they're dead, like Jude and Charley, while others, like Henry, Debra, and a laundry list of others, walk around like they're still alive. Whether they just don't want to accept their fate, or it's just too farfetched to fathom, I don't know. All I can think about is Bruce Willis' character in *The Sixth Sense*. He's walking around, doing everyday things like he's still alive, not knowing he's haunting that poor little child.

That boy's dialogue is one I can now relate to because I'm living it. He said he sees dead people walking around like normal people. They see what they want to see. And they don't know they're dead.

I shiver because this is no Hollywood film.

The Fade is another name for limbo. In short, if that's possible, Jude roams Earth because he didn't "step into the light." Jude is a ghost...and I've fallen in love with him.

I need a drink.

Jude is right. I do have to help Henry. He helped me, and one good deed incites another. If it weren't for him and Jude, I would be standing on the end of the denial stick, too.

The question is, where do I start? How do you tell someone they're dead?

"Hey."

Looking up from my—Mrs. Anderson's front porch, I see Charley guiltily standing by the bottom step with Jäg nestled and purring loudly in her arms. Seeing her and Jäg out here in the open, I can't help but think how unfair life is.

"I found—"

I don't allow her to finish. I pounce down the stairs and throw my arms around her breathing frame. Tears leak from my eyes as I whimper. "I'm sorry, Charley." She begins to sob, realizing her ruse is up.

It's still inconceivable how real she feels. How all of this feels. I can feel the breeze on my freshly washed skin, hear the rustle of the newly fallen leaves; I can smell the batter from the pancakes which pop and sizzle, and I can see Charley's tears when she breaks our embrace.

She wipes them away, embarrassed. "So Jude told you?"

"Yes. He showed me. It seems my mind has fabricated situations to deal with my current predicament—being in a coma." It sounds so farfetched, but it's the truth.

Charley's lower lip trembles. "Are you okay?" I shrug. "I'm sorry I didn't tell you. I just—"

But I wave off her apology. "You've got nothing to apologize for. I understand."

She seems relieved. "What happens now?"

Jäg purrs loudly as I scratch under his chin. "I don't know. I know that the people I've spoken to, actually had a two-way conversation with are either dead or in a coma, except Angus. He's special, but I always knew he was." The thought of Angus hurts my heart. I know when I find out his story, I'll be a mess once again. "Jude seems to think I'm here because I have a connection to him and Henry. Maybe we're all connected because of what happened that night. I can't go on living with myself knowing that two men died because of me without helping them."

"Helping them means—"

"I know what it means," I sadly interrupt.

Charley lowers Jäg, who jumps on the small round garden

table, waiting to be fed. Some things never change.

"Jude is right, Tori. We're all here for a reason." When she lowers her eyes, I know what's about to come. "We all want to tie up loose ends before we hopefully end up in the big house in the sky."

"Is that why you're here?"

She meets my gaze, nodding. "I died two years after graduation. A brain aneurysm. Can you believe it? I was on my way to a Christmas party. One minute, I was feeling festive, ready to embrace the holidays with two hands, and then the next…well, the next I was watching my body being wheeled to the morgue."

"Oh, Charley." I cover my mouth, shaking my head. "I'm so sorry. That is awful. I can't even imagine what you went through."

"Thanks." She smiles, but it's somber. "That's why I probably look the same way you remember me. I've been stuck here ever since. For the first few years, I was angry, so angry. I didn't understand why this had to happen to me. My whole life was ahead of me, but now I was doomed to wear this red ball gown forever." She pulls at the tulle.

I sniffle out a laugh, thankful for the comic relief.

She turns serious, her eyes focused in the distance. "Once people accept they're dead and settle old scores, they go to the light. I've seen it. Everything we've read about the afterlife, it's mostly true. If we're lucky enough to be given a second chance, then there's a reason for it."

"What's your reason?" I ask, afraid.

"I saw you come into the hospital. It nearly broke my heart. That's how I knew about you." She pauses before confessing, "I think my reason is…you and Jude."

I gulp down my surprise. "Us?"

She nods, her ponytail bobbing with the momentum. "I was nineteen when I died. I never got to say goodbye. To anyone. Not my mom, my dad, my little brother, or you. I wasn't lying when I said I thought of you. I did. Dying really brings forward your priorities.

"The way I've seen you and Jude interact, knowing what he is and what you are, I think I understand what true love is all about. It's about sacrifice. I think I'm here to learn from that love and let go of regrets. My regrets have tied me to the past, and finally, I think I'm ready to move forward."

I wipe away my tears, my chest jerking in uncontrollable sniffles. "I don't want to say goodbye."

"I don't either," she softly cries. "It's not my time, not yet. But I can feel it. It's coming. Soon."

This is all too much. I slump into the chair. Cradling my head in my palms, I'm overwhelmed with what I should do. Can Jude feel his end, too? I can't even stomach that thought without getting sick.

"Charley, if I stay here, I die. I never see my mother, father, sister…I never breathe again. But if I choose to live, I lose Jude.

I've made this world my home, but I can't help but feel I'm defying the gods by being here. I had to die to find out who I want to be and who I want to be *with*. It just seems so unfair." Charley's warmth sheathes me tightly in comfort.

"My boyfriend and best friend are ghosts, and me, I can see dead people. And animals apparently." Jäg purrs on cue.

I hate to quote a movie, but it's the truth. "It seems I'm not alive, nor am I dead. I'm stuck in a coma where I'm suspended between life and death. My body is physically in that hospital bed, unable to wake, but my spirit has never been more alive. How messed up is that?"

I hate that I'm so feeble, considering I'm one of the lucky ones and still have the option of choosing which path I want to take. Jude, Charley, Henry, and millions of others don't have the luxury of deciding.

A warmth skips through my center, alerting me that only one person is standing feet away. Charley kisses my head, leaving me alone with Jude. It takes me a while before I feel confident enough to face him without bursting into tears.

"Hey." I try my best to smile. "How're you holding up?" My smile suddenly trembles.

I'm trying my hardest to be strong, but seeing him breaks me. I want to give him my life, or at least a part of it so we both can live. But I know it doesn't work that way. Ultimately, I will have to make a decision.

Jude offers me his hand. "Take a walk with me?" He doesn't

have to ask because I'll go anywhere with him. The familiar charge warms my belly when we connect, highlighting how unfair things are.

We walk in silence. There seems to be a lot of silences between us of late. I can't stand it. I need to fill the void.

"So I figured out why my pupils were so well behaved. It appears I've been teaching an imaginary class." I'm trying to lighten the mood, but it only makes me feel worse. Thinking hard, pulling back the layers, I see that I'm standing in an empty classroom. I thought I was teaching a room full of students, but it was all in my head. I saw what I wanted to see.

"Tori, I'm sorry. I know this is hard for you."

He leads me to the dock's edge, pulling me onto his lap when he sits. We look out into the quietness, only wishing this is what our future holds. "What happens now?"

"Only you can decide that." He kisses the side of my neck. "I should have told you from the first moment we met, but I was selfish. I still am."

"You may think you're selfish, but you're selfless. You helped me when I didn't even know I needed help. You saved me, Jude. You've saved me time and time again."

"I'm flattered you think that way, but I can't let this go on." Every hair on my body stands on end. I attempt to turn around, but Jude embraces me tighter. "I can't stand to see you in pain. I'd do anything to take that away, and I think I can."

"No," I cry, attempting to wiggle free. I need to see him,

need to make sure he's still here.

But he continues. "I'm holding your heart hostage, and I'm tearing us into two. I have to let you go. I knew it would come to this, but nothing could prepare me for how empty I feel."

I struggle, thankful when he releases me. Spinning, I brace both shaky palms to his cheeks. "No, you don't get to decide that for me."

"Let me help you."

"Help me how?" I'm almost afraid to ask.

"To wake."

"No!" I violently shake my head in protest. "If I wake up, I never see you again. What kind of a future is that? I may be alive, but without you, it means nothing."

His stormy eyes sink, just like my heart. "I can't watch you do this to yourself. It's tearing me apart." He places a fist over his chest, squeezing tight. "I will try with Henry to get it through his thick skull. I shouldn't expect you to stay. You have a life; you *had* a life before me. Maybe you could try again with Bryan?"

His depraved suggestion has me almost gagging on the thought. Before he can speak another word, I place my finger over his wavering lips. "*I* will make Henry see the truth. I owe him that. As for me getting back together with Bryan..." I scrunch up my nose. "That will not happen in this or any other lifetime. I love *you*, Jude, and yes, our love may not be conventional, but everything happens for a reason. You're my future, my destiny, and we will work this out together."

I sag in relief when he nods. "If this ever gets too hard, or your life is in danger, we end it. Promise me?" I turn away, unable to stomach the thought. "Promise me, Victoria."

His resolve is clear. "I promise," I finally reply.

"Good." Without warning, he fiercely secures my face in his large hands and smashes our lips together.

I'm in the midst of tearing off his T-shirt when he suddenly freezes, a chuckle following soon after. "I hope you're not laughing at my attempts to seduce you," I mumble against his incredible tasting lips.

He bites my mouth, eliciting a guttural moan from deep within. "We have company."

"We have...oh." He doesn't need to explain. My cheeks flush as I quickly straighten my clothes and hair.

Once I'm decent, and Jude's tucked his shirt back into his pants, I gingerly peer over his shoulder to see Angus on the lawn, flying his kite. "How did you...?" I don't bother asking, as Jude seems to be in tune with the world.

I have so many questions regarding Angus, but I don't want to push.

Jude helps me stand, and we make our way over to where he happily plays. When he sees us, his sweet little face lights up. "Hey, buddy." Angus waves and signs quickly to Jude.

We're a few feet away when I pause, a realization dawning on me. We were yards away when Jude addressed Angus, too far away for him to lip read. Our first encounter flashes before me, and I remember how terrified he was. I thought it was because he was getting bullied and because I inadvertently mentioned Rose, but I now know that's not the case at all.

Angus *was* indeed scared because of the bullies, but not because he wasn't brave. It was because those bullies were ghosts—ghosts he could *hear*. "He's not deaf, is he?" I ask, almost in a state of tears.

"No, he's not." I don't press any further because Angus waves me over, gesturing I'm to take over as kite captain.

"Hey, little wombat," I sign, not wanting anything between us to change.

His dimpled grin melts my heart. "I missed you," he signs, passing me the spool.

"I missed you, too." I remember all the tips Angus taught me, full of pride when the kite takes to the wind. Jude cuddles his son tightly, kissing the top of his head, reveling in his fragrance as they both watch me.

As they chat amongst themselves about everyday father and son stuff, I think over everything that didn't make a lick of sense. But now, I understand it all. The night we went to the movies, Jude could see the connection Angus and I shared, especially when he asked me to be his date for the dance. We were getting too close, which would have been fine if our circumstances were different. The entire town already thinks Angus is a freak, so I can only imagine the city being rife with rumors if he turned up to the dance with an imaginary date on his arm.

From Angus's lack of speech, I think it's safe to assume he was born this way. I knew he was special, but this just confirms it. It seems both Angus and I can see dead people.

Angus laughs, drawing my attention to the limp butterfly dragging along the grass. Looks like I better leave it to the pros. "Can I play with Jäg?" he asks Jude, who nods. He runs off happily, none the wiser that I'm seconds away from scooping him up into my arms and never letting go.

Jude walks over to me, scratching his heavy scruff. He appears nervous, apprehensive to how I might react to the bombshell he just dropped. Even though Angus may not be theoretically deaf, hearing spirits daily is enough of a reason to switch off. I have no doubt he can still hear them, but signing might deter them from talking so much. He hides beneath this ruse. Maybe he's hoping if he can mute them, if he shuts them out, that eventually, they'll go away.

"Are you all right? Jesus, I seem to be asking you that a lot lately." Jude runs a hand through his hair, leaving a mohawk in its wake.

I rub my arms, suddenly feeling a chill. "I'm okay. I just… wow."

"I know. I'm sorry I didn't tell you. I just…there was just so much going on, and I didn't want to add to the shit pile."

I step into his open arms. "How long has this been going on?"

"Since he was born. It was evident by age three his imaginary friends weren't so imaginary."

"*What*?" My heart sinks even further.

"I always knew he was special, but Rose, she refused to accept it. She didn't want to deal with special. Neither did Henry, which is ironic, considering his current predicament." He sighs. "Rose took him to see doctors, but it was all done in secret. She didn't want her name attached to the stigma of a boy who was different. The doctors confirmed he wasn't deaf. They said to give him time, as his behavioral issues could be linked to autism or other learning disabilities. But as time went on, it was obvious something wasn't right. Rose would try to force him to speak, but that only made him retreat further into his shell." His lip curls in disgust. "I didn't know what was wrong, but I did know he was special. I tried to talk to him, but how do I try to explain something I don't fully understand? How do I explain to him that he can see and hear dead people?

"He's always been a strong boy, but Rose ignored it, pretended it wasn't there. I didn't know where to send him because he wasn't a lab rat, and I wouldn't allow doctors to treat him that way. He was ostracized enough. The only thing I could do was respect his decision to switch off and send him to a school that would cater to his needs. They taught him sign language, and for the first time in my life, I finally saw my son happy. The teachers were wonderful. They made an exception because of who Angus was." He sighs. "But I was stupid. I should have taken him away years ago. I regret my decision to stay every single day. Rose didn't understand. I told her what I believed was happening and why he chose to be the way he was. But she refused to believe it, ignoring his wishes, and in turn, she just disregarded the issue at hand. She treated him like an idiot, but he's the smartest person I know."

His lament is clear, but I suppose he did what he thought was right.

"I know you've been wondering why Rose left. Well, it was because she was sick of special. Just like the rest of this small-minded town, she thought Angus was a freak."

I feel ill inside.

I suppose it shouldn't surprise me, considering the person Rose has been painted to be, but still, that is just so cruel. It's also cowardly. "She doesn't deserve him. I'd give anything to have a child as remarkable as Angus. She sees his gift as a curse, but I see it as him being chosen, acknowledged as someone who is special."

"I don't think I could possibly love you more than I do right now."

It feels nice to be loved. Even when engaged to Bryan, I never felt this kind of connection. But I guess Jude and I share something pretty incredible.

"Do you think his specialness is due to the accident?" Debra mentioned Rose running off the road the night Angus was born. It might explain why he has this extraordinary gift.

Jude exhales, the memory still raw. "I don't know, but I guess it could be the reason. What I do know is that regardless of his limitations, nothing will stop that boy. He'll make me proud. My side of the family certainly doesn't have any psychic abilities," he adds as an afterthought. I pull back and arch a brow. He smirks, the sight setting my body alight.

Turning serious, I ask a question which has been playing on my mind. "Why didn't you leave after Rose left?"

"Because this is Angus's home. He likes his school, and for the most part, people, living and otherwise, leave him alone. Can you imagine moving someplace like New York? LA? Angus wouldn't last five minutes."

He's right.

"Does Angus know…what we are?"

Jude blows out a hollow breath. "What you are is exceptional." He kisses the top of my head. "But I think so…I just haven't been able to tell him. Each time I do, I think about what I—" He takes another breath. "What I ultimately have to do." He means saying goodbye. "I'm just not ready to take that final step."

We stand huddled together, enjoying something that feels beyond words. Just as I'm about to fall asleep standing up, Angus runs over, signing faster than a freight train.

Jude lets go, looking at me with concern because he knows what my reply will be. "That sounds great, Angus. Tell Grandpa we'd love to have dinner tonight." Angus runs off, fist pumping his delight.

When he's out of earshot, Jude clucks his tongue. "Are you sure about this?"

"Yes," I reply firmly. "He deserves to know. What he decides to do with the information is entirely up to him. We can lead a horse to water…"

"When did you get so smart?" he teases with a lopsided smirk.

"Right around the time you told me you loved me," I reply, never missing a beat.

At 6:59 p.m., Angus, Jude, and I stand at Henry's front door. I get a terrible sense of déjà vu.

Tonight can go one of two ways—bloody brilliant or a bloody mess. I'm really hoping it's not the latter.

The door opens, interrupting my thoughts. Henry stands before it, stunned to see both Jude and me. We make no secret that we're crashing dinner. Just as Henry's lips shape into a deeper scowl, I cheerfully step forward and give him a loose hug. "Thanks for inviting us."

"You were not—"

"Whatever's cooking, it smells simply delicious. I'm starved." I push past him, hoping he and Jude don't fight before we step through the door.

The home looks exactly how I remember it, down to the smell of roast lamb. Jude's comment about Jillian losing her mind has me wondering just how bad she is. The fact Henry acts like he would if he were alive makes me think he's slowly driving Jillian over the edge. He's haunting his own home, and as a result, he's haunting his wife. Poor Jillian.

"Where's Jillian?" I ask, subtly peering around the room.

"She's upstairs getting changed." He tugs at the collar of his crisp shirt.

Angus switches on the TV in the living room, making himself at home, while it's anything but homey in here as Jude and Henry glare at each other something fierce. "Why are you here?"

"Because we need to talk." Jude folds his arms across his chest, not at all impressed.

Henry scoffs. "Unless you have something I want to hear, then you're wasting my time."

Great. Let the mediation commence. "Henry, I'd really like some wine." I'm being awfully bossy and rude, but it's the only thing I can think of to stop them from fighting.

He clenches his jaw, but nods, leading us into the kitchen silently.

When we march into the kitchen, Jude stands while I take a seat at the breakfast bar. As Henry is pouring us each a glass of wine, my gaze floats to the refrigerator and the invite which sits on the silver door. I know without a doubt Jude and I will need all the ammo we can arm ourselves with to convince Henry that things are not what they seem.

"The ball is tomorrow?" I gesture with my chin to the invitation.

Henry nods, but something in his demeanor tells me he's not as excited as he should be to attend. "Yes, but I'm not sure if I will attend. Jillian hasn't been feeling well."

"Oh, that's awful. I'm so sorry to hear that. What's wrong?"

He takes a sip of wine before passing me my glass. "She has been complaining of migraines, and she's unable to sleep. The doctor said she's suffering from insomnia. She hasn't been herself since Rose left." He doesn't keep the contempt from his tone as he glares at Jude.

I hold my breath, waiting for an explosion, but thankfully, there isn't one…well, for now, anyway.

When Henry's gaze turns soft, I know what's about to occur. "There she is…my love."

Jillian staggers into the kitchen, looking like a ghost of her former self. While she once emitted radiance, she now looks lost, clouded. She's wearing the same cream dress I saw her in nights ago, but her long snarled hair hangs scrappily around her drawn face.

Jillian announces in a robotic tone, "I hope you like lamb. It's Henry's favorite." Once upon a time, I thought she was talking to me, but now I can see she's talking to no one. She's talking to herself. She's acting out an event which once took place when Henry was alive.

Surely, Henry can see her wasting away before his eyes. If she continues this way, she'll be joining him very soon. I try my best to smile, but I just want to cry.

Henry leads us into the dining room, his lips pulled in tight. I dart for the chair next to Jude's because I'm not interested in playing Rose for the night. Henry clenches his jaw. He's obviously not too happy I've strayed from his plans.

Jillian enters a moment later, the front of her cream dress coated in a brown liquid where she obviously spilled the gravy. She hobbles over to the table, setting the food down with shaky hands. She takes her place, looking lovingly and reminiscently over to Henry. He mistakes the gesture as her doting on him, rather than see what's really going on.

Closing my eyes, I focus just how I did when I saw that world through Jude's eyes. The room transforms from light to dark, showcasing what's actually happening underneath the fictitious layer we see. There is rotten meat, decaying vegetables, and mountains of dinnerware scattered across the tabletop. The tablecloth is blemished with stains that have been there for months. A vase of wilted wildflowers lays knocked over in the center of the table, the same flowers I saw when dining here before. I wonder how long she's been living this way. The military precision I once remarked on now looks like a wasteland of broken dreams. I suppress a scream when a cockroach scurries across the table.

Jillian sits staring vacantly at Henry's chair. A memory must cross her mind because she smiles. She may be alive, but she may as well be lost in our world because her will to live is long gone. I want to reach out and comfort her, but I don't.

Jude's reassurance in the way of a gentle touch against my thigh has everything returning to an alternative reality—Henry's reality. Dark becomes light once more. I discreetly wipe my eyes.

Jillian recites the same prayer I heard weeks ago while I shake my head. This is getting almost unbearable.

"The dead see what they want to see, and right now, Henry's feelings are influencing what we see," Jude whispers, evidently able to read my anguish. "He's distorting reality."

"Is it always this way?"

He doesn't reply for the longest of moments. But when he does, I understand why the pause. "Sometimes."

Henry ignores Jude and me and begins talking to Jillian about his day. He speaks to her as he would if he actually did the things he claimed he did. Jillian sits and stares, her hands crossed in her lap. Henry reads her docility as interest while I break through the façade and see her true form. She's broken and vacant. Nothing is going in. Nothing is coming out.

"How long has she been this way?"

"Since Rose, but it got worse once Henry…" He leaves the sentence unfinished. "She sits here, talking to herself every night. She is acting out a normal family dinner as if Henry were alive. She lives in this decay, stuck in a loop, while Henry sees it as anything but that."

"We have to help her. He's *haunting* her."

Jude nods. "To help her, we have to help him." He doesn't hide his struggle.

Henry slows down his chewing, the room suddenly dropping to a sub-zero climate. "Something wrong with your lamb?" He points at Jude's dinner with his knife.

Jude pushes his plate out in front of him, leaning casually back in his chair. "No, I love lamb. But you must be sick of it, seeing as it's all you've eaten for the past nine months."

I close my eyes and rub the bridge of my nose.

Henry sits tall. "And what's that supposed to mean?"

Jude glares at him like he's an imbecile. "Oh, c'mon. You don't think things have been a little weird around here? Maybe even a little *Groundhog Day*-ish?"

Henry huffs. "The only weird thing around here is you bringing your *date* to my home. Have you no respect? Look how you've upset Jillian." On cue, Jillian sobs, covering her face with her hands.

"I'm not the one who's upset Jillian. You have." He folds his arms defiantly.

"I beg your pardon!" Henry stands, kicking back his seat. "I will not allow you to speak this way to me in my own home. Leave."

"I'm not going anywhere," Jude states firmly. "I may have

had to put up with your shit when Rose was around, but now that she's not, I have no qualms about telling you what an asshole you are!"

I cover my mouth as I peer up at the ceiling, conceding defeat.

Henry stabs a finger into his chest. "I'm an asshole? How dare you? You're the one who drove Rose away!"

Henry's comment was intent on wounding Jude, but all I see in Jude's bearing is annoyance. "Wake up, Henry! Rose left because she's a self-centered bitch. She doesn't care about anyone but herself."

"That's not true."

"Yes, it is true. You're so damn blind. She left us behind because she couldn't care less whether we live or die." I taste his pain.

Henry refuses to believe that. "She may not care about you, but—"

"But what? She loves you? Jillian? Have you seen what she's done to Jillian?" Jude points at Jillian, who is still weeping.

"We're her family." The fire behind Henry's arguments is slowing burning out.

"She has a new family now," Jude reveals. "One that includes a grandchild you've never met!" He stands, thumping his fist onto the table. My heart hurts, remembering his pain when he found out the truth while Henry looks as though he's about to be sick.

"What are you talking about? How do you know that?"

Jude realizes he's said too much. "Nothing. Forget I said anything."

But Henry's not about to forget. The corded veins in his neck pop. "You son of a bitch. You know where she is, don't you?"

Jude raises his eyes to the ceiling, fed up with this pointless conversation. "No, I don't. If only you'd open your eyes and see"— he sweeps a hand around the room—"then you'd understand what your epic asshole behavior is doing to everyone."

"Oh, my eyes are open." He glares at me like I'm public enemy number one. "Get out of here, the both of you. Leave my grandson. He deserves to live a normal life, not with an adulterous father and a home wrecking whore."

"*Excuse me.*" I snap my head his way. I've kept my mouth shut, but he's just crossed a line.

Just as I'm about to set him straight, Jude clenches his fist, his nostrils flared. "Don't you *ever* call her that. Try it again, and I won't be so understanding of your predicament."

Henry curls his lip. "What predicament? My life was perfect until you walked into it."

"You are such a narrow-minded fool. Look around you. Things are not what they seem."

"Jude." I stand, shaking my head. This is not the way. I know he's upset, and Henry doesn't deserve our compassion, but this is not the way to tell him.

However, as expected, Jude doesn't listen, and storms over to where Jillian sits still, almost corpse-like. A sniffle wracks her tiny body every so often. "Hello, Jillian! Can you hear me?" He waves a hand in front of her face while she doesn't bat an eyelash.

"Jillian!" he shouts louder this time, now waving both hands in a wide circle inches from her face. "I'm sorry your husband is such a jackass."

I rub my brow.

"Get out!" Henry roars, storming over to Jude.

But Henry's threat doesn't deter Jude in the slightest. "Jillian, wake up!" he bellows into her ear. She remains stone-faced and entranced.

Henry tugs on Jude's forearm, spinning him around to face him. His flaring nostrils, twitchy eye, and heavy breathing all expose he's seconds away from punching Jude in the face.

I squeak, unbelieving how that went from naught to one hundred in a second. "Stop it!" I urge, but I may as well not be here.

"I should shut that smart mouth of yours for good," Henry threatens, glaring, his lip coiled.

"Go on then, hit me," Jude mocks, stepping forward, not intimidated in the slightest.

Henry growls, and it appears he's about to take Jude up on his offer. He's in good shape, but Jude's towering frame overshadows the sheriff. "I won't feel it," Jude taunts. Henry misinterprets Jude's comment as Jude calling him weak.

Pandemonium erupts. I shout for Henry to stop when he dives forward to strike Jude while Jude stands proud, challenging him to give it his best shot. The only voice of reason is when Jillian sobs. "I miss you so much. None of this makes any sense."

Henry freezes, pain etching at his face. "Jillian?" He no doubt has heard her say these words before. Hearing them again, I now understand what she means.

"Look at her!" Jude shouts, pointing at Jillian. "She's broken. No matter how much of an asshole you are, I know you're not stupid! Deep down, you know something isn't right. Let us show you why." Jude exhales, pulling at his hair with both hands.

I watch with bated breath. Just when I think he's going to throw us out, he remarkably nods. "Fine. But I'll meet you there."

Jude shrugs, uncaring. "Have it your way. Meet us at Saint Mary's Hospital. Room 201."

I'm expecting to see shock, confusion, or horror swarming around Henry, but all I see is dread.

Eighteen

I'm quiet on the drive, but my silence reveals there is anything but stillness crawling around my mind.

No matter how hard I try, I can't get Jillian's lost, vacant look out of my head. She's a shell, a husk of who she used to be. I can't help but wonder if looking at Jillian is like looking into the future. Is that what I have to look forward to? Living in the past and finding comfort in my memories. I blink back my tears as I stare out the window, not wanting Jude to read my sadness.

We park the car, then walk into the hospital in silence. Thoughts continue to plague me. I wonder if we have to drive. I marvel at a lot of things. I eat, although I can't really taste. I sleep, although I don't need the rest. A sense of sadness overwhelms me.

"Jude." It's the first word spoken in what seems like forever.

"Yes."

"Do we have to drive? Or sleep? Or bathe? I mean, no one can see us." As if on cue, a nurse marching down the hallway walks through…yes, through me. I yelp. I didn't feel a thing, but still, it just cemented my point.

Jude sighs. He suddenly looks so tired. "I live how I would if I were alive. I don't *have* to drive, or eat, or shower, but I do. It's the only way I can stay here and stay sane."

I can see how difficult this is to talk about, so I let it rest. But his theory seems understandable. But it also drives home the point that we're both testing fate. Jude slides his hand into mine, an instinctive action which reinforces the fact that he's now a part of me.

Suddenly, the closer we get to my room, the more trapped I feel. Will my coma self remember Jude if I choose to wake, or will all of this feel like a dream? My chest squeezes, unable to accept a reality so bleak.

Focusing on why we're here, I pull back my shoulders and try my best to stay strong. Henry is leaning against the wall, looking more than unimpressed that we dragged him here. "You have two minutes."

Jude snickers, shoving past him. "I only need one." He never lets go of my hand as he slowly opens the door to my room. He peers down at me, ensuring I'm all right. I nod even though my legs are trembling.

Henry waits for a second before he pushes off the wall and

marches into the room confidently. I watch as he turns solid, his entire body seizing up. We can all see the grisly sight before us of me lying deathly still in the single bed. My dark hair contrasts the stark white of the pillow, my sealed eyes contradicting what I'm currently seeing. The machines are humming, keeping me breathing for another day.

I will never grow comfortable seeing myself this way. The old me versus the new me. Which person do I prefer?

"What the hell?" Henry gasps, shaking his head.

Jude doesn't sugarcoat the truth. "Henry, this is Victoria. She's been in a coma for nine months. If it wasn't for you, she'd be dead."

"If it wasn't for the both of you," I correct, squeezing his hand.

"This is not possible."

"Yes, it's very possible," Jude amends.

I don't know what Henry's reaction is, but I know it's probably not good. "Henry..." Stepping out from Jude's cocoon, I walk toward Henry and stand by his side. The closer I get to myself, the sicker I feel. Ignoring the nausea, I continue. "Jude is right. Nine months ago, I got"—I take a centering breath— "shot. I would have died if it weren't for Jude and you. Jude came to my rescue, sacrificing his life for mine. And you called it in."

"I what?" Risking a glance, I see that his mouth is jarred open, his eyes riveted to the bed.

"I know this doesn't make any sense, but please believe me

when I tell you, you and Jude, you're both—" But I can't. The words get strangled in my throat as I gag on them.

"We're dead, Henry," Jude concludes, using the word I still can't accept. "You must have felt something wasn't right for a long time now. People ignoring you? One day blending into the next? Waking up not remembering what happened the day before? Feeling more alone than you've ever felt in your entire life?"

I lower my eyes, saddened that Jude is retelling this story from personal experience.

"The reason is because you're not really here anymore. Neither of us are. We're ghosts. No surprise it seems you hate me as much in this world as you did in the previous."

If Henry weren't already dead, I'd be afraid he was seconds away from having a heart attack. He knows what Jude is saying is true, but he doesn't want to accept it. How can anyone accept something so farfetched?

He finally tears his eyes from my sleeping form, looking at me as though he's seen a ghost. "Is what he says true?" It appears Jude was right all along.

"Yes. I'm so sorry, but yes. I know it's a lot to—"

He doesn't let me finish, though, and storms toward me with his fists clenched by his side. "He put you up to this, didn't he?"

"*What*? N-No." I fumble over my words, his hostility out of left field.

"Bullshit! You're both trying to trick me."

"Trick you how?" Jude's voice no longer holds contempt or anger. He simply sounds defeated.

"I-I don't know, but I don't believe a word that comes from either of your mouths."

"Henry." I try to comfort him, but he recoils so quickly, he almost falls backward onto the bed.

"Don't come anywhere near me. Either of you."

I don't know what else to say, so I raise my hands in surrender, indicating he's free to leave.

He takes the offer and runs from the room, his feet slipping on the linoleum as he disappears down the hallway. Looking at Jude, I sigh. "Sorry." I was foolish to think Henry would believe me.

"It was never going to be easy. But we've planted the seed."

"So what happens now?" I ask, slowly turning around to face him.

With a slow swagger, he makes his way over to me. Swathing a hand around my waist, he draws me to his broad chest. "We watch it grow."

"And what if—"

I don't get to finish because I'm silenced when he plants his finger against my mouth. "Life is too short not to eat the cake."

A ghost of a smile touches my lips. "What does that mean?"

"It means he'll come around."

"When did you get so smart?" I whisper around his finger.

Flicking my bottom lip, he replies, "Right around the time you told me you loved me." It's exactly what I need to hear. Just as he lowers his delicious mouth to mine, the door opens, and I wheeze in horror.

Bryan looks just as he did the last day I saw him. However, when he looks over at the bed, I no longer see the love I once saw. The door locks with a gentle click, but it suddenly feels amplified in the small room.

He stands silent, hands dug deep in his pockets. "Hi, Tori. I'd ask how you are, but I know you're not going to answer." He ambles to the foot of the bed, looking down at me miserably. "I don't know what to do, baby. You were the smart one in our relationship, and if you were here now, you'd tell me what to do. Sometimes, I feel you, like right now—" He touches my leg through the blanket, but I don't feel a thing. "But most of the time, I don't.

"The strange thing is, wherever you choose to go, I know that place makes you happy. So maybe I'm being selfish by keeping you here. Maybe your parents are right, and I have to let you go. I at least have to give you the option to choose. If I do that and you come back to me, then I know it was your choice. If you don't"—he shrugs with a sigh—"then at least I know you were given the choice to choose.

"Being hooked up, we're taking away your free will. And I couldn't bear it if we were keeping you here and you didn't want to stay."

Tears spill down my cheeks. I don't bother wiping them away because I know more will take their place.

"So I'm here to tell you that…I'm letting you go. You always loved Sunday morning sunrises. You said there was magic in the air—that we survived another week, and you looked forward to living another seven days with me. So I think it's fitting that this Sunday is your day.

"It's all up to you now, Victoria. Know that whatever decision you make, I'll respect it. I don't deserve you after everything I've done. I don't blame you for staying hidden away. But know that Matilda and I miss you. So much. The future is in your hands now." He wipes away his tears with the back of his wrist before kissing me on the cheek.

I gasp. His kiss lingers. I can feel his whiskers; smell his cologne. How is that possible? He walks past where I'm standing and stops. He looks directly at me, lost in thought. I know he can't see me, but can he feel me? He shakes his head as if to dispel any thoughts and leaves a second later.

I don't bother moving as actions escape me right now. My gaze flutters to Jude. He's slouched against the far wall with his boot braced behind him. His shoulders are drooped, and his head is lowered, his gaze affixed to an invisible spot on the floor.

I know what he's thinking. I know what he's going to say.

"Take me home?" I whisper, afraid he'll say no. He nods with a stiff upper lip, not meeting my eyes.

We walk to the truck in a deadly silence. I don't bother

looking where I'm going. I've accepted that I'm transparent matter in this world, but I'm very much alive in another. He opens the door for me, still refusing to look me in the eye.

"Jude?" I beg, but he turns his cheek when I attempt to console him. I jump in, feeling deflated and hollow. The engine roars to life after he slams his door shut. The harsh sounds mimic his enmity. I can't stand this emptiness between us, but I need to give him time.

He wants me to go back. He doesn't need to say it. Bryan affirmed what we both knew to be true. Time is running out for me. I need to choose, and I need to choose now. But how can I? Either way, I lose. Tears sting my eyes, but I discreetly wipe them away with my sleeve.

The fleeting landscape of towering trees, lush greenery, and picturesque, rolling hills flashes before me, and I wonder if what I'm seeing is really there. Jude did say the dead see what they want to see. Am I just like Henry, fabricating what I want to see? Feel? Touch? A whimper escapes me, betraying my fears.

Without so much as a warning, I brusquely bounce into the passenger door as Jude takes a sharp turn and speeds down a dark gravel road. I hold the door handle, my body jarring from the force. Jude doesn't slow down. His knuckles are white from gripping the wheel so firmly. He's wound up so tight, I'm afraid to see what happens when he's ready to let go.

The tires skid over the dirt as he pulls to a jarring stop, killing the engine, before jumping from the truck. He doesn't bother closing the door. The headlights capture his transition from man to caged beast when he paces feverishly, hands interlaced behind his neck. He tilts his head, eyes raised to the heavens as his chest rises and falls.

I'm afraid as I unbuckle my seat belt and step from the truck. The trees rustle and sway as the wind blows around us with a punishing force. "Jude?" My voice is small, fearful.

He freezes, buried under a blanket of pain. "We have to end this, Victoria. I won't be the cause of your death."

"But you'll allow me to be the cause of yours?" I bite back, squashing down my sorrow.

He places a hand over his heart. "It's too late for me, but it's not for you. You've got your whole life ahead of you. Live for me. Live the life I couldn't live." He charges over to me, the force pushing me two feet back. "Knowing my death gave you life is enough. I think I can…leave now."

"Leave?" My lower lip begins to tremble. A June beetle sounds in the distance, the echo hollow, just like my heart.

He looks solemn as he confesses, "Yes, I was never supposed to stay here. I'm on borrowed time, and I have a feeling my number is almost up."

Charley's words ring loudly in my ears. "No!" I cry. "You can't go."

"I have to. It's the only way."

His determination drives me forward. "Why can't we just wait and see what happens when Sunday comes? Why do we have to choose?"

His heartfelt reply brings tears to my eyes. "Because you don't belong here. You never did. That's the way things are supposed to be. You're alive for a reason, Tori. You're destined for great things. I can feel it. And you can be rest assured that I'll be watching you every step of the way."

His comment drives home how elaborate our situation really is. "I don't know what's real and what's not anymore. Without you, everything I've experienced won't feel real."

He steps forward, his wild fragrance engulfs me. "I'm real. What we had was real. No matter what universe we're in…I'll never forget it."

"But what if I do?" I whisper, my fears catching on the wind.

"Remember now." His touch is warm against my cheek, affirming his words.

Leaning into his palm, I candidly confess, "I have one foot in each world, but my tie to reality is fading each day. My north is you, Jude, and I know it's only a matter of time before I slip and land in your world for good."

He pulls his hand away with a hiss. "No, I won't allow it. I can't stand by and watch you die."

"It's not your choice to make."

"How can I live with myself knowing the sacrifice you made? No." He stubbornly shakes his head.

"We don't even know what will happen. I may not be able to go back." He turns somber at the prospect. "My heart belongs here with you. It's useless in a body that can't feel. Can't love."

He closes his eyes for a moment before opening them and revealing his torture. "Don't say that. I want you to live. Do everything you've wanted to do. Go back to Australia. Or back to Bridgeport. Find l—" He stops, exhaling painfully before continuing. "Love. Have lots of babies. I can't give you that," he reveals with an inconsolable frown.

"Jude." I step forward, careful to give him his space. "This has to be real, the life I'm destined to live because I've never hurt so badly before. This pain eating away at me"—I tug at the front of my sweater—"is unlike anything I've ever felt. It hurts. Leaving *you* hurts. That shows me I'm alive."

"No, Victoria. Don't make this harder than it already is. Please." He turns his back, digging his hands into his pockets.

A thought suddenly occurs to me. One that hasn't before. "Is the thought of being with me for eternity that awful?"

"What?" Disbelief engulfs him as he spins around.

I raise my shoulders limply. "Maybe you're having second thoughts. About us. I know I'm stubborn, relentless, and headstrong. Maybe I'm not the person you want to spend forever with." I wipe away a tear. This belief makes me feel sick. "If that's the case, then…"

He doesn't let me finish. He reaches me in two huge strides, the anger humming out of his taut frame. His ferocity takes my breath away. It invades every pore in my body, and an ache builds within.

"Don't you ever say that!" he exclaims, silencing the distance between us. "Do you think this is easy for me? Do you think I want to say goodbye? The thought of another man loving you, touching you"—he thrusts his left hand into my hair and tugs firmly—"is unbearable to me. I wanted to rip off Bryan's arms and beat him to death with them." A low growl erupts from his chest. "The thought of another man inside you"—he tightens his hold, fisting my locks—"drives me insane. I have an uncontrollable urge to hurt anyone who touches you. So don't you dare say I don't want to spend forever with you because forever is not long enough.

"I want to consume you just as you've consumed every… single…part of me." A bottomless black overcomes his irises. "Everything I am, I give to you. Mind. Body. Soul. You own every part of me. That'll never change. Regardless of our circumstances, I'll love you for eternity."

It's a pledge, an ode that whatever happens, we will fight until the end. It's all I need to hear to cement my decision. I know which path I've chosen, but honestly, there was never a choice to be made.

But all vows are put on hold because the moment Jude slams his lips over mine, nothing else matters but becoming one. This kiss is fueled with desperation, longing, and need. We both know this may be the last night we share together, on whatever dimension we're in. That certainty is no better incentive than to make this union eternal.

I paw at him, needing him imprinted onto every part of my body. We're pressed together from chest to thigh, but the contact isn't close enough. He lifts me as though I weigh nothing at all and slams my ass onto the hood. I open my legs, and he settles between them before latching onto my waist and sliding me down. We're now the same height, and he devours my mouth like the strong man that he is, fisting the back of my hair, controlling the kiss, controlling me.

Our mouths move in a frenzied rhythm, unable to keep up with the need to consume the other whole. His tongue tangos with mine, stoking a small fire in my belly and below. His hands hungrily wrap around me, cocooning me into the warm cavern of his body. I've never felt safer.

His passion takes my breath away, our kisses getting hotter, and messier, and needier. My body spoons around his perfectly, shaping the angle of our union idyllically. I brazenly rub against him, whimpering when I feel an impressive bulge nudge at my entrance. Memories of how good he felt have me boldly and hastily unbuckling his belt and almost ripping his zipper clean off as I need to feel flesh.

I don't wait for permission and thrust my hand inside his jeans. We both groan when I palm his hot erection, the contact sending us both wild. With our lips still locked, I begin stroking him, savoring every hard inch of him. His size is mouth-wateringly large, evoking a dampness to pool between my thighs.

He sucks my tongue before heatedly breaking our connection. I don't have time to question him because, within seconds, he's ripping at my sweater, my white cotton T-shirt following in quick succession as both garments are tossed to the ground.

I'm sitting on the hood in my black bra, blue jeans, and Chucks, the headlights our only lighting, but they set a dreamy, clandestine mood. Jude takes a step back, admiring me with a look of feral possession. He scans my body, and his gaze lingers on my breasts. As he ascends lower, he does a double take when he sees my tattoo.

"I like your ink." His voice is heavy with emotion as he undoubtedly knows his tattoo was the inspiration behind mine.

"I like yours, too." My gaze drops to his clothed flank. "Although I think you're imperfectly perfect."

"Well"—he licks his upper lip—"you're just perfect." He emphasizes his comment by growling when his stare lands at the junction between my thighs.

I can't stand the separation any longer, so I reach forward and drag him toward me by the collar of his shirt. Our lips are like a moth to a flame, and we reconnect, kissing fervently, intent on ravaging the other whole.

Tiny goose bumps prick my skin when he skims his hand down the length of my neck, over my shoulder, and down my side. He rubs two fingers over my tattoo, before unsnapping the button on my jeans. My heart skips a beat when he goes in for the kill and rubs over my ripe center. I scream into his mouth, the sensation shooting a current all the way to my toes.

He continues his exploration, but we both want more, and more is what I get when he inserts two fingers inside me. I buck into him with eyes squeezed shut, groaning when he lowers his head and kisses the tops of my breasts while never missing a beat below. I bow backward, not afraid of toppling over as Jude has a firm hold around my waist. He's in total control, and I love it.

While he's working my body to a delirious pulp, I can feel my climax speeding closer and closer to the edge. But this time, I want the pleasure thrumming through both our bodies. He's somehow managed to push one bra cup down, allowing him full access to my pebbled nipple. He's suckling and lapping, his tongue a rod of pure pleasure. I'm moments away from exploding, but with what little sense I have left, I grip the lapels of his shirt and rip them open with a force so great, the buttons pop off and scatter along the ground. His chest feels divine under my hungry fingers, but I want the whole hog. He helps me tear off what's left of the offending garment, so we're now equally clothed.

With our lips still locked, I reach around and unhook my bra, not caring where it lands as I toss it over my shoulder. I slide down the hood, pressing our chests together, feeling our hearts beat as one. Needing more, so much more, I tug at the waistband of his pants, indicating I want them off—I want this last piece to be stripped away for good.

It's a blur of hands, lips, tongues as we undress each other with a desperate need to be bare. When we're unclothed, I attempt to dive for Jude's well kissed lips, but he stops me. Not understanding what he's doing, I'm about to protest, but go willingly when he picks me up and walks me to the back of the truck.

He begins kissing me, this time with a slow, sluggish speed. I cross my legs around his lower back, holding on tight because I never intend to let go. His length presses against me, sending my heartbeat into an unhealthy staccato because I know in minutes it'll be buried deep inside me.

He climbs into the back of the truck and lays us down, using a blanket to cushion us. I settle back, his weight feeling impossibly perfect as he sinks into me. Our kiss is heavy with desire, both starved for one another, needing this final union to seal our fates forever.

With our lips still locked, he slips a hand between us, testing to see I'm ready for him. He hisses when he feels how eager I really am. He rubs his thumb over my budding center, teasing me this one last time. My eyes roll into the back of my head.

Opening my legs wider, he positions himself, groaning when we touch. I'm desperate to feel him inside me, so I arch my hips in a silent invitation, a plea. Just as he inches into me, he freezes, a tremor passing through his body. My eyes snap open because I don't understand why he's stopped.

"Jude?" I whisper, stroking my hand down his whiskered cheek and over his neck, toying with his pendant. "What's the matter?"

The moonlight exposes his heaviness. "I'm afraid I won't be able to let you go when the time comes."

His confession is nothing short of heartbreaking. "Then don't. I belong to you. Now and always."

He clenches his eyes, a look of unadulterated happiness passing over him. "Now and always," he repeats before closing the agonizing distance between us and making us one.

I cry out, unacquainted with such a delectable intrusion, and Jude stills, allowing my inexperienced muscles to bear his girth and size. It doesn't take long, and I raise my hips, needing to feel more of him.

He complies and works his way inside me, each stroke sending my body into sensory overload. When I'm filled full, he pauses while I hold my breath, basking in this sensation of absolute pleasure. He bends down and lays a kiss over my racing pulse, before moving inside me with a measured, long stroke. It feels unlike anything I've ever felt before.

He continues moving unhurriedly as if savoring this dreamlike connection between us. His length brings tears to my eyes, filling me to the brim each time he hits my core with exact precision. I can feel he's holding back—most likely afraid he'll hurt me—but I want all the shackles around us to be broken; I want to lose myself in him completely and perpetually.

With that thought in mind, I buck my hips and loop a leg around his waist, drawing him deeper. We both moan. He stares into my eyes as he drives into me fiercely, letting go of reservations and claiming me as his. The speed of his thrusts is almost punishing, but I like it. I take everything he gives and match his intensity as I meet him stroke for stroke.

"You feel incredible," he groans, cupping my heavy breast as he thumbs over my nipple. "Am I hurting you?" I'm unable to vocalize anything but moans and grunts, so I shake my head. "Nothing has ever felt more real," he hums, relishing in our connection.

His shaft is hot and swollen as he pushes into me, rocking with a speed that has me gasping for breath. I wrap my arms around his broad shoulders, his flesh sticky and warm; he's never felt more alive. My orgasm is skimming so close to the surface, I have to rein it back in because I want to take pleasure in this feeling as long as I can. Jude lowers his lips and kisses me passionately, his tongue in sync with his movement below. He lowers his chin, growling when he sees our connection. The sight invokes an untamed passion. "I love you, Victoria." He emphasizes each word with a prolonged stroke.

I pant and whimper beneath him. "I love you, too." A look of victory passes over him.

He rocks into me, stroking every part of me, but when he suddenly breaks our connection, every fiber in my body screams in protest. However, when he flips me over and draws me back, hinting he wants me on all fours, my body screams for an entirely different reason.

He sinks into me, the angle hitting me in the just the right way, sealing our intimacy so not a whisper of air can pass between us. He propels into me faster and harder, ensuring I don't fall forward as he wraps both his big hands around my waist. I buck backward, taking every hot inch of him, shattering when he circles his hips and stabs at my core with a direct hit. He continues this for minutes, his primeval growls alerting me that he's close.

Arching my neck back, I look into the star-filled sky and appreciate that what Jude and I have knows no boundaries. This shouldn't be happening, but it is. This incredible man crossed my path for a reason, and I'll be damned if that reason will be in vain.

Everything aligns, and things have never looked clearer. As he thrusts into me over and over again, I absorb his essence, drawing him into my body as I clench my muscles, never planning on letting him go. He shouts and grunts before slipping a hand between us and flicking over my inflamed core. We groan in harmony, and I explode with an ear-splitting howl. "I love you. I love you," I chant, every part of my being surrendering to him.

Jude hums in complete satisfaction before he drives into me with two vigorous pumps. He growls and explodes inside me, the speed of his rhythm drawing out every last ounce of my orgasm. Tears spill from my eyes because I can't remember a time when I felt happier, more fulfilled. I'm completely spent, and my body is well-sated.

Still rooted deep inside me, he bites over my thundering pulse, the heat from his body sending my body lax. At the precise moment, we are drawn to the skies, and a shooting star flashes before our eyes, leaving a shadow of enchantment in its wake.

Jude kisses the shell of my ear before whispering, "Make a wish."

But what he doesn't realize is that all my wishes have just come true.

Nineteen

I'm numb—comfortably numb.

I'm surrounded by the only smell which reminds me of home. Not wanting this moment to ever end, I snuggle into Jude's chest, intent on staying this way forever. A deep rumble makes me remember the profound sounds Jude made as he buried himself so deeply inside me, I never thought he'd be found.

Kissing over my eyelids, he chuckles. "Good morning."

I groan. "No, it's not morning yet." I don't want to open my eyes because I know what today holds. Once I face the harsh light of day, I know that today is the day that changes everything.

"No, you're right, it's not," Jude whispers.

Before I can question him, I feel the silk sheets being

wrapped around us, shielding us from the sunlight streaming in from the curtains. He kisses me just as he did last night and stirs the same longing as he did hours ago.

We made love countless times, each time sanctioning my decision. The desperation to stay together could be felt each time he touched me; each time he told me I was his forever.

Opening my eyes, I feel a blush tint my cheeks when I see Jude watching me with ferocity. He remembers every kiss, every promise we made, and his fervor takes my breath away. "Hi," I manage to say.

The sheets are over our heads, blanketing us from reality. "Hi," he replies, kissing the slope of my nose. "You feeling okay?" His warm breath floats across my cheeks.

"Never better. Although…" I leave the sentence hanging deliberately.

His lips press together as he scrunches up his face. "Although what? Last night was…"

I can't help but smile since I know what he's thinking. "Last night was amazing. Although you still owe me a date."

He exhales in relief. "Every day I spend with you is a date."

"Cheapskate," I mumble under my breath, grinning.

His mouth falls open before he tickles my side while I squirm, giggling. "Okay, fine. I suppose you're right." His fingers pass over my tattoo, stroking tenderly. When he turns serious, I know what he's thinking. It's a reality we both have to face. "There's one thing we have to do beforehand."

"I know," I reply, fingering over his lips. Silence surrounds us. We both know we have to help Henry.

This quite possibly may be my last day wherever I am, and I can't let go without trying one last time. The thought makes me incredibly sad, and I can't help it showing. Jude brushes the hair from my brow, sliding his thumb down my cheek. "Is there anything, in particular, you'd like to do?"

I shake my head, thankful for the change of pace. "You choose. Anywhere with you is perfect."

He lowers his forehead to rest against mine, rubbing my nose with his. "You smell unbelievable," he hums. "I can smell myself all over you." His possessive words are avowed when I feel something hard and incredibly brilliant stir below.

I bite my lip, and a soft moan escapes me. I want him again. I don't think I'll ever stop. Jude reads my thoughts, and a playful grin tugs at his lips.

When a small knock sounds on the door, we both know who it is, and smile. "Just a minute, buddy," Jude calls out to Angus, who is standing outside the bedroom door.

Jude kisses me quickly before tugging the sheets off us and jumping up to find our clothes.

We dress in seconds, and when I'm completely clothed and collected enough, Jude opens the door. The mood instantly changes when I see Angus. When he sees me, he smiles with a sigh. It's a look of relief. Does he also know what's lurking around the corner?

I pat the bed, and Angus runs over to me, throwing himself in my arms. I look at Jude, who appears teary-eyed to see us connect so closely. "Did you sleep okay?" I ask Angus when he lets me go. He's still in his red, fire truck pajamas.

He nods, but I can see the distress in his big blue eyes. "What's the matter?"

He shrugs and looks over at Jude and signs. "I had a dream you and Daddy left me."

His fears are my own, but I try to stay strong. "Victoria and I will always be with you," Jude says, walking over and crouching down in front of him. He takes his small hand into his large one. "Even if you can't see us, know that we're watching over you. Always. Okay?"

I discreetly wipe at the tears in my eyes.

"Okay, Dad." Jude squeezes Angus's shoulder before kissing him on the cheek.

"Who you talking to, little monkey?" Grace peers around the doorjamb, almost appearing afraid to step into Jude's room.

Angus looks at Jude, who nods. "Daddy," he signs.

Grace's lower lip trembles. It's the first sign of weakness she's shown. But I suppose I see her in a different light now. All those times when Angus mentioned Jude, she thought he was talking to an imaginary friend to deal with his grief. "What did Daddy say?"

"He said that even though I can't see him, he'll be watching over me."

Tears well in Grace's eyes, just as they do in mine. "That sounds like something Daddy would say."

With a deep breath, she enters slowly, peering around as if absorbing the sight for the first time. Her response has me guessing she hasn't been in here since Jude's accident. I rub over my scar, feeling an ache deep within.

As she gazes around, tears spilling down her cheeks, I understand her resentment is because she misses Jude. He mentioned it was only him and her, so I can appreciate how lonely and lost she must feel without him. She buries her pain under her tough skin. I suddenly feel that Grace and I would have been great friends.

Jude looks at her, frowning when she runs her finger along his dresser, admiring a silver frame that holds a picture of them hugging Angus. They were a happy family once, but now, all Grace has is memories. She wipes at her tears with the long sleeves covering her hands. "Why did you leave us, Jude?" she whispers.

Jude swallows, his pain breaking my heart. "Buddy, can you do something for me?" he asks, his eyes glued to Grace as she wanders around the room. Angus nods. "Tell your Auntie Grace that I'm really proud of her."

Grace stops by Jude's closet, suddenly opening the doors and moving the garments from side to side. The hangers scrape along the bar, revealing her anger and pain, but most of all, her sadness. When she passes over a navy sweater, she rips it down and fists the material in both hands. Angus walks over to her slowly and signs.

She sniffs, hugging the sweater to her chest. "Thanks, little monkey." Both Jude and I can read her disbelief, but Jude perseveres.

He takes a step toward her, facing her as if she can see him. He lowers his chin. "I miss you, Grace. And I'm sorry to have left you alone. When Rose left, I took all my anger out on you, and that wasn't fair. I'm sorry. I want you to know that I am so proud of the woman you've become." She draws the sweater to her nose, sobbing. "You may not be able to see me but know that I am here, watching over you, watching over you both. I know you can feel me. I've heard every word you've said. I love that you still leave the porch light on for me, just in case I come home. When you're alone at night, crying in the dark, know that I'm sitting right beside you, holding your hand and telling you everything will be all right."

Grace stares at Angus, her vision clouded with tears. Tremors rack her body; she's barely able to speak. "Is D-Daddy really here?"

Angus nods, looking up at Jude with a smile. Grace follows his vision and gasps. "I m-miss you, Jude." It's the first time I think she's spoken to him aloud. Whether she believes Angus or not, I don't know, but she appears to need this comfort.

He steps forward, his footsteps creaking along the floorboards. With the most delicate of touches, he runs his fingers an inch away from her cheek. Her mouth falls open. She feels him. "I miss you, too…little monkey."

Tears roll down my cheeks. This nickname appears to be a special one, one that Jude called his sister, and now his sister is calling his son. She's keeping his memory alive. Angus runs over to Grace, hugging her tight. Jude watches with nothing but melancholy in his eyes.

We stay quiet for minutes, the realization of what is about to happen settling in. I know what Jude is doing. This is the first time in months he's spoken to Grace. He's doing so because he's tying up loose ends. He's saying goodbye.

A sharp pain suddenly kicks me in the chest, and I wheeze, falling back onto the mattress. "Victoria!" Jude bellows, running over and scooping me into his arms.

I can't breathe.

Air escapes me, and I feel like I'm seconds away from passing out. Lights flash before my eyes, and I smell…iodoform. "Tori, please, breathe. Not yet," Jude begs, kissing my temple, my eyes, my lips. His touch overrides the wave bound to drag me under, and in seconds, I'm gulping down three deep breaths.

"What's happening?" I ask, unable to keep the tremble from my voice.

Jude's silence reveals he knows, but he's not going to tell me until it's time.

The car ride into town is silent, and for once, I don't mind.

After guzzling three bottles of Gatorade, I feel remotely better, but I know it will be short-lived. Jude won't tell me what happened when I almost blacked out, but I have a feeling I'm hours away from finding out.

Jude parks his truck in a no-standing zone. Looking up at the sign, I say, "You can't park here." Jude smiles sadly. It's easy to forget we're not actually here.

The thought has me wondering. "When did you know you were…?"

"Dead?" Jude fills in the blanks. I nod, chewing my lip. "I knew right away."

As we step out onto the sidewalk and see Henry marching up the stairs in a tuxedo, I suppose Jude is right. "You ready to do this?"

He wraps an arm around me, drawing me into his side. "Yes. It's now or never, right?" Jude kisses my brow in response, which somehow makes me feel worse.

The lavish ballroom is decorated quite elegantly and packed full of men and women in uniform. Although chatter fills the air, a sense of sadness dominates the tone because the reason for this gathering is not a happy one. That fact is confirmed by the large screen which sits behind the lectern on stage.

Sheriff Sands' photograph is the main focus, sitting dead center, reminding everyone why they are here. Regardless of the fact that Henry may have been an ass, he seems to have been loved by many. As Jude and I walk around the room, we hear many people talk about Henry and what a great man he was. His colleagues, no doubt, admire him, and his absence is definitely felt throughout the room.

Jude holds my hand and navigates me until we locate Henry. He's standing by a middle-aged man who seems to have captivated the crowd around him. We stop a few feet away, remaining hidden as I know Jude wants to work this slow.

The uniformed men and women laugh at something he says. Henry joins in also, but I can see he's out of sorts. An older gentleman with hair the color of snow slaps the man on the arm lightheartedly. "Make sure you go easy on me, Sheriff, I'm an old man. I can't tee off like I used to."

Henry laughs, straightening his tie, but he knows this comment isn't directed his way. He replies anyway. "Old? Lieutenant Holms, you're nothing of the sort."

The sheriff smiles, appearing to have settled into Henry's role quite well. "You're lucky I'm a charitable man."

I lean into Jude's side, feeling incredibly sad for Henry. He surely knows something isn't right, but he's too stubborn to accept the truth. But so am I. No one can blame Henry for living in denial because the alternative is just too hard to digest. My chest begins to ache once more, but I quash down the pain, not wanting Jude to know.

He leads me over to a table at the back of the room, and we sit, anxiously waiting for this night to get underway. My knee bounces, and I'm unable to sit still because the only thing I can think is what happens next. Whether Henry believes us or not, there are roughly twelve hours until my time is up. Until I'm doomed to choose where I belong.

"Are you all right?"

Gazing around at my current surroundings, at the people who will never know my name, never know my story, I know the answer is no. I will never be all right again.

A silence pervades the air, alerting us that it's time. We both watch as the audience takes their seats, and the sheriff climbs the stairs to stand behind the lectern. I can just make out where Henry sits, surrounded by colleagues who don't even know he's there.

The sheriff looks out into the crowd, waiting for silence, and it doesn't take long until he has the floor. Clearing his throat once, he turns and looks at the image of Henry in uniform behind him. "We're here tonight to honor our fallen brother, Sheriff Henry Sands."

I sigh, knowing this is not going to end well.

"I never had the pleasure of working alongside Sheriff Sands, but I know from the many stories you've all been kind enough to share that he was a good man. Sheriff Sands loved being a policeman, that much is clear. He dedicated his life to the force, ensuring the townsfolk could come home to a safe and protected community." He takes a moment, meeting the eyes of the crowd. "He died protecting his community, and for that, we will never forget the sacrifice he made. So tonight isn't about remembering Sheriff Sands' death, it's about honoring his life."

The room is deathly still, and when I look at Henry, I can see that that stillness has overcome him. He is unmoving, his mind no doubt processing everything he's just heard. But nothing prepares us all for what the sheriff has to say.

"There is no better person to honor Sheriff Sands' life than his wife, Jillian Sands."

The crowd claps vociferously as the sheriff steps down from the podium and walks over to the corner of the stage. He pulls back the red curtain to reveal a frail-looking Jillian standing alone, just off stage left. I latch onto Jude's hand, frightened. Henry stands but remains frozen.

We watch as Jillian fearfully peers out into the crowd, her eyes darting nervously around the room. The sheriff whispers something into her ear, which has her holding back her tears. When she takes a small step forward, she's greeted with a standing ovation. The sight seems to give her the confidence she needs.

She looks fragile standing behind the podium, her hands fluttering as she shuffles her cue cards. The audience takes a moment to settle, but when they do, each and every one of them gives their undivided attention to Jillian.

She adjusts the microphone to suit her small frame. "T-thank you everyone for coming tonight." She takes a deep breath. Her hands tremble so badly, the cue cards fall from her grip.

The shine from the sheriff's shoes catch the bright lights as he saunters across the stage to pick up Jillian's cards. She accepts them, wiping away her tears.

"I had a speech planned, but things always sound so much better in your head than they do aloud." I nod, understanding her completely. "If Henry were here…I know he'd be overwhelmed. Henry may have been a hard man, but he was my man." She chokes down her tears. "He was far from perfect, and he knew that, but in the end, he always tried to do what was right."

I remember seeing Jude's death through his eyes. No matter what a hardnosed bastard Henry is, there is still a layer of good buried underneath his firm exterior. He may not remember it, but when push came to shove, he was there for Jude. He could have left him for dead, but he tried his best to save him, to save us both.

This is the reason Jude is so unrelenting. He wants to help Henry because Henry helped him. Once the scores are settled…I know what happens then.

"My Henry would have been so grateful to see you all here. I want to say so many things, but let us just remember him in our own way. Thank you for remembering the man he was."

The audience stands, clapping and cheering at full volume. Jillian turns and sobs into her palms when she sees photographs of Henry flick across the screen. When the final picture of Henry in full uniform comes to a standstill, the entire room raises their hands to give the sheriff his final salute goodbye.

The entire time, I couldn't bear to watch Henry, as his reaction would most likely leave me in tears. But now I know I must because this is where it begins. The moment I see him, I can see he now believes, but the question is, what is he going to do now that he knows?

Jude stands tall beside me, his towering height alerting Henry to our presence. My insides squirm when Henry locks eyes with Jude. "What happens now?" I ask, unable to move.

"We wait."

"Wait for what?"

Jude waits a hair's breadth before pointing. "That."

Henry storms over to us, pushing anybody who stands in his way. Of course, there is no one there, but he does so nonetheless. When he reaches us, he doesn't hesitate and swings wide, intent on hitting Jude in the jaw.

Jude doesn't flinch, he doesn't even move because Henry's fist passes straight through him. The sight makes me gasp, as I've never seen anything so surreal before. Every time Jude and I have touched, I've felt him, so I can't imagine what thoughts are racing around Henry's mind.

"What the—?" he admonishes, looking down at his clenched fist.

"Stop," Jude scolds, standing proud with his hands folded across his chest. "You're embarrassing yourself."

"You've done this. All of this," Henry persists, desperately clutching at straws.

"No, Henry, this is all you. This is your fantasy." Jude circles two fingers around the room. "You're dead. We both are. The sooner you accept it, the sooner you can move on."

"You're crazy. You both are."

Just as he attempts to lunge at Jude again, I step forward, blocking his flight path. I'm too quick, and he ends up falling straight through me and onto his ass. A small shiver passes over me. "Henry, stop it. Jude is right. Look around you. You're the guest of honor because this gala is in memory of you. You died nine months ago."

"No." He stubbornly shakes his head.

Looking down at him, I offer him my hand. "If you don't believe me, then believe Jillian."

Those magical words seem to be the key because something in his demeanor unlocks. He peers up at the stage where his picture still sits, watching Jillian talk to the new sheriff as he shakes her hand. She dabs at the corner of her red eyes with a white handkerchief, looking exactly what she is: a grieving widow.

Jude and I may not be able to convince Henry, but I know Jillian can. He blinks once, then twice, and I witness the moment he sees the world under the layer he's built. "Look, really look and listen to what's happening around you." I keep as calm as I can, considering my circumstances.

Henry, still on the floor, peers slowly from left to right. At first, he sees the world through Henry-tinted glasses, but I recognize the moment things become clear. He gasps, shaking his head quickly.

"No, it can't be."

I don't speak. I allow him time to absorb the world because he's seeing it for the first time in months. He snaps his head my way, desperation and helplessness marring his soul. "This is really happening?"

I nod, saddened by his pain. "Yes, Henry. I'm so very sorry." My words can never reflect the sorrow I feel. Offering him my hand once more, I hope that instead of words, maybe he can touch my grief.

With apprehensive fingers, I hold my breath as he extends his arm forward and hesitantly slips his fingers into mine. The moment we touch, however, something unexpected happens. The room begins to spin, and all the voices around us get sucked into a spiraling whirlpool of colors. A chill passes over me. I cover my mouth, certain I'm seconds away from being sick. Before I can blink, we're standing in a bedroom I've never seen before.

It takes a moment to find my feet, but when I do, I instantly look for Jude. I exhale when he's standing behind me. "What's going on?" I ask, swallowing down my nausea.

His lips pull into a thin line. "We're running out of time. The clock has somehow fast-forwarded to this." He doesn't need to elaborate.

"Where are we?" I ask.

Henry answers for me. "We're in my bedroom."

Floral wallpaper gives the room a feminine feel, not what you'd expect to see adorning the bedroom of the town's sheriff. But peering around, I see this entire room is garnished with girly trinkets and pastel pinks.

"This is Jill's favorite room," he reveals as if reading my thoughts. "She would spend hours decorating, wanting to make our house a home. I hated that blanket, but Jillian, she loved it."

His eyes fall to the center of the bed where a delicate Jillian lays, curled into a ball as she sobs into her hands. She's still in the same black dress she wore to the ball. Her heels sit at the foot of the bed where she stepped out of them and collapsed... how many hours ago, I don't know.

The diamond in her wedding ring snares the glow from the lamp, highlighting her ubiquitous devotion to Henry. Her tears are guttural, coming from deep within. Anyone with a heart can't help but cry with her.

"What, what's the matter with her?" Henry asks, his voice

broken. Numerous bottles of pills are strewn on her bedside table.

"You need to let her go," Jude replies, his jaw firm.

"Let her go?" Henry doesn't conceal his dismay. "But I can't. I love her." He holds vigil by Jillian's bedside, examining his wife with tears in his distinctive, hard eyes.

Jude looks at me as he rests against the wall. "All the more reason to let her go."

We're all silent, lost in thought as this moment touches each of us in a different way. "Henry," Jillian weeps. Henry jolts, his eyebrows shooting up into his hairline. "I can still feel you. Hear you. I think I'm going crazy. I miss you and Rose so much." Henry holds his breath. "This world is full of suffering. Maybe it's my turn to end the pain."

The lamp bulb flickers, sending a chill down my spine.

"No, Jill, I'm here!" Henry cries. But that's the problem. He's not. None of us are. We're voyagers on a journey, using this, wherever this is, as our pit stop.

He sits by her side, stroking her cheek with nothing but love. She sniffs, closing her eyes, his touch appearing to comfort her. "Please, Henry, if you're here...please, let me go. I can't go on living this way. I feel so empty inside."

Henry lowers his chin. "I can't let go," he whispers. "If I do, it'll mean goodbye. I'm not ready to say goodbye."

His pain cuts me deep because it's exactly how I feel. No one wants to say goodbye. Hoping I'm not out of line, I gently walk to where he rests and place my hand on his shoulder. "In the words of someone pretty remarkable, your grandson, it's not goodbye, it's good night."

Jude inhales painfully.

Henry turns over his shoulder and looks at me, really looks at me. This is the hardest thing he's ever had to do in his life, but love is about sacrifice and putting the person you care about first—that's true love in its purest form.

He nods.

I give him space because I understand how he feels.

Jillian's sniffles assail her fragile body, the sight visibly tearing her into two. Henry lowers his body and spoons her from behind. I can imagine this is the way they slept, him protecting her and using his body as her shield. "I'm sorry, Jill. I truly am. I never deserved you. You were always too good for the likes of me. Your kindness made me want to be a better man." He shuffles closer, securing his arm tightly around her. "I'm sorry for so many things. I'm sorry for blaming you when Rose left. It was no one's fault. It was Rose's decision to leave. I see that now."

Jude blows out a silent breath. It's the reprieve he's been looking for.

"I wish I could have told you how much you meant to me because I loved you every day of my life. I may not have shown you, but I did." He sniffs back his tears.

"But most of all, I'm sorry for not being the man you

deserved. I failed you in life, but I won't do so in…death. I'll let you go, Jillian. Live your life and be happy. That's all I want for you. Live the life I couldn't live. I love you. Take good care of our grandson."

I want to stand by Jude, but I can't. I know the moment I do, I will latch on and never let go. We watch as Henry lays a soft kiss on Jillian's cheek before rising and wiping away his tears.

He stands, unfastening his bow tie and unbuttoning the top button on his shirt. "So what happens now?" He's attempting to be strong, but that speech was heartfelt.

Jude pushes off the wall. "You let go of this life and accept the next."

"I have let go."

"There is something holding you back," Jude explains, coming to rest at my side. His warmth calms my nerves.

"I've said my goodbyes." Henry looks completely perplexed.

Jude wraps his arm around me, drawing me into his side. "No, you haven't."

"I…" His mouth falls open. "It's Rose?" His question can be perceived as a statement also.

Jude nods slowly.

Henry's face turns sallow. "But she's my baby."

"No one is asking you to forget her. No one can take away your memories." The pain in Jude's voice reveals he's done the same.

"But I…I need to know where she…" Henry suddenly

pauses, peering over my head, astounded.

I don't know what's transfixed him so, but I don't bother turning around because this expedition isn't mine to see. His pupils dart from left to right; he's chasing something. He's being subjected to a manifestation that is meant for his eyes only.

I lean into Jude's side, suddenly feeling drained. He kisses the top of my head. "What's happening?" I whisper. Jude's response is hugging me tight which leaves me nervous.

Henry snaps from his trance, stumbling backward as he gasps for breath. "That motherfucker shot me." He rubs over his stomach. Jude nods, never breaking our embrace. It appears Henry now knows the truth. "He shot you, too. And you." He looks at me sadly.

The only word that echoes over and over in my head is *acceptance.*

"My obsession with finding Rose finally killed me. The ironic thing is, I still don't know where she is," Henry says, pulling at the collar of his shirt as if it's suddenly strangling him.

"She's meant to stay lost, Henry. That's just the way things are." It's an awful reality, but Jude is right.

Henry nods slowly. "Why did you tell me he knew where Rose was? You didn't have to do that. You could have died taking that secret to your grave."

Jude snickers playfully because that comment is such an oxymoron. "You didn't have to call in my location or Victoria's. You could have left us for dead. I suppose death puts everything into perspective. It separates the saints from the sinners. Why did you turn left, instead of right? Why did you follow me? The answer is everything is mapped out for us from the moment we were born. If I didn't tell you, you'd probably still be alive, but you'd be living an existence which wasn't your own. This was supposed to happen. It was in our destinies." I bite my lip, hating we all couldn't be saved. "It's because of you Tori is alive. I can't ever thank you enough for that."

For the first time, I don't see disgust when Henry marvels at me enfolded in Jude's arms. "So it appears we don't hate one another after all."

Jude scoffs teasingly. "I wouldn't get too carried away."

Henry smirks, before turning serious. "I was a terrible father-in-law. You're right. Rose did…leave us behind. I blamed you, but in reality, she was at fault all along. I'm sorry…kid." I can see how hard that confession was for Henry to make.

Jude's body goes slack. I feel the weight lift from his shoulders. "I'm sorry, too."

The moment those words leave Jude's lips, Henry tilts his head to the side and listens closely. I unfold myself from Jude's embrace, watching with wide eyes. He turns in a slow circle, gasping at whatever he sees. All I see is wallpaper.

The room becomes terrifyingly still. I can see the dust particles travel along the ray of light emanating from the lamp. I can feel something otherworldly. My skin pricks.

"I'll be damned." Henry's footsteps are heavy as he trudges

slowly, turning to look at Jillian one last time. With a bittersweet smile, he says, "Goodbye, Jill, or as someone wise once said… good night."

His words ring on the evening breeze, but one moment he's there, and the next, in a blink of an eye…he's simply not. It's that easy? A sadness defeats me. *This* is how it ends?

"All of this is possible because of you," Jude says.

"I'm just one person," I whisper, not seeing the brilliance everyone else seems to appreciate in me.

"One person who can change the world," he soulfully reveals.

After a few significant moments, I think I understand what he means. Everything comes down to Jude and me, and the night we met.

I suddenly feel the need to sit down.

Jude catches me as I almost crumple to the ground. "Hey?"

"I'm fine," I lie, gripping his bicep tightly to stop the room from spinning. "Just lightheaded." He doesn't look convinced as he leads me to an oversized armchair in the corner of the room. As I catch my breath, I smooth out the worry lines etched on his brow.

Jillian stirs, thankfully diverting the attention from me. With a yelp, she shoots up, her eyes darting from left to right. Brushing the hair from her brow, I've never seen her eyes look clearer. When she turns and peers at the bottles of pills on her bedside table, she frowns. Does she remember? Standing, she collects the bottles and marches into the en suite, where she tosses them into the wastebasket.

My mouth pops open. I've never seen this side of Jillian, but I like it.

With hands braced on either side of the basin, she looks into the mirror, really looks at her fatigued reflection. I think this may be the first time she's seen herself in months. She splashes water onto her cheeks and straightens out her hair. She finally looks happy—no longer plagued by the ghosts of the past.

My stomach turns, and I break out into a cold sweat. But I'm determined to see how this pans out.

Her bare feet pad softly along the floor as she reaches for the cell off the dresser. Jude exhales deeply. We're both engrossed in what's transpiring before our eyes.

"Hi, Grace, it's Jillian."

I tilt my chin to look up at Jude, who is standing behind me. He seems…relieved.

"Yes, I know. It has been a long time." She pauses, appearing nervous at what she's about to say. "I'm sorry to call so late, but would it be okay if I said good night to Angus?"

I gasp. Did her subconscious hear us? Jude places a hand on my shoulder. "She knows he isn't deaf?"

"Yes. She knew the entire time. She's the only one who accepted him for him. She was also the one who opened Henry's eyes. I know he loved Angus, loved him in his own way. And it's because of that love I gave him a second chance."

"Thank you," Jillian says, drawing us back to the now. "Oh, Grace? Maybe one day you and Angus could come over for lunch. Or breakfast. Or dinner. Whatever suits you best?" A genuine smile lights up her face. "I'd like that, too."

She waits a moment, running her fingertip over a frame that holds Henry's picture. She looks lovingly at it, rather than mournful. So this is what letting go, closure looks like.

"Hello, little monkey." I blink back my tears. "Grandma just wanted to say good night." There is a long delay before she confesses, "I know I haven't been a very good grandma, and I'm sorry. But if you'll let me, I'd like to make it up to you. I love you so much. Good night."

She waits for Grace to come back on the line. A few seconds pass before she covers her mouth, tears stinging her eyes. "Tell him yes, Grandpa is now protecting the people in the sky."

Jillian hangs up, hanging onto the cell for minutes after. When her gaze flutters to the photo of Henry once more, I see acceptance—acceptance that it's her turn to live. "Good night, Henry." She walks into the bathroom a new woman. It feels good to know I helped. The moment the door closes, though, I'm suddenly hit with excruciating pain. I slump forward, a pained scream ripping from my throat. The sound only amplifies the pain.

"Tori?" Jude darts around the chair, dropping to his knees in front of me. He places his hand on my thigh, which fosters the pain. Everything inside my head is blaring, echoing off the walls. I'm certain someone is wielding a pickax and is digging away at my soul.

I press my palms over my ears, needing to shut out the noise. Something solid gets wrenched from my throat, and I gag. Coughing madly, I look up at Jude and wipe away my tears. "What's happening to me?"

"You're pulling toward reality," he reveals. "The weaker you get here…the stronger you are in the real world. The moment someone you touched makes their peace, a piece of you goes with them."

"No." I shake my head. "That's not fair. I don't have a choice?"

"I'll take you home." He doesn't need to reply. We both know the answer. I don't bother arguing and allow him to help me up.

Taking one final look at the floral papered walls, I appreciate that although I'm breaking, I'm happy my loss has helped someone gain their life back.

*Butterflies adapt and make it
through incredible obstacles.*

The Fourth Stage: Adult Butterfly

Twenty

We walk to my house in silence. There seems to be a lot of that lately. I have no idea where Jude's truck ended up—not that it matters because it's not really there. There is no truck, and my house isn't even my home. None of this is real, except this stabbing pain eating away at my heart and mind.

Jude never lets me go, and for that, I'm thankful, as I doubt I'd be able to hold myself up.

Jude is right. I'm losing this battle. Each breath I take is harder than the one I took before it, but I won't give up. Not yet.

As we walk down my driveway, Jude kisses the top of my head. His touches linger; he's savoring whatever time we have left together. The thought breaks my heart into a million irreparable pieces.

"Did you want anything to eat? I can grab you something from the store."

His kindheartedness hurts me even more. Sniffing back my tears, I breathlessly tease, "You o-owe me a date, mister." We stop walking. I'm thankful to take a breather.

Jude sighs, holding me out at arm's length. "Victoria…"

But I shake my head. "You're not getting out of it that easily. Just because we witnessed some batshit crazy things doesn't mean you're off the hook." I poke him in the chest playfully.

His lips twitch. It's nice to see him smile. "Are you sure?"

Stepping toward him, I nod. "Yes. I've never been more certain of anything in my life. What time should I come over?"

"I can come get you," he offers.

I swallow past the lump in my throat. "I'd like to see Angus…if that's okay." I leave the inevitable lingering.

He looks like I've just clubbed a baby seal to death. "Of course. Come over around twelve. That'll give us plenty of time to…watch the sun rise."

What he really means is watch me die. "Will Angus be awake?"

He sweeps a strand of hair from my brow. "He will be when you arrive."

I melt into his touch. "I'll see you at twelve."

"Okay." Licking his full lips, he bends down and seals his mouth over mine.

Desperation and longing are the driving force behind this

kiss. I hate myself for doing so, but I memorize the shape of his lips, the curve of his body, and the vibrancy of his flesh. These small keepsakes will help me remember when things turn gray, and I need help recollecting. When he matches my despair, I know he's doing the same. We will both revert to these memories when that's all we have left—the only mementos that will get us through.

He tugs my bottom lip before pulling away slowly, and a whimper escapes me. "I'll see you soon." His voice is heavy, coated with so many layers of emotion. I nod, too afraid to speak.

I watch as he walks away.

When I can no longer see him, I amble to the front stairs, not even bothering to search for my keys, as I can't stomach this façade any longer. The moment I step foot inside, the interior flashes from what I see to what's really there. Dark is replaced with white, old submerged with new. My wounded mind concocted this reality, knowing life as I know it was just too painful to front.

My boots sound against the floorboards as I take in my surroundings because I'll miss this place. The place, which was my sanctuary, and the place I called home.

I skim my finger over the top of the regal chair, just as I did with the piece of furniture that started this chapter. These things may not physically be here, but they are in my mind, and that's good enough for me. They provided me comfort and made me feel human. For a small moment in time, this was mine. But I know in a few small hours, nothing will be the same.

"Can I help you get ready for your date?"

Tears well in my eyes when I see Charley holding Jäg. She's dressed in her red ball gown, the sight binding what I know to be true.

"I'd love that. Thank you."

We walk up the stairs, the air heavy with emotion. But I won't allow my last moments with her to be tainted with tears.

She moves around the bedroom with ease, positioning me on the end of the bed and placing Jäg in my lap. He purrs loudly when I pat him, turning in a circle before settling into my warmth.

I watch as Charley opens the closet, hunting through the garments to find the perfect date outfit. "What about this?" she suggests, holding up a royal blue summer dress.

I'd forgotten I owned this outfit. It's casual but still dressy enough for a first date.

I strip off, allowing Charley to fuss because we both need this normalcy. As she sits me in front of the mirror and begins brushing my hair, one could forget our dire situation. But when her reflection reveals a tear trickling from her eye, there is no luxury of forgetting what's bound to come.

"You look so beautiful," she whispers, arranging my tresses of hair into a messy bun. "I finally figured out why I've been here for so many years."

I can't speak. I can only watch her through the mirror.

"I'm here because I just wanted to be a girl. I never had a chance to do trivial stuff like this. I never had a chance to live. But coming here and seeing you and Jude, I know there is more to life...whatever life you live. I may be...dead...but there's something more out there. You being here proves that."

I bite my bottom lip, blinking past my tears.

"I was scared, Tori, so scared of what was on the other side, but now, I'm not frightened anymore." Her shoulders shudder, but she appears calm. "I'm here to let go. Let go of what could have been. And it's because of you that I've finally found where I belong. I know I'll find my path. Wherever it may take me, I'm ready to go."

A sob echoes in my chest. "This is goodbye, isn't it?"

Charley looks ethereal as she peacefully pins the final piece of hair in place. "No." She smiles. "It's just the beginning."

She touches my shoulders, her reflection a portrait of faith and acceptance. "You're ready."

When the air shifts, just as it did with Henry, I know what's to come. Standing, I turn to face my best friend and reach for her hand. "So are you."

Motionlessness carries a certain beauty to it; an opportunity to inhale the world around you and simply be. If I could take back my life, would I? Would I give up the chance of living a life so extraordinary? When Charley's lips part and a small breath escapes, I know the answer is no. It's through suffering that I have come to love the person I am. I make a difference.

"I'm glad I'm wearing my Sunday best," she says, astonished, her eyes widening when she peers over my head.

Leaving her to gaze into the future, I make my way over to the bed where Jäg still sits. I never knew what happened to him. One day, he simply didn't come home. Regardless of my efforts to find him, he remained lost. It hurt so much to lose him, but seeing him this one final time is like I've been given a second chance to say goodbye.

Picking him up, I rub my cheek against his fur, finding comfort in his heavy purring. "Be happy, little buddy. I'll always remember you." He nudges my chin with his head.

Charley waits, allowing me the time I need. "Take good care of him." I hold back my tears as I gently pass him over to her. He goes willingly, appearing to have found his home.

How do you say goodbye to someone you love? You don't. Sniffing back my tears, I wrap my arms around them. "Good night, Charley." Charley sniffles before bursting into a quiet sob. Charley thought I was here for her, but little does she know, she was here for me.

We stand for minutes hugging, needing this final moment to reinforce this reality as being real. As we both weep, a thought scratches at the surface, one that has been there all along. I know what path I've chosen; my mind was made up nights ago. I, like Charley, was also scared, but now, things have never looked clearer. I'm prepared, ready to accept my decision, and I'll be damned if I don't at least try.

Charley breaks our embrace, her mascara running black rivers of sorrow down her cheeks. She takes a deep breath, brushing away her tears. "I know you won't give up."

"How do you know?" She's right…Of course, she's right.

She begins walking toward her destiny. When she's feet away, she turns over her shoulder, stroking Jäg tenderly with a tranquil smile. There is an unearthly glow around them. They both look like…angels. Charley's angels. A tear streaks down my cheek. It's a sight I'll never forget. "Because love doesn't give up on you."

Those parting words are our final goodbye.

Squeezing my eyes shut, I take three deep breaths knowing that when I view the world again, I'll be standing in it alone.

Turning around with my eyes sealed shut, I feel a wave of sickness choke me. I know what's happening. Like Jude revealed, I'm slowly dying, fading from this world, which means I'm alive in the real world. All my anchors in this reality are no longer here except for him. There is no reason for me to stay but him, but he's the *only* reason that matters.

I'm the person in charge of my destiny, and I'll be damned if I don't go down fighting.

Finding the courage I need, I peel open my eyes and admire the mirror image of someone who exudes nothing but a will to live. I know Jude will fight me, but this isn't his choice to make.

I take one final look around my room. This place will

forever be etched in my mind, but I know I'll see it again. With a sense of urgency, I bound down the stairs and run out the front door. Seeing Jude has never been more imperative. I know he'll try to talk me out of my decision, but my mind is made up.

My legs burn as I take off in a dead sprint, the feeling confirming that no matter what this place is, it's my home. It's where I belong. It's where I choose to stay.

I get to Jude's in minutes and don't bother knocking as I burst through the front door. "Jude!" I call out, searching each room, suddenly frightened he's somehow gone. When he appears at the top of the stairs, I almost sag in relief.

"Tori?" He looks down at his watch, seeing that I'm early. "Is everything all right?"

Now that he's here and I can catch my breath, I realize my entrance was a little dramatic. Before I can answer, however, Angus steps from his room, rubbing the sleep from his eyes. Jude was right. We're all connected. A simile of hope.

Calming my nerves, I smile. "Hey, wombat. What are you doing up so late?"

"I heard your voice," he signs, yawning.

I need to be near him, near them both, so I climb the stairs, hoping my shaky legs hold me up. When I reach the top step, I can feel the perception humming off Jude. He knows what I've decided, and he'll do everything in his power to ensure I don't follow through.

Ignoring him, I close the distance between Angus and me

and open my arms. He steps into them, hugging me tightly.

"You look pretty," he signs once we break our embrace.

"Thank you." I gently run my fingers through his hair, the silky strands slipping between my fingertips.

Jude smiles proudly, devotion swimming in his eyes. He knows it's time. "Buddy, I want you to listen real closely for a few minutes, okay?" He crouches down in front of him. Angus gives him his undivided attention.

There is no doubt he's in visible pain, as this is the hardest thing he'll ever have to do. "I'm so proud of you," he says with conviction. "You're the best thing I've ever done with my life. I want you to know that. There are going to be times when things are going to get tough, but you'll always have Grace and Grandma. And Victoria." Adding me to the list reveals he believes I won't be here come morning.

"What about you?" Angus asks, frowning.

Jude swallows, running a hand through his hair. "I'll be watching over you every day, but you won't be able to see me." I hold back my tears. "I have to go."

"For how long?"

"For a long time," Jude signs after a pregnant pause. Angus lowers his eyes, pondering over what Jude just told him.

As he's processing the fact that this is the last time he'll ever see his father, Jude slips the silver chain out from under his T-shirt and gently places it over Angus's head. "I want you to have this, buddy. My mom gave this to me when I was your age. It's Saint Jude."

Angus fingers the medallion with care, understanding the importance and significance this gesture holds. Without a lick of fear or uncertainty, he asks, "Is he an angel, too?"

A gasp escapes me while tears sting Jude's eyes. "You know what I am?" His question is split into two. It's a desperate plea that Angus shed some light on what he, what we are. But it's also filled with surprise that Angus knew this entire time.

Angus nods, placing his tiny palm against Jude's cheek, before removing it to reply. "Yes, Daddy. You're an angel." Lifting his blue eyes, he signs. "And Tori is an angel in training."

I mute a sob behind my hand.

"That's right." His voice wavers. He's trying to keep it together. "You'll always have two angels watching over you."

I don't know if Angus knows the true meaning of his words, but either way, he's always known that we've been something… else. Jude was never a ghost. He's an angel.

"Know that I love you. So much. Forever." Jude pulls Angus toward him and crushes him into his chest.

The sight is my undoing, and a stream of tears cascades down my cheeks.

Jude doesn't let Angus go for minutes, murmuring how much he loves him and to never forget him.

For the first time ever, my decision to stay doesn't feel so clean cut. If I stay here, I stay with Jude, but if I leave and return to the world I know, there is a possibility I'll see Angus again.

Jude reads my indecision over Angus's shoulder. If I live, he'll still be dead. But his legacy is a living reminder of just who Jude was. I pull it together, determined to stay strong.

Jude breaks their embrace, holding back his tears. Angus looks over at me and rubs his watery eyes. Dropping to my knee, I smile. "Thanks for teaching me how to fly a kite."

"Thanks for being my friend," he replies without pause.

"Good friends," I sign, just how he once said to me.

With a smile, he peers down at Jude's chain, appearing to be deep in thought. A moment later, he slips it off from around his neck. It dangles from his fingers, the medallion like a hypnotizing pendulum swinging from side to side.

Breath evades me as Angus slides the chain over my head. The metal cools my skin the moment it settles between my breasts. Toying with the medallion, I'm speechless to why Angus would give it to me.

He explains a second later. "I already have enough angels looking over me. Now, you have your own angel watching over you." I draw the medallion to my lips, kissing it with tears.

Can Angus see something that I can't? Does he see that come morning, the best thing in my life will be snatched from my fingers and lost into thin air?

Hiding my worries, I smile. "I'll wear it and think of you. I'll think of you both," I add, focusing on Jude.

As I hug Angus tighter than I've ever hugged him before, a sense of disembodiment comes over me. It's happening.

Another piece of me is lost. "I love you," I whisper, kissing his hair, cheeks. "Grow strong, and be happy."

My heart feels broken. I don't think it'll ever heal. I'll never be ready to let Angus go, but as a cold sweat coats my sticky skin, I know I don't have a choice. Angus kisses my cheek. He wipes away my tears. He is far wiser than his young years. He knows it's time to let go.

"Bye, Angus." A sob gets caught in my throat.

But Angus shakes his head, looking at both Jude and me. "It's not goodbye. It's good night."

A laugh coalesced with tears escapes Jude. "You're right. It is good night. We'll never say goodbye because you'll always be in here." He places a fist over his heart. "No one can ever take that away from me. I love you, my son."

Angus smiles. "The heart sees what is invisible. I love you too, Daddy." He runs over to him. This is the last goodbye. Jude bends down and scoops him up into his arms. His hug is near suffocating, but there is no place either would rather be.

I give Jude some privacy to say his farewells as I quietly walk down the stairs and open the front door. The cold breeze is like a punch to the guts, and I wheeze, clutching at my chest. Time is running out for all of us.

With no place to go, I take a seat on the top step, contemplating on where we go from here. I know I'm mere hours away from all of this ending one way or another.

"You've decided, haven't you?"

Jude's voice from behind me carries the weight of the world. He knows my mind is made up. I don't bother answering him because it would be a waste of breath.

His footsteps sound around me as he walks down the steps. I'm expecting a lecture, or for him to argue why I need to live. But he doesn't. He stands in front of me and extends his hand. He doesn't wipe the tears from his eyes, and I do the same. "Shall we?" Peering up at him from under my lashes, I don't see a hint of defiance or defeat. He appears relieved.

We walk to his truck in silence, our footsteps the only resonance filling the stillness between us. We're both lost in the inevitable. For some strange reason, it calms me somewhat that he's just as anxious as I am.

I don't question him to where we're going because as long as I'm with him, I can handle anything fate throws my way.

He looks incredible, but he always does.

"Where are we going?" I finally speak. I don't bother asking if he's okay because I know that wound will always weep.

"It's a surprise," he replies, his eyes crinkling. I'm thankful to see a half smile.

"Of course, it is."

A melodic country tune fills the truck as we drive toward destination, unknown. I allow myself to get lost at this moment because it's one I'll hope to never forget.

The road becomes more deserted the farther we drive. It also becomes greener and more tranquil, too. Rolling hills surround us on either side, the beauty almost appearing like a painting. About forty minutes in, my nose is practically pressed to the window, unable to take in the elegance fast enough.

When Jude turns onto a gravel road, I sit up taller. "Are we having a picnic?"

"Maybe," he replies, his voice light. We continue driving into a thick forest, civilization long gone.

When he finally pulls up by a huge oak tree, I unsnap my belt. "Patience was never a virtue of mine," I reveal when he chuckles. Regardless of our circumstances, I know this will be the last memory I make of this place in this lifetime, so I want to cherish every second.

He switches off the engine, which is my cue to get out and absorb Mother Nature. The moment my feet touch the ground, I'm filled with a sense of freedom, and I kick off my shoes. I dig my toes into the dirt, closing my eyes and feeling the thrum throughout every organ and limb.

When Jude slips his hand into mine, I can't help but sigh, as I've come to crave his touch. He makes me feel alive. "Keep your eyes closed," he softly instructs, adding to the mystery of where we are. I do as he asks, trusting him completely.

The ground feels divine under my toes, the cool soil refreshing. I lag behind him as he leads us through what I'm assuming is dense bushland as he tells me to duck, weave, and bob a handful of times. The moment I hear running water, I almost take off in a dead sprint.

Jude squeezes my hand, sensing my excitement. "We're almost there." I don't care where "there" is because I know I'll love it. We walk for about a quarter of a mile before Jude stops.

A small squeak escapes me. "Thank you for taking me here."

"You don't even know where you are. You could open your eyes and be confronted with so many different scenarios." The heaviness hurts my heart.

With our hands still interlocked, I step forward, feeling vulnerable and exposed, but I swallow down my fears because this is what living is about. "It wouldn't matter because I'm here…with you. Any place where you are is…beautiful."

Two fingers slip underneath my jaw, and a delicate kiss is placed on my cheek. The hair on my arms stand on end, sending a shiver from head to toe.

"Open your eyes," Jude whispers, his warm breath like a kiss to my soul.

I take my time, slowly taking in my surroundings as I allow the world around me to sink in. The first thing I notice is the wide river only feet away. Rocks line the edge and lead into the clear water, the perfect steppingstones to stand in the middle of nature. All I'm surrounded with is vegetation. My own personal greenhouse. The hills are enormous, the trees towering, giving us the right amount of privacy and legroom.

"It's perfect," I whisper, unable to remember a more seamless sight.

Jude smiles, and with our hands still linked, he leads us

over to an aged, weeping tree. He shakes out the red blanket he's brought along, placing it on the ground.

"Are you hungry?" he asks as I settle on the blanket.

"A little." He sits down beside me, his signature fragrance making my mouth water.

I watch as he opens the basket, producing every food known to mankind.

I can't help but laugh. "How long do you plan to be out here for?"

A sadness drapes above him as he pours us some wine. "If I had my way…forever."

His admission has me thinking about why we're here. "You're okay with what I've decided?" I don't see the point in sugarcoating anything because time isn't on our side.

Jude pulls in his lips and sighs. He looks so tired. Standing, he doesn't answer my question, but instead, he rests by the river's edge. He turns his back, his head bowed. "Grace and I used to come fishing out here when we were kids. I wanted to take you someplace nice. Somewhere that means something to me."

My fingers instinctively seek out the pendant. Feeling it gives me the strength I need.

"I don't agree with your choice, but I'll respect your decision. When the time comes, I will allow you to decide." I celebrate prematurely. "But I ask that you do the same for me."

"What's that supposed to mean?" I sit up tall, my pulse

beginning to spike.

"It means I don't know what's going to happen. I'm scared, Tori."

"I am too."

But he shakes his head, his shape appearing so broken. "I'm not scared for me. I'm scared for you."

Standing, I need to close the distance between us because I suddenly feel so alone. "Jude, look at me."

He hesitates but finally turns. He looks heartbroken. "Grace was the only family I ever had. We used to come here to escape the monotony of our lives. Life was simple back then. It was hard, but it was the only life we knew. But now, I know we live many lives. And I was meant to die in this lifetime to live my life with you. If it was only for a moment, a mere whisper in time, then I want you to know it was worth every second."

"Why do I feel like you're saying goodbye?" I speak softly, the earth humming beneath my toes.

"I'm not. I'll never be able to say goodbye."

"Good, because you'll never have to. I choose you, Jude. Wherever that leads at this stage, I don't care. As long as I'm with you and you love me, the world can fall into place around us. We don't know what's going to happen, but let's face it together."

He digs his hands into his pockets, his chin pressed to his chest. "I'm a selfish bastard because you've just made me the happiest man in the world." His comment is contradictory to his deflated stance.

But I understand. How can one be happy when they've just agreed to potentially watch the one they love commit suicide? By staying here, I'm taking my own life. That fact is true.

"Jude…" I walk toward him. "I can't live in a world where you don't exist." He turns his cheek, his jaw firm. "So if this is the only way…then I accept my fate."

Acceptance.

How that word appears to be the sole beat I'm marching to.

I unfold his fists from his pockets and loop them through my own. "You once said you couldn't wait to see me spread my wings and fly. Well, I've emerged a butterfly, and it feels good to be free."

"So it's our turn to fly?" he asks, untangling from our union to wrap his arms around my middle.

"Yes." His warmth quietens down the noise.

"See how she flies," he whispers, drawing me into his chest. "For she is beautiful and free." I settle into his arms, closing my eyes.

"Tori…"

"Yes," I reply moments later.

"Promise me… you'll leave if you have to. If you're pulled in that direction, or you're in pain, you'll go. Promise me," he presses when I don't reply.

With arms cocooned around him, I snuggle into his chest, basking in his scent. "I promise."

His shoulders sag, appeased by my pledge. I, on the other hand, keep my eyes sealed shut, beset with guilt because my pointer and middle finger are crossed over tightly, with no intention of keeping a promise I would ever make.

Twenty-One

"I'm stuffed full." I place my hands over my bloated belly. Jude grins, and the sight, as always, takes my breath away.

For the past few hours, we've eaten, talked, kissed—repeat.

As each second turned into minutes, I felt myself grow weaker, drifting from this world. The red and oranges are on the verge of piercing the horizon, suggesting what's looming around the corner. I used to love sunrises, but now, I think I'd rather live my life in the dark.

Jude packs away the remaining items of food, his mind elsewhere; I can see the conflict on his face. This is a disquieting time for both of us. The unknown is what frightens me because we don't know what we're dealing with. If we knew what monsters were lurking in the dark, we could come prepared and fight until the end. But we're going in blind, having faith that our love is stronger than whatever this is.

"Come sit with me." Jude motions for me as he nestles against the trunk of the tree. He doesn't have to ask me twice.

I settle into his lap, my back to his front. He draws me backward, his arms enfolded around my waist. We're both looking into the same star-filled sky, both awaiting the final step. "Are you nervous?"

I shake my head, eyes transfixed on the horizon. "No. My renaissance will be beautiful. And so will yours." And I believe it will be. The pangs of pain are unremittingly bobbing under the surface, but I'm stronger than they are.

We sit for minutes, lost in our own worlds. Sunrise will be here soon. I can smell it.

Sitting this way with Jude, I can almost forget we're awaiting the unknown. But life is an adventure. It offers you a second chance —it's called tomorrow, and come tomorrow, I refuse to regret today.

"You're the bravest woman I've ever met, Victoria." He shatters the silence. "I want you to know that. No one has ever fought for me. I was never someone's reason to live. Thank you for making me yours." He kisses my temple, the quiver to his lips shooting a fearful current all the way to my toes.

"Jude…" I attempt to turn around, but he tightens his hold. I'm trapped. The blood whooshes through my ears. My mouth gets dry. "What's going on? Let m-me go. Sunrise is minutes away."

He ignores my demands.

As an orange hue breaks the horizon, hot, angry tears stab at my eyes. How could I have been so blind? "You lied to me." He was never going to stay. He made the choice for me.

"You lied to me, too." Jude knew all along what I had planned. I was not prepared to accept any other future than one with him in it. Even if I was pulled to go, I was always going to stay. He knew I was not going to wake up.

"No!" I shout, fighting him like a caged dog, wiggling and bucking wildly. "We don't even know what will happen. Don't go. No." His grip is firm, and I'm suddenly so fragile. The darkness begins to ebb away. "No!" I scream a guttural cry. "Let me go. Please, Jude, let me go."

"I am letting you go. I knew you wouldn't leave, so I've made the choice for you. I have to let go of the one thing keeping me here. *You.* I don't belong here anymore. But you do. You always did. If I go, there's no reason for you to stay."

I can't breathe. My lungs are starved for air. I continue fighting, however. I will do so with my last breath. I push back, but he's so damn strong, and me, I'm suddenly so weak. "Jude… no, please. Don't do this." I cry, choking on my paralyzing pain. "Going means you don't exist. Wait for me."

He kisses my temple once again, while placing a hand over my heart. "I'll always be in here. Whether you remember me or not, it doesn't matter. I can die knowing I was someone's reason to live. And you can live knowing you were loved. That you were the reason I found hope again."

"No! No!" A surge of adrenaline swiftly shoots through my veins, and I buck backward, throwing him off balance. He tumbles to the side, his hold loosening as he grunts. I will fight to the bitter end.

I find my footing and jump up, ready to fight him—fight for him to stay. He stands facing me, a look of defeat marring his soul.

"D-don't l-leave me. Please." I sob, dropping to both knees, interlacing my hands.

His stormy blue eyes are lucid as he looks into the skies. He knows it's time. Dropping to his knees in front of me, he caresses my cheek. "I have to. There are so many reasons we met. Why the stars were aligned that fateful evening. You've helped me let go and love again. To let go of regret and accept." He lowers his hands and rubs over my tattoo.

Flashes of red and orange begin to spark across the skies. "Stay with me. Stay with me," I repeat, torrents of tears drowning every pulse thrumming throughout my body.

Jude remains poised while I'm seconds away from falling into a black abyss with no safety net. "I can't, butterfly. It's your turn to fly. I can't let you end your life. You'd sacrifice your life for me but…I'm already dead. I'm not even here."

The moment he says those words, his warmth, his presence begins to grow fainter. He's leaving me.

"The most important reason I'm here…" His voice echoes. "I'm here to help you cross over and accept that you're alive."

A sob so deep and raw cuts through the air; the heavens are charged with a burning electricity. The atmosphere pops around me as I reach out, and my hand passes through Jude's cheek. He's fading. "I don't care what world this is. It's real. This pain is real. If I'm not supposed to be here, then why does the thought of leaving you kill me inside?" I wrap my hands around my middle, weeping hysterically.

He frowns and lowers his eyes, but as each second passes, his shape flickers in and out, like a TV searching for a signal.

Lightning flashes across the sky as the heavens split open, spewing out deafening, thunderous rain. Raindrops splatter against my cheeks, merging with my salty tears. The drops are heavy and sizeable; I automatically think they're tears of every angel watching this tragedy unfold. "You said you'd never say goodbye!" I struggle to hold onto him, to grip him by the shoulders and yank him from fading because I can't feel him anymore.

He smiles, but it's bittersweet. "It's not goodbye, Tori…it's good night. I love you. For eternity. Live, Tori. Live…for…me." A burst of orange lights up the sky, the stars on the cusp of slumber. "Promise me, please watch over Angus."

Jude is no longer solid. He's walking toward the light. He watches me with tears in his eyes, surrendering to our predestined fate. He raises his chin and spreads his arms out wide. He's accepting his destiny without giving me a choice. But we both knew it would always come to this. There was never a way we could both subsist without sacrifice.

Still on my knees, I desperately attempt to grab him, but my fingers swipe through air. "No! Please, God, no! Stay with me. Please don't leave me. Jude!" My sobs are now soundless tremors convulsing through my body.

The downpour continues to pound down around me as the sun rises and the shadows are overcome by light. Daylight passes through Jude, turning my dress a crimson red. He smiles and extends his hand. I now understand why Jude couldn't watch me die. This feeling is one I cannot...*will not* accept.

Acceptance. I accept that this is why I was brought here all along. This is my final destination, and I'm ready to descend.

"Are you sure, Mrs. Armstrong?" a voice booms down from the sky, deafening me. I scream, covering my ears.

But the relentless voices won't stop. "Yes, Victoria would want it this way."

The beeping of machines are like a hammer striking steel... over and over again. It pierces my temple. I buckle, sagging forward, but I plant my hands firmly into the slick mud.

Jude's eyes widen, and he speaks, but I can't hear the words coming from his mouth. He's flashing in wordless animation.

"Vitals are good. Turning off life support." The clamor gets louder and louder. I can barely breathe. The rain showers me, hammering against my flesh, and I'm drowning.

A paralyzing stabbing evades every fiber of my body. I know that I'm dying. With nothing for me here, I'm being pulled to the real world. But I fight it. There's nothing for me there.

Clenching my teeth and clawing until my fingernails split into the dirt, I fight with every ounce of strength I have left. Jude, who is now just a glow, shakes his head, pain slicing across his face. I can't hear him, but it's evident when a scream rips from his horrified mouth. He's begging me to go, but this is my life, and it's my choice whether I live or die.

With that thought in mind, I evoke all the emotions that Jude awakened in me and focus on where I want to be. I remember the first time we met, how we had an inexplicable connection from the moment I laid eyes on him. I remember the first time we kissed. That kiss had never felt more real. I go on to recall every single moment Jude made me feel more alive than anyone has in my entire existence.

"Victoria, no!"

I can suddenly hear Jude. It's distant, but he's here. My memories are bringing him back to life—to the life we both know. Jude may have thought this was our destiny, but fuck fate—I'm the commander of my own vessel. I recall his hands, mouth, body on me, in me…how he brought me back to life. And now, it's my turn to return the favor.

I collapse onto my stomach, stars flashing as the world spins and spins like a merry-go-round in fast-forward. I smell antiseptic, my sister's perfume. But I push those scents aside and concentrate on him.

"No!" Jude's voice is louder. I smile, my cheek pressed into the dirt.

My arms are without sensation, but I will my hand to move and grip the medallion digging into my heart. This final piece is my anchor. With one hand clutching it so tightly, I begin to bleed. I reach the other out blindly in front of me, hoping he'll reach out and meet me halfway. I know he won't let me go. Regardless of what he thinks is right and wrong, he won't leave me. He thought leaving would make the decision easy for me, but he's wrong. I don't belong there. Not anymore.

I wait for breathless seconds, unsure if this will work. But moments later, his fingers envelop mine. I'm shot with agonizing pain and light converges with black. The raindrops form a puddle around me as I sink into the ground.

I'm left gasping for breath, my fingers clawing at the mud, the thickness alive under my hands. Lying on my side, I look into the heavens and hum when I see that it's dark. Lifting my weary body, I'm certain every bone is broken, but the pain is worth every punishing blow when I see where I am.

I'm home.

The dock is feet away. I remember many moons ago thinking about what'll happen when I swim to the other side. Now I know. It's the difference between life and death.

"She's preventing herself from waking up."

"Why?" A hysterical scream bounces through the air. "Why

would she do that?" My mother sobs.

I begin to claw my way toward the dock, appreciating the finesse of a snake as it makes its way home. My name is being shouted over and over again. The caller is Jude. Somehow, I dragged him into my reality, but the question is, are we reborn?

When my sister's, Bryan's, my parents' voices come crashing down from the thundering, torrential sky, I know the answer is no. I'm still caught between two worlds.

"Victoria! Stop!" This voice is Jude's.

Usually, I would, but I know what he wants. He wants me to stop fighting. He knows there is still time for me to live.

Hell to the fuck no.

I crawl faster and faster, wincing when I drag my lifeless body along the wooden dock and toward the water's edge. I'm paralyzed from the waist down, but my upper body strength from the daily swims is all the vigor I need.

An animalistic impulse controls me, and in seconds, I'm peering over the edge, my frenzied features mirrored in the tranquil, crystal water. Water is a conduit to all worlds. Its importance is imperative to every human being. Without it, we die. But with it…we can be baptized. We can be reborn.

Jude's pounding steps vibrate off the dock; I know he's going to stop me. With that thought in mind, I close my eyes and choose…life. The water is like tiny needles pricking my skin as I hit the surface. My natural instinct is to swim, but I compel my body to relax and allow the darkness to drag me under.

"We're losing her!"

A thousand track runners are using my heart as a trail, all shoving and kicking as they race to the finish line, stretching the walls until I'm certain it'll explode from my chest. My lungs begin to fill with water, air escaping me as I descend further and further.

I can feel Jude the moment he breaks the water's surface. It's like I'm caught in a tsunami.

His pleas only encourage me to sink farther as I tuck myself into a ball and visualize that I weigh ten thousand pounds. I submerge deeper and deeper, the freezing temperature shutting down my organs as I begin to die.

"C'mon, Tori! Breathe." I barely remember this voice as Bryan's. My mind is furling in on itself.

I'm drowning, being sucked into a hollow black abyss, but I know there is a light at the end of the tunnel. I accept that. I accept that this is my time. I was never meant to wake. This is my home.

With that as my final thought, I seal my lips shut and pinch my nose. Jude is begging me to swim, but I'm tired, so tired. I'll never get to the other side without him. But that was the final piece. I always wondered what would happen when I got to the other side, but this, right here, split right down the middle, this is my other side. A compromise.

"Tori, go. Be free." It's the last voice I ever expected to hear. The voice of my sister is filled with nothing but sincerity. She understands I don't belong there any longer. I've found my peace. I've found my forever.

Sobs sound around me as my heart begins to slow. My starving lungs fill with water, and I take my final breath. It's peaceful. I no longer hurt. This is my world. This is my calm within the chaos, and it's beautiful.

"I'm sorry, we did all we could. She's…gone." I'm dead, really dead. The shackles on my heart break free.

This time, there was no one to save me but me, and I did.

Jude screams out for me, but I can't move. Fear overtakes me. What's happening? I'm no longer stuck between two worlds. I've chosen where I want to be, so why can't I move?

My legs feel like they're caught in quicksand, and my arms are a mountain of jelly. "Jude!" I call out, but he's suddenly not there.

I'm alone, suspended in blackness, hooked by invisible talons. I try to calm my heart, but I realize it's not beating, nor am I breathing. Fighting against an invisible threat, I struggle and writhe, desperate to disengage from the shadows and find my light.

A thought knocks me backward. Maybe there is no light? No, that's not possible. All of this was not for nothing. "Jude!" I bellow, but everything is so dark.

I grip onto the only light I have in this darkness. The moment I secure my fist around Jude's necklace, I catapult through the water, the shadows soon becoming a bright white.

Visions flick so quickly before my eyes, and I can't keep up.

I will myself to focus, and when I do, I see that the movie playing before me is my life. It's from the day I was born, amalgamating into important events in my life—the events which shaped me into who I am today.

My life flashes forward so quickly, I can't keep up, but small snippets sink in. I see Matilda, my mom, dad, Bryan, and how important they were to me. I laughed, cried, smiled, just like everybody else who existed around me. I lived a happy life. But the moment it flicks over to the night of my twenty-seventh birthday, it slows down and pauses, the noises decelerating to a sluggish speed, which is impossible, seeing as I'm still flying.

The moment Bryan drops to one knee, the person with my life remote control pushes the pause button. The still image hurts my eyes. I try to squeeze them shut, but I can't. I'm being shown this for a reason. An unbearable stabbing punches at my chest, and I gasp for air. Lights flood around me, and I get spat out of this nightmare, landing face first.

I'm almost too afraid to open my eyes. Sounds, sights, smells, they are all too familiar, but I can't pinpoint why.

The moment I hear Jude scream, I forget everything. Nothing else matters but finding him. Is he hurt? The light abruptly gets turned off. My pupils adjust to the natural hue, but I suddenly wish I was blind.

I'm bowled over when I see where I am.

No. This can't be.

Epilogue

"**H**old up, I have to tie my laces."

I blink, attempting to take in where I am. Everything looks and feels the same, but in some ways, it doesn't. The street I stand on is poorly lit, shrouding it from full view. Snapping my head from left to right, I see we're alone.

"Turn around, would you? I can't do this with you looking at me." His voice has me gasping as I'm certain I've heard this phrase before.

As I attempt to process where I am, an acute pain penetrates my temple. It's so sharp it robs me of my breath. I press the heel of my hand against my brow, hoping the pressure will help alleviate the darkness.

I know where I am, but how did I get here? And why do I

feel like I've been in this exact same spot before?

"Tori, please, just this one time, can you do what you're told?"

Bryan is reciting from a book I've read before. But unlike the first time I read it, I don't want to know how it ends.

"Bryan?" My voice is filled with bewilderment. "What are we doing here?"

He looks exactly the same as I remember, but in contrast to all the times I looked at him before, I feel nothing.

He reads my turmoil and stands, seriousness replacing his smile. "What do you mean? You look like you've just seen a ghost." The moment the word slips past his lips, a cold chill passes through my body.

Before this second, this fleeting moment in time, what's the last thing I can remember?

Dinner at my favorite Italian restaurant. I had a glass of red. The ravioli Florentine was delicious. Everything was perfect. The food, the company, the place—it was the best birthday I've had.

Birthday.

It's my twenty-seventh birthday.

"Baby? What's going on?"

Bryan's voice, although expressing nothing but concern, sounds and feels so wrong. The comfort he once provided now makes me nauseous.

Why?

What can't I remember? There is a hole in my memory. A big black hole sucking down anything that may feel familiar.

"What day is it?" I ask, my eyes wide as I scope out my surroundings.

"It's Saturday. September twelfth. Are you okay?" When he attempts to comfort me, I involuntarily take a step back.

Bryan cocks his head to the side. That's *never* happened before. I've always craved his touch. But now, I crave the touch of someone else. Someone with eyes the color of the clearest blue sky. I just can't remember who that someone is.

"I'm fine," I lie when Bryan stares at me as if I've grown a second head.

"Did you have too much wine with dinner? Maybe it's something you ate?" His questions are giving me a headache.

This time when Bryan tries to comfort me, I don't turn away. He wraps his arm around me; his cologne, the scent I used to love, now makes me gag. I long for something warmer, deeper, and manlier.

I quash down this disconcerting feeling that something massive is about to happen and allow Bryan to lead me down the sidewalk. His hands feel clumsy, his touch comparable to being in the arms of a cold fish. I subtly shift out of his hold as I feel like I'm seconds away from suffocating.

What is the matter with me? Maybe I am getting sick? I *was* out in the rain with Jude.

I leave skid marks as I come to a screeching halt. Who the

hell is Jude? Every inch of my body shrieks in protest, punishing me for not knowing his name. I should know his name, but why?

"Okay, now you're freaking me out. I'm taking you to the hospital."

Beep.

Beep.

Beep.

I was in a hospital once, the machines keeping me alive. Images flash for a mere second of me lying in a peach room.

"I think I need to sit." I don't wait for Bryan and run over to a bench seat. I slump down into it, cradling my head in my palms.

Why is everything so fuzzy? Why are the memories I think I made hours ago feel like they were made in a different lifetime?

Bryan's voice is a distant murmur because I can't focus on the noise. I need to concentrate and break through the shadows clouding my vision. As I rub absentmindedly over my chest, a blanket of déjà vu tucks in around me, and I gasp for breath.

"So…what do you say? Want to marry me?"

I have no idea how long Bryan has been talking, or what he's said other than the fact he just asked me to marry him.

My heart begins mounting to an unhealthy rhythm. *Marry him?* Is he serious? I don't even love…him. I haven't for a very long time.

"Victoria?" He's nervous, concerned that I'm seconds away

from throwing up my ravioli. "Will you marry me?"

"If I go, there's no reason for you to stay." A whisper raps gently against my temple, but when I hear his voice again, I'm certain a sledgehammer has replaced the undertone. *"I die every night just so I can meet you again."*

Oh, god.

A kaleidoscope of colors, voices, events crashes into me, leaving me winded as I try to piece together what's happening. Stormy blue eyes, pink bowed lips, ever-present whiskers come together to form the face of a man I know. A man I love. But who is he?

Clutching at my hair, I squeeze my eyes shut, desperate to see more because those memories are fresher than any others before it. *"Who are you, and why are you standing in my yard?"*

The corner of his mouth tips up into a hint of a smile, and the simple gesture has me wondering how he'd look with both corners lifted—handsome, no doubt.

"What makes you different…makes you beautiful."

Memories sputter from my subconscious, forming a moving picture of my life. I don't remember the things I'm seeing, but I know they happened. It's so surreal to watch yourself and not remember engaging so vividly in milestones that made you happy.

I spring up in my seat, my heart about to punch a hole straight through my chest as I attempt to catch my breath. Bryan is standing feet away, his hands raised in surrender. He's paler than a…ghost.

I instinctively reach up and latch onto a smooth, round medallion. Gasping, I blink once, twice…I remember. No, how is this…how is this even possible?

Does the flap of a butterfly's wings in Brazil set off a tornado in Texas?

Hell yes, it does.

"I need to go!" I jump up like the seat is on fire and push past Bryan, who stumbles backward with the force.

"Tori!" he beseeches, begging me to explain what's going on. He's clutching onto the ring box, cementing this is real.

Looking down at my watch, I see I have mere minutes to play god. "I don't love you, Bryan. I'm sorry. I did, but things, they change. I changed." I hear a bottle skate along the pavement, bringing back memories I never want to remember. "Run to your car, lock the doors, and drive home. Forget you ever met me."

He shakes his head animatedly. "I'm sorry I asked you to marry me. I know you're not ready." He snaps the lid shut and shoves the box into his pocket. He believes my outburst is due to the fact he just popped the question, and it went down as the world's worst proposal.

Looking over my shoulder, I know I'm being watched. Closing the distance between us, I place my hand against his cheek. "I would have married you…in a heartbeat…in a different lifetime. I know that much is true. Goodbye, Bryan."

Before he has a chance to protest, I kiss his lips briefly.

He's speechless, his mouth opening and closing like a goldfish, but he'll soon understand this is for the best. He'll find comfort in my sister, and that reality makes this farewell a sweet goodbye.

Before I turn on my heel, I extend my palm. "Can I borrow your cell?" He stands thunderstruck, wasting precious time. Manners long forgotten, I hastily reach into his pants pocket and retrieve his phone. "Thanks."

I push past him and run. "Tori! Wait! Victoria! Come back!" But I do neither.

Flashes of when I was last here cloud my vision. But unlike last time, I've come prepared. When I bump straight into a pungent smelling mass, I don't yelp, nor do I apologize profusely for not looking where I'm going.

I meet the small, beady eyes of a destitute looking man who changed my life forever. He sneers, his yellowed, long teeth akin to that of a sewer rat. "Nice necklace."

The scenario, the words may have changed, but they've changed for the better. "Thank you, it is," I confidently quip, stalking toward him instead of away. "It's Saint Jude. The saint of hope."

Just as he opens his mouth to emit filth, I raise my leg and knee him straight in the balls. The force is so hard; I actually think I've broken my kneecap. He falls to the ground, wailing in pain. "And you better hope you get a merciful judge."

I dial 911, rattling off my location, describing my victim, who ironically was once my assailant. I don't feel guilty when I tell the operator he attacked me. He may not have done so in this lifetime, but we all pay our dues sooner or later.

"What did I ever do to you?" he howls, clutching his junk as he gasps for breath.

"You're in no position to ask questions." Taking back my freedom has never felt so good. I have saved so many people from heartache. I have saved lives, and it feels good.

Bryan is standing frozen behind me, just as he did when I saw him through Jude's eyes.

Jude.

Leaving the man who changed my life forever, I take off in a dead sprint to meet another man who did the same. But this man…he's unlike any man I've ever met before. I can't believe it's only been a few minutes since I last saw Jude. How is it possible to miss someone so much after a fraction in time?

With everything I am, I hope this works. I've altered history, changed events which shaped me into the person I am today. I just hope I haven't lost a piece of my soul doing it. It only takes a moment to change your future. I only hope I'm not too late.

I saw Jude's past through his eyes, so I know exactly where he'll be. My legs ache, and I'm seconds away from falling into a breathless heap, but when I turn the corner and see a green truck, nothing else matters. A tall, towering man with a commanding poise stalks over to his truck, hood drawn over his bowed head.

My heart swells, and every inch of my body hums in exhilaration. Not thinking, caring, or questioning, I sprint across the road toward Jude. I don't know how this is possible because it shouldn't be. But our love, it knows no bounds.

His back is turned, so he doesn't know that he's seconds away from being mauled. My footsteps thrum loudly against the pavement, alerting Jude that I'm behind him. Just as he turns, I throw myself into his arms, clutching onto him like a deranged koala. I've never experienced such bliss—this is heaven.

I wrap my arms around his nape, basking in this familiar sensation. It's amazing how one single scent can bring back so many memories. He feels stronger, firmer, and I know it's because he's really here. We're both alive, breathing in the same world.

He doesn't say a word, his harsh exhalations warming my body from head to toe. He wraps his arms around my middle, pressing us chest to chest. Beating heart to beating heart. I could stay this way forever. Tears stream down my cheeks, but there's not a trace of sadness within them.

"Um, hi." His hoarse voice has me humming, closing my eyes in bliss.

"Hi." I latch on tighter, never intending to let go.

"I don't mean to be, er, rude. But do I know you?"

My eyes pop open.

Caught up in my excitement, I completely forgot that

although I remember, Jude does not. I should be sad, but I'm not. What we shared will be my secret because I can save Jude from knowing the heartache of our past.

Sliding down his body, I shyly brush the hair from my face. I can't meet his eyes. Not yet. I remember Jude once told me he died every night just so he could meet me again. I now can walk a mile in his shoes. I too feel a kinship to these feelings because I'd happily die a thousand deaths just to see his face again.

I take a breath, but it's in vain. I stop breathing when he places two fingers under my chin. An inhalation leaves my lips as I meet his warm, gentle eyes. I could stare into the inky depths and get lost forever. He cocks his head to the side while tonguing his upper lip. He's watching me closely while I remind myself to breathe.

He traces the curve of my brow, the slope of my nose, before scoring my lips with his slow, torturous movements as he outlines the seam of my mouth. I'm certain he can see my heart slamming in my chest, but I allow him to examine me because I have the upper hand.

When we first met, he knew who I was and what I had been through. But now, the tables are turned because I have seen the future—and it's beautiful. He pulls back his hand, shaking his head as if to snap from his daze. "I'm so sorry. That wasn't at all creepy," he quips while I smile.

"It's fine. I did just violate your personal space seconds ago, so I suppose we're even." He laughs, the resonance a harmonious sound.

We stand staring at one another, both captivated by the electricity sparking around us. "I'm Victoria." I extend my hand, a glutton for his touch.

He peers down at it and takes it, not letting go. "I'm Jude." We continue shaking well after introductions have passed.

As much as I want to stand here forever, I'm ready to start living in the real world—our world. "Can I buy you a coffee?"

"Sure, I'd like that." He finally releases me. We both frown at the separation.

I try not to linger and stand off to the side as he reaches into his pocket and produces a yellow envelope. I know what's inside, but does he? When he tosses it into the truck and locks the door, I can't help but ask, "Do you know what's inside?"

He slips the hood from his head, running a hand through his thick, tousled hair. "Yes, but it doesn't seem as important as it once did."

We walk with a small space between us, indecently close for strangers, but we both appear to yearn for the other's touch. When we round the corner, I bump straight into someone, yelping when memories, ones I'll never forget, rise to the surface. The older lady walking her Chihuahua apologizes before walking off.

When my racing heart stills, I realize Jude's hand is wrapped loosely around my waist. He appears startled, confused as to why he feels compelled to touch me. When his eyes drop to my chest, and he sees my medallion, he pulls in his lips. "At the risk of sounding like a creep once again, who are you? I feel like—"

"Feel like what?" I press.

Nothing but worship and affection stares down at me. "I feel like I've met you before. That's crazy, right?"

He's waiting for validation, but all I can do is thank the stars that aligned on this magical evening—they changed our lives forever. Stepping closer, I press my palm to his chest, over his heart, a heart which beats strong. "If you're a creep, then I'm completely batshit crazy when I say…you once saved my life… and it's now my turn to save yours."

A shooting star graces the heavens, a reminder that our love knows no bounds. "Make a wish," Jude whispers, brushing a strand of hair sticking to my tears. I know if this were another lifetime, this would be the moment he took his final breath. Although these scenarios have played out before, life is giving me a second chance—I better not screw it up.

Standing on tippy toes, reservations long gone, I lay a single kiss on his whiskered cheek. He sinks into my touch, humming softly. With eyes closed, I inhale his essence. With so much to say, I say the only thing fitting—the thing which kick-started my heart. "Jude…I know we're going to be great friends." This time, there is no speaking in the past tense, and it feels bloody incredible.

We stand, hugging on the sidewalk, uncaring that we're two strangers who aren't really strangers after all. There are simply no words to explain what's happening between us because what we have, what we went through to find one another, is beyond words. Feelings, however, we will never be beyond feelings. Or love. And what I feel for this man could fill volumes and volumes of books. An epic love story of two broken people who battled against all odds and found love…in this lifetime…and the next.

Acknowledgements

I lost my beloved father in July, so these past few months have been tough. I wouldn't have been able to get through this difficult time without my family and friends. Elle Kennedy, Vi Keeland, L.J. Shen, Lisa Edward, Christina Lauren, Natasha Madison, Kylie Scott, SC Stephens, Helena Hunting, Tina Gephart, Kimberly Brower, Danielle Sanchez, Jenny Sims, Gemma, Louise, Ryn Hughes—thank you from the bottom of my heart for being there for me.

To my author family—Vi Keeland, Elle Kennedy, Susan Stoker, Natasha Madison, BJ Harvey, Pam Godwin, Jay Mclean, Adriane Leigh, Helena Hunting, Penelope Ward, Christina Lauren, Stina Lindenblatt, Carrie Ann Ryan, Sawyer Bennett, Geneva Lee, Kristen Proby, Natasha Preston, L.J. Shen, Critical thinking can and should be taught from at least 3 rd grade up. Jen Frederick, Audrey Carlan, Heidi McLaughlin, KA Tucker, Meghan March, Sarina Bowen, Kristy Bromberg, Beverly Preston, Lisa Edward, Rachel Brookes, Len Webster, Debra Anastasia—thank you for my beautiful flowers. I was so touched.

My wonderful husband, Daniel. I love you. Thank you for

always believing in me. You're my favorite.

My ever-supporting parents. You guys are the best. I am who I am because of you. I love you. RIP Papa. Gone but never forgotten. You're in my heart. Always.

My agent, Kimberly Brower from Brower Literary & Management. Thank you for your patience and thank you for being an amazing human being.

Kimberly Whalen—Thank you for believing in this book from the very beginning.

My editor, Jenny Sims. What can I say other than I LOVE YOU! Thank you for everything. You go above and beyond for me.

My proofreader—Lisa Edward—More Than Words, Copyediting & Proofreading. You are amazing.

Sommer Stein, you NAILED this cover! Thank you for being so patient and making the process so fun. I'm sorry for annoying you constantly.

My publicist—Danielle Sanchez from Wildfire Marketing Solutions. Thank you for all your help. Your messages brighten my day.

A special shout-out to: Cheri Grand Anderman, Staci Hart, Mia Sheridan, J.L. Beck. Tijan, Aleatha Romig, Kat T.Masen, Danielle Norman, Carmen Jenner, Ben Ellis—Tall Story Designs, Nasha Lama, Natasha Tomic, Sali Benbow-Powers, Heyne, Random House, Kinneret Zmora, Hugo & Cie, Planeta, MxM Bookmark, Art Eternal, Carbaccio, Fischer,

Bookouture, Egmont Bulgaria, Brilliance Publishing, Audible, Hope Editions, Buzzfeed, BookBub, PopSugar, Aestas Book Blog, Hugues De Saint Vincent, Paris, New York, Sarah Sentz, Ria Alexander, Amy Jennings, Gel Ytayz, Jennifer Spinninger, Aurelie Dee, Vanessa Silva Martins, Amz Bourne, Amalie— Amalie Reads, Megan—Steamy Reads Blog, Kim Nash, Lauren Rosa, Kristin Dwyer, and Nina Bocci.

To the endless blogs that have supported me since day one—You guys rock my world.

My bookstagrammers—This book has allowed me to meet SO many of you. Your creativity astounds me. The effort you go to is just amazing. Thank you for the posts, the teasers, the support, the messages, the love, the EVERYTHING! I see what you do, and I am so, so thankful.

My reader group and review team—sending you all a big kiss.

My beautiful family—Mum, Papa, my sister—Fran, Matt, Samantha, Amelia, Gayle, Peter, Luke, Leah, Jimmy, Jack, Shirley, Michael, Rob, Elisa, Evan, Alex, Francesca, and my aunties, uncles, and cousins—I am the luckiest person alive to know each and every one of you. You brighten up my world in ways I honestly cannot express.

Samantha and Amelia— I love you both so very much.

To my family in Holland and Italy, and abroad. Sending you guys much love and kisses.

Papa, Zio Nello, Zio Frank, Zia Rosetta, and Zia

Giuseppina—you are in our hearts. Always.

My fur babies— mamma loves you so much! Buckwheat, you are my best buddy. Dacca, I will always protect you from the big bad Bellie. Mitch, refer to Dacca's comment. Jag, you're a wombat in disguise. Bellie, you're a devil in disguise. And Ninja, thanks for watching over me.

To anyone I have missed, I'm sorry! It wasn't intentional!

Last but certainly not least, I want to thank YOU! Thank you for welcoming me into your hearts and homes. My readers are the BEST readers in this entire universe! Love you all!

About the Author

Monica James spent her youth devouring the works of Anne Rice, William Shakespeare, and Emily Dickinson.

When she is not writing, Monica is busy running her own business, but she always finds a balance between the two. She enjoys writing honest, heartfelt, and turbulent stories, hoping to leave an imprint on her readers. She draws her inspiration from life.

She is a bestselling author in the U.S.A., Australia, Canada, France, Germany, Israel, and The U.K.

Monica James resides in Melbourne, Australia, with her wonderful family, and menagerie of animals. She is slightly obsessed with cats, chucks, and lip gloss, and secretly wishes she was a ninja on the weekends.

Connect With

MONICA JAMES

Facebook: facebook.com/authormonicajames
Twitter: twitter.com/monicajames81
Goodreads: goodreads.com/MonicaJames
Instagram: instagram.com/authormonicajames
Website: www.authormonicajames.com
Pinterest: pinterest.com/monicajames81
BookBub: bookbub.com/authors/monica-james
Amazon: https://amzn.to/2EWZSyS
Join my Reader Group: http://bit.ly/2nUaRyi

CPSIA information can be obtained
at www.ICGtesting.com
Printed in the USA
LVHW080809071219
639769LV00002B/34/P

9 780648 467885